D0193580

TIGERS AND DRAGONS

DATE DUE

DEC 12 '97			
OCT 2 5 2004			

TIGERS &DRAGONS

JON HENDERSON

Tyndale House Publishers, Inc.
Wheaton, Illinois

FOR
SG, LMV,
AND
ELB

Fiat veritas

Library-of-Congress-Cataloging-in-Publication Data

Henderson, Jon,   date
  Tigers and dragons / Jon Henderson.
    p.   cm.
  ISBN 0-8423-7309-8 :
  1. Political crimes and offenses—China—Fiction.   2. Nuclear
industry—Security measures—Fiction.   3. Persecution—China—
Fiction.   4. Christians—China—Fiction.   I. Title.
PS3558.E4853T54   1993   93-13834
813'.54—dc20

Printed in the United States of America

99 98 97 96 95 94 93
7   6   5   4   3   2   1

The night had closed in rain, and rolling clouds blotted out the lights of the villages in the valley. Forty miles away, untouched by cloud or storm, the white shoulder of Donga Pa—the Mountain of the Council of the Gods—upheld the Evening Star.

The monkeys sang sorrowfully to each other as they hunted for dry roots in the fern-wreathed trees, and the last puff of the day-wind brought from the unseen villages the scent of damp wood-smoke, hot cakes, dripping undergrowth, and rotting pine-cones.

That is the true smell of the Himalayas, and if once it creeps into the blood of a man, that man will at the last, forgetting all else, return to the hills to die. The clouds closed in and the smell went away, and there remained nothing in all the world except chilling white mist and the boom of the Sutlej River racing through the valley below.

Rudyard Kipling, *Namgay Doola*

I

Tibet

The storm howled through the deserted streets of Lhasa.

Ganden Nesang fought his way around a corner, his arm held protectively in front of his eyes as a shield against the sleet that stung and tore at his face. As he came full into the teeth of the wind, his foot slipped on a patch of ice. He staggered, and the wind threw him to the pavement.

He sat up, fighting to regain his breath, then dragged himself into the relative shelter of a doorway. Ganden ran his gloved hands worriedly over his thick sheepskin jacket. "Please," he whispered, "don't let what I carry this night have been damaged by my clumsiness." He pulled himself to his feet and continued down the street.

Ganden hurried past a vegetable stand, shuttered against the gale, then froze as headlights appeared down the street. He slowed his walk and averted his face, as if against the wind. A spotlight mounted on the vehicle bathed him in its actinic glare. He sucked in his breath and forced himself to remain calm as the People's Liberation Army jeep swerved across the street and stopped beside him.

"Your papers!" a voice in the darkness ordered.

1

As Ganden Nesang reached inside his jacket and pulled his identity folder out of his shirt pocket, his hand brushed against the edge of something else he carried beneath his coat. *They mustn't find it*, he told himself. *They must not. We cannot go on without it.*

The soldier tucked his flashlight under his arm and examined Ganden's folder. "Why are you out at this hour?" he barked. "It's after curfew!"

Ganden suppressed the part of him that wanted to strike out at the hated invader. "As you can see, sir," he replied, fighting to keep his voice deferential, "I work at the People's Glory Power Plant."

"So? Your shift was over hours ago!"

"I am a technician. It is the end of the month, and I stayed late to finish the power generation reports. My supervisor says it is important for Beijing to have current information." Ganden stared at his shoes, in case the repugnance he felt at such submissiveness showed on his face. "His authorization for me to stay beyond the end of my shift is on the back of my employment card."

"Then why are you headed this way?" the soldier snarled. "Your address is two blocks behind you!"

Ganden looked up, shielding his eyes from the light. "I was going to borrow some cigarettes from a friend. I ran out this afternoon and didn't get to the shop because I had to stay—"

"*Silence!*"

Ganden tensed, ready to flee if the man got out of the jeep. He could hear a whispered conversation. *If they find what I am carrying, it is the end of us all. . . .*

A crumpled, half-full pack of cigarettes appeared at his feet.

"Now, go home," the soldier ordered, handing him his identity folder.

"Yes, sir. Thank you, sir," Ganden said as he obsequiously

scooped up the pack. He turned around and hurried back the way he came. As the jeep sped past him, one of the soldiers shouted obscenities. Ganden slowed, keeping his eyes on the jeep. Once it was out of sight, he reversed course again.

✦ ✦ ✦

Headquarters, 165th Motorized Rifle Division, Semipalatinsk, Kazakhstan

Colonel Grigory Markov pulled the cork from the bottle with his teeth. As the clear liquid splashed into the glass on his desk, he stared glumly out into the night.

Those fools, he thought bitterly. *Those miserable fools. Here I am, a full colonel in the Red Army and the commander of a rifle division, stuck in this miserable backwater. They ignore my situation reports and promise to bring us home as soon as "conditions permit."*

Markov gulped the vodka and winced as it burned on its way down.

My last bottle, and it's not even Stolichanya. I had to borrow it from my division sergeant, and he had to barter with the local peasants for it!

The coarse vodka chafed the officer's resentment into flame.

How long has it been since we had good Russian fare instead of the Kazakh slop we buy here? I don't remember the last time I had sausages, potatoes, and black bread.

Markov thumped his fist on the desk.

And now it's to the point where we're having to trade our clothes for food! We've been reduced to the level of serfs, while in Moscow they argue over how to divide up the samovars and silverware. . . .

A knock at his office door interrupted Markov's mental diatribe.

"What is it?"

His staff sergeant, a slight, older man, slipped into the room. He looked at the bottle for a long moment. Then, knowing what it meant, he addressed his commanding officer.

"Someone to see you, Grigory Ivanovich," he said deferentially.

"Who?" Markov demanded to know. "If it's that fool of a mayor, tell him to go away!"

The sergeant shook his head. "It is no one from the village." The sergeant lowered his voice. "He claims to be an Afghan."

Markov sat up. "Why," he asked suspiciously, "would one of those bandits be nosing around here?"

"I don't know, Colonel. But he did ask me to give you this." The sergeant held out an envelope.

Markov took the envelope. It was Red Army stationery. The address in the corner read:

Headquarters,
Central Asian Military District
Alma-Ata
Kazakh S.S.R.

He tore it open. Inside was a note from his old friend Pyotr Tallin, commander of the garrison at Alma-Ata.

Grigory Ivanovich,

While I am sure that you are dining on caviar and frolicking with the local maidens, we are starving. As you have undoubtedly come to realize, those idiots in the Kremlin have left us to the tender mercies of the "indigenous peoples" we have worked so hard to repress. It is a sad state of affairs, and an ending unworthy of our Motherland.

"You are right, as always, Pyotr Dimitrovich," Markov muttered. He drained his glass.

4

It is also, however, an ending unworthy of *us*. Therefore, allow me to introduce Yousef Bey. He is an Afghan, and therefore not to be trusted, but he is also someone that I have found I can do business with. I would advise you, old friend, to listen carefully to what he will propose.

Soon I shall collect Natalia and head west—perhaps to Germany, perhaps even to America. I suggest you do the same. We have nothing left here, and I have heard that the CIA treats defectors well.

Until better times, comrade,

Pyotr

The colonel opened his desk drawer, pulled his SIG SP220 out of its worn leather holster, and snapped the safety off. Then he laid the pistol in the open drawer.

"Very well," Markov told the sergeant, "send in the Afghan."

Ganden turned right off Xingfu Donglu and into Yak Alley. He walked slowly, careful to step over the sleeping worshipers who had spent the day inching their way on their bellies around the Jokhang Temple. Not even the brisk north wind could entirely dispel the stench from the meat markets that lined the alley.

Bearing left, Ganden stepped into a nameless pathway between two rows of buildings at the rear of the Barkhor Bazaar. He stopped before a nondescript door. After a furtive glance in both directions he knocked, waited, then knocked again. The door opened, and for a brief instant a sliver of warm light made the blowing sleet glow like fireflies.

Ganden slipped inside, and the door closed behind him. The room was in the back of a flower seller's shop, and the perfume that lingered from the day's deliveries mingled with the rich aroma from the yak-butter lamps called *chome* that filled the room with golden light.

"*Toshi dili*, Ganden," a chorus of voices called. Someone barred the door behind him, and Ganden returned the greetings.

The room was bare except for a table surrounded by chairs, the butter lamps arranged in a row down the middle of the table. A young woman got up. The six other people in the room smiled as she rushed across the room and threw her arms around Ganden. He smiled and pressed his cheek to the top of her head.

"I missed you today, little one," Ganden whispered as he toyed with one of the 108 braids she wore in the traditional hairstyle of the Khampa nomad. *It's so good to be able to speak my real language*, he thought as he held her, *and not the foreign tongue of the hated Han Chinese.*

Puzhen looked up at her fiancé. "You're late," she said accusingly. "We're not even married yet, and already you prefer your work to me." The smile in her eyes defused the accusation.

Ganden didn't return the smile. "I was stopped by the police. Over on Yanhe Donglu."

Puzhen's eyes widened. "What did you tell them?"

"The truth. That I had worked late and was on my way home."

"You don't think they suspected anything, do you?" a plump woman asked.

Ganden shook his head. "Would I be here if they had?" He looked at one of the men seated at the table. "It was a good thing that you gave me that permit, sir. I don't think they would've let me go without it."

The man nodded. "Good service should always be rewarded. That's what it says in our lesson tonight." The older man looked sharply at Ganden. "You didn't lose it, did you?"

"No sir," Ganden replied sincerely. "Would I be here if I had?"

2

As the laughter around the table subsided, Ganden reached into his jacket. Very carefully, he took out a sheaf of onionskin paper covered densely on both sides with the Sanskrit-like characters of the Tibetan alphabet. He breathed a prayer of thanks that it was undamaged and gently placed it on the table. Ganden's employer took a much larger stack of paper from the table in front of him and set it on top of Ganden's contribution. The middle-aged man looked at those around the table.

"This is a great day," he said solemnly. "Ganden's trip to Kathmandu has borne wonderful fruit." Overcome with emotion, the man closed his eyes. "Our copy of the Gospel of Luke, the only one in our own language, is now complete." Tears ran down the face of the plump woman who was his wife. "It is a time for prayers of thanksgiving, brothers and sisters." Everyone nodded. Then the man smiled.

"It is also a time for celebration!" He gestured at Ganden and Puzhen. "Next Sunday we shall have our first wedding!"

"Thank you, Pastor!" Puzhen said excitedly. Beaming, she looked shyly at Ganden. "I will spend all week rubbing the finest yak butter into my hair, so that it shines for my husband!"

A knock on the door silenced the delighted applause. All eyes went to the entrance to the small room.

"It must be Tenzig," the pastor said. "He told me that he was sick, but he hoped to be able to come anyway." He gestured to Ganden. "Open the door."

Ganden unbarred the door. The instant he slid back the bolt, the door flew wide, hurling Ganden to the floor. The butter light glinted off the rifle barrels that were thrust through the door and from the red stars set in the middle of the beaked caps. Soldiers rushed into the room, followed by a lieutenant in the Chinese People's Liberation Army.

The pastor came to his feet. "What is the meaning of this?"

"You would know that better than I," the lieutenant replied calmly, "since it is you who claim to be schooled in the meaning of this so-called religion." The lieutenant's voice went cold as the snow that was drifting in through the door. "This is an unauthorized meeting of a sect outlawed by the Beijing government. All here will be taken away for self-critique and rehabilitation."

Using the muzzles of their rifles, the soldiers began prodding the pastor, his wife, and the others toward the door.

Ganden reached for Puzhen's hand as the huddled knot of believers reached the door. The lieutenant stepped between them.

"*Almost* all here," the officer said, "will be rehabilitated." He reached into his pocket and took out a wad of bills. "There is one here who, earlier tonight, chose wisely." The lieutenant handed the bills to Ganden. "I believe this is the amount we agreed upon."

Ganden didn't move. "You lie," he whispered from between clenched teeth. He could feel the eyes of Puzhen and all the rest on him.

"I think not," the soldier replied. He pointed at the pastor. "It is this man and that Christ of his that are the liars."

Enraged, Ganden threw himself at the officer. A rifle butt

caught him in the stomach and knocked him down. Ganden struggled to get up, but the pastor wrapped his arms around him.

"No, Ganden," he whispered. "This is not the way." He helped the gasping young man to his feet. "Truth will prevail."

The lieutenant threw the money at Ganden's feet. Puzhen looked at it, then up at Ganden, her face ashen. Tears filled her eyes. Ganden fought back his blind rage. His eyes never left hers as he slowly shook his head.

The army officer shrugged. "It would seem that you want to wait until the others are gone before you claim your reward. As you wish." He gestured to the soldiers. "Take them away," he barked.

The soldiers prodded the group outside and into a waiting truck. One of them kept his rifle trained on Ganden as he backed out the door. When the soldier had climbed into the truck Ganden darted outside. He looked into the back of the truck, but could not see Puzhen.

As the truck pulled away, Ganden began to run. Legs pumping, arms outstretched, he tried to grab the truck's tailgate. A rifle butt again lashed out at him, and flame erupted from another rifle's muzzle. Ganden ducked as the bullet whined off the road beside him. He hit a patch of ice with his foot and went sprawling into a puddle of filth. The last thing he heard before consciousness fled was Puzhen's cries of "Ganden! Ganden!" as they were carried away on the wind.

Inside the house church, the wind scattered the pages of the Gospel. Snow began to cover the floor. One by one, the candles guttered and went out.

"You don't look Afghan," Markov remarked as the immaculately dressed man seated himself on the other side of his desk.

Yousef Bey smiled. "If you wish, Colonel," he said in flawless Russian, "I will go get my tarboosh and scimitar. In

9

these times, however, I find it more expeditious to dress in an intercontinental fashion."

Markov grunted. He started to push the bottle across the table, then stopped. "Muslim, aren't you?" he asked.

Bey nodded. "You are an astute man, Colonel Markov." The Afghan gestured at Markov's uniform shirt. "But I would expect that of someone who wears both the Order of Lenin and the Hero of the Soviet Union."

Markov leaned back in his chair. He fingered the gold star that was the Soviet equivalent of the Medal of Honor. "You read decorations well, Afghan. You speak Russian well, too." *And you do both better than my own men*, Markov thought bitterly. *Forty of my last sixty recruits were Kazakhs who speak no Russian at all.* "Now, why are you here?"

Bey set an expensive leather briefcase on Markov's desk. "I represent a consortium that is interested in doing business with those in positions such as yours."

Markov stared at the case's finely tooled Moroccan leather. "And, just what *is* my position, Afghan?"

"It is, Colonel—to put it delicately—untenable." Bey held up his hands, quelling Markov's incipient outburst. "I happen to know that, for the last week, your men have been living on nothing but bread and milk."

"Nonsense. My men are given their full daily ration of food."

"Then why are they seen in the bazaar bartering their equipment for foodstuffs?" Bey smiled wryly. "I believe that the current rate of exchange is one combat knife for one loaf of bread." He looked at Markov over steepled fingertips. "Your desertion rate is up, and your men are near rebellion."

"Lies! All lies!" The colonel banged his fist on the desk. "My base is at full operational readiness." He glared at Bey. "Marshal Gagarin himself was here not three days ago to inspect, and he found all to be in order!"

Bey returned Markov's unwavering stare. "Marshal Gagarin flew here in response to your alert that the soldiers were about to form a strike committee. He brought his own food—" Bey looked at Markov's bottle of cheap vodka "—which he obviously did not share with you. The marshal told you that there was nothing the Supreme Command could do to help you, then he left."

Markov rubbed a fist across his mouth. "How do you know these things, Afghan?" he asked quietly.

Bey shrugged deprecatingly. "A liter of vodka and a glass have the most amazing effect on a conscript's tongue." The arms merchant snapped open the ornate silver clasps of the briefcase. As he lifted the lid, embossed initials flashed in the harsh overhead light. "My clients are prepared to provide you and your men with immediate aid, in the form of food and clothing."

"What could we possibly have to offer you?" Markov asked, already afraid that he knew the answer.

Bey took a sheet of paper out of his briefcase. "These are the items in which we are interested. Consider this to be a shopping list." He handed the sheet to Markov.

The blood drained from the colonel's face as he ran his eyes down the list. "You must be joking!"

"Not at all, Colonel," Bey replied quietly. "My clients are quite serious, I assure you."

With reflexes developed as a boy during the siege of Stalingrad, Markov whipped his pistol out of the drawer and leveled it at Bey's chest. "Get out of my sight, Afghan," he growled.

Bey didn't move. "Very well, Colonel. As you wish." Slowly, his eyes never leaving Markov's, Bey closed and locked his briefcase. "There are others more desperate, or perhaps more willing to listen to reason, than you appear to be." He stood. "May I leave you my card, on the off chance that you will tire of your diet of bread and vodka?"

When Markov didn't reply, Bey, with infinite care, reached inside his suit coat. He took out a business card. "I can be reached at this number." He set the card on the desk. Markov glanced at the card. The telephone number was the only writing on it.

"Call me if you change your mind, Colonel," Bey said pleasantly. He picked up his briefcase, turned, and strode out of the office.

Markov put the pistol away. He looked again at the card. Something glinted underneath it. The colonel flicked the card out of the way with a fingernail and found himself looking at an Imperial. It was the first gold ten-ruble coin he had seen in years.

✧ ✧ ✧

The hard-toed boot of a Public Security Bureau policeman roused Ganden from unconsciousness. "Get up, you!" he ordered.

Ganden took a shuddering, painful breath. He was shaking with cold, and his head ached terribly. As he tried to push himself to his hands and knees, he found that he could not. His face seemed to be stuck to the pavement. The PSB man kicked him again, and the blow brought Ganden off the ground. He gasped with pain as the skin of his face, glued to the dirt by the frozen blood that had seeped from his abrasions, tore loose. Ganden came unsteadily to his feet. He could feel blood running down his neck.

"You are either a worshiper who has chosen this area in which to sleep," the policeman said simply, "or a drunk who has had too much *chang*. Neither of which is permitted." The PSB man reached out imperiously. "Your papers!"

"I am neither," Ganden replied as he fumbled for his ID folder. "I slipped on the ice and fell." He handed his papers to the PSB officer. "I've hurt myself. Would you please help me get to the clinic?"

The policeman looked at Ganden's papers, then pointed his flashlight at the young Tibetan. The side of Ganden's head was caked with dirty, clotted blood, and the cold night air caused steam to rise from the fresh blood that oozed from the scrape that covered half his face.

"Would you please help me get to the clinic?" Ganden repeated quietly.

"See?" the PSB officer said with self-satisfaction. " I *was* right. In your drunkenness you passed out and fell."

Ganden bristled at the calumny. He also realized that if he told this man the whole truth, he'd never see Puzhen again.

"Now go home and make yourself presentable," the policeman ordered. "You're lucky that I don't arrest you for being a public embarrassment." The PSB man started to leave, then turned and struck Ganden with his nightstick. "I said *move!*" As fast as he could, Ganden shuffled away.

His journey home was an unending trail of icy snow and fiery pain. Each time he stumbled and fell to his knees it took a greater effort of will to rise. At last he found himself leaning against his dormitory room door. He batted at the latch with numb, useless fingers. Finally the door opened, and Ganden fell through.

When he regained consciousness, the first thing he saw was his bed. The blanket looked wonderful. Ganden dragged himself up onto it. He swallowed, and pain tore through the side of his face. *Must clean it*, he thought, *then go to the clinic in the morning.*

Ganden grabbed hold of his dresser and pulled himself up. He took the cleanest of his towels and punched it through the thin crust of ice that covered the water in his bowl. He winced each time the coarse cloth touched his raw skin. When the water that dripped from the cloth had turned red, he threw himself onto his bed.

Lord, he prayed as his eyes closed, *you have preserved me for a purpose. Please let me know what you wish of me.* . . . Before his prayer had ended, sleep enveloped him.

3

Image Processing Facility, CIA Headquarters, Langley, Virginia

"AOS in thirty seconds," the technician reported.

"I've got to go, hon," Greg Miahara said into the phone. "No, I can't talk right now. See you at lunch." He hung up and shook his head in exasperation.

"Acquisition of signal . . . now," the technician said.

Greg turned to a console. "How's it look?" he asked his colleague Susan Kirkcaldy.

"Much better than the previous passes. Signal's five-by-five." The optoelectronics technician nodded approvingly. "Looking straight down is a decided improvement over an oblique angle."

Launched by a recent space shuttle mission, the imaging radar satellite, the latest in a series code-named Indigo-Lacrosse, was the first to be placed in an orbit that carried it over much of the Commonwealth of Independent States and China.

"Parameters for the pass?" Susan asked.

"Let's see what we're going to be looking at." Greg punched some keys. He thought for a moment, then his eyes lit up. "Feel like trying out our new toy, Mrs. Kirkcaldy?" Greg asked theatrically. "Warm it up and bring it on-line," he instructed. "Just over the horizon is the perfect spot to take a peek."

The commands Susan typed in at her keyboard were sent to a geostationary satellite orbiting twenty-three thousand miles over the Atlantic. From there, they were relayed via laser to the low-flying reconnaissance satellite.

"Command acknowledged," she reported.

"Good. Let's see what it sees."

From her seat at the console, Susan looked up at Greg. "Sure they won't notice us as we go by?" she asked the senior imaging officer.

Greg shook his head. "Don't think so." He typed a command on the console's keyboard, and latitude and longitude lines appeared on the high-resolution flat-panel screen in front of them.

"Notice where we're snooping today." His finger traced an arc over the screen. "Right now, those folks down there are much more worried about their neighbors than they are about us." He grinned. "When the woods are full of bears, you *don't* take time out for stargazing."

They watched as the image began to build up slowly on the screen. Billions of bits of information were being downloaded by the spy satellite via the Tracking and Data Relay Satellite System to the TDRSS ground station at the White Sands Missile Range in New Mexico. There, the data went by secure landline to Greg Miahara and Susan Kirkcaldy at the Image Processing Facility. As the information was processed by the Cray YMP supercomputer in the basement, more and more detail was added to the picture.

Watching the image grow, Greg was reminded of the sidewalk artist he and his fiancée, Cathy, had seen the previous weekend. The painter had first done a rough charcoal sketch, then he had filled in the fine detail. *Just like these*, Greg realized.

Too bad, he thought with a grin, *that none of my pictures are painted with visible light. . . .*

"You're from Hawaii, aren't you?" Susan asked, not taking her eyes from the screen.

"Born and bred on Maui," Greg replied. "Why?"

"Jeremy and I want to visit the Islands while we're out here on the west coast. Since you're a native, we thought you might have some suggestions."

The young Asian nodded. "Sure thing. Cathy and I can set you up with our families. They'll show you around." Miahara grinned. "Be sure and try some *puu-puus*."

Susan looked up at Greg. " 'Poo-poos'?"

"It's Hawaiian for appetizer. Water chestnuts wrapped in bacon then dipped in honey and deep-fried, spring rolls, barbecued pork, that sort of thing. Good stuff!"

Greg glanced at the top of the screen. Across it was the message,

PASS: 224 INCLINATION: 62.2°
ASPECT RATIO: 1 x 1.435   12:24:56.37EST

The image was three-quarters complete when it was suddenly replaced with rows of letters and numbers.

ABNORMAL TERMINATION OF MODULE
ASSERT_CRC

CYCLICAL REDUNDANCY CHECK
OVERRIDE FAILED

SUDDENDEATH (903) AT 0ED2A7(H)

CORE IMAGE DUMP STARTING SECTOR
1322952

PREMATURE LOS

TX TERMINATED—12:37:21.62EST

Susan slapped her leg in annoyance. "Bother! I thought we had that one!"

Greg stared at the error codes. "Must be something in the spectra-encoding algorithm, but I'll be darned if I know what it is." He took a deep breath. "Start downloading the coredump."

"It should be ready by the time you're back from *lunch*," Susan said. She pointed at the screen, which now read, 12:40.05.73EST.

"Great, just great." Greg muttered as he grabbed his jacket. "Now Cath is going to coredump all over me, too."

Susan's quiet chuckle trailed behind him as he raced from the room.

4

A breeze tugged at the balloons tied to the posts of the rail fence surrounding the lawn in front of Joel and Pat Dryden's Trenton, Maine, home. Pat moved among her guests, greeting them and receiving their congratulations on her sixtieth birthday. Off to one side, in the shade of a maple tree, more wellwishers sat chatting at flower-laden tables.

Jake MacIntyre came out of the Dryden kitchen to find a stranger standing on the back porch—someone who hadn't been there when he went in. Jake set the tray he was carrying down on a white wicker table.

"Lemonade?" Jake asked the man who was leaning on the porch rail.

The stranger turned away from his view of the rocky coastline. He glanced at the glasses on the tray, hesitated, then looked at Jake. "No, thanks."

Jake looked at the man in front of him. Tall and powerfully built, the sandy-haired man held himself with the lithe, easy readiness of a fighter. Jake saw something in the man's gray eyes that he recognized.

"Hang around," Jake told the unexpected arrival. "I'll be right back." He went back into the kitchen.

Jake returned with two bottles of cold beer, and the smile that flickered across the man's face told him he had guessed right.

"Cheers," the man said, raising the bottle that Jake had handed him.

"Hold it," Jake replied. The man paused, the bottle halfway to his lips. "I never drink with a stranger."

The man looked disconcerted for an instant. "Sorry," he replied with a rueful shake of his head. "I'm not used to introducing myself." He grinned and stuck out a large hand. "Randy Cavanaugh."

Randy's grip was as strong as any Jake had felt. "Jake MacIntyre."

"Yes," Randy replied. "I know. The famous photojournalist." He took a swig of beer. "I've heard of your work."

Jake rested his elbows on the porch rail and looked out over the lawn. "You a friend of Pat, or Joel?"

Randy frowned in confusion. "Pardon?"

Jake rephrased the question. "Did Pat or Joel invite you?"

"Neither of them, actually," Randy admitted.

"Kind of peculiar, then, isn't it?"

"What's kind of peculiar?" Randy replied casually.

"Crashing a stranger's birthday party."

Randy smiled. "Now that you mention it, it is."

The tension between them grew as Jake waited. Something about the way Randy looked at him told Jake that Randy had been in this kind of situation before. He appeared to be in his mid-thirties. While there were several single women at the party, they were all friends of Pat, so it seemed unlikely to Jake that Randy was someone's date for the afternoon. Jake's next thought caused him to frown.

"Do you know Anne?" Jake asked, an edge to his voice.

"We've met," Randy admitted, his face guileless. "Why?"

"Just trying to figure out what you're doing here," Jake replied. He gestured toward the birthday guests. "You show up out of nowhere, and you don't exactly melt into that crowd of Kennebunkport types."

"I heard that," a voice called from inside the kitchen. The screen door swung open, and a lean man in his sixties stepped out. "First off," Joel Dryden continued, "the view's better here than down in Kennebunkport, and, secondly, at least we're willing to acknowledge what we're looking at—"

Randy turned, interrupting Joel's lecture.

"Randy Cavanaugh!" Joel exclaimed. He shook Randy's hand warmly.

"You know this guy?" Jake asked Joel.

Joel nodded. "Randy's boss used to work for me." Jake shrugged and turned away.

"What brings you up this way?" Joel asked Randy.

"I came up with Cathy and Greg."

"Just to attend Pat's party?"

"I thought that we were just going to bum around for the weekend," Randy explained. "I didn't realize that there was a party involved." He grinned as Jake, feeling rather excluded, watched from the sidelines.

"When Greg told me that he and Cathy were going to Maine for the weekend," Randy continued, "I just sort of invited myself along." Randy closed his eyes. "It wasn't until they showed up at the airport this morning that Cathy found out Greg had suggested that I come with them." Randy chuckled. "She was *not* happy. Greg also didn't tell me that the two of them had plans for the day." He shrugged. "The best plan I could think of was for me to come here until they get back." The young man looked steadily at Joel. "I hope you don't mind. I really needed to get out of D.C."

Joel grinned. "No problem. You're more than welcome." He gestured at the table. "Besides, there's lots of food."

"True," Randy agreed, surveying the table. "But, is there anything besides quiche and fruit salad?"

Joel laughed. "As a matter of fact, I was down in New York the other day, so there's a pound of Carnegie Deli pastrami waiting in the kitchen." He gestured at the quiche. "I prefer something a bit more substantial myself."

One of the figures on the lawn below turned toward them. Randy looked at the slim, auburn-haired woman. "That's Anne?"

Joel nodded. "It's been a few years, hasn't it?"

Randy noticed Jake's expression, and filed it away for future reference. "Think I'll go say hello." He started down the porch steps.

Joel watched as his daughter turned, smiled, and gave the newcomer a hug. Then he glanced at Jake and tried not to laugh at the younger man's expression.

✧ ✧ ✧

"I could just *kill* Greg", Cathy muttered as she helped Anne wrap up the leftovers from the party. "I was ready to send him back to Hawaii—permanently." She shook her head. "I couldn't believe it. We get to the airport and there's Randy, flight bag in hand, grinning like an idiot."

Cathy picked up the box of cellophane wrap and looked speculatively at its serrated metal cutter. With a savage jerk she ripped off another piece. "Greg didn't even tell me that he'd invited Randy along!" Cathy grabbed a pan of leftover quiche and started wrapping. "When I asked him why he hadn't bothered to let me know, he just stared at me. Then we're running late, and the two of them see no problem in just dropping Randy off unannounced." Cathy slammed the quiche pan down onto the cutting board. "I didn't even get to introduce him to you. We just dropped him off, right in the middle of your mother's birthday party, like he was a hitchhiker or something."

Anne's eyes traveled from the shattered quiche crust to the

young woman. It was clear that Cathy was angry over more than just Greg's indiscretion.

"Cath," she began, carefully formulating her questions. "Is there something else—something between you and Greg, maybe—that you're upset about?"

Caught off guard, Cathy gaped at Anne and attempted to stammer a reply. She was saved by the doorbell and by Jake's shout from the foyer.

They rushed out to the foyer, where Jake stood with a duffel in one hand and his other arm around a young woman in sweatshirt and jeans.

"*LEE!*" several voices cried. Anne rushed over and threw her arms around the woman.

Randy Cavanaugh and Greg Miahara stood back and watched as the Drydens and Cathy took turns hugging the new arrival. Jake walked over to where Randy was standing.

"Lee Parker, Annie's best friend," Jake explained.

Randy nodded. "I know."

Jake suppressed a grimace. Apparently this mystery man knew a lot about Anne—and Jake wasn't sure he liked it at all. "She's been overseas all summer," he continued. "We weren't expecting her—last we heard, she was touring Russia."

Randy wasn't listening.

"Lee," Jake called, "you remember Greg Miahara? And this is Randy Cavanaugh."

"Hi, Greg," Lee said. She looked at Randy and smiled. "Nice to meet you, Randy."

Anne saw Lee run her hands through her hair and tug at her grubby sweatshirt. She caught Jake's eye. "Why don't you take Greg and Randy down to the dock and bring back the lobsters? By the time the water's boiling, Lee will have freshened up."

Jake headed toward the door, motioning for Greg and Randy to follow him.

"Mama," Anne continued, "will you set another place?"

"Your *father and I* will be happy to," Pat said. She looked pointedly at Joel, who had been about to leave with the rest of the men. Joel sighed and stepped back toward his wife.

Randy and Greg followed Jake down the slope that led to the dock.

"Is something the matter with Joel?" Greg asked Jake as they made their way through the blueberry bushes. "The last time I saw him, he was about to go charging off with you to Peru. Scullery work doesn't seem to be his style."

"Joel had a mild heart attack a couple of months ago," Jake replied. "It didn't kill him, but this enforced rest period just might."

The path led past the Drydens' driveway. Randy stopped to admire an immaculately restored 1965 MGB-GT, its chrome gleaming in the setting sun.

"Yours?" he asked Jake.

Jake smiled fondly at his pride and joy.

"Nice car," Randy commented. "Restoring and maintaining one of those babies is *not* cheap. I didn't realize that photojournalists made that kind of money."

"They do when they're the only witness to the assassination of the decade," Greg said. In response to Randy's blank look, Greg continued. "Remember the Moncrief affair?"

"You mean those killings over in Egypt?"

"Exactly. Remember the week when all the newsmagazines had a photo of the assassins on their covers?"

Randy looked at Jake. "You mean that was *your* photo?" Jake nodded.

Randy shook his head. "Some luck."

"Jake made his own luck," Greg replied. "Like all top photojournalists do."

"*Jake,*" Jake said, "got himself in way over his head. Only a large dose of divine intervention kept this photographer's skin intact."

They walked down a gangplank and onto the floating dock. The incoming tide caused the platform to stir restlessly beneath them. Jake hauled on a yellow nylon line tied around one of the pilings, and a seaweed-encrusted wooden crate slid up out of the water and onto the dock. He opened the lobster trap and peered inside.

"Six . . . seven . . . eight," Jake counted. "All two pounds plus, it looks like." He swung the trap's door shut, causing the blue-gray shapes inside to flap wildly.

Randy looked puzzled. "Wait a minute," he said. "I thought lobsters lived on the bottom of the ocean. How did eight prime specimens end up in a trap hung over the side of your dock?"

"Easy," Jake replied with a grin. "Last night Pat came down and explained to them how many she was going to need today. She always includes a couple of extra, so that they can have lobster omelettes for breakfast the next couple of days."

Greg, standing behind Randy, covered his eyes and shook his head.

"Pat then leaves them to fight it out for the privilege of being served up at one of her dinner parties. I come down the next afternoon, and here they are. Of course," Jake laughed, "if you ask her, she'll tell you that she calls Tony the lobster-man, and he drops them off on his way home. But don't believe her."

Jake gestured at a large bucket that he had brought down to the dock. "How about if you fill that with seawater and lug it up the hill."

Randy grabbed the bucket by its handle and lowered it over the edge of the dock. When the bucket was full Randy stood, holding ten gallons of salt water well away from him. *Strong*, Jake thought as he looked at the brimming bucket. *I wouldn't want to wrestle this guy. . . .*

"Why the seawater?" Randy asked.

"If you boil them in tap water," Jake replied, "the fresh water sucks all the juice right out of them." He grinned. "If you've never had lobster this way before, you're in for a treat."

"Need a hand with them?" Randy asked. "I've got one free."

"No, thanks. I can manage." Jake hoisted the crate to his shoulder. "Let's get this show on the road."

❖ ❖ ❖

A platter mounded with scarlet, steaming lobsters provided the centerpiece to Pat's birthday dinner.

"You work with Jake?" Lee asked Randy as she deftly extracted the meat from a lobster claw. Pat had seated the unexpected arrivals across from one another at one end of the table.

Randy set down the tools with which he had been struggling to crack open his lobster's shell. "No, I don't." He took a sip of wine before continuing. "Actually, I didn't even know him before today. I just sort of showed up."

Lee arched her eyebrows. "Oh?"

Randy shifted uncomfortably. "I know the Drydens, and I needed to get out of D.C. for a few days, so I took Greg up on his offer to come up here." He looked sheepish. "Greg didn't tell me that he and Cathy had been invited to a party. I thought that we were just going to hang out."

A basket of rolls was passed to Lee, who offered one to Randy. "Are you on vacation?"

Randy hesitated. "Not exactly." He picked up the nutcrackerlike tool that he had seen Lee use, placed one of his lobster's claws in it, and squeezed. The claw shot out of the cracker and, trailing an arc of juice, landed halfway between Randy and Lee.

A sound from across the table caused him to look up. Lee, shoulders shaking, was trying unsuccessfully to hide her laughter behind her napkin.

Randy rested his chin in his hand and looked across the table at her.

"I'm sorry, Randy," Lee was finally able to gasp. "But the look on your face was priceless." She smiled at him. "I really am sorry."

"No, you're not," Randy replied flatly. Lee hesitated, unsure, until she saw the smile in his eyes.

"You're right," she agreed with a nod. "I'm not." *He recovers well*, Lee thought approvingly.

Randy surveyed his plate. "Hmm . . ."

Lee waited, then asked, "Yes?"

Randy looked at her, seemingly lost in thought. "Jake offered me some quiche and fruit salad for lunch today, and I was just wondering if there was any left."

Lee studied Randy. *He's handsome, clever, and not supposed to be here. Let's take a chance and see what happens.*

She rested her elbows on the table, bringing her face into the candlelight. Her hair fell in soft curls around her ears. Lee looked at Randy's lobster, then brought her eyes up to his. "Would you like a hand?" she asked.

Randy smiled. "Please."

Make that handsome, clever, and charming, Lee thought as she reached for Randy's lobster.

"I'm going to bed, Daddy," Anne called through the door to Joel's study. "Is there anything you need?"

"Another plate of cookies for these two young wolfhounds would be nice," Joel called back. Anne came in and retrieved the plate. Randy glanced at the papers on Joel's desk, then at Anne as she left.

"Don't worry about it," Joel said pleasantly. "Annie grew up in a house full of classified documents. If it wasn't marked TOP SECRET or above, I let her color on the backs of the pages." He smiled. "She took one of her works of art to school once, in second grade." Joel chuckled at the horrified expression on Greg's face. "For show-and-tell. I thought the director was going to have a stroke when I told him about it."

Anne returned, carrying a plate heaped with cookies that she put on the desk. "Mama says don't be all night," she told her father as she kissed him on the forehead. "Remember, you need your rest." Joel grimaced as Anne turned to Greg and Randy. "You two know where your bedrooms are?" she asked. Both men nodded. "Breakfast is serve-yourself—it'll be there whenever you get up." Anne closed the door behind her.

"I don't think that you would've ticked Cathy off without a good reason," Randy told Greg. "So why am I once again sponging off the Drydens?"

Greg shrugged, then snagged an oatmeal cookie from the plate Anne had brought in. "You needed a break, and Pat's birthday was a good excuse to come up."

"Are you expecting a tough time at the subcommittee hearings?" Joel asked Randy.

Randy shrugged. "Not really, I guess. Senator Rutherford's a reasonable man. Once we explained to him that the suddenness of the coup required an immediate response on our part, he got over being miffed about not having been notified before the operation." He took a bite of cookie. "Rutherford's one of the few on the Hill," Randy admitted through a mouthful of crumbs, "who doesn't believe that the American public has a right to know everything that its government has going on."

"But," Joel interjected, "he has to *appear* that he does, so you get raked over his subcommittee's coals."

"Exactly. Fortunately, it's my boss that has to testify, and not me." Randy grinned. "That's why they pay him the big bucks." He shook his head. "Still, it's entirely too close to the spotlight for someone like me, so I decided to blow town for a couple of days."

Greg nodded sagely. "Spoken like a true Company man. When the going gets public, the covert-ops types bug out."

Randy raised an eyebrow. "Food's better here than at Langley, too."

"It's been a while since you've been up here," Joel said to Greg. "What's new?" He grinned. "Cathy does seem more than a little miffed at you."

Greg made a face. "Tell me about it. She wants to get married, and I don't want to talk about it until my reputation's more established." He closed his eyes. "Which, at the rate I'm going, won't be anytime soon."

"Why is that?" Joel asked. "I showed that paper of yours in *Optoelectronics Journal* to a physicist at Bowdoin. He was quite impressed."

"The theory's no problem," Greg replied. "It's putting it into practice that's giving me grief. I'm field-testing a new type of sensor, and it isn't behaving itself. It acts up days, and Cathy acts up nights." He threw up his hands. "Life is the pits."

Joel looked interested. "Visible light sensor?"

"Nope," Greg said. "Hyperons."

"Forgive this poor, humble spook for not knowing, O long-haired professor type," Randy said, "but what's a 'hyperon'?"

"Subatomic particle. Given off as a by-product of nuclear decay."

"So?"

"So, the Indigo-Lacrosse bird that the shuttle *Atlantis* launched on its last military mission has a hyperon detector built in."

"This was your idea?" Joel asked.

"Partly," Greg admitted. He leaned back in his chair. "Remember that Soviet missile sub that went down off the Carolinas a few years ago?" Both men nodded. "Well," Greg continued, "when the Navy nosed around that boomer, they found a missile nearly intact, with its payload undamaged. There were plenty of warheads to go around. Somehow, the boys over in the basement of the NSA ended up with one."

"Why is it," Randy said, "that the prospect of a hydrogen bomb in the hands of a bunch of civil servants on the outskirts of the nation's capital makes me very unhappy?"

"Don't worry about it," Greg advised. "Langley is less than a mile from where they're playing with it." He shrugged nonchalantly. "If they fumble the warhead, you'll never know it."

Randy rolled his eyes.

"Anyway," Greg concluded, "they fooled around with it in all sorts of ways. One of the things that they found out was that weapons-grade plutonium—that is, stuff that's at least 60 percent plutonium-239—decays with a recognizable signature."

"And, " Joel asked, "the hyperons are the signature?"

"Exactly. The NSA bunch found that plutonium refined from ore mined in the U.S. emits hyperons with an entirely different spin than plutonium refined from Russian or Chinese ore."

"Let me get this straight," Randy said. "Hyperons spin?"

"Not exactly," Greg responded with a smile. "*Spin* is a term that the nuclear physicists invented to differentiate between the various forms of a subatomic particle. Just as light has different frequencies, hyperons have different spins."

Frustrated by his ignorance, Randy grabbed a cookie from the plate on Joel's desk and bit it in two.

"Don't worry, Randy," Joel assured him. "You're doing just what field operatives like you do so well."

"What's that?" Randy mumbled.

Joel grinned. "You're asking questions . . . and eating."

Joel turned back to Greg. "Why the new technology?" he asked. "I thought that between the adaptive optics of the Keyholes for when it's clear and the synthetic aperture radars of the

Indigo-Lacrosses for when it's overcast, you could spot stuff down to a few inches in diameter."

"We can," Greg agreed. "And that's the problem."

"Sure is," Randy concurred. "Now he can catch me when I'm over there reading girlie magazines instead of shooting at the bad guys."

"With resolution down now to a few inches," Greg explained, "the problem isn't a lack of information but an over-abundance of it. The new high-resolution radars can generate information thousands of times faster than the priority-one tracking channels can download it. We've got three satellites in orbit, at over a billion dollars apiece, and they're already swamped."

"How about preprocessing the data?" Joel wondered.

"Once we get supercomputers the size of your PC over there, we'll stand a chance. Nothing we've got right now that will fit in a shuttle's cargo bay is worth bothering with." Greg shrugged. "Anyway, even when we do get the data downloaded it takes way too long to process it. It used to be that once a month or so we checked to see that the Soviet ICBMs were still in their silos. We could check that infrequently because that's how long it took them to move one of them. Now, even daily checking can't keep up with an SS-20 that's mounted on a mobile launcher."

Greg took a sip of coffee. "So we get the data. Somewhere in that data is the SS-20, but *where?* Teaching a computer to recognize the electronic signal that matches the known return from a fixed, unchanging object like an ICBM silo is one thing. Teaching it to recognize a mobile ICBM launcher that's trying real hard to look like a tree is something else entirely."

"Any luck with data fusion?"

"Not yet. And that's the really frustrating part. We know that each form of sensor has its blind spots: The optical technology can read the license plate on that mobile launcher—

something the radar can't. But we need the radar to tell a real launcher from a plastic decoy. The trouble is, we're barely into the prototyping stage on systems to integrate all this information. The software especially is giving us fits."

Greg shrugged. "That's the whole point of my new toy. I've been heavily involved in treaty verification—SALT, START, and so forth—and this is an attempt to acquire a large amount of very specific information, information that'll tell us exactly what we need to know without overloading the Tracking and Data Relay Satellite Station."

Lee knocked, then looked in. "Could one of you help me get the lobster trap back down to the dock?"

Randy came to his feet. "Excuse me, gentlemen. Duty calls."

5

"This is madness," Grigory Markov told Pyotr Tallin as they walked together in the woods near Alma-Ata. Water dripped from the leafless, tendril-like branches that hung down from the silver beeches around them.

"You are right, comrade, it is," his old friend agreed. "But, these days, what isn't?" Sodden leafmold muffled their footsteps. "Moscow has discovered that it can change the laws of nature. They have repealed our law of gravity—the constitution that held us together—and now, not surprisingly, we are flying apart." Tallin looked down at his short, stocky friend. "The question is, Grigory Ivanovich, which way do you want to fly? Into light, or into darkness?"

Markov stuffed his hands deeper into the pockets of his greatcoat. He frowned as a drop of water marred the polish of his boot toe. "But," he protested, "what about our oath to the *Rodina?*"

"*What* Motherland?" Tallin snapped, his voice bitter. "Russia is controlled by drunken embezzlers, Germany has sold herself to the West, and the so-called republics are doing their level best to wipe each other off the map."

"Moscow *will* recall us," Markov insisted.

"Yes, they will." Tallin's breath formed a plume of fog in the still air. "But," he asked gently, "to *what?*"

"They have promised us all jobs."

Tallin nodded. "So they have." He paused. "Grigory, how much is one of your MAZ driver-mechanics paid?"

"You know that as well as I do: twenty rubles a month."

Tallin nodded again. "So we have a trained soldier, responsible for the maintenance and operation of a mobile launcher that carries a strategic nuclear missile, paid less than half that of the trolleybus driver who takes the soldier's fat *babushka* wife to the store." The tall, thin colonel shook his head. "There will be no jobs for us, Grigory. There will not even be work for the driver, and at least he can *do* something."

"Our pensions, then," Markov persisted stubbornly. "We can retire."

Tallin whirled. "Listen to me, you *dooriik!* What pensions? The party *nomenklatura* have looted the treasury! Russia is broke! And if it is broke, the army is broke!" The two stared at each other for a moment. Tallin chuckled. "Ah, Grigory Ivanovich, you have managed to get me worked up once again."

Markov smiled at his bookish friend and laughed heartily. "I have always said that it was good for you, Pyotr. I doubt that you would have ever married Natalia had I not whipped you into a lather first by pretending to steal her from you." Markov frowned. "So, what do we do?"

Tallin clapped his friend on the shoulder. "You know that already, old friend. Or else you would not have driven here like the hell-bent tank driver you once were." Markov smiled at the memory, and his ears filled with the roar of his T-72's seven-hundred horsepower engine. "Our little stroll has taken us near my *dacha*. Come in, and have some Stolichanya and pickled eggs." Tallin smiled as Markov's eyes widened in anticipation.

Pyotr Tallin set down a bottle and glasses, along with a

plate of eggs. As Markov helped himself to both, Tallin left the room, then returned with a piece of paper and a map.

Markov lifted his brimming glass. "*Saw Zdoroviectem!*"

"Good health to you too, Grigory," Tallin replied. He handed Markov the sheet of paper. "This is what I have sold to Yousef Bey."

Markov looked the sheet over. He whistled. "How much did you get for all this?"

Tallin smiled. "Enough to keep Natalia in the style to which you made her accustomed." He leaned forward. "But," he said, quite serious now, "no more than you will make if you sell Bey the rest of the items on the list."

Markov squinted to bring the list into focus.

"SS-1 SCALEBOARDs . . . SA-7 GRAILs . . . FROG-7s . . . 152-, 180-, 203-, or 240-mm artillery shells . . . ADMs . . . " The colonel looked up. "I have all of those."

"I know, Grigory," Tallin said quietly, "I know." He lifted his glass. "Now, let us drink to the Motherland. May she rest in peace."

✧ ✧ ✧

Ganden awoke and found that his eyes wouldn't open. He knew he was in his bed; he could feel the weight of blankets. He pulled one hand from beneath the covers, cautiously rubbed the stickiness from his left eye, and was rewarded with the sight of a rectangle of sunlight on the wall of his room. When Ganden reached for his right eye and could not touch it, he sat up. The sudden movement caused his head to throb, and he cried out in pain.

"Lie still, Ganden." Firm hands pushed him back down onto his pillow. "You have been very sick."

"Tenzig," Ganden asked his best friend, "what's wrong with my other eye?"

"It is bandaged," Tenzig replied. "As is half your head." Tenzig moved his chair into Ganden's field of view. "When I heard what had happened, I went to Drapchi Prison and inquired about you and the others."

"Did you see Puzhen?" Ganden asked eagerly.

"No, I didn't. I'm sorry. They would tell me nothing about any of them. All they would tell me about you was that, since you had collaborated with the PLA, you had not been arrested." Ganden started to get up again. "Lie still," Tenzig ordered. "Even if I believed for an instant that you would do such a thing, it is not up to me to judge you for it."

Tenzig got up and walked over to Ganden's dung-fueled stove. He ladled some soup from a pot on the stove into a large cup. "It's *tukpa*," Tenzig explained. "My mother made it for you. Sip it slowly." Ganden pulled himself into a sitting position and took the cup, breathing in the aroma of the noodles and bits of savory meat.

"After visiting Drapchi, I came here." Tenzig smiled as Ganden slurped hungrily at the soup. "I found you delirious with fever. You were burning to the touch, and your face was badly infected. When I went to the clinic to fetch a doctor, they refused to come because you had been blacklisted as a insurrectionist."

Tenzig smiled grimly. "You must admit that they are clever. They tell us that you are a Chinese sympathizer, and they tell their fellow Han that you are fomenting revolution." Ganden ran his hand over his bandages. " A nurse at the Tibetan hospital," Tenzig explained, "was able to give me some soap and bandages. I washed you as best as I could and bandaged you up."

"And you've been here since?"

Tenzig nodded. "Except, of course," he said with a laugh, "when I went home to get the *tukpa.*"

Ganden set down the empty bowl and lay back against the pillow. "Do you remember the story that the itinerant preacher told to us when he passed through a few months ago?" he asked. "The one about the Good Samaritan?"

"Yes. It's in our copy of the Gospel of Luke."

"Just like him you bandaged my wounds, took me in, and took care of me. You are my Good Samaritan." Ganden closed his eyes. *"To duo chay,* my friend. You saved my life."

"You're more than welcome. You would have done the same for me." Tenzig tossed some more dried yak dung into the stove, then covered Ganden with a blanket. "Sleep now. I'll be back tomorrow."

Public Security Bureau Inspector Hua Chen picked up a rock and threw it irritably into the Kyichu River. He had stayed up all night caring for his ailing mother, and his throat hurt from chain smoking Mild Seven cigarettes.

Long nights were hard on Chen. They reminded him of the dark night in 1970 when the Red Guards had kicked opened the door to his family's modest Hangzhou home. The sweating, excited band of men, not much older than the twelve-year-old Chen, had announced that his father, a professor of English at Hangzhou University, was to be taken to the country for "re-education." When Mrs. Chen had gone to their bedroom to fetch her husband, she found the bedroom window open and her husband gone.

Two days later a note arrived from Chen's father, telling them to meet a boatman friend of theirs at the waterfront on the south side of the Pearl River in Canton. The boatman would take them to join Professor Chen in safety on the island of Taiwan. After another long night, just as the sun was rising behind their mountainous island haven, the small boat had been intercepted by a U.S. Navy frigate. Its captain explained that, at the request of the Kuomintang government, they were helping to protect Taiwan against "revolutionary infiltrators" from the mainland. For years afterwards Chen's mother had cried herself to sleep in the desolate labor camp to which they had been banished, and the sound of her sobbing and the face of the American captain had infiltrated Chen's dreams.

After Mao's death, Chen's English skills, a legacy from his father, had enabled him to get a job in the *Wai Shi Ke*, the branch of the Public Security Bureau that dealt with foreigners. However, because of his "demonstrated unreliability" as a child of twelve, he was posted to Tibet. Two years ago, after much scrimping and saving, Chen had been able to afford to have his aging and broken mother join him. Chen's job consisted mainly of dealing with tour groups, monitoring the few legal expatriates living in Lhasa, and issuing exit orders to unauthorized travelers. To those he deported he bore no ill will. He was saving his fury for others.

Jarmalinka at five, said the note left for him on his desk this morning. Because he spoke fluent Tibetan, Chen had assumed the role of PSB contact with the local ring of snitches, double-crossers, and turncoats. At 4:30, eager to find out what one of his informants had for him, Chen left his office. Not wishing to attract attention with a car, he took one of the bright-blue canopied pedicabs down to the shore of the Kyichu River opposite Jarmalinka Island. Chen paid the driver, then handed the crone huddled in the gatekeeper's shack a ten-*fen* note and strode across the prayer-flag festooned footbridge. The inspector walked the length of the island, past picnicking couples and groups of small boys playing in pools of stagnant water. When he arrived at the copse of trees at the far end of the island that was his usual rendezvous with an informant, the grove was empty.

Arms crossed, Chen stared across the Kyichu. A herd of sheep, white spots against the dark green undergrowth, wended its way across a hillside. Downstream, clouds blackened with rain flowed over jagged peaks. Chen watched the rainclouds advance, then glanced at his watch. *Ten more minutes. If I get wet, I'll take it out of that fool Xongnu's hide.*

Chen whirled at the sound of hurried footsteps. "It's about

time," he snapped at the small, nervous man who scuttled toward him.

"I'm sorry, *genla*," the man greeted Chen politely. "I had to come across the river." He pointed to a small, yak-skin boat that had been beached upstream.

Chen frowned. "You live on this side of the river, Xongnu. Why did you come in a boat?"

The informant glanced around nervously. "I had to make sure that no one saw me."

Chen was suddenly interested. *Xongnu is the laziest man in Tibet. Everyone knows that he makes his living selling information to us. What could he have that would terrify him into expending such effort?* "What is it this time?" he asked with feigned indifference. "Yet another list of black-market moneychangers?"

Xongnu's eyes flicked from side to side once more. He reached into a jacket pocket and took out a battered Polaroid photograph. "Found it yesterday," Xongnu said proudly as the policeman inspected the photo of a bootmaker working at his bench. "In Yak Alley. A tourist took it, then threw it away." Chen reached for the picture, but the Tibetan snatched it back. "Double my usual price for it."

Chen glared at the man. "Why double? I don't even know who he is."

Xongnu laughed. "I know you don't, *genla*. You haven't been here long enough. But your superintendent will know who this bootmaker is. Double."

"Tell me who it is, then I'll decide how much to pay you."

The informant's eyes glittered shrewdly. "His name would mean nothing to you, but much to those you'd tell it to. Double my usual, or I throw it in the river."

The inspector regarded his informant narrowly. *He's repulsive, but reliable.* Chen pulled a wad of bills from his pocket. "This had better be worth it," the inspector warned as he peeled off four 50-*yuan* notes. "If you're trying to swindle me, I'll personally feed you to *Lukhang Chu*." The Tibetan blanched at the mention of the water dragon rumored to inhabit the nether regions of the Jokhang Temple, and Chen grinned mirthlessly.

"It's worth it," Xongnu replied as photo and money exchanged hands. He looked at the younger man archly. "I'd show that to your superintendent right away, if I were you." Pocketing the cash, the small man headed back toward his boat.

Chen waited until Xongnu was out of sight. Then he slipped the photo into a pocket of his coat and started back to the footbridge.

6

Pyotr Tallin's sergeant walked over to the command car and saluted smartly. "Truck loaded, sir. We're ready to move out." Tallin, who was watching the preparations, made no reply.

"Sir?"

The colonel looked at the enlisted man as if seeing him for the first time. "Yes, Sergeant? What is it?"

The sergeant had served in the Red Army long enough to know better than to point out to a colonel that he hadn't been listening. "Ready to move out, sir," he repeated noncommittally. The sergeant had also worked for Tallin since the day he was commissioned. "Anything wrong?" he asked after a long look at his superior officer.

Tallin smiled. "I am fine, Mikhail Petrovich." He gestured to the second of the three trucks. "But, I will be a lot better when we get that nest of vipers to Semipalatinsk."

The sergeant nodded his agreement. He looked at the column of men waiting to board the first and last of the three trucks in the convoy. "The men are afraid of the bombs, sir. It would help if I could explain our mission to them."

Tallin bristled. "They are soldiers in the Army of the

Sov—" He stopped, shook his head, and smiled. "In the Army of Russia," he finished quietly.

"As are we now," the sergeant said gently. "But, unlike us, those boys will never know the glory of serving in the Red Army." Tallin glanced at what was left of the sergeant's left hand. The rest had been blown off by an Afghan mine in the hills near Kabul. "They are half-trained conscripts who have no pride, but who *have* heard all about Chernyobyl." The sergeant looked at Tallin. "They are scared."

Tallin smiled, liking this man who reminded him so much of his dead father. "Very well, Sergeant," he said with a pretended brusqueness that made them both smile. "Tell the men that, by order of no less than the president himself, all tactical nuclear arms here at Alma-Ata are being recalled to Russia. They have the privilege of guarding the very first of these historic shipments!" Tallin winked. "That ought to do it."

The colonel watched as the sergeant briefly addressed the occupants of both trucks. Tallin got into the car as the sergeant trotted back.

"That did the trick, sir," the sergeant reported as he slid behind the wheel. "I told them that this would be a day to tell their grandchildren about." He grinned at Tallin. "That ought to be enough to keep them in dirty jokes until we get to Semipalatinsk."

The command car took the lead as the convoy moved out.

❖ ❖ ❖

As the convoy neared Ayaguz, it descended into the small valley through which ran the Ili River. The road meandered down to the valley floor along a small ravine that cut across the river valley, and a rusting iron bridge spanned the Ili at the point where ravine and river met.

The command car was halfway across the bridge when Tallin saw a ball of red flame erupt in the rearview mirror. An instant later the car was rocked by a tremendous concussion.

As Tallin and the sergeant threw themselves out of the car and ran back along the bridge, soldiers began to scramble out of the first truck. The sergeant shouted and pointed. Men had appeared on the cliffs above the river. As they watched, one of the men brought a weapon to his shoulder and sighted along it. Flame spouted from the end of the RPG-75, and a projectile rocketed toward the first truck.

"*Nichevo!*" the sergeant screamed in fury as the missile struck. The 75-mm HEAT warhead detonated, and the truck vanished in a ball of white light. Tallin heard something whistle past his head. A soldier, in flames, ran screaming into the river. Then other men appeared on the clifftops, pouring automatic rifle fire into the panicked troops.

The sergeant reached the convoy first. He scooped up a fallen soldier's AKM assault rifle, braced the butt against his hip, and sprayed the cliff face with bullets. One of the attackers tumbled down the cliff and crashed to the ground. The veteran soldier shouted orders in a futile effort to subdue the chaos that raged around him. Then, as suddenly as they had appeared, the men on the cliffs vanished. The pinging of cooling metal replaced the crackle of gunfire as the only sound in the valley.

Tallin and his sergeant searched the small battlefield. They found no one alive. Each deep, rapid breath filled their nostrils with the acrid stench of scorched metal and charred flesh. The two men made their way around to the rear of the convoy. The sergeant pointed to a large crater where the third truck had been.

"Land mine, sir. From the size of the crater, I'd say they used a PDM-42." He mopped the sweat from his face with his sleeve. "They knew we were coming." He pointed at the second truck. Except for a few tears in its canvas cover from shrapnel, it was undamaged. "Looks like they know what they want, too."

"Let's get back to the command car and call this in," Tallin ordered. "I'm sure our attackers will come get us when they're ready."

Tallin was about to turn away when the sergeant grabbed his arm. "Look." From the far side of the river, a car was making its way across the bridge.

The gold Rolls-Royce Phantom VI was waiting for them when they got there. As the soldiers approached, the front doors of the Rolls flew open. Two men jumped out and leveled automatic rifles at them. Tallin and the sergeant stopped. Another door opened, and a well-dressed man got out.

"*You!*" Tallin hissed.

Yousef Bey slipped on a pair of dark glasses as he walked toward Tallin. "Really, Colonel," he said amiably, "you are surprised to see me?" Bey stopped before him and looked at Tallin quizzically. "I believe that this is where we agreed to make the exchange."

The sergeant looked at Tallin. "You know this man, Colonel?"

Tallin ignored him. His rage focused itself on Bey. "You said *nothing* about this," he whispered, gesturing at the carnage behind him. "You said it would be a *peaceful* exchange."

Bey shook his head. "And you wonder why you lost the Afghan war. What did you expect to do, Colonel?" he asked scornfully. "Stop the convoy and hand me the keys?" Bey gestured elegantly toward the smoking wreckage of the trucks. "This is good training for my men, and it will give your military police something interesting to investigate." The Afghan reached into his jacket. "Now, about your payment."

The confusion on the sergeant's face was replaced by horror. With a screamed curse he backed away and started to bring up his pistol.

"Kill him," Bey ordered without looking at the man.

One of Bey's bodyguards pivoted and fired. The burst caught the sergeant in the chest and threw him over the side of the bridge.

"For a moment," Bey remarked, "I thought that you had acquired a partner." He handed Tallin a thick envelope. "Inside is your account number at the Zurich branch of Credit Suisse, a German passport, and a British Air ticket from Delhi to London. How you get to Delhi is your concern."

Tallin accepted the envelope. He stared at it for a moment, then leafed through it.

"All is in order, then?" Bey asked. Tallin nodded numbly. "Do forgive me, Colonel Tallin, if I do not say that it's been a pleasure doing business with you." Bey took off his sunglasses and held the colonel's gaze. "After all," he told Tallin, "it was your army that bayonetted my wife and children to death before my eyes." Bey got into the car.

The Rolls backed to the far end of the bridge and stopped. Then a radio-controlled detonator ignited the plastic explosive hidden in the passport, and Pyotr Tallin's life ended in a cloud of red mist.

7

Grigory Markov shook the snow off his greatcoat as he entered the building. He stuffed his gloves in one of its pockets and handed the coat to an aide as he strode toward his office. The colonel had not eaten since the alert was announced twelve hours ago and the base at Semipalatinsk had been sealed. Nor had his midnight patrol of the base perimeter in an open jeep improved his mood.

"Report!" Markov growled as he passed the communications station.

"Nothing new, sir," the radio operator replied, trying to stay as inconspicuous as possible. "Still no word from Colonel Tallin."

"Do we know why we weren't informed that a convoy was in transit here?" Markov demanded to know.

"Still working on that, too, sir."

In his office, the colonel scowled as he surveyed the dispatches on his desk. *Twelve hours*, he thought disgustedly. *More than half a day since this mysterious convoy from Alma-Ata disappeared, and still they cannot find it.* Markov shook his head. *Not surprising, given the level of expertise of the searchers.* He smiled as another possibility occurred to him. *Perhaps they don't want to be found. Perhaps they're in Rybache, reveling in a night of R&R....* His smile disappeared. *That would explain the whereabouts of the rest of them, but what about Pyotr? Even if he's with them, he's much too married for that sort of thing.*

Markov opened the humidor that occupied a corner of his desk and pulled out a Cuban cigar. It was an Hoyo de Monterrey Double Corona, the last from a box given to him by his brother, one of the few Soviet advisers left on the island. He looked at it, rolled it between his fingers, and cursed Moscow because after this one was gone there would be no more. Markov started to put it back, then bit off one end. He spat out the plug of tobacco with such force it bounced off the far wall of his office.

The son and grandson of field-grade officers, Markov had been raised with little love for uncertainty. As a cadet in the Young Pioneers he had learned how orders were to be carried out; as an officer in the Army of the Soviet Union he had learned how they were to be given.

Now he was faced with a situation for which no orders existed. Everyone at Alma-Ata would tell him only that "Colonel Tallin is currently unavailable." It never occurred to him to call Supreme Command—Markov had learned early that you don't make marshal by running for help. A late-night call to Tallin's home had resulted only in Natalia's sleepy voice exhuming within him the specters of memories and desires he had thought long forgotten.

Markov had just exhaled the first lungful of sweet smoke when the radio operator stepped into the office and saluted.

"They've found the convoy, sir."

Markov set the cigar in an ashtray made from the casing of an artillery shell. "Where?"

"In the Ili, sir."

Markov frowned. *"In* the Ili?"

"That's what it says here, sir. *In* the Ili. Near Ayaguz."

Markov sat down. "Dismissed." The operator saluted again and left. *Even with Azerbaijani drivers,* Markov wondered, *how could three ten-ton ZIL-135s and a command car end up* in *a river?*

His phone rang. It was Alma-Ata.

Ganden looked up from his reading as the door to his room opened. Tenzig came in, followed by a man Ganden didn't recognize.

"Did you have any luck at the prison today?" Tenzig asked.

Ganden began to answer, then stopped abruptly. He looked at the man standing next to Tenzig, then at his friend.

"It's all right," Tenzig assured him. "This is Kailas Barabise. I've told him what happened."

Ganden shook his head glumly. "They won't even tell me if she's there or not. And they won't tell me about any of the rest, either."

"I'll see what I can find out for you," Barabise offered. Ganden turned his head toward him, and the man frowned. "How did that happen?" Reflexively, Ganden's hand went to his cheekbone. Beneath his fingertips he felt the patch of hard, slick scar tissue that was appearing as the scabs fell away.

Ganden looked at the man before him, who appeared to be in his fifties. Short, but with the build of a champion weightlifter, the man wore both the high boots of the Khampa nomad and camouflage fatigues. Eyes glittering with experience-sharpened intelligence gazed out at Ganden from beneath grizzled eyebrows. A luxuriant mustache, the only other hair on his head, completed his air of confident ferocity.

"Well?" It was not a question.

As Ganden proceeded with his explanation, both his bitterness toward his persecutors and his attraction to this man grew. Barabise nodded occasionally, his eyes never leaving

Ganden's. When Ganden credited Tenzig with saving his life, Barabise gave the young man an approving nod.

"Let me get this straight, major," Markov growled. "You're telling me that *we* were not notified that a convoy was in transit here because *you* were not notified of its departure?"

"That is correct Colonel Markov. I was away from the base day before yesterday—at the air base in Iliysk."

"And Colonel Tallin was with you?"

The voice on the other end of the line hesitated. "Don't you know, sir?"

"Know what?" Markov snapped.

"Colonel Tallin is dead, sir. He was commanding the convoy." The ash dropped from the end of Markov's forgotten cigar. Unbalanced, the cigar fell out of the ashtray and onto the desk blotter. "Colonel Markov?"

"Still here, Major." His mind raced. *Pyotr, you idiot, why didn't you let me know you were going ahead with the deal?* "Do you know what the convoy was carrying?"

"No sir, not yet. Our inventory isn't finished. All we know for sure is that one of the convoy vehicles is missing completely."

Markov swore under his breath. "Were there any survivors?" He waited tensely.

"Three. Two draftees, and Colonel Tallin's staff sergeant."

"Very well, Major. You're in command now. I'll be there in ten hours."

After breaking the news to Natalia Tallin, Markov sat for a long time in stony silence. At last he noticed the smoldering cigar, and snuffed it out with a single blow of his massive fist.

Ganden finished his explanation. For a moment, Barabise said nothing. Then he sat down on the edge of the desk. Ganden managed to avoid flinching under the intensity of the man's gaze.

"Tell me about your education," Barabise said at last.

"The Han sent me away when I was eleven," Ganden replied. "To the Hongguang Middle School. In Tianjin, near Beijing. Three thousand kilometers from here. For four years I studied there, and not once was I permitted to visit my family. My parents offered to pay my way, but it did no good. I was not allowed to return home for summer vacations or for my sister's wedding." His voice grew cold. "Not even for my parents' funeral."

"How did they die?" Barabise asked.

"They had been shopping. On their way home a group of protestors ran past them, chased by a pair of Security Bureau jeeps. One of the jeeps stopped, and the PSB men accused my parents of being involved in the protest. My father stepped in front of my mother to protect her, and they shot him." The life fled from Ganden's face. "Then they shot my mother. Carefully. She was eight months pregnant. It took her four days to die."

The room echoed with silence.

"After the four years at Hongguang," Ganden continued, "I was allowed six weeks here before being sent back for three more years of study. Then, after another six-week vacation, because I had been a good student, the Han rewarded me with four years in exile at the University of Shanghai." Desolation filled Ganden's eyes. "Twelve weeks. I had twelve weeks with my family in almost twelve years."

Ganden looked at Barabise. He saw in the man's eyes neither pity nor compassion, but instead the grim, uncompromising understanding of one who has also endured the unendurable. And that understanding did more for him than any amount of compassion ever had.

"What languages do you speak?" the older man asked.

"They made me learn Mandarin, and I picked up Shanghainese at the university. Some English, too."

Barabise nodded. "And your major?"

"Electrical engineering. I've been posted at the People's Glory Power Plant as the foreman in charge of renovation."

"Any experience with high-speed electronic devices?"

Ganden frowned. "Some. Why?"

Barabise said nothing. He looked at Tenzig, barely nodded, and left.

"What was that all about?" Ganden asked after the door had closed behind Barabise. "Isn't he a bootmaker over in the Barkhor?"

Tenzig nodded, then smiled. "He's also someone who can help us. He hid me from the police after the raid, and helped me get the bandages for you. And he meant what he said when he promised to try and find out about Puzhen and the others."

"How can a simple cobbler do all these things?"

"A 'simple cobbler' cannot. But a Khampa warrior who has dedicated his life to breaking the Han stranglehold on his country can." Tenzig paused. "With help. Our help."

"Even if what you say is true, how could we possibly be of help to him?"

"It's getting dark. Light your candles, sit down, and I'll explain. . . ."

8

Markov strode unannounced into the office marked **Maj. M. Rozhin.** The man behind the desk started to bark out a reprimand, then stopped abruptly as he looked up at the officer who loomed over him like Mount Lenin.

"Are you Rozhin?"

The major nodded, then took off his glasses and scrubbed his face with his hand. He had been up all night, preparing for this man's arrival.

"I am Markov, from Semipalatinsk."

Rozhin smiled faintly. "So I assumed."

"Have you figured out what's missing?"

Rozhin picked up a sheet of paper. "We finished the inventory while you were on your way here. In addition to one ZIL-135 and four SA-7 GRAIL surface-to-air missiles, we're missing a variety of—"

"Tactical nuclear weapons," Markov interrupted. "Including 203-mm nuclear shells for the S-23, FROG-7 artillery missiles, and Atomic Demolition Munitions."

Rozhin's amazement overcame his prudence. "How did you know?" he blurted.

Because I remember what was on the list that Pyotr showed me that day in his dacha, Markov thought. "That," he roared, "is none of your concern!"

"But, Colonel," the hapless major protested, "I'm in charge of security here."

"Not any more, you aren't," Markov replied quietly.

The calmness worried Rozhin even more than the bellowing. Shouting superior officers were a fact of army life. Calm ones made him very nervous. "In my capacity as acting commander of the Central Asian Military District," Markov said, "I put you in command of this base. That means *you* are responsible for the lost weapons, and *you* are responsible for finding them." Rozhin winced as the jaws of the trap closed around him. "Now, take me to Colonel Tallin's staff sergeant."

The doctor in the infirmary started to say something to Markov, then shook his head as he thought better of it. "I was going to tell you not to tire the sergeant out, but go ahead and take all the time you want. He'll be dead before he's tired."

"When was he brought in?" Markov asked.

"This morning. A search party found him about a hundred yards downstream from the bridge."

"Has he said anything?"

"Not that I've heard."

"And he stands no chance of surviving?"

The doctor shrugged helplessly. "Between spending a night in near-freezing water and the size of the bullet holes in him, I'm surprised that he's alive at all." The physician turned away. After a glance at Rozhin, Markov went into the room alone.

The face of Pyotr Tallin's staff sergeant was barely visible beneath a tangle of tubes. Markov glanced at the IV bag on its stand next to the bed, saw that it read MORPHINE, and nodded grimly.

"Can you hear me, Sergeant?" he asked quietly.

The man's eyes opened slowly. He glanced at the three stars on Markov's shoulderboards and tried to sit up.

"At ease, soldier," Markov ordered gently. He sat down, carefully, on the edge of the bed.

"Colonel Tallin?" the soldier rasped. He took a breath, then winced as if breathing hurt. From the size and color of the stain on the bandages around the sergeant's chest, such a reaction didn't seem unreasonable to Markov.

"Dead," Markov replied.

A little of the remaining light left the sergeant's eyes.

"Any . . . others . . . alive?"

"Two. They're being debriefed now. But you were the only one close to the incident on the bridge. Can you tell me anything?"

The sergeant swallowed, coughed, and fought his way back to consciousness. "Three men . . . in a car. One claimed . . . he knew the colonel."

"Did Colonel Tallin seem to know him?"

The sergeant frowned, then nodded. Markov took a deep breath. "Describe them," he ordered.

"Foreigners . . . Kazakhs, maybe."

"Could they have been Afghans?"

Another nod, more feeble than the first. "Do you know . . . who they were, Colonel?"

Let this old man die in peace, Markov thought. *He doesn't need to know.* "Afghan informers. Colonel Tallin was their contact. It would appear that they've turned renegade. Don't worry, Sergeant. We'll find them."

Markov stood. He took a black leather case out of his jacket pocket and snapped it open. "One more thing, soldier." He held the case in front of the sergeant's face.

The sergeant's eyes fluttered open, tried to focus on the object before them, then went wide with recognition.

"The Order of Lenin—"

"For exceptional bravery and service to the Motherland. You are now a hero of the Soviet Union."

"But I didn't—"

"You served the *Rodina* long and well, Sergeant." Markov smiled sadly. "Besides, this is perhaps the last time this decoration will ever be awarded." The colonel pinned the Order of Lenin and the Gold Star Medal onto the pillow next to the sergeant's head. Then he brought himself to full attention and saluted.

"Thank you, sir." The old sergeant smiled. His eyes closed.

"Well done, soldier," Markov replied.

The colonel turned to leave, then stopped. The flow of morphine into the sergeant's veins was controlled by a stopper clamped onto the tube that led into his arm. Markov glanced at the man in the bed, then thumbed the stopper wide open.

"*Dosvedanya*, comrade."

"I want a jeep and supplies," Markov ordered on their way back to Rozhin's office. "I'm driving back to Semipalatinsk—I want to inspect the site where the convoy was found."

"Very good, Colonel." *It's not my problem if this madman wants to drive eight hundred kilometers in freezing weather.*

"Call your quartermaster. I'm leaving immediately."

Eight hours later, Markov stood in the center of the bridge over the Ili. Below him the river, swift-flowing but shallow, gurgled and muttered in its bed. All that remained of the raid was the crater, now dusted with snow. Markov had found nothing, and he looked around him as if casting for a scent. The sun came out from behind a cloud. Through the holes in the metal flooring of the bridge, a glint caught his eye.

The colonel gritted his teeth as he waded into the frigid waters in the bridge's shadow. He waited patiently until he saw the gleam again, then plunged his arm into the river. Markov frowned as he pulled his fist from the water, then grimaced as he opened it. In his hand Markov held a pallid, cold finger. The glint that had attracted his attention was from Pyotr Tallin's wedding band. With a curse Markov flung the finger far into the river. As he turned to leave, he noticed another gleam.

This time his fist opened to reveal a gold Imperial.

He held the coin in his hand and stared at it, his lips compressed into a thin line. Then he muttered, "Yousef Bey."

9

After helping with the breakfast dishes, Anne went into the family room. Jake was sprawled on the couch, his feet propped up on an ottoman, lost in thought. Anne sat down next to him and rested her hand on his.

"Anyone home?" she asked.

Startled, Jake looked up. "Where is everybody?"

Anne ran down her mental checklist. "Mama's answering service just called, Lee and Cathy are catching up on each other's news, and Greg and Randy are talking to Daddy in his study." She looked at Jake. "And as for you, you've been far away all morning. If it's someplace exotic and terribly romantic," she teased, "then may I join you there, please?"

"It's nothing," he said quietly. "Just a little restless, that's all." Jake's massive hand enveloped Anne's small one.

A sudden realization caused Anne to look at him. "It was Dave Stevenson, your boss at Global, who called a little while ago, wasn't it?"

Jake nodded. "He wants me in New York on Monday. The old skinflint wouldn't tell me what was going on, but I could tell that it's something big."

"His tone of voice?" Anne wondered.

"Yeah. The same one that he's used in the past when he's been *really* excited at me." Jake looked at the large photo of Machu Picchu that dominated one wall of the family room. "I think he's got an assignment for me." He hesitated. "Dave asked if my passport was still current," Jake added quietly, "so I might be gone for a while."

Anne's hand went to the hollow of her throat. Her fingers toyed with the pendant, polished tourmaline set in gold filigree, that Jake had given her for Christmas. "I thought that, this time, you were going to be able to stay for a while."

Jake shrugged. "So did I. But Dave made it real clear that if I don't show on Monday, I'm history."

"Oh. Well, at least we have some time to do something." Anne brightened. "I know. We can go sailing! I'll ask Cathy and Greg, and Lee and Randy." Anne missed Jake's sharp glance. "We'll pack a lunch and take *Turnstone* down to the picnic area at Pretty Marsh Harbor." *Turnstone* was Joel's twenty-four-foot Stone Horse class sloop. It had been purchased with the enthusiastic support of his wife and his cardiologist, both of whom wanted him out of the house.

"Sorry, lady. No can do."

Anne's face fell. "Why not? You can fly to New York Monday morning."

"I was going to. But Joe Denton, who was going to cover the president's United Nations speech tonight, broke his ankle getting out of the shower this morning."

"And you volunteered to take his place."

"Yep. That means I need to leave here in an hour."

When Anne didn't say anything, Jake reached out. He brushed her thick auburn hair back over her shoulder, then ran a forefinger along her collarbone. Even though she was more than a little annoyed at him, still Anne trembled at his touch.

"It's just until Monday," Jake told her, ignoring her plans

for a picnic. "I'll tell you what. I'll fly back Monday night, if it works out, and then stay as long as I can before I have to ship out." He smiled. "I'll make it up to you."

Anne said nothing. She thought she had become accustomed to Jake's comings and goings, *thought* she had worked out a way to handle it. But she discovered that as her feelings for him deepened, her battles with expectations grew more fierce. In her mind, she knew that he had a responsibility to his work. But her heart wanted—desperately, at times—for him to feel a similar responsibility toward their relationship.

It hurt, this feeling that she cared more about him than he did about her. And the hurt made her angry—at him, at herself, at the world.

With a sigh of resignation, Anne opened the box in her heart marked MEN, stuffed in her disappointment, and slammed the lid.

Jake yawned and stretched, then grabbed the shoulder that had stopped a Viet Cong bullet while he was an army Ranger. He grimaced in pain.

"It serves you right," Anne said reprovingly. "I saw you carrying the lobsters and showing off, as usual." She shook her head in disapproval.

Jake looked at her out of the corner of his eye. "Of course I was showing off. The things I have to do to impress you—"

"—do not include," Anne finished primly, "solo lobster lugging." Jake laughed. Anne laid her cheek against his shoulder, wishing that it didn't hurt him. "Take off your shirt, and I'll get the ointment Mama prescribed."

Randy, his hands in his pockets, sauntered along next to Lee as they wandered their way up Freeport's Holbrook Street. "That was a great dinner. What was the name of that place?"

"The Harraseeket Inn," Lee answered. "Annie and I have lunch there when we go shopping." She paused. "At least we *used* to have lunch there. We haven't been shopping much since she started seeing Jake."

Randy nodded understandingly. "It's the same way with guys: One of my friends starts dating, and we never see him again."

Lee looked up at him sharply, but Randy didn't see it.

"Twelve minutes until we clear the horizon," Susan Kirkcaldy reported. The middle-aged woman leaned back in her swivel chair and looked piercingly at Greg Miahara. "Well then, what is it? Don't you love her?"

Greg shifted uncomfortably in his chair. His account of his disastrous weekend with Cathy had met with little sympathy. "Well," he said slowly, "I guess I do. . . ."

"'I guess I do'? What kind of answer is that?" Susan harrumphed derisively. "What would you do if you were sitting on a dissertation panel over at Georgetown University and one of the doctoral candidates answered a question with a wimpy 'I guess I do'?"

Greg flinched, then looked defensively at the heavyset, gray-haired woman. "OK. Yes, I *do* love her."

"Then, what's keeping you from marrying her? She's made it obvious enough that she'll have you, though why she possibly would want to I'll never know."

The warmth with which Susan looked at Greg diffused the harshness of her words. She and her husband, Jeremy, had come to the U.S. the year before on a CIA-sponsored exchange program with the British intelligence agency MI6, and the couple had taken an immediate liking to the then newly engaged Greg and Cathy. Jeremy Kirkaldy, a small, sparrowlike man, was a brilliant theorist, while Susan was one of the best optoelectronics technicians in the world. They had met in a bunker underneath London during World War II, and they adored each other.

"Well?" Susan demanded.

"It's just that it's so—" Greg groped for words. "So *confining* to be married."

Susan struggled to keep from laughing. "You've got a point there," she agreed. "Marriage means that you'd have to cut back on your exhilarating social life." She waited until Greg looked suitably relieved, then continued. "No more twenty-hour shifts in this garden spot."

"Well, then," Greg protested, "what about excitement? There's no spontaneity when you're married."

"Hah!" Susan laughed. "You want excitement? Try a newborn with bronchitis at 3:00 A.M. in the middle of a blizzard! You want spontaneity? There's *nothing* more spontaneous than carrying on a love life in a house full of kids!" The youngest of the five Kirkcaldy children was now studying astrophysics with Stephen Hawking at Cambridge.

Greg gulped. "How did you ever get Jeremy to marry you, anyway?"

Susan smiled. "It took the entire population of the village of Lochgilphead and a good deal of rope, but he finally managed to persuade me."

A light began blinking, announcing that the satellite scan had begun. "Well now," she said, turning to her console, "let's see what the laddies have been up to today."

When the green rectangle glowed, Greg frowned. "Are we having telemetry problems?" he asked.

Susan shook her head. "Nothing on my screen."

"We are still Priority 1 with the tracking station, aren't we? If they've bumped us down in the queue, we could be losing data." The fact that the allocation of TDRSS time slots was a military secret sometimes made life interesting for intelligence analysts.

Susan picked up a phone and called White Sands. A minute later, she shook her head. "No problem there. Tim says that we've got the high-band relay for the next seven minutes."

"Doesn't make sense," Greg muttered. "We're only getting half the targets displayed that we did on Friday. Maybe it's a hardware glitch. Run level-two diagnostics."

"Everything shows normal," Susan reported three minutes later.

Greg thumped the console with his fist. "Something must be wrong with the discernment code. How long will it take to download the diagnostic report and reload the software?"

Susan called the tracking station again. "Best extended-duration uplink Tim can give us is preempted Priority 3. At those transmission rates, and considering that *Discovery* is aloft, it will take around seven hours."

"At that speed, I could almost fly over there and count 'em myself." Greg grimaced. "OK, let's get it set up."

Susan held up a hand as he started to sit down next to her. "I'll do it. Why don't you—"

"I'll go hack that new mass-calibration code I'm writing!" Greg interrupted. "That way we can begin to determine the relative yields of the warheads we find." He grinned happily.

"*You*," Susan said firmly, "will go take Cathy to lunch and talk to her."

"About what?"

"About how you feel about your relationship."

"Why do we need to talk? Can't I just buy her flowers and take her out?"

Susan rolled her eyes. *Well, at least it beats the way Jeremy always suggests that we make up.* "Because talking about the two of you is important to her."

Greg shook his head. "You sound just like she does."

Susan smiled. "That's because she's taking lessons from me. Alternate Tuesdays, at three. Now run along with you."

❖ ❖ ❖

That evening Randy, hands in pockets, sauntered along next to Lee as they wended their way up Freeport's Holbrook Street. "That was a great dinner. What was the name of that place?"

"The Harraseeket Inn," Lee answered. "Annie and I have lunch there when we go shopping." She paused. "At least, we *used* to have lunch there. We haven't been shopping much since she started seeing Jake."

Randy nodded understandingly. "It's the same way with guys: one of my friends starts dating, and we never see him again." Randy didn't see Lee look up at him.

From their table in the courtyard of Jameson Tavern, Lee and Randy watched the package-laden tourists streaming out of L. L. Bean.

"You work with Uncle Joel?" Lee asked over an iced cappuccino.

Randy took a sip of his Samuel Adams. His white wicker chair creaked as he shifted his weight. "Not exactly," he hedged. "I sort of work where Joel used to." *Gotta get off this subject*, he thought. "Joel's your uncle?" he asked.

Lee smiled. She tilted her head to one side, and Randy's pulse quickened. "Not really," she explained. "Joel and Pat have known my mom and dad forever. They're my godparents, just like my folks are Annie's. 'Auntie' and 'Uncle' is something Annie and I picked up when were little."

A street musician carrying a mandolin paused beside their table. Bowing low, he launched into a rendition of "Honeysuckle Rose," which was rewarded with applause and the five-dollar bill Randy gave him. Randy turned back to find Lee frowning.

"Was five too much?" he asked. "I play mandolin sometimes, and that guy was *really* good."

"You used to date Annie, didn't you?" Lee asked.

Randy blinked, taken aback by the abruptness of the question. Then he grinned. "You mean you don't know? I thought girlfriends told each other all about that sort of thing."

Charmed by his casual self-confidence, Lee laughed. "Moses had less trouble getting water out of rocks than I do getting any sort of gossip out of Annie." Lee looked at Randy expectantly.

Randy pointed at himself. "Me?" he asked diffidently. "I'm hardly the sort to kiss and tell." He paused, enjoying Lee's start of surprise. "Actually it was no big deal. Anne and I hung out together a few times one summer. Like we're doing tonight." Randy smiled. "She's kind of like a kid sister."

Inwardly bristling at the implication, Lee nodded nonchalantly. *I'll 'kid sister' you, Mister Randy Cavanaugh. . . .*

Randy frowned as something occurred to him. "If you two are so inseparable, how come I haven't met you before?"

"I was an exchange student at the University of Guadalajara the summer you and Annie . . . 'hung out together.'"

"Ever make it to Puerto Vallarta?" Randy asked.

"I flew there every weekend. *Langostas* on the beach, and being serenaded by the cutest *mariachis.*"

"You really get around, don't you?"

Lee stared at him.

"Travel-wise, I mean," he added hastily.

Lee nodded. "I love to go places and meet people. Have you ever been to Russia?"

Suddenly very alert, Randy was careful to keep his face expressionless. "Why do you ask?"

"I was in Russia earlier this summer," Lee replied breezily. "You said that you traveled a lot for the government, so I thought that you might have been there before."

Randy groaned inwardly. *Great. Just great. Now I've got to file a Potential Contact Report. Five forms, at twenty minutes a form. Crud. Some date this is turning out to be.* He watched as Lee took a sip of her cappuccino. *There is no way someone that gorgeous could be a Russian plant. I've seen their female agents—they're all built like Russian tanks and come on to you just as subtly. There's just no way. In any event, I bet she's gonna be worth it. . . .*

"Yeah, I've been there," Randy found himself admitting. He finished his Pale Ale. "The beer's a lot better here, though."

They joined the other couples strolling along Main Street. When they passed Ben and Jerry's, Lee declined Randy's offer of an ice cream cone. Then, as they sat on a park bench underneath a gas lamp, she stole bites from Randy's scoop of *Chunky Monkey*.

Randy finished, then rose and offered his hand to Lee. Neither of them relinquished the other's grasp as they continued their promenade.

Propped up by her pillow, Lee laced her fingers behind her head and watched the shadows of the trees outside her window as they flickered across the ceiling of her bedroom. *Better revise your list,* she thought contentedly. *To 'handsome, clever, and charming' gets added tonight's entry: Randy Cavanaugh* really *knows how to kiss.*

Lee stretched languidly and closed her eyes. In the back of her mind a small, strident alarm was sounding, but it was muffled by the warm glow within her, and she fell asleep without heeding it.

10

"I'm glad you came, Ganden. Sit down." Kailas Barabise motioned to the chair across the desk from his. "First, tell me why you're here."

Ganden glanced around as he took the proffered chair. The room in the back of Barabise's shop was furnished only by a desk, the two chairs, and a large, solid-looking cabinet. Harsh light flooded the room from the bare bulb dangling from the ceiling by its wire. Through the thick, stone walls the midafternoon bustle in the Barkhor Bazaar reached them faintly.

Ganden sat nervously on the edge of the chair and searched for words.

Barabise saw Ganden's hesitation. He smiled. "I assume you talked to Tenzig last night?" he offered.

The younger man nodded. "Is everything he told me about you true?"

Barabise laughed. "Knowing Tenzig, he told you that I am the reincarnation of Genghis Khan, returned to once again strike terror into the heart of the civilized world." He shook his head. "No, I am just a simple nomad who happens to love his country very much."

"But," Ganden protested, "all those things Tenzig told me. About Litang Monastery, and Chou En-lai, and America."

Barabise leaned back in his chair. He studied Ganden for a long time before answering. "Because Tenzig trusts you," he said at last, "I will too. What Tenzig told you is true. I was at Litang in 1956, when the Chinese bombed and strafed my people's encampment. I watched as the shrapnel from the fragmentation bombs shredded my family. It was their aircraft against our primitive rifles. With the rest of the survivors I spent that night hidden nearby, listening to the screams as the soldiers ravished and tortured our women and children. We were too few; they were too many."

Ganden saw the pain in Barabise's eyes. What else he saw made him shudder. Ganden watched Barabise as he continued his story, but he couldn't get the warning chill out of his mind.

"Fifteen thousand of my tribespeople, driven from the plains that were their ancestral homes, fled south and west. Proud herders and farmers were now displaced refugees, reduced to menial labor just to stay alive. It was then that those of us who were able formed the resistance movement called Four Rivers and Six Ranges."

Barabise paused at a distant shout. He watched the door behind Ganden for a moment, then continued.

"And yes, I was with Chou during the uprising of 1959. The People's Liberation Army was about to reduce the Potala to rubble when Chou intervened."

Ganden's eyes widened at the thought of the destruction of the winter home of twelve centuries of Dalai Lamas. The magnificent palace, perched high on the Marpori above Lhasa, was part of his life.

"Chou pledged his life to the Potala's defense and asked the help of Four Rivers and Six Ranges. We agreed, and together we held the palace until the PLA backed down."

"My father was there!"

The Khampa chief nodded. "Your father was a good man, Ganden."

"And you have been to America?"

Barabise nodded again. "In 1958 a man came to Four Rivers and Six Ranges. An American. He said he was with the CIA and asked us if we would like help. Since we were starving, harried, and on the edge of extinction, we agreed. The man—I never found out his name—flew us to America. To a place called Camp Hale, in the state of Colorado. There we were trained in modern warfare and weapons by members of the 87th Mountain Infantry of the U.S. Army. They called us something strange— *guerrillas*—which they said meant 'warrior.' The army taught us how to use automatic weapons, how to slide down vertical rock faces, how to kill, silently and instantly, in the night." A smile flickered across the nomad's face. "In exchange, we taught them how to *ride*. I showed the Americans how to pick a handkerchief off the ground with their teeth, at a full gallop.

Then we came back. For a while, as at the Potala, the fight went well." Barabise's smile disappeared. "But the supplies began to dwindle, and expected replacements never arrived. Our American contact disappeared. Slowly, one by one, we died—some in battle, some in prison. Finally, the three of us who were left escaped into Nepal. That was twenty years ago."

"Why have you returned now?" Ganden dared to ask.

"Because it is time. The old men who rule in Beijing are near death, and their grip is weakening. And the old warriors here, like myself and your father, are dying off, too. The next generation in Beijing is being raised up, so a next generation in Tibet must be made ready as well—a generation willing to fight and die for its country." Barabise stared intently at Ganden. "If the next generation of leaders here presents their *peers* in Beijing—" He waited until he was sure that Ganden understood his emphasis. "—with a free and defiant Tibet, they *will* listen."

71

Something in Ganden's heart warned him against trusting Barabise. There was a wrongness about him, a darkness . . . even though his words made sense to the mind. But Ganden pushed aside his doubts. He had to know more.

"How will all this be accomplished?"

"All that will come later. First, will you join us?"

Barabise waited. Ganden's mind returned to his long discussion with Tenzig the night before. . . .

From his bed Ganden had eyed his friend. "Just how long have you known this man?"

"A few years. I met him when I got out of school. Kailas arranged my first job in a photo studio, and got me my camera."

"But what do you know about *him?*"

"I know that he gets things done." Tenzig had smiled and leaned closer. "Remember that theft of guns and ammunition from the police armory last year? Kailas masterminded that, and I got to go along. The weapons are safely hidden, ready when we need them."

"That's stealing," Ganden had replied, shocked. "The eighth commandment forbids stealing."

"True. But in the very next chapter of Exodus God tells us to avenge any serious wrong 'eye for eye, tooth for tooth, hand for hand, foot for foot, burn for burn, wound for wound, bruise for bruise.'"

"That doesn't apply here!"

"You're right. It doesn't. If we were to take's God's commandment to heart, we'd ravage China the way it's ravaged us." Tenzig had jumped up, knocking over his chair. "Wake up, Ganden! You've been among the Han too long! Look around you. Where are the forested hills that we climbed as boys? They've been stripped to provide paneling for the homes of the leaders of the 'People's party.'" Tenzig paused. "What is the Chinese name for Tibet?"

"Xizang."

"And what does it mean?"

"'Western storehouse'."

"A strange name for our country, don't you think?" Tenzig had asked mockingly. "Could it have something to do with the fact that the high plains of our ancestral homelands are now uninhabitable because they're littered with Chinese nuclear waste? When was the last time you saw a book in Tibetan? I watched as the PLA heaped our books in the Barkhor and burned them all—except, of course, for the Tibetan version of Mao's Little Red Book. *So now people like you are forced to risk their lives to smuggle books in page by page.*"

Tenzig had spread his hands in frustration. "What would you have me do? Sit quietly by and watch as we're exterminated? Since China's 'peaceful liberation' of Tibet, a quarter of our people have been killed." The young man's knuckles whitened as he gripped the back of the chair. "My sister's first child was ripped from her womb in the ninth month, and then she was sterilized. Former playmates of ours have been accused of 'counterrevolutionary activities.' The lucky ones were executed immediately. The rest were disemboweled, skinned alive, or dropped into vats of leeches." Breathing hard, Tenzig sat back down. "No, my friend. Our response has been mild." He watched the candle as it flickered in its bowl. "So far."

Exasperated, Ganden had glared at Tenzig. "But what about Romans 13? What about the verse that tells us, 'Everyone must submit himself to the governing authorities'?"

Tenzig glared back. "You know as well as I do that chapter teaches that the state should only be obeyed if it is a terror to evil." Tenzig banged his fist on Ganden's table. "The Han government here in Tibet isn't a terror to evil; it's a terror to good!" He threw open the door. "You can serve evil," Tenzig said over his shoulder, "or you can serve good. Your choice, Ganden. I've made mine." The door closed behind him. . . .

73

✧ ✧ ✧

"I found out about Puzhen," Barabise said quietly.

Ganden jerked out of his reverie. "Where? When? How is she?"

Barabise's gray eyes caught Ganden's and held them. "She's dead."

"How?" It was the barest of whispers.

"She was given to the guards. What they started, a cattle prod finished."

Ganden stared past Barabise. Through him, into the night. To the Dragon King Pool, beside whose waters they had so often picnicked. To the drawer in his room, where the silver, turquoise, and coral necklace he had bought in Kathmandu as her wedding present waited to be warmed by her skin.

I was going to surprise you, little one. After our wedding feast I was going to sweep you onto the back of my horse and whisk you off to the Yarlung Valley, where I would have already set up my yurt. You would have lit candles inside the tent while I unloaded our supplies. Then, as Vajra rose over the mountains and the hoarfrost glittered outside, beneath a mound of sheepskins and blankets I would have gathered you to me.

Again he saw her face as she looked up at him, again he heard her frantic screams from the back of the truck. Unconsciously he ran his hand over the ruined half of his face, touching as he did his withered spirit. "I will join Four Rivers and Six Ranges."

Barabise shook his head slowly. "No, Ganden, you will not. Four Rivers and Six Ranges belongs to the old men. Different times demand different ways. And young men. Tenzig has named your movement."

"And what," Ganden asked intently, "is the name of *my* movement?"

"Tigers and Dragons."

II

New York's infamous traffic blared in the street below as Jake put his feet up on a corner of Dave Stevenson's battered desk. The office walls of Global's chief of photographers were covered with badly hung, award-winning photos, more than a few of which were Jake's. A map of China was Scotch-taped to a blackboard behind Stevenson's desk.

Jake picked an empty film canister off the floor and sank a field goal in the wastebasket across the office. "What I don't get is how we can do this on such short notice. I mean, the equipment leaves in two days and we go the day after that. How'd you pull that off?"

Dave grinned. "Peerless management, impeccable preparation—"

"And large bribes," Jake interrupted.

"That, too." Dave turned to the map. "Actually, Global's part in this is like Spencer Tracy's description of Katherine Hepburn: 'There's not much there, but what's there is real choice.'" He pointed to a spot in central China. "You, Geoffrey Sheffield, and Sheila Atherton will catch up with your gear here, in Chengdu, five days before the shoot. From there, you'll fly to Lhasa and get acclimated for a couple of days. Then Geoff goes west to Shigatse, Sheila stays in Lhasa, and you—" Dave jabbed a finger at Jake, "go to Everest. Rendezvous back in Lhasa the day after."

"Are three of us enough for all of our chunk of Tibet?"

Dave pulled a couple of Diet Cokes out of a small refrigerator that sat grumbling in the corner. "Enough to get all the interesting stuff. After all, there's not much news being made there. How many pictures of yaks do we need?" He rummaged around on his desktop and came up with a sheet of paper. "Plus, you'll have local support."

Jake sat up. "Not those 'cultural advisor' types telling me what I can and can't photograph—"

"Nah. For once, the Chinese government is being vaguely cooperative. You'll be assisted by some good local talent. Take this guy, for example." Dave handed Jake the sheet of paper. "Good photographer. He was a stringer for us while he was going to school near Beijing. Got some shots of the Tienamen Square demonstrations that went national."

"Sounds OK." Jake peered at the paper. "If what this says is true, he's got the experience. Not to mention the fact that I can pronounce 'Ganden Nesang.'"

The head of every man standing in front of Portland's International Jetport swiveled to follow the racing-green MG and its driver as she slid the car deftly into a parking space against the curb. Their interest dissipated into a ripple of envious shrugs as a large man climbed into the coupe's passenger seat.

Jake gave Anne a quick kiss, then his head was snapped back against the headrest as she whipped the car into a break in the line of traffic.

"I'm beginning to wonder if teaching you to drive this thing was such a good idea," Jake remarked, massaging his neck. Anne flashed him a smile, then shot the car onto Interstate 95, heading north.

✧ ✧ ✧

"You missed a great picnic," Anne told Jake later as they finished their fish and chips. Outside Graham's Diner, the lobster boats were arriving at their anchorages in Machiasport Harbor, laden with mounds of distinctively striped buoys and stacks of barnacled traps. "It was a beautiful day. Lee did the sailing while Randy and I reminisced." Jake watched as she smiled, a smile that didn't include him. "Randy tells the *funniest* stories."

She looked up to find Jake dousing his french fries with ketchup. "Ugh. I don't see how you can do that to poor, unsuspecting potatoes."

Jake shrugged. "Someone's got to make up for your slathering everything in yogurt." He capped the bottle. "This way, it evens out."

"What did Dave have for you?" she asked.

"You know those big picture books that are a day in the life of someplace?" Anne nodded. "Well," Jake continued, "Dave says that Global has been retained to do a big chunk of the next book."

Anne beamed. "Wonderful! Where is it a day in the life of? Barbados, maybe?"

Jake grinned and shook his head. "Tibet."

Anne's eyes widened. "Wow."

"'Wow' is right," Jake agreed. "Forty photographers from around the world will spread out over Tibet. Then they'll all spend the same day taking pictures." Anne saw Jake's eyes light up. "It'll be the greatest photo essay ever done."

"And Dave wants you to go?" she asked, already knowing the answer. Jake nodded. *It's Christmas in April for him,* Anne thought.

"On top of that," Jake added, "Dave wants me to organize and head up Global's participation—supervise the photographers and plan our part of the shoot. We were lucky to get the Chinese government's permission at all. As it is, it's a real bang-bang schedule once we're in China: a day or two to get there, a few days' prep, the day of the shoot, then home."

The waitress brought them each a slice of blueberry cream pie and a cup of coffee.

Jake looked past Anne, out through the diner's front window, and far into the gathering darkness. The light in his eyes grew brighter. "Tibet is one of the few remaining wild places in the world. It's the chance of a lifetime." He rested his elbows on the table and leaned forward, looking at her over his hands, the intensity of his gaze stirring her. "We'll be there in time for *Monlam*, the Tibetan Great Prayer festival, and it'll be springtime on the Kangba Plateau." Anne could feel his excitement, and it both warmed and worried her.

She looked at him fondly. "And what plum has the expedition leader set aside for himself alone? What part of Tibet is yours?" she asked.

Jake questioned her with his eyes.

"I know you too well, love," Anne said with a smile. "You wouldn't have agreed to it unless Dave had promised that you'd be more than a tour guide. You're a doer, not just an organizer."

"Chomolungma," Jake replied instantly. "At moonrise."

"Is that a place, or a person?"

"It's a mountain. It's *the* mountain." Jake rubbed his hands together in anticipation. "Mount Everest." She saw his fingers tense, as if reaching out into the night. "Everest in the moonlight is mine."

"When do you leave?"

"Tomorrow."

"*What?*"

"Not for Tibet. I have to go back to New York tomorrow. I'm meeting with my staff at ten."

"Why the rush?"

Jake smoothed his hair back in frustration. "I just told you. After months of about-faces, the Beijing bureaucrats finally slipped up and actually gave us permission. We've had the logistics ready for most of a year; we've just been waiting for them to make up their minds."

Anne chopped off the tip of her slice of pie and began mashing it flat with her fork. The anger swelled in her—that now-familiar anger born out of hurt, the hurt of being over-looked, of being left behind. "You mean that you've known about this for months and haven't bothered to tell me?"

Jake looked at her quizzically. "I didn't see any reason for you to know. Other than a couple of meetings with Dave, it hasn't been a big deal." He swallowed a mouthful of pie. "Until now."

"You could at least have mentioned it to me."

"Why?"

Because the part of me that thinks about you all time needs to know these things. Then Anne saw the honest incomprehension in his eyes. She shook her head. "Never mind." The silence gathered between them as Anne stirred a packet of sweetener into her coffee. "When do you leave for *Tibet?*"

"Five days from now." Oblivious to the look she gave him, Jake continued explaining. "Lord alone knows why, but one of the codicils in the agreement the Chinese signed requires us to be in and out by the end of the month." Jake grinned. "Right now, agencies around the world are busting themselves getting ready to go." He nodded with satisfaction. "But, thanks to Dave, Global's all set."

Anne poked at her pie until it became a mess of syrupy blueberries under a pile of flat whipped cream. "Do you have to go?" she asked after a while.

Jake looked up at her from the remnants of his pie. "Of course I have to go." He frowned. "What kind of question is that?"

Anne's coffee-cup reflection stared back at her accusingly. She wondered briefly why she had asked such a stupid question.

"It's just that," she said slowly, "you haven't been around much lately."

He leaned back in the booth and crossed his arms, obviously irritated.

"I'm here every weekend I can make it." His tone turned the statement of fact into an indictment, and his palpable annoyance made her feel petty and childish. She didn't deserve to feel that way, and the implicit accusation in his expression fired her anger even more.

"Which doesn't seem to be very often," she lashed back.

Jake looked at her in angry disbelief. "Well, what do you expect? I can't live forever on what I made from the Moncrief photos, you know."

"Can't you get some work around here?"

Jake laughed scornfully. "Like what? Photographing hog judgings for the *Lewiston Sun-Journal*? Or maybe you want me to open a Kinderfoto in Presque Isle?" He finished his coffee. "If I'm going to eat, I need to be where the news is. Which is *not* around here." Jake spread his hands. "What do you want from me?"

"How about showing up for my birthday?" Anne suggested, her voice sweetly vitriolic. "Since you obviously don't remember, let me remind you that I'll be celebrating it just about the time you'll be arriving in Tibet!"

The blank look on Jake's face set a match to the tinder of Anne's temper, and she flung her wadded-up napkin down on the table. "I don't believe it!" She stopped. "No, I take it back. I *do* believe it, because this is so exactly like you! You come and go as you jolly well please, without the least shred of consideration for anyone."

Anne's tone caused the waitress to look up. She shook her head in amusement and went back to her crossword puzzle.

Jake massaged his temples wearily. "In case you hadn't noticed, I have other things to do with my life."

"I most certainly have noticed! When you're not off somewhere taking pictures in the middle of a revolution, you're racing that car of yours."

"They're not races; they're rallyes."

Anne's months of pent-up anger erupted. "Whatever they're called, you obviously prefer their company to mine." She glared at him. "I am sick and tired of your not being here, of your not calling me between assignments, and of your generally gallivanting in and out of my life whenever you please."

"I don't do that."

Anne tossed her head. "No? You were off somewhere for our first anniversary, and now this!"

"I beg your pardon," Jake said with quiet sarcasm. "How stupid of me. The 'somewhere' I was off to, as you well know, was fulfilling a commission from the president to take his official portrait. The one that's going to hang in the White House *forever*." His eyes bored into her. "*Of course* I should have jumped up in mid-session and dashed out. I'm sure the president would've understood *perfectly* when I told him, 'Just hang around, Mr. President—I'll be back after I spend the evening with this babe I kissed for the first time a year ago tonight.'"

"Don't you dare talk to me that way, Jake MacIntyre!" Anne came to her feet. "Now, please take me home. I have a long day tomorrow."

"Going to be retelling Randy's funny stories?"

"If you must know, I have a teacher's inservice meeting in Camden, and it's a long drive." She held the shards of her voice together just long enough. "Please, take me home."

A crescent moon was emerging from behind Sargent Mountain by the time they reached the Dryden house. As Anne slammed her parents' porch door behind her, gravel from the spinning tires of Jake's MG rattled against it.

❖ ❖ ❖

"I'm sorry, sir, but I cannot give out that information," the receptionist at the telephone office stammered.

Grigory Markov smiled. "Quite all right. I understand completely. Allow me to rephrase the question."

The receptionist stifled a scream as Markov's SP220 appeared from beneath the counter. He pointed at the card he had laid on the countertop. "This is a phone number in this city," he said calmly. "I want the address that goes with it."

Very quickly, the woman scribbled an address on a piece of paper and handed it to the colonel. Markov glanced at it, then stuffed the scrap into the pocket of his fatigues. He thanked the ashen-faced clerk, then went outside and got into his jeep.

The address was only a few minutes' drive across Taldy Kurgan. Markov pulled up in front of a pleasant *dacha* sequestered behind a grove of cedars. After checking to see that the street was deserted, he reached under the driver's seat and pulled out a Kalashnikov assault rifle.

The combination of a burst from the Kalashnikov and Markov's booted foot tore the door from its hinges. He stepped into a richly furnished front room, where a uniformed maid stood transfixed. In the center of the floor a young woman sat with a baby, gazing up at Markov in wide-eyed fear.

Markov walked over to the young woman. With a swift, lithe motion he tore the baby girl from her mother's breast. Markov held the squalling infant at arm's length and pressed the Kalashnikov's muzzle against her swollen belly.

"Now," he said in grim, fluent Pashto, "you will tell me all about Yousef Bey."

12

The bartender at Eat at Joe's didn't even look up when the man walked in. He was used to seeing the type: deserters, smugglers, and other forms of the renegade clientele that frequented his establishment. Indian music, broadcast from Calcutta, blared in the background. The stranger looked around, then strode purposefully over to a table in the corner of the Kathmandu bar.

Kailas Barabise waited to acknowledge the new arrival until he had eaten his fill of the pork and peanut dish called *gong bao rou ding*. The nomad chieftain handed the rest of his meal to a beggar who squatted by the table. As the man scuttled off, clutching the bowl, Barabise looked up.

"Kailas Barabise?" the new arrival asked in flawless Tibetan.

"And if I am?"

The man snorted derisively. "I was told I'd find you here. I was also told what you are looking for." He swept the grubby room with a gesture. "Who else in this den of drunks, beggars, and thieves could possibly be interested in my services?"

Barabise laughed. "It's good to meet you, Yousef Bey. We have business to do."

✧ ✧ ✧

The door to Hua Chen's office banged open. He looked up, then smiled tolerantly.

"What's this about a job?" Tenzig asked breathlessly.

Chen reminded himself to be patient. He had, after all, summoned the man. Chen leaned back in his chair, letting Tenzig catch his breath. He then handed the Tibetan a piece of paper. "This just came in from the Ministry of Tourism in Beijing."

Tenzig glanced at the paper, then frowned. "It says that a group of Americans are coming in. So? China International Travel Service, the government-run travel agency, has its own guides."

Chen smiled, liking Tenzig and amused at the younger man's impetuosity. "*Read* it, Tenzig."

A moment later, Tenzig looked up in disbelief. "Photographers! *American* photographers! Coming here!"

Chen nodded. "Their visa was issued today. Plus—"

"What?" Tenzig demanded.

"They'll be needing some help." Chen handed Tenzig another paper. "Beijing has authorized the local CITS office to provide each photographer with a qualified assistant." Chen laughed at Tenzig's expression. "You're not listening," he chided. "I said 'assistant,' not 'guide.'"

"When do they get here?"

"Four days from now. Naturally," Chen continued with mock officiousness, "all assistants will have to be approved by the local official of the *Wài Shi Ke.*" Tenzig waited expectantly. "Of course you're approved, Tenzig," Chen said with a grin.

"And Ganden?"

Chen frowned. "Will he be well enough in time?"

Tenzig nodded vigorously. "He's almost healed now."

Chen nodded. Then he regarded Tenzig over steepled fingers. "It's a good thing you weren't involved in that band of counterrevolutionaries that was arrested the other night. If you had been, there'd be no way that I could approve you as an assistant."

Tenzig hoped that Chen didn't see the spasm of loss that arced through him at the mention of his friends. "But, Ganden was," Tenzig said quietly. Another spasm, this one of guilt, followed the first.

"So he was. Only the fact that he collaborated has saved him." Tenzig started to protest, then thought better of it. "Saved him so far," Chen added ominously.

"What's going to happen to the—the 'counter-revolutionaries'?"

Chen hesitated. "We know they have foreign contacts here in Lhasa. They'll be interrogated until they provide us with names." Chen's phone rang, shattering the growing tension. "Now go," he said, gesturing toward the door, "and tell Ganden the good news."

"Stop waving the paper around and let me see it!" Ganden shouted. Tenzig calmed down long enough for Ganden to snatch the paper from his friend's hand. Ganden read it, then looked up at his friend.

"No wonder you're excited," he said increduously. "Three hundred FEC for a day's work! Sure this isn't some kind of joke?" FEC were Foreign Exchange Certificates, the "hard" currency used by foreigners under China's dual-currency system.

Tenzig shook his head emphatically. "Inspector Chen told me, and I checked over at the CITS office. Some American photographers are going to be here to take pictures for a day. Each one needs a local assistant, and each assistant gets paid three hundred FEC." Tenzig grinned. "With that I could open my own photo studio, get married—"

"And, undoubtedly, be asked to carry the Dalai Lama piggyback over the Himalayas. Calm down."

✧ ✧ ✧

Kailas Barabise stood up. "Come. This is not the place to talk."

Bey followed the Khampa nomad out of the saloon and into the bedlam of Durbar Square. Hawkers peddling flutes, prayer shawls called *khatas*, yak-wool *yakets*, and necklaces of chunky turquoise shouted beseechingly. They crowded around the two, shoving their wares into the mercenaries' faces and grabbing at the Afghan's expensive briefcase until Barabise threateningly slapped the daggerlike *thupta* he carried in a sheath on his belt. As the street vendors fled, the Tibetan purposely quickened his pace. Barabise, with the Afghan matching his stride, turned left into Pig Alley, a narrow, filth-laden lane that ran down to the river. Bey swatted at the clouds of flies their passage disturbed. Barabise's room at the Monumental Lodge was Spartan and dingy. He motioned Bey into the only chair, then stretched out on the sagging bed.

"It's good to work with another hill man," Barabise said. "That little stroll would have left most foreigners panting like a frightened yak in heat."

Bey nodded his understanding. "What," he asked, "is that incredible stench?"

Barabise leaned over and threw open the shutters. Below the window, on one of the jetties thrust into the river that forms the southern border of Kathmandu, smoke rose from a still-smoldering funeral pyre. As they watched, workers began shoveling the embers into the river.

"Hindu funeral," Barabise explained. "They have dozens here every day. At least," he added, "the rich ones do. They just toss the corpses of the poor into the river at night." Barabise turned and grinned. "A man's funeral was a quite popular attraction up until not too long ago."

"Why was that?"

"Because, until the Indians got sticky about it, *suttee* was a popular practice. Everyone would gather to watch the widow, overcome as she was by grief, throw herself onto the blazing pyre to join her husband in nirvana."

The Afghan toyed with his luxuriant moustache. "And if she was reluctant to do so?"

"That's why everyone showed up," Barabise explained. "At the first sign of reluctance on the part of the bereaved, they got to assist her in starting her journey." He shook his head. "No burning for me. When my time comes, I want a sky burial."

"Which is?"

"On a large, flat rock open to the sky my flesh will be flayed from my skeleton. My bones will be crushed and mixed with *tsampa* flour, and all will be left for the hawks, ravens, and vultures. As food for others I will gain merit with the gods." Barabise pondered the filthy river as it flowed by. "With only the sky above me, I am free to join my ancestors."

Yousef Bey hid his revulsion. *Barbarians*, he thought disgustedly. *Insensate pigs that care nothing for human life.* "Let's get down to business, nomad," he said tersely. "I don't want to spend the rest of my life here." The armsmonger opened his satchel. "I have a variety of weapons of mass destruction to offer." He took out a sheaf of technical specifications. "Depending on your objective, these arms will either eliminate a specific target or kill from ten to ten thousand. . . ."

13

Lee waited, leaning silently against the doorframe, until Anne had leafed listlessly through the entire magazine, then cleared her throat. Startled, Anne looked up.

"What's with you?" Lee asked.

Anne shrugged. "Nothing, really. Just tired, I guess. I didn't get much sleep."

Lee shook her head. "Uh-uh," she said firmly. "That's *my* excuse. You were sound asleep when I got home the other night." Lee sat down on the other end of the bentwood sofa that occupied a large portion of the Drydens' sun porch. "What's more, you deprived me of a chance to shoo Jake away, curl up, and tell you all about it."

"It? What 'it'?"

Lee made a face. "My night out with Randy, silly."

"Ah, yes. Your big date."

"It was not a date!"

"No? Then, what was it?"

"I had to go to Freeport," Lee replied primly, "so I just asked Randy if he wanted to come along."

Anne nodded sagely. "I see. Well, then, don't you want to show me what you bought? You always do after one of your shopping sprees."

Lee shrugged noncommittally.

"Don't tell me that you didn't buy anything!" Anne feigned surprise. "Surely you must've picked up *something*. You were gone long enough to clean out Bean's."

Lee grabbed a cushion and tossed it at Anne. "Cut it out! You know perfectly well that we went to dinner and a concert."

Anne laughed. "Did you have a good time?"

Lee nodded happily. "He's sweet." Then she frowned. "Didn't you have dinner with Jake?"

"That man is absolutely impossible!"

Lee's eyes widened. "Oh." She looked at Anne who, lips pursed with anger, was busy staring out through the screen, across the water, and into the depths of Acadia National Park. "I see. Want to tell me about it?" she asked softly. Anne bit her lip and nodded.

"I knew something was wrong," Lee said. "This was the first time I've ever seen you go through an entire issue of *Christianity Today* without a word. When you don't either love or hate something you've just read, I know you're really upset." Lee tucked her feet underneath her. "Now, talk to me."

A rectangle in the corner of the screen turned green, indicating that the processing of the Indigo-Lacrosse image was finished.

"Pretty slick," Greg said with a whistle. "Check out that resolution. Looks like the new asynchronous timing code we uploaded is doing the job." He smiled at Susan with satisfaction. "Remind me," Greg told her, "to tell HP that their new cesium-beam clock is a real winner."

Susan studied the image. "Are you sure it's working?" she

asked with a frown. "This doesn't look much like what we've seen before."

"OK, then. Let's find out. Pull up the images from the last pass."

The current image compressed until it filled only the top half of the screen. Below it, the corresponding image from the previous pass appeared.

Greg's eyes swept over both images. *Cripes. I don't like the looks of this at all. . . .*

"Next image ready."

"Put it up." The pair of images appeared on the screen. Greg frowned. "Where's the eastern horizon on this pass?"

Susan clicked a mouse button, and a small window appeared on her screen. "We start losing resolution at about ninety degrees east longitude. After ninety-five degrees, our confidence level drops rapidly to zero."

Greg reached up and pulled a copy of the *Nuclear Weapons Databook* from a shelf. He flipped through its pages, glancing back and forth from the screen to the report. "Doesn't look good," he said a minute later. "This edition of the *Databook* was published only a month ago, so its information should be pretty accurate." He handed the book to his friend and mentor. "See what you think."

Susan went through the same process. Frowning, she overlaid the new image with a composite LANDSAT map of the world. Slowly, her finger traced a line across the screen. "Merciful Saint Swithin," she muttered. "If this means what I think it means . . ."

Greg turned to Susan. "Dump both sets of images to the printer." He looked again at the screen. "I want copies of both passes, and I want them *fast.*"

"D'ye ken what's goin' on?" Susan asked.

Greg smiled at Susan's habit of reverting to the dialect of

her native Scotland in moments of stress. "No, I don't know what's going on, but I know somebody who will."

Greg grabbed a phone and began dialing. By the time he hung up, Susan had the prints for him. Greg stuffed them in a folder. He stopped with one hand on the door.

"Are you going to see Cathy today?" he asked. Susan nodded. "Will you tell her that I won't be able to make dinner?"

Susan nodded again. Then, grinning, she slowly drew her finger across her throat.

✧ ✧ ✧

Thanks for letting me come up on such short notice, Joel," Greg said as he sat down in Joel's study.

"Pleasure's mine," Joel replied. "Got me out of a shopping trip. What's up?"

Greg pulled a sheaf of photographs out of his folder and spread them out on the desk. "These are prints of two passes over a part of eastern Asia taken by one of our newest birds." He sorted the photos into two sets. "They were taken, six days apart, over what was the southcentral part of the Soviet Union and is now Kazakhstan, Kirghizia, and Tadzhikistan."

Joel examined one of the photos. It was a computer-generated topographic map covered with what appeared to be pinpoints of light. "This obviously isn't optical, so they can't be letting you play with one of their new KH-12 Keyholes." He frowned. "If this is infrared, it's pretty crude."

"You're half right," Greg replied. "It's pretty crude, but it's not infrared."

Randy joined Joel in studying one of the prints. "Since there's no natural terrain, it can't be ambient light or radar." Randy peered at Greg. "Some sort of weird radar mapping?"

"Nope. These are the first usable images generated by my hyperon imager."

Joel picked up one of the photos. "I don't see," he told Greg, "why you want me to see these. While your hyperon

technology is interesting, particle physics is hardly my baili-
wick."

"I know," Greg agreed. "But you do a lot better job of
keeping up on what's going on in the world than I do. I just
process the data and pass it along to the analyst types."

"Who grossly misinterpret your data," Randy interjected,
"and then send lowbrow types like me off to some godforsaken
spot to get shot at. I wouldn't mind so much," he added reflec-
tively, "if it wasn't usually the *wrong* godforsaken spot."

Greg handed the photos to Randy. "Recognize the terrain?" Randy studied the photos, then frowned and shook his
head. "It's part of your old stomping grounds," Greg added.

Randy shrugged. "Haven't had much practice reading
these computer-generated topo maps," he confessed. "Usually,
all I get to use is a Swiss army knife and a wet finger to hold up
in the wind."

"Those three concentrations of lights that you see in the
first photo," Greg explained, "represent clusters of tactical
nuclear warheads." He pointed to three spots on the photo.
Greg got up and walked over to a map of the world that covered
one wall of Joel's study. Published by the Department of Defense, it was both extensive in detail and newly updated.

"Those clusters are—or, I should say *were*—located *here*,
here, and *here*." Greg jabbed at three spots in the middle of Asia.

He pulled a sheet of paper out of his briefcase. "See if these
mean anything to you, Randy." Greg peered at the paper.
"Coordinates for the three sites are:

43.15.12N, 76.57.22E
38.33.42N, 68.48.17E
50.30.29N, 80.10.05E."

Randy's head shot up. He strode over to the map. "Where did
you say they were?"

"That's what I'm hoping you can tell me," Greg replied. "All I have right now are latitude and longitude."

Randy looked at the coordinates, then studied the map for a long time. He turned away, and glanced at Greg. "I wouldn't worry about whether your detector is working or not. From here, it looks like it's working way too well."

Frowning, Randy sorted through the photos and extracted three. "Take this one, for example. 43.15.12N, 76.57.22E." He pointed to a spot near the Pakistani border. " Alma-Ata, capital of Kazakhstan and site of the former headquarters of the USSR Central Asian Military District. A Russian motorized rifle division is still stationed there—Moscow can't afford to bring them home—and it's also the location of a FROG battalion equipped with at least four FROG-7 launchers."

"Let me get this straight," Greg interjected. "Nuclear frogs?"

"Yeah," Randy replied. "The Sovs got the idea from our plot in the sixties to assassinate Castro when he was skindiving by blowing him up with an exploding clam."

Joel winced at the painful memory of the fiasco. He caught Greg's disbelieving look. "I'll tell you about it sometime," he said.

"Actually," Randy continued, "FROG means Free-Rocket-Over-Ground. That's NATO's acronym for a nasty little nuclear-tipped division-support missile with a range of about sixty-five kilometers. The Soviet eastern divisions inherited them after the elite outfits in East Germany and Czecho-slovakia were upgraded to the longer-range SS-21."

Randy tapped the map a thousand kilometers southwest of Alma-Ata. "Next is 38.33.42N, 68.48.17E. Dushanbe, capital of Tadzhikistan. Another motorized rifle division; another FROG outfit." Randy smiled sardonically. "One charming thing about this little garden spot is that the FROGs might actually be in Frunze. Frunze is the capital of Kirghizia, which, when I was last there, was on speaking terms with neither Tadzhikistan nor Kazakhstan."

"Last, but certainly not least, is *here*. 50.30.29N, 80.10.05E. Fifteen hundred kilometers north of Alma-Ata, a place called Semipalatinsk. I've never been there, but I've sure heard about it. It's sort of like our Los Alamos. Big nuclear weapons research, development, and testing facility. Lots of FROGs, and lots of nuclear-capable artillery. Not to mention a whole brigade of SS-1s. You might remember them as SCUD-Bs, our little friends from the Gulf War."

Greg sorted through the pile of satellite images. He picked up two and held them up. "Notice any difference?" he asked Randy.

"Oh, crud! Where is this?"

"According to you," Greg replied, "Alma-Ata."

"It figures," Randy replied grimly. "That place is a giant candy store for someone with big bucks and a world-class grudge." He circled part of one photo with a forefinger. "See how there are a lot fewer points of light in today's photo?"

Greg nodded. "That's exactly what brought me up here."

Randy shook his head in disbelief. "That can mean only one thing. They've gone and done it," he said to no one in particular. "Those idiots have actually gone and done it."

"Done what?" Joel asked.

"They've gone and sold the store." Randy looked bleak. "The question is, who did they sell it to?"

"What does it mean, Randy?" Joel asked quietly. "You look as if you've just seen a ghost."

Randy snorted. "A spook who's just seen a ghost. I like that." He studied the map in silence for a full minute. "If I'm right, then we've got a lot of work to do in a real quick hurry." Randy looked at Joel. "Greg's appointed you our 'big-picture' man. So tell us your analysis of the current state of the former Soviet Union."

Joel studied the young man in front of him. *I recognize that look in his eyes,* he thought. *It's the same one I had when I was thirty.* Joel managed to suppress his smile. *Good luck, Randy, and God help you. . . .*

Joel leaned back in his swivel chair. "The Soviet Union that we knew and loved," he began, "has been formally dismantled for almost two years now. In that time, the now-independent republics have had varying degrees of success in everything from democracy to doughnuts."

Joel got up and walked over to the wall map. He drew a circle in the vicinity of Germany. "Poland, who admittedly had a head start, is doing quite well, as is Ukraine." He drew a second circle to the southeast of the first. "Both are flourishing both economically and socially. But, it would seem that the farther east the republic, the worse things get."

Joel pointed at a spot northeast of Turkey. "Georgia is a mess, and so is Azerbaijan." His finger traced a line along the map. "And the eastern republics are impoverished, authoritarian, and locked in destructive internal conflict. Democracies in the west, and dictatorships in the east. Just like it's always been, only now on a smaller scale." Joel looked at Randy. "How am I doing?" he asked rhetorically.

"Too well," Randy replied grimly. "You're telling me all the things I *don't* want to hear."

Greg picked up one of the satellite photos. "So what does all this wonderful news have to do with our 'thousand points of light'?"

Joel and Randy began to speak at the same time. When Randy started to defer to Joel, Joel held up his hands. "Rule number one," he said, "is always listen to the man who's been on the scene."

Randy looked sharply at Joel. "How did you know about *that?*" he stammered.

Joel shrugged. "Your boss used to work for me."

Seeing Randy's obvious discomfort, Joel smiled. "Don't

worry about it," he said. "Sometimes when I'm down in Washington I have lunch with him. Afterwards we play cribbage at his club. If I win, then he has to tell me what all the young turks in my former department are up to."

Randy looked pained. "Why," he wondered, "do I feel like I'm wearing dark glasses, a cheap wig, and a black trenchcoat with **SPY** written on the back in big letters?" He turned to Greg. "Anyway, as Joel already appears to know, a few weeks back I was over in Uzbekistan keeping an eye on their coup of the month, the one the subcommittee's so interested in. After the festivities died down, I took a little sidetrip through the eastern republics, to see if I could get an idea of how those boys were treating their nuclear toys."

"And?" Greg asked.

"Everyone I talked to promised me that they didn't want them there, had no intention of trying to use them, and wanted them to go away as soon as possible."

Greg frowned. "But it's been almost two years since they went independent. Why are the nukes still there?"

"That's the rub," Randy replied. "The strategic stuff—the ICBMs and long-range bombers—are going to stay right where they are. Russia's got control of them and is going to keep them. At least," he added, "until the START treaty is fully implemented." Out in the night, a rabbit screamed as it became an owl's dinner. "That part of it's all right. We know how much of it there is and where it is, and we get to verify that it either stays there or gets scrapped. It's the little stuff, the tactical stuff in the kiloton range, that's making us nervous."

"Why is that?"

"For starters, there's so much of it. Thousands of warheads in short-range missiles, artillery shells, and ADMs."

"ADMs?"

"Atomic Demolition Munitions," Randy explained. "Charming little devices intended to impede the enemy's progress by taking the top off a mountain and throwing it into the valley next door." Randy grimaced. "This hardware is scattered all throughout the republics. A lot of it is on mobile launchers, and what isn't is easily transportable in the back of a truck."

"Why then," Joel asked, "if the republics have disavowed the usage of nuclear weapons, are they still around?"

"You probably know that as well as I do," Randy replied with a grin, "seeing as how I never can manage to beat my boss at cribbage." He pointed at the map. "Before the breakup, Russia managed to maneuver the Baltics out of their tactical nukes. Just as Moscow was about to pull the same stunt on Ukraine, the boys in Kiev wised up and realized that there's gold in them thar bombs." Randy waved his hand over Greg's photos. "Almost a billion dollars' worth of weapons-grade plutonium in the weapons deployed in Ukraine alone. So, understandably, they told Moscow to pony up if they wanted their weapons back. And no rubles, please—hard currency only. Naturally Russia didn't have the cash, so there the warheads sit."

He got up and swept his arm in an arc over the map. "It's the same in the rest of the republics. The nukes sit like plums on a tree while their new owners try to decide if they can get away with selling them to the highest bidder."

Greg frowned. "What about the Non-Proliferation Treaty?"

"Fine and dandy," Randy responded caustically, "if it's being applied to a republic's archenemy neighbor. But point it out to them, and they politely remind you that they don't happen to be a signatory of the Non-Proliferation Treaty." He picked up the pile of photos. "That's why what you've got here makes me so nervous."

Branches from the apple tree outside rattled against the window as Randy sat down. He sorted out three pairs of photos. "In six days, we've gone from *this*," he held up the photos covered with dots of light, "to *this*." He held up the second, and much darker, set. "Any way of telling how large each of these warheads is?" he asked Greg.

"Not yet," Greg replied. "But we just got in a new Cray floating-point coprocessor unit." He smiled in anticipation. "Once we get it on line we should be able to calculate the size of any individual warhead."

"I think," Randy told him, "that you'll find that most of them are in the twenty- to fifty-kiloton range. That's the size of most tactical nukes."

"Doesn't sound very big."

"Maybe not, when you compare it to a hundred-megaton thermonuclear weapon. But let me put it in a perspective I bet you can understand: We dropped a twelve-kiloton bomb on Hiroshima."

Greg Miahara nodded slowly as he remembered the pictures of twisted, fused metal and of human shadows etched forever into stone walls. In his mind he heard anew the wails of his grandmother as she mourned for relatives who had vanished in an incandescent instant.

"That was a crude, low-yield warhead," Randy finished. "These are efficient, high-yield, state-of-the-art weapons. And, there are thousands of them."

Randy stared at the map. "From the 'Kazakh' in *Kazakhstan* we get our English word *Cossack*." He paused, and the silence in the room grew heavy. "Genghis Khan came out of that part of the world."

"So did Alaric the Goth," Joel added quietly. "And he brought down the Roman Empire." Outside, it began to rain.

14

"And just what was that all about?" the president snapped as the door closed behind the Russian ambassador. From across the Oval Office he glared in confused annoyance at his chief of staff.

Mike O'Brien returned his boss's stare impassively. He had known the president since college and had learned that the truth was always an acceptable answer.

"Beats me," O'Brien said with a shrug. "But old Josef sure was ticked off about *something.*"

The president strode over to his desk and picked up the only piece of paper on it. As a matter of routine, even the *Far Side* calendar his grandchildren had given him for his birthday was locked away when foreigners called.

"It is with great regret," the president intoned in a vicious mimicry of Josef Panshin's cultured English, "that I am instructed by my government to deliver this note." As he brandished the note, light from the chandelier glinted off the blue and gold seal of the president of Russia that was embossed at the top of the page. The small, spare man took a pair of reading glasses out of his pocket and placed them on the end of his nose.

"'Mr. President.'" He stopped and looked at O'Brien.

"What kind of greeting is that? I've known Boris for years, and now I get 'Mr. President'?" The president sat down behind his desk and resumed reading. "'As you well know, there has been considerable unrest in the former Soviet republics that are now Tadzhikistan and Kirghizia. While Russia has monitored the situation closely, it has respected the sovereignty of those two nations and has refrained from intervention.'"

"Only because they couldn't get away with it," O'Brien snorted derisively.

"'It is therefore with the greatest alarm that I have found out from a highly placed source—'"

"Russian spooks inside Tadzhikistan or Kirghizia," O'Brien interpreted.

"'Which has been corroborated by local officials—'"

"Rebels caught and interrogated by the former KGB goons."

"'That at the height of the unrest an agent of your Central Intelligence Agency was known to be active in the area.

"'Mr. President, I feel it my duty to inform you that, while this action did not take place on Russian soil, any future attempts by an *agent provocateur* to foment revolution in the former republics will be interpreted as a direct threat to the security of Russia herself.'"

The president leaned back in his chair. "That part I can understand. Some local talent of the Company's got caught with their pants down and fingered the Imperialist West. Doesn't happen as much as it used to, but it still happens. It's this part that worries me." He held up the note to the light that filtered through inch-thick panes of bulletproof glass.

"'Furthermore, you are reminded that any attempts to aid the former republics in acquiring nuclear weapons will be considered a direct violation of both the Non-Proliferation Treaty and the treaties between our two nations. Such attempts will be responded to in an appropriate fashion.'"

The president tossed the note onto the desk. "We need to find out what went on over there. Get Elliot French in here now."

"The deputy director of operations for the CIA? Can't. He's in closed subcommittee hearings."

The president removed his glasses and pinched the bridge of his nose. "Great. Whose?"

"Rutherford's. The Foreign Affairs special investigation."

"This is getting better by the minute. The CIA's director is in intensive care with a stroke, and his fair-haired boy is testifying before a bunch of Democrats."

"Rutherford's OK. He voted for the Intelligence Appropriations Bill. And French is a former trial lawyer. He can hold his own."

The president smiled. "Mike, you know as well as I that all's fair in love, war, and politics. Unfortunately, politics rarely has the decisiveness of war, and it *never* has the potential of love." A light on his phone began to blink insistently. "Get someone over to the Hill, and get French back here ASAP."

As Elliot French ran the gauntlet of reporters outside the subcommittee's chambers, a large man in a gray suit fell into step beside him.

"Yes, Watkins?" French asked.

"I brought your car, sir."

French gauged the noticeable limp with which Kyle Watkins walked. "How's the leg?"

"Better, Mr. French. Doctor says I'll be playing rugby again in a month." Earlier in the year Watkin's femur had been shattered by a bullet from a Peruvian drug lord's submachine gun.

"What's up?" French asked once they were out of earshot of the reporters.

"You're wanted at the White House."

"Any idea why?"

"No, sir. They called, and I was told to come get you."

French's stomach growled as the Lincoln limousine neared Pennsylvania Avenue. "Got any crackers?" he asked Watkins. "The only thing that got grilled today was me."

Watkins leaned over and spoke to the driver, who made a sharp right.

"Kyle," French protested, "the White House is over *that* way."

"Yes, sir." Watkins grinned. "See that pushcart up ahead? This guy makes the best Polish around."

✧ ✧ ✧

"Don't worry, Elliot," the president said after shaking hands and sitting down. "I realize that you can't talk about the hearings." Then he looked at French and waited.

"No, sir, I can't. But I can say that the administration's position is receiving a fair hearing."

"Spoken like a true lawyer." He handed French the Russian president's note. "What I can and do expect you to tell me about is this."

French read the note. "I haven't seen this before."

"Not surprising," O'Brien explained. "It just arrived today. Josef brought it himself."

French's eyebrows went up in surprise. "They must be really bent out of shape if they persuaded Joe to bestir himself from the embassy. He's just like the rest of them. A former minor official in the Russian bureaucracy who rode to power on the president's coattails."

"Wasn't he considered for foreign minister?" O'Brien wondered.

"Yeah. But he's neither as tough as Gromyko nor as smart as Schevardnadze."

The president pointed at the note. "We need to know about this."

"First, sir, let me say that the agent involved is one of our best—"

The president held up a hand. "You don't have to sell it to me, Elliot. If you recall, I had your job for more than a few years."

French smiled. "Right. After a day of hearings, it's hard to shuck the doublespeak. Anyway, the guy involved is Randy Cavanaugh. He was making a routine run through the CIS when this little dustup down south broke out. We thought someone should go check it out. So, when Cavanaugh reached St. Petersburg, the station chief there delivered to him a TALISMAN-encoded message. It instructed him to go to Frunze, the capital of Kirghizia, and evaluate the situation."

"'Evaluate the situation.' That's all he was instructed to do?" the president asked sharply.

"Yes, sir."

"You said that he was sent down there because of the large number of nuclear weapons in that area." French smiled to himself. He hadn't said that, but he realized that the president knew his stuff. "Did he have any specific instructions regarding them?"

"He was told to evaluate the potential of their being used."

"Was he in any way to encourage their use?"

"No, sir. If anything, he was to dissuade the factions involved from considering using them."

The president scratched his neck meditatively. "Then the Russians must be using this as a red herring."

"How so?" O'Brien asked.

"Our friends the Sovs," French explained, "have a long history of what magicians call misdirection. Whenever they really blow it, they distract attention from the foul-up by pointing a very public finger at something else. Like when Khrushchev made such a big stink about that U2 being shot down. Normally, there would've been a few nasty communiqués, and we would have traded a jailed KGB officer for the pilot.

Instead, Khrushchev made a crisis out of it to cover up the fact that he had been caught turning Cuba into a giant missile silo."

"So," the president wondered, "what is it that they don't want us to know about?"

"I have no idea at the moment, sir," French confessed.

"We'll need to talk to Cavanaugh."

"I'd rather we didn't."

"Why not?"

"As I said, Cavanaugh is as good an asset as I've got. He's experienced, speaks fluent Russian as well as several dialects, and has never had his cover blown. While Senator Rutherford is on our side, he still needs someone for the pillorying the public demands whenever an operation is uncovered. In this case, it's to be Cavanaugh."

The president nodded. During his own years as deputy director of operations he'd had to play this game often enough, and he understood it all too well. "Plus," he noted, "the Russian agents here will take note of his arrival, and someone in Moscow will add things up."

"Anyway," French finished, "I couldn't bring him in if I wanted to." French and the president exchanged a glance. Both men began to chuckle.

O'Brien stared at the pair. "Why not?"

French smiled. "Because just before the hearings started, I told Cavanaugh to get lost, which he promptly did. I have no idea where he is. That's the only way that I could honestly tell the subcommittee that 'the whereabouts of the agent in question are currently unknown.'" The DDO grinned at O'Brien. "You can't subpoena someone who doesn't exist." He looked at the president. "If you make me bring him in from the cold now, he's finished."

The president nodded assent. "When does he next check in?"

"Tomorrow. After the hearings are over."

"Make sure he knows that we need to talk to him *pronto.*"

The president grinned. "Poor guy's probably holed up in some flophouse somewhere, living off White Castle triples with cheese. Bet he's dying to get back."

"See?" Lee asked. "It's that little island, right there." She removed her arm from around Randy's waist and pointed to a finger of stone that jutted out of Somes Sound about thirty yards offshore. "The nest is in the top of the tree." A single lodgepole pine, ravaged by age and storm, clung precariously to the top of the spire. They sat down at the base of a sandstone cliff, its sea-blue shadow a pleasant contrast to the warm light of sunset that flooded the island.

"What's that thing on top of the tree?" Randy asked. "It looks like it needs a haircut."

"That's the nest, silly. Use your binoculars."

Randy found a hollow in the base of the cliff that made a perfect backrest. Lee stretched out on the still-warm sand in front of him and leaned back against his drawn-up knees.

Randy trained his binoculars on the intertwined jumble of sticks that formed the nest. "Pretty ugly," he commented.

"Bet it's better decorated than your apartment," Lee retorted. She squealed with laughter as Randy reached down and tickled her ribs.

"So where are these birds of yours?" Randy inquired. "All I see is that dump of a nest and a big old stump on one—"

"Whoa!" he breathed as the "stump" turned to face him. "*Big* bird! Must be two feet tall."

"That's the mama fish hawk," Lee explained. "Dad's out getting dinner."

"What did you call her?"

"A 'fish hawk.' Only people from away call them ospreys."

"I wouldn't have thought it possible, babe," Randy replied as he stared through the binoculars, "but you're making even less sense than usual. What's 'away?'"

"Maine slang. Anyone who hasn't lived in the same spot in Maine since before the Pilgrims is from 'away.'"

The head and shoulders of a second bird appeared above the rim of the nest.

"That's one of the babies!" Lee exclaimed. "It's a lot bigger than before I went to Russia. It's almost fully fledged."

As they watched, the young osprey pulled itself onto the edge of the pile of sticks. It flapped its wings vigorously, rose a few inches into the air, then fell heavily backwards into the nest.

"Kind of fun, isn't it?" she asked when they had stopped laughing.

"What's kind of fun?"

"Spying on them like this." Lee paused. "Too bad it's kind of a busman's holiday for you."

When Randy said nothing, Lee zipped her binoculars into their case, then turned around and folded her arms across Randy's knees. She rested her chin on her hands and looked up at him.

"I know what you do for a living," she said quietly.

Randy lowered his eyes to hers. He shook his head.

Lee smiled gently. "It really is all right. I'm used to it. I've known for years what Uncle Joel did—"

"Does," Randy corrected.

"*Does*, and I think my dad's helped him a couple of times." Her smile spread to her eyes. "It's a job that needs doing, and it's all right with me that you're doing it."

Randy regarded her for a long moment. "Part of me," he said at last, "feels just like that adolescent ospr— *fish hawk* out there."

Lee watched and waited.

"All through high school and college I was just about as successful as my young friend out there. I'd get all ready, flap my dating wings madly, and then end up in a crumpled heap on the floor." He smiled at her smile. "Maybe that's why I accepted so eagerly when the Company offered me a job. They gave me someplace to hide." Randy stared out at the islet. "I was a senior at Bowdoin, majoring in international relations. Not one of the hotly recruited professions. Joel was my senior adviser, so I jumped at the chance when he suggested I talk to some friends of his." He shook his head. "Ever since then women have been either completely turned off by what I do or have expected me to perform like James Bond."

"I'm not, and I don't," Lee said quietly. The shrill cries of the fish hawks mingled with the evening wind in the pines.

Randy looked back at her. He reached out and ran a fingertip down her sunburned nose. Lee looked up at him, and he smiled as the offshore breeze tugged at her hair. "C'mere, you." He pulled her to him.

"Where is everybody?" Pat asked as she came into the kitchen with the mail.

Anne slid dinner into the oven, closed the door, and wiped her hands on her apron. "Lee said something about taking Randy to look at the fish hawks, and Daddy's on the phone."

Pat regarded her daughter for a moment. "Want to talk about it?"

Anne frowned. "Talk about Lee and Randy?"

"No, about you and Jake. I had to restrain your father the other night, you know."

"He wasn't going to come downstairs, was he?" Anne asked, horrified.

"No, but Jake's tearing out of here woke him up, and he thought it was that pack of summer boys again. I had to restrain him from calling the police." Pat smiled. "Given the circumstances, I didn't think that having to bail Jake out of jail at two in the morning would've helped matters much."

Anne found herself caught up in her mother's quiet, infectious laugh.

"You OK?" Pat asked.

"Not really."

Pat repeated the offer. "Want to talk about it?"

"Can we take a walk, Mama?"

"It's lovely outside right now," Pat said as she opened the kitchen door. "Let's go."

Anne pulled her sweater more tightly around her shoulders as they left the grove of trees surrounding the Dryden house and turned onto the road that ran along the clifftops. Built a century ago to connect the marble quarry on the Dryden property to their deep-water dock, the road had borne the enormous altar columns destined for the cathedral of Saint John the Divine in New York.

Anne walked beside Pat, head down, hands in the pockets of her sundress. "I don't think it's going to work, Mama."

"Oh? Why not?"

"We can't seem to talk. About anything. I tried to explain to him how I feel about his waltzing in and out of my life, and he just stared at me like a big dope. That's what our fight was about."

When Anne had finished describing Jake's Everest assignment, Pat smiled. "Jake's not telling you about China was thoughtless, love, but it wasn't wrong." Anne stared at her mother. "Until you're married to him you have no inherent claims on a man's time, and he has no obligation to inform you of his whereabouts. The reverse is true as well; Jake has no special right to know where you are, either." The psychiatrist held up a hand to quell her daughter's incipient outburst. "I know you want him to be here with you. Like all women, you want your man to express his undying devotion to you by sitting at your feet and gazing soulfully into your eyes."

Anne wrinkled her nose. "If Jake tried that, the clumsy oaf would probably sit on one of my feet." The two women laughed together.

"Most men aren't very good at it," Pat agreed, "despite

what the perfume ads would have us believe." She broke off a sprig of lilac and breathed in its fragrance. "But they do try. And Jake, contrary to what you may believe, *is* trying."

"Well," Anne said petulantly, "if he is, then he needs to try harder."

Pat stopped. She waited until Anne turned and looked at her. "Annie, it's not Jake who needs to try harder. It's you."

Anne heard her mother's "doctor" voice and knew better than to say anything.

"Yes," Pat continued, "Jake has a lot to learn. But it's *you* who has to try harder, not Jake. He's already trying as hard as he can, while you haven't even started yet."

"I don't understand."

"Who's beside you in our pew every Sunday he's here? Who spends every minute he can spare learning from your father? Joel is a demanding mentor, and he's very pleased with Jake's progress." Pat smiled gently. "Think about how Jake's mealtime graces have grown in confidence and depth. Remember, not everyone was raised in the faith like you. Jake's had his whole life turned upside down, and he's still sorting things out." Pat resumed their stroll.

"But," Anne protested, "when I try to explain to him how I feel, or why I need him to be a certain way, he just looks at me like I'm crazy."

"When you were in Cairo, did you understand what the vendors were shouting at you?"

Anne frowned. "Huh? No."

"What you're saying to Jake is, to him, just as incomprehensible. Look at the words you just used: *feel, need, be.* In general, these words are not part of a man's basic vocabulary. Some men, certainly, are more adept at expressing their feelings than others, but even men who are innately sensitive have a lifetime of macho expectations to overcome." Pat smiled at her daughter. "I understand what you're saying," she went on, "but

Jake won't." She paused. "It's not that he can't, it's that he doesn't quite know how. Not yet, anyway."

Pat smoothed back an errant wisp of Anne's hair. "Intimacy is a learned behavior—more so for men than for women, I think. But men *can* learn to express intimacy in ways we can recognize. Give him time."

Pat squeezed her daughter's hand and looked into her eyes. "You've led a sheltered life, love, and now this hulking, loud, hairy-chested thing has rudely encroached upon it." Pat laughed quietly. "And, just like the rest of us, you've fallen in love with him."

"So, what do I do?"

"Until he learns better, try to recognize Jake's attempts at intimacy. Your father calls it 'trading in the other person's coin.' I can think right now of one thing Jake does that shows how much he cares for you." Pat saw Anne's hand go to the pendant at her throat, and she shook her head. "No, this is something much more precious than anything purchased. This is something *given.*"

Anne looked helplessly at her mother. "His car," Pat whispered.

"What?"

Pat nodded. "You know how much he loves that car. He hasn't even let Joel drive it. But you get to."

"Last time I drove it I got a flat. I'll trade that for some chocolates and roses any day."

Pat put her arm around her daughter. "It's more than that. I know his coming and going infuriates you, and understandably so. But have you noticed how, every time he's going to be gone for any length of time, he leaves the MG here?"

"That's because I look better in it that he does."

"It's also because he's trying to say, as best he can, 'I'm trusting you with my most important possession. I know you'll take care of it for me and that it'll be there when I get back.' He's giving you his trust, and what is love but ultimate trust?"

A flash of color caught Pat's eye. "The daffodils have bloomed!" she exclaimed. "I think I'll pick some for the dinner table."

As her mother picked flowers, Anne wandered to the cliff's edge. She spotted the rocky offshore spire topped by the fish hawk's nest. *I wonder,* she thought, *if Lee and Randy are anywhere to be found. Dinner's almost ready—they can walk back with us.* Then she looked down at the beach.

"It's been nice knowing you," Jake said as he devoured another chunk of steak.

Dave stared at him across the food-laden table. "You know something that I don't?"

Jake gestured to the massive, hickory-smoked sirloin that covered the platter in front of him. "When Accounting finds out that you took me to Gallagher's for dinner, you'll be lucky if all they do is string you up."

Dave waved dismissively with one hand as he sopped up the juice from his prime rib with the piece of sourdough that he held in the other. "It's not often that I get to take the ace of my staff out to dinner."

"Yeah," Jake agreed. "Usually it's ham-and-pineapple pizza with Stephanie and the kids at your house. By the way, why aren't we eating pizza with them?"

"Steph's started a women's Bible study. A bunch of her friends bring their kids to our house." Dave laughed. "We men thought of starting a study of our own, but the idea kind of fizzled when we realized that the study would eliminate Monday night football. So, one night a week I'm on my own for dinner." He cut off another slice of prime rib. "You know, this sure beats my usual Monday-night fare."

"Which is?"

"Chicken nuggets, fries, and however much of a chocolate shake is left after sharing with Forrest and Mackenzie."

Dave set down his knife and fork. "It's also not often that the ace of my staff looks like last week's meatloaf. What's up, friend? You look terrible. Surely that staff meeting this morning wasn't all that rough?"

"No, but driving here last night was."

"You *drove* here? From Maine?"

"Sure did. Got here just in time for the meeting."

"That explains why you said so little today. I just thought that you were dumbstruck with awe at my executive prowess in getting this thing organized."

"*Awe's* the word for it," Jake agreed. "Aw—" Jake stopped, grinning.

"I bet I know what's up," he told Jake. "You tore out of here last night because you were going to have dinner with Anne. You told her about Tibet, right?"

"Uh-huh."

"And she went through the roof."

"How'd you guess?"

Dave shook his head. "I've been married for thirteen years. No guessing involved." He finished his iced tea. "Got any idea why she went ballistic on you?"

Jake winced at the memory. "Not a clue."

"What was she the maddest about?"

Jake shoved his plate aside and rested his elbows on the table. "Well, she was not at all happy about not being told about Tibet."

"You hadn't told her?"

Jake shrugged. "It was just a back-burner possibility until this week. Didn't see any reason to mention it."

Dave's eyebrows arced. "Oh."

"Anyway, after chewing me out about the trip, she went on and on about how I'm never around."

"Are you?"

"Whenever I can make it up there."

Dave smiled at his old friend. "Notice any connection between the two things she's mad about?"

Jake thought for a moment, then shook his head.

"Has Anne ever, even once, told you she was busy that weekend when you showed up on her doorstep on a Friday night?"

"No."

"Have you ever not been there when she wanted you to be?"

Jake grimaced. "You mean like her birthday next week, when I'm going to be photographing Everest?"

Dave grinned. "You're beginning to get the point." He waited while the waiter cleared the dishes. "You thought about marrying her?"

"Some, I guess."

"However much you've thought about it, I guarantee you that Anne's thought about it more. Now she's made up her mind."

"Well, if she doesn't want to," Jake said acidly, "that's all right with me."

"Just the opposite. She's waiting for you to ask her." Dave savored the look on Jake's face. "She's committed to you, man—she's decided that you're the one. The question is, are you committed to her?"

"Of course I am!"

"Does she know it?"

"Why shouldn't she?" Jake replied defensively.

"Because women equate commitment with security, and you've done exactly nothing to make Anne feel secure."

"I'm not following you."

"I've known you a long time, old friend, and I've seen this in you before. For years—until recently—I've watched the women come and go in your life. And every time old Jake showed up in my office, eager to take that four-week stint photographing penguins in Tierra del Fuego or some other assignment that no one else was willing to touch, I knew that another relationship had just gone south on you. You were a runner, Jake. When the going got tough, you got going."

Feeling cornered, Jake just frowned at Dave. "It's different with Anne," he said at last.

"I believe you. It's different because *you're* different. You're proof positive of 2 Corinthians 5:17: 'If anyone is in Christ, he is a new creation; the old has gone, the new has come!' But Anne hasn't known you as long as I have. All she sees is what remains to be changed, not what has already changed. And, she's a woman. I'll bet that each time you come and go as you please she lies awake and thinks."

"About what?"

"About sitting in a kitchen, holding a newborn baby. It's growing dark outside, and she's watching the kitchen door wondering where you are and when you'll be coming home."

"But if we were married, I'd tell her where I was!"

"Then, since you're thinking about marrying her, why not start making her feel secure now? Do something that makes her feel like she's a permanent part of your life."

"Like what?"

"For openers, try saying, 'I love you, and I'll be back.' Stef says it to Mackenzie when he doesn't want to be left at Sunday school, and I say it to Stef when I kiss her good-bye each morning. Works real good."

Dave stood. "Come back to the house. You can help tuck the kids in, and then I'll have Stef tell you about how she used the first time I proposed to her to teach me to check in."

"The *first* time you proposed?"

"Yeah. I'd just breezed back into town after an extended, unannounced business trip. I had bought an engagement ring in Antwerp. I had also missed Stef something fierce, so I called her and asked her out. That night I reached across the table at

Sardi's, handed her the ring, and popped the question. She looked at the ring, smiled, then dropped it in my soup on her way out. Didn't see her for two weeks." Dave shook his head ruefully. "Worst two weeks of my life."

"Sounds like Stephanie."

"Don't it, though. Let's go."

15

Hua Chen eyed the young man struggling in the grasp of a burly PSB policeman. "Caught him writing 'FREE TIBET!' on a wall near the Barkhor, Inspector," the officer explained.

Chen frowned. "That's not like you, Tsenring. This is the third time this week that you or one of your friends have been caught promoting insurrection. What's going on?" Tsenring glared defiantly at Chen. "Is someone putting you up to this?" the inspector asked.

When he received no response, Chen motioned to the officer. "Put him in Drapchi until he decides to talk. Don't forget," Chen reminded the young Tibetan, "what we do with splittists."

Tsenring's eyes went wide at the use of the PSB jargon for "revolutionary," which he knew carried a death sentence. The officer led him away. Deep in perplexed thought, Chen leaned against his desk and stared out his office window.

Barabise handed Yousef Bey a worn leather satchel. "Here's half your money, Afghan. The other half when we get to Lhasa." Bey took the case and put it in his flight bag. "You aren't going to count it?" Barabise asked, surprised.

Bey smiled. "You are an honorable man, nomad." *And if the money is not all there, or if you attempt treachery of any sort, I will handcuff you to one of your purchases and then watch from a safe distance as you get your money's worth.* "Besides," Bey continued as both men laughed at his joke, "the arming instructions for your selections have already been sent to Lhasa, and only I know where they are."

Barabise looked the Afghan over with a critical eye. "It would be wise for you to obtain some new clothes."

Frowning, Bey fingered his cashmere Burberry topcoat. "This is warm enough," he protested.

"Undoubtedly. However, it is also conspicuous. In Lhasa, dressed as you are, you will stand out like a yak on a snowfield. I know a merchant over in the *Cheez Beez Bandar* who will trade you clothes left by the Everest expeditions for what you are wearing."

Bey, who had long ago learned that a high profile was not an asset when dealing in stolen arms, reluctantly agreed.

Three hours later, feeling very uncomfortable in a down vest, plaid flannel shirt, and canvas pants, Bey strode alongside Barabise into the central truck depot.

"Imagine!" he snorted. "Only two thousand rupees for my briefcase." The smuggler swore. "That thief!" Barabise ignored him, mentally calculating the kickback from his Tibetan friend who ran the Jawalakhel Surplus Shop.

"How do you plan on getting both us and your purchases to Tibet?" Bey asked.

Barabise pulled back the flap of his dilapidated Landrover. Inside were piled canvas duffel bags with expensive bicycles heaped on top. "A group of American tourists want to bicycle the High Road from Tibet. On the recommendation of one of my men who works in the Lhasa CITS office they had their supplies flown here." The Khampa grinned mirthlessly. "They were so appreciative when we were able to arrange transport."

Bey shook his head. "Bicycle over the Himalayas from Lhasa? They are crazy."

The Tibetan nodded agreement. "They are also rich."

"What about the border checkpoint at Zhangmu? How are we going to get past inspection?"

Barabise grinned hugely. "What day is it, Afghan?"

Bey looked warily at the Khampa chieftain. "Wednesday. Why?"

"Those of us who deal in contraband have divided up the border guards, one day each. I own Wednesdays." The nomad threw open the door to the Landrover's cab and slid behind the wheel. "Let's go."

From his table on the terrace of the Farakhat restaurant, Markov stared out through the poplar and acacia trees at the Pamir mountains that ringed Dushanbe. His inquiries at the city's three hotels and its airport—even when reinforced by his Red Army ID card—had proved fruitless. Savagely, he tore a piece from the loaf of *obi non* on the table. He wrapped it around his shiskaboblike *shaslik* and pulled a lump of the charcoal-broiled meat from its skewer. Markov chewed morosely as he thought over what to do next.

Before dissolving into hysterical pleas for her baby's life, the woman in Taldy Kurgan had admitted to being Yousef Bey's mistress. He had been there two nights before, but had left the following day for Dushanbe. Markov had barely made the afternoon flight that lurched across the Tien-Shan foothills and then dropped into the long, narrow Dushanbe valley in a terrifying series of tight, descending turns.

Why here? Markov wondered. *Why come to this repulsive little backwater? Who's he going to peddle his wares to here? The semiliterate goatherding nomads who infest these mountains? They never really were part of the Rodina, and now they have nothing to rebel against even if they desired to.* Markov picked up the skewer of *shaslik* and tore off another bite. *But if not here, then where? Not his homeland—the Afghan war is over, and his side won. Nor can it be the Pakistanis. From what I hear about their weapons development program, he's already been through that territory. Perhaps the Sikh rebels in northern India—they're both desperate and fanatical enough to use his toys. . . .*

The sudden realization that someone was approaching him from behind shattered Markov's reverie. In a single motion he lunged out of his chair, his knife appearing in his hand. Markov found himself facing a young man, who started so violently at the sight of the knife that his gold-embroidered *tubeteyka* flew off. He glanced at the round cap that now lay at his feet, then licked his lips nervously.

"Colonel Markov?"

"How do you know who I am, boy?" Markov seemed to loom even larger over the terrified youth.

"I work at the Hotel Vakhsh, sir. I overheard you asking the desk clerk about someone. An Afghan."

"So?"

The gangly youth looked up at Markov. "The desk clerk was lying, sir. The man you're looking for checked out this morning."

"Where is he going?"

The boy reached for a pocket, then froze as the point of Markov's knife pricked the skin of his throat. "I have his departure card," he whispered hoarsely. Markov nodded. Very slowly, the boy pulled it out of his pocket. Markov took the proffered card and glanced at it.

"*Nichevo!*"

The epithet was meaningless to the boy, but the expression on Markov's face told him all he needed to know. "The card is helpful, sir?"

Markov, his brows beetled in thought, nodded as he stared past the young Tadzhik. His knife hand dropped to his side.

The youth gathered all his courage. "You said something to the desk clerk about a reward, sir."

Markov smiled at the young man. "You've got pluck, boy. I like that." He took a bill out of a pocket. The youth stared at it for an instant. Then he grabbed it, scooped up his *tubeteyka*, and fled.

The former Red Army colonel threw another bill down on the table and stalked out of the restaurant.

The agent at the Dushanbe train station was sound asleep, his chair tilted back against the station house wall. Markov looked at the man in disgust, then kicked the chair out from underneath him.

"I want the manifests of all transshipments for the past week," he demanded.

The agent came to his feet. "Just who do you think you are?"

Markov's ID card appeared in one hand, his SP220 in the other. He repeated his demand.

The agent seemed unimpressed by either credential. "Very well," he said tiredly. "This way."

Inside the gloomy station house, Markov took the ledger the stationmaster gave him over to the flyspecked window. He ran his finger down a page, then another, the agent watching quietly. Markov went past an entry, then back to it.

"What's this?"

The stationmaster peered at the ledger. "One crate. A hundred forty-seven kilos. Came in yesterday morning."

"From where?"

"Alma-Ata."

"The contents?" Markov asked, his voice now grim.

The agent peered again. "'Machine parts,' it says here."

"And you, of course, fulfilled your duty as a stationmaster and inspected the contents." The silence in the dilapidated building grew taut as the two men stared at each other.

The agent shook his head. "No need to. You know as well as I that Alma-Ata's a big manufacturing town—"

The stationmaster went cross-eyed as he tried to stare down the snout of Markov's pistol, which was now resting against his lower lip.

"The truth," Markov said quietly.

This time the agent didn't hesitate. "I was paid well not to notice."

"By whom?"

"A foreigner." Markov prodded the man with the pistol.

"It was a stranger," the stationmaster protested. "I don't know who he was!"

"Did he pay you in gold?"

Wide-eyed, the man nodded.

"And where is the shipment now?" Markov's voice had a dangerous edge to it.

The man said nothing.

Markov placed his thumb on the hammer of his pistol. "Gold or steel, smuggler." Slowly, he drew the hammer back until it cocked. "Your choice."

The man seemed to wilt. "I heard one of the men who picked up the crate say that they had to hurry—that they had to leave before the airport shut down for the night."

Markov parked the jeep two blocks from the Dushanbe airport. He stuffed his Kalashnikov into his duffel, padded it with clothes, and slung the bag over his shoulder.

The new nation of Tadzhikistan was eager both to prove its sovereignty and to enhance its commerce, and so a crop of booths for the airlines of neighboring countries had sprung up in the shabby, corrugated-tin building that passed as an air terminal. Markov strode up to one and, with the combination of his military passport and a large amount of cash, secured a ticket to the destination marked on Yousef Bey's departure card.

I will follow you everywhere, Afghan, Markov thought as he waited for his flight. *If your trail leads me into hell, then so be it.*

A departure was announced. As Markov walked toward the gate, he glanced at what the airline agent had written on the top of his ticket: FLIGHT 947: KATHMANDU.

16

Joel handed Randy the phone. "It's for you."

Randy frowned at both the unexpected call and at the grin on Joel's face. He took the receiver. "Hello?"

"Randy, this is the president." Joel chuckled silently as Randy stared at the phone in disbelief. "Your boss told me where you were as soon as you checked in," the familiar voice told him. "You've picked a good place to hide—nobody keeps a secret better than Joel Dryden. Randy, I want you to take a look at something for me." A piece of paper was sliding out of Joel's fax machine. Joel handed it to Randy, then pressed the button on his speakerphone.

"Did you have anything to do with this?"

Randy read the Russian president's note again, just to make sure this was really happening. "No, sir, I didn't."

"Did anyone order you to do this, and then cover it up?"

"Answer the question, Randy." Elliot French's voice interrupted Randy's hesitation.

"No, Mr. President. To the best of my knowledge, nothing of this sort has been attempted." Randy heard what sounded like several sighs of relief.

"You were just over there. Have any idea what's going on?"

"Yes, sir, I do. While I was in Russia—"

"Hang on a sec," the president interrupted. "Elliot, do you want to hear this? The subcommittee hearing isn't over yet."

"Miss this?" French snorted. "Not on your life. I haven't had a chance to talk to young James Bond yet. Randy, ask Joel if this is his secure line."

"It is," Joel replied through the speakerphone.

"OK. Then what Randy's about to tell us is to be classified EchoFoxtrotFive. That way none of the committee members will be cleared for it. Code name is—" French paused. "CRUCIBLE. Mr. President, will you sign the directive?"

"Just send it over. Fire away, Randy."

"Mr. President, despite the reassurances given by your Russian counterpart at the Summit, things are coming apart in the CIS. While we know about the civil and economic unrest the breakup of the Soviet Union has caused, not much attention is being paid to its effect on the *intelligentsia*.

"The technocrats, both civilian and military, are being squeezed from both sides. The State, which formerly was their lifeblood, is broke; and, unlike in the U.S., there's no commercial market for their technology. They'll do anything for hard currency with which to continue funding their research. Witness, for example, the world-class Russian computer talents who are forming into so-called 'consortiums' and doing hack programming jobs for American hi-tech firms. They're desperate."

"What do you mean by *desperate?*" the president asked.

"Exactly that, sir. It's getting to the point where they'll do anything for money. One of our informants is a high official in Rosengoatom, the agency that operates Russia's nine nuclear power plants. He reported that his nuclear engineers haven't received a full paycheck yet this year, and that the agency is owed billions of rubles by its customers with essentially no possibility of payment. Maintenance has been halted, sabotage is up, and he suspects theft."

"Of fissionable materials?" French asked.

"No," Randy replied. "Of sophisticated electronic components highly sought after on the black market. Fissionable plutonium, in its raw state, is really tricky to steal and transport."

"What about the military?" O'Brien asked.

"They're even worse off. Unlike the scientists, they can't sell their skills to the highest Western bidder. Instead of the pension and dacha they were promised, the officers in the elite Soviet missile forces are now suddenly homeless and out of work. Surrounded by extremely marketable hardware as they are, I wouldn't put it past one of them to hold an impromptu yard sale."

"Any guess as to who might have done it, Elliot?" the president interjected.

The four men waited as the DDO thought. "Probably one of the crack East German units. They have access to both the technology and Western lines of transportation. Randy?"

Joel watched as Randy shook his head vigorously. "Can't say I agree with you, Boss. When I was last through that part of Germany there wasn't a nuke in sight, and the few remaining Red Army officers were busy selling their medals in order to work up the cash to buy a used Trabant from the locals."

"Thank you, Randy." They heard the president's line go quiet for a minute. "We'll go with your analysis, Elliot," he announced. "Get cracking."

"Yes, Mr. President. I'll allocate the necessary resources immediately. Randy, I need you in my office tomorrow morning. Start packing."

"Yes, *sir.*" Joel grinned at Randy. In a longstanding mockery of the FBI's traditional formality, CIA field agents used honorifics only when they were extremely displeased with their superiors.

"Good to talk to you again, Joel," the president finished. "Say hi to Pat for me."

"That I will, Mr. President. Good night." Joel waited until the president hung up, then punched the speakerphone's off button.

"I happen to agree with you," Joel told Randy. "I wasn't about to undermine Elliot's authority in front of the president, but I will call him tomorrow."

"Thanks." Randy shook his head. "Darn. And just when it was starting to go so well."

"With the subcommittee hearings?"

"No. With Lee."

Chairman of the Joint Chiefs of Staff Jaime "Roddy" Rodriguez arose from his place at the end of the long mahogany Situation Room table. A stocky fireplug of a man with a grizzled regulation crewcut, he had spent the last three decades working his way up through the ranks of the Marine Corps. He still remembered his days as a scared recruit who spoke little English, and that memory brought an element of compassion to his demanding leadership and battlefield ferocity.

"What you got for us, Roddy?" the air force chief of staff asked.

Rodriguez pressed a button on the console before him, and a map appeared on the rear-projection screen at his right hand. "This, gentlemen, is a map of the southeastern portion of the border between the former Soviet Union and the People's Republic of China. At 1730 hours yesterday, a routine overflight of the area by a KH-12 surveillance satellite revealed an unexpected massing of Russian troops along the border." Rodriguez picked up a laser pointer from the table, and a small spot of brilliant red light appeared on the map. "Troop concentrations were discovered here, east of Kum Tekei, and also here at Naryn."

"What sort of troops, General?" the president asked.

"What we'd expect, sir. Infrared analysis revealed the heat signatures of M-1973 self-propelled guns, T-72 tanks, and MAZ heavy-duty utility vehicles." Rodriguez turned back to the map. "These units are believed to be from the Fifteenth Tank Division based in Ayaguz, as well as from the SU-24 Fencer Regiment based in Iliysk."

The army chief studied the map. "Do we know for sure?"

"No, we don't. But we're pretty sure. At 2300 hours last night, pursuant to orders issued by the secretary of defense, the shuttle *Discovery* changed course and overflew this part of Russia and Kirghizia. Photo-recon of the installations at Ayaguz and Iliysk revealed a significant absence of armor."

"*Discovery* is on a civilian flight," O'Brien said sharply. "If news leaks about this unauthorized side trip—"

"*I* authorized it, Mike," the secretary of defense interrupted. "Remember that the Department of Defense paid for most of *Discovery.*" He smiled disarmingly. "As a matter of fact, I've got the pink slip in my desk." O'Brien glowered as a murmur of laughter went around the table.

"And don't worry about word getting out," Rodriguez added. "The only crew member privy to the real reason for the course change is the mission commander. He's a bird colonel who really wants his star before he retires." The chairman smiled grimly. "There'll be no leaks."

"What about the 165?"

Rodriguez shook his head. "Beats me why, but they haven't budged."

The president looked up inquiringly.

"General Harker is asking about the 165th Motorized Rifle Division, a crack infantry unit based along the border. Our wargame scenarios have traditionally shown them as spearheading any advance into China. But *Discovery*'s recon showed no activity whatsoever either at Alma-Ata or Semipalatinsk."

Rodriguez spread his hands. "We don't have a handle on that one yet."

"Your recommendation, General?" the president asked.

"I'd like your permission, sir, to call Defense Condition Four."

"Is that really necessary?" O'Brien asked.

Rodriguez suppressed his growing dislike for the chief of staff. "The troop movement alone requires some sort of response on our part. Add to that our little surprise visit from Ambassador Panshin, and we can't afford to just sit on our thumbs." He stared at O'Brien. "All DEFCON Four will do is make official the steps we've already taken—increased surveillance and security. The press will report the tightened security, which makes us look proactive." *For a change.* "No one goes anywhere or does anything dangerous."

The president nodded. "So ordered. Keep us informed, General." He strode from the room, followed closely by the whispering O'Brien.

❖ ❖ ❖

A rat squealed as Ganden stepped on it.

"Silence!" Barabise ordered. "If they catch us here, we die."

Ganden followed the nomad through the dusty, cobwebbed warehouse toward a sliver of light. Barabise pushed a massive packing crate out of the way, and Ganden blinked at the sunlight that streamed through the intricate latticework window. Below them, a high wall topped by broken glass and razor wire surrounded a bleak concrete courtyard.

"Drapchi Prison," Barabise whispered. "Something's about to happen that I want you to see."

As Ganden watched, the steel door to the prison courtyard clanged open. Two guards stepped out, followed by six gray-clad prisoners. A People's Liberation Army officer stepped into the courtyard and closed the door behind him. The prisoners stood facing him as he took a piece of paper out of a pocket and began reading. Straining to hear over the wind, Ganden caught the words "counterrevolutionary activities." Suddenly, the prisoners turned their backs on the officer.

"No!" Ganden gasped as he saw their faces. "Pastor Ling!"

Ignoring the irate PLA officer, the members of Ganden's house church formed a circle. Joining hands, they knelt. Ganden, his faced pressed against the latticework, tried to reach out to them. He felt the skin tear as he attempted to force his hand through an opening.

Barabise jerked Ganden's arm back. "Say and do nothing, boy," he whispered fiercely. "You may wish to join them, but I do not. Attract any attention, and you die where you stand." The wind flung sound to them, and Barabise looked out the window. "Are they singing?" he asked.

Ganden fought back the tears. "The Doxology," he whispered. "A song of praise."

The infuriated officer flung down the paper. He drew his pistol, stepped behind the nearest prisoner, and pressed the pistol's barrel against the base of her skull. Ganden heard a *crack!* and Pastor Ling's wife slumped over. Ganden clutched the latticework, blood dripping from his fingers as he watched the officer make his way around the circle. Each successive *crack!* silenced another voice. Finally, the wind carried only Pastor Ling's rich baritone. The pistol jerked once more, and the pastor fell across his wife.

"Did they die well?" Barabise asked.

Ganden forced himself to turn away from the window. "What?"

The Khampa chieftain repeated the question. It seemed to Ganden that his voice was coming from very far away.

Ganden looked at the nomad. "For us, death is only the doorway to eternal life. But yes, they died well." The song of thanksgiving, lifted on the wind by a lone voice, echoed in Ganden's mind.

"Then they are now martyrs to your cause," Barabise declared.

Ganden shook his head. "Pastor Ling taught us that death does not *make* someone a martyr, it merely *reveals* a person as one."

Barabise pointed toward the prison. "I wanted you to see just how effective this pacifist doctrine you used to follow is. They are dead, and the Han will bill their families for the cost of the execution. But because you now follow me, you are still alive." He turned to leave.

Ganden glanced through the latticework. The bodies were gone. A guard stood hosing down the concrete, and blood swirled down the courtyard's drain in a red-stranded whirlpool.

17

Lee struggled to remain calm. "I can't go with you," she said quietly.

The Drydens' floating dock shivered as Randy spun around angrily. "Why not? If you don't want to go away with me for the weekend, then say so!"

"That's just it. I *do* want to go with you."

Randy stared at her. "Then what's the problem? If you don't feel like going to Washington, we can go somewhere else."

"It's not that. It's not *where* we'd go at all. It's *why* we'd go." She looked at him. "Why do you want me to spend the weekend with you?"

Randy shrugged uncomfortably. "You know. To spend time together. Get to know each other. That sort of thing." Lee said nothing. "I don't have to spell it out for you, do I?" Randy finally exclaimed.

Lee smiled gently. "No. And that's just it. 'That sort of thing' is really the whole reason for the trip, isn't it?"

"OK, it is. So what?" Randy huffed in exasperation. "I thought you'd be more comfortable if we went away someplace."

Lee laughed in spite of herself. "Annie's my best friend, and she and her parents have seven graduate degrees between them. I think they *might* figure it out."

"I really do want to get to know you," Randy backtracked.

"You can do that here."

"I *have* been doing that here!"

"So you have. And it's been fun." Lee paused. She looked up at him. "What's my favorite color?"

"I don't know." Randy grinned. "But I'd like to know."

Lee placed her hand on Randy's arm. "You'd like to know *now*. But would you want to know, or even care about knowing, after we'd had sex?"

"What's that got to do with it?"

"Everything. Everything I hold true. Sex comes last, not first. It *has* to. After she's reconciled herself to the fact that he not only watches football but falls asleep and snores during the games. After he's accepted that she can't cook to save her life. And after they've made a commitment—a public, *lifetime* commitment—to each other and to God. Then, and only then, are they entitled to God's precious wedding present." Nearby, a gull looking for its breakfast dropped a mussel onto the rocks. "That's why it's called *consummating* a marriage. To 'consummate' means to complete, or make perfect." She looked at him tenderly. "You can't 'make perfect' something that doesn't yet exist."

"Is that why you stopped me the other evening on the beach?"

Lee nodded. "I'm sorry I let things go as far as they did. I had no intention of leading you on."

"Obviously," Randy said bitterly.

"Please don't be angry. This isn't easy for me, either."

"Who's angry?" he replied sarcastically. "It all makes sense now. Let's go nowhere fast. But, let's go *together*. Thanks for clueing me in." He turned to leave. "I'm outta here."

"Please stay. I enjoy your company very much."

"That's wonderful to know, but I've got better things to do with my time than birdwatch." Halfway up the gangway, Randy turned. "Now I know why you talk about marriage so much. With your attitude, talking about it is as close as you're ever gonna get." He shook his head. "Later. Maybe."

Stung, Lee lowered her eyes. As she listened to his receding footsteps, the dock's weathered planking darkened in teardrop-sized circles.

❖ ❖ ❖

"I suppose you're here as Randy's second to challenge me to a duel over Annie," Jake remarked as Joel sat down. Soft gray light filtered through the skylight in the room of Jake's apartment that served as his personal studio.

Joel grinned and accepted a can of Diet Coke. "Not hardly. No way I'm getting involved. You and Annie can sort this one out. Just as soon as both of you get back."

Jake frowned. "Both of us get back? Where did Annie go?" He hastily suppressed a vision of Anne eloping with Randy.

"To her apartment," Joel replied. "Seems that Lee got into some sort of swivet this morning, so she and Annie cut all the pizza and ice cream coupons out of the *Portland Press-Herald* and took off." Joel was relieved to see Jake chuckle. "You need to talk about it?" he offered.

"I'll live." Jake put his feet up on a rung of a battered stepladder. "Greg's already done a good job of recruiting me to spy for him, so I suppose you're here to deliver the *coup de grace.*"

"Not really," Joel replied. "If anything, I'd be inclined to talk you out of it. Sending someone into the field is never something I've been eager to do." Knowing that Joel wasn't finished, Jake waited. "But," Joel continued, smiling at the inevitability of the word, "it needs doing, and you can do it."

"Of course I can do it, but why should I?" Jake asked skeptically. "'It needs doing' is no reason—in Texas, up until recently, 'he needed killing' was an acceptable defense for murder."

Joel nodded. "When the need for action is determined by a man crazed with bloodlust, I'll agree with you. There are, however, other, less subjective standards by which need can be determined." Through the skylight, Jake watched a 747 on final approach to La Guardia. "Greg's scans show fissionable material disappearing from three sites in the former Soviet Union. Those discrepancies might have been caused by legitimate transfers of weapons to a site or sites outside of the scanner's field of view. A week later, however, weapons-grade plutonium appears in Lhasa. Again, this might have been a legitimate transfer by the Chinese government. But we just don't know."

"And," Jake mused, "since we obtained the information via spy satellite, we can't exactly ask them what's going on, can we?"

"Exactly. But we do need to know in order to decide how to proceed." Joel paused, then looked at Jake. "We're in a somewhat untenable position: We know that something's wrong, but we don't know just how wrong it is. Until we get the information we require, we don't know whether to make a big stink about this or not." Joel pulled a Bible from Jake's bookshelf. "Remember the story in Numbers 13?" Jake shook his head. "Moses was in the same sort of position that we are. A primitive, nomadic tribe was being threatened by the inhabitants of another country. And Moses, too, had differing scouting reports about the hostile territory."

Joel, you're too bald to be Moses, Jake thought. *But I bet you sound just like him. . . .*

"So Moses did what any sensible field commander would do. He sent someone he trusted in to do a little recon work."

"Joshua," Jake remembered.

Joel nodded. "Moses told Joshua to go 'into the hill country. See what the land is like and whether the people who live there are strong or weak.'"

A shutter banged against a window as Joel looked at Jake. "We need you to be our Joshua. We need reliable information. Just like Moses, we need to know whether or not there are giants in that land."

✧ ✧ ✧

"Going away present for you." Greg set the gleaming, all-black 35-mm SLR on his desk.

Jake glanced at the camera. "Thanks, guys, but I have all the cameras I'm going to need."

"Not without this one, you don't," Greg replied. "Check it out."

Jake picked up the ordinary-looking Nikon F3, then frowned as he turned it over in his hands. "The controls are wrong for an F3, but I know I've seen them somewhere before. . . ." Jake's frown deepened as he thought, then he looked up in surprise. "Is this a DCS?"

Greg nodded. "It's a standard Kodak Digital Camera System—"

"With," Joel interjected, "a few of Greg's own touches."

Jake set the camera down. "Thanks again, but I don't think so. I've seen demos of digital photography, and it just doesn't have the resolution for my kind of work, let alone yours."

Joel nodded agreement. "You're right. The commercial models are still little more than expensive toys." He gestured at Greg. "Some time ago, however, we sicced young Frankenstein here on them."

Greg shrugged. "I thought about it for a while and then realized that the LZW-encoding algorithm currently being used could be maximally optimized by—"

Jake held up his hands in a *T* signal. "Time out. I'll take your word for it. What I *won't* take your word for is that this'll produce images that I'm happy with."

"Give it a try," Joel suggested. "We use it all the time for rapid-access imaging, and I hear that the Desert Storm guys were really happy with it, too."

"What's different about it?" Jake asked.

"For one thing," Greg explained, "it's got the new Mega-pixel CCD array incorporated into the F3's back. At over 1.3 million pixels in the array, it's about three times as dense as anything else available."

"So," Jake offered, "that means three times the resolution, right?"

Greg shook his head. "Just over ten times, actually."

Jake looked at Joel. "Now I know why Cathy's so ticked off at him. This sort of thing is his idea of big-time fun. How many exposures?" Jake asked.

"Twenty-four."

"How'd you manage that? The lower-resolution cameras store twenty images on a diskette." Greg nodded. "But," Jake protested, "the more detail, the more information that has to be saved, right?" He paused, then looked the camera over again. "Speaking of which, where does the diskette go?"

"There isn't one. In order to accommodate the resolution we need, I changed the recording technology. Instead of a diskette like the 'still video' cameras use or an IC memory card like the rest of the digitals, this uses a thirty-two megabyte static VRAM cache to store up to twenty-four images. Plus, there's a hard drive that goes with it."

Jake frowned. "Hold it. I've seen those drives. They're about the size of one of Anne's purses, and they're tethered to the camera by a sort of leash arrangement. No, thanks."

Greg smiled. "New technology. Conner Peripherals has come up with a hundred-megabyte, one-inch form-factor hard drive. I got one, ruggedized it, messed around with its controller some, and installed it in the F3's motor drive. It holds seventy-nine images."

Jake stared at the Nikon. "Does the motor drive still work?"

"Two-point-five frames per second. Plus, there's a couple of other goodies for you: the Megapixel array doubles the effective focal length of your lenses—"

"So it will seem as if I'm twice as close as I actually am."

"Useful when dealing with restless natives," Joel added.

"And," Greg finished, "you can dynamically change your film speed from ISO 20 to 4000."

Jake whistled appreciatively. "Sounds OK to me. What about color saturation? That's an important element in my work."

"Full thirty-two bit color mapping."

Joel, who had been staring out the window, looked at Greg. "Thirty-two bit mapping gives you around 4 billion different light intensities and colors, right?"

Greg nodded. "Far more than the eye can discern."

Jake caressed the camera. "This is a great toy, gentlemen. How much does one of things run?"

"Tricked out the way yours is, around fifty grand," Greg told him.

"Terrific. I can see me trying to explain losing this to my insurance agent." Jake leaned back in his chair, crossed his arms, and frowned. "Now, what's it going to cost me to use it?"

Joel smiled. As he began to explain, Jake's frown deepened.

"Thanks for coming, Senator." Mike O'Brien motioned to a sideboard laden with food and silverware. "Help yourself to coffee and pastries."

As the senator sat down on one of the overstuffed leather couches in the chief of staff's anteroom, he looked sharply across the coffee table at the man sitting next to Elliot French.

"You Cavanaugh?" he asked with the residual drawl of an Ozarks childhood.

Randy nodded.

"Where have you been for the past six days?"

"I can't say, sir."

Rutherford's piercing blue eyes narrowed. "I hope you realize, Mr. Cavanaugh, that it is within my authority—"

French held up a hand. "The hearings are over, Darren." Rutherford glanced at the DDO, then busied himself with his coffee. "As chair of the Foreign Affairs Subcommittee, you've been invited here, as a courtesy, to be briefed on an operation we're planning." French smiled. "We realize that we broke form by not notifying you of the last one, so this is our way of reassuring you that it won't happen again."

Mollified, Rutherford nodded magnanimously.

"We've recently received some information we believe requires further investigation."

"Such as?"

"It concerns the escalation of the lethality of the violence committed by the parties involved in the coup that was the subject of your subcommittee's investigation." French waited until Rutherford blinked. "In other words, Senator, we believe they've received a supply of weapons from an external source. Weapons that dramatically alter the nature of the conflict."

"What sort of weapons?"

"A variety of missiles and antipersonnel devices."

Gotta admit the man's right, Randy thought as he struggled not to grin at French's adroit maneuvering. *Nuclear artillery shell would make one heck of a fragmentation grenade.*

"Is this information reliable?"

"It comes from a top-level source."

Rutherford smiled. "So one of our moles is finally earning his keep, eh?"

"You might say that, Senator."

Standing behind Rutherford, O'Brien smiled as he tried imagine what the president of Russia would think of being labeled a "mole," a highly placed official who is persuaded to spy for the enemy.

"Why, Mr. French, should we continue to spend time and money on what you only yesterday described on the record as 'an internal squabble between two relatively minor factions'?"

"Good question. We like to think of this particular operation as the CIA's equivalent of the old Soviet May Day parade. We're not out to accomplish anything definite. We just want to put on a show of force. "

"Who are you trying to impress? The KGB no longer exists."

"True. But its successor, the SVR, exists with a vengeance."

"The SVR?"

"The Russian Foreign Intelligence Service. Under the guise of doing credit and background checks on Westerners who want to invest in Russia, these guys have been trying to steal everything from electronic banking software to computer games. Their motto is Why Pay for Technology When You Can Steal It for Free?"

"So? Sounds to me like what goes on in Silicon Valley any day of the week."

"If that's all it was, we'd hand it over to the FBI. But our SVR comrades are also trying to recruit Americans as spies. They've contacted NASA workers at the Johnson Space Center, as well as embassy staffers in Germany."

Rutherford shrugged. "Same sort of thing that's been going on for forty years. Sure you aren't engaging in a little threat inflation in order to justify your budget, Elliot? It seems to me that 30 billion a year for espionage ought to be enough."

"That's the Appropriations Subcommittee's concern, Darren," O'Brien chided gently.

"It gets worse," French added.

Randy picked up his cue. "While I was over there, one of my informers tipped me to a scheme to recruit sailors at the Hampton Roads Naval Base in Norfolk."

The senior senator from Virginia sat up. "Are you sure of that? The Russian ambassador has been suggesting a bilateral ban on espionage."

"Senator," O'Brien asked, "can you *really* imagine a Russia without spies? We can't afford to ignore this increased recruiting activity. Russia has anted; we must stay in the game."

"And if they raise?"

"We call," French said quietly. "That's why Randy has to go back over there. Since there's nothing fair about the intelligence game, it'll be really helpful if he's able to mark their cards."

Rutherford looked at Randy. "How long will it take you to come back with proof of this?"

"I'll be back in two weeks, tops."

The senator stood. "I'll expect a full report then. Thanks for the briefing, gentlemen." He winked at Randy. "And, while you're at it, see if you can throw a scare into one of those 'relatively minor factions,' OK?"

"You got it, Senator," Randy said after the door had closed. "But, if I scare the wrong faction, I've just started World War III."

❖ ❖ ❖

"Here's the other half of your goodies," Greg said. What he handed Jake was about the size of an oversized paperback book.

"Laptop PC," Jake observed.

Greg nodded. "Intel Pentium-based; with a color, active-matrix LCD display. Fairly run-of-the-mill stuff. Except," he added with an enigmatic smile, "that the boys over in Communications have messed around with it some."

Better the boys over in Communications, Jake thought resignedly, *than the boys over in Ordnance. At least that means it won't blow up. Maybe . . .*

Greg powered the computer up. "It's fully functional, so there'll be no problem with security at airports. Aside from replacing the DOS printer drivers, all we've really done is this." He spun the little machine around. "See this port marked PRINTER?"

Jake nodded.

"Don't try to hook a real printer up to it," Greg cautioned. "We've reprogrammed the port to talk to this." He handed Jake a device that looked like an old-style flashbulb reflector. Roughly a foot long, it had a collapsible aluminum reflector on one end. On the other was a connector designed to plug into the printer port.

"This is what you're going to use to transmit images to us. This is an antenna that will generate a krypton-argon laser in the milliwatt range. Whenever you've got something to send, plug this into the printer port." Greg snapped the antenna into place. "Then open up the dish." With a fingertip he unfurled the "reflector."

Greg handed Jake a cable. "Plug this end of the cable into the external sync connector on the F3's motor drive. The hard drive is hooked up to it. Next, plug the other end into this port marked EXTERNAL HDD." Greg pointed to a small plug shaped like an elongated *D*. "That'll connect the hard drive to your laptop." Greg glanced at Jake. "Still with me?"

Jake nodded, wishing that he wasn't.

"Power up the machine. Then, when you're in Windows, click on UPLOAD. The program will respond with WAIT-ING. That's your cue to start waving the dish around the eastern sky. When the program locks onto the homing signal from a geostationary satellite out over the Pacific, it'll say AOS. Click on SELECT, and you'll get a menu asking what you want to transmit. Click on OK, and it'll start transmitting. When it's done you'll see TX COMPLETED. After that, you can just shut it off."

"How long will this take?" Jake asked, fending off visions of police beating on his hotel room door.

"About thirty seconds, assuming a good linkup." Greg grinned. "I've also put a couple of other things out on your hard disk. A previewer to let you look at your images and a really great new game called 'Shadowcaster.' It's the hot new thing over in Operations right now."

As Jake turned the antenna over in his hands, Cathy brought a tray into Greg's den. "Iced tea?" she asked.

Jake surveyed the hardware arrayed before him, then looked up at Cathy. "Shaken, not stirred."

18

"Well, if it isn't the boy wonder!"

George Delgado, Global Photo's equipment manager, strode across the room and shook hands with Jake. "Where you been keepin' yourself, man?" he asked amiably.

Jake grinned as he surveyed the cavernous room. Shelves covered with neatly stacked equipment reached the ceiling; tripods, backdrops, and brushed aluminum cases holding camera bodies and lenses. At a workbench in the middle of the room, a technician was replacing the flash tube in one of the elements of a Norman PS-2000D lighting system.

"Just like you to wait until the last minute on this Tibet thing," George said chidingly.

Jake shrugged. "I've been kinda busy."

Delgado winked at Jake. "The place has been crawling with guys wanting equipment, but I saved the good stuff for you." He pulled open a drawer. Camera bodies sat in cut-outs in the foam that lined the bottom of the drawer.

"Let's see." George held up a 35-mm body in each hand. "You'll be wanting to use the new Nikons, right? I just got these two in."

Jake shook his head. "Thanks, but not this time. Actually, I'm just here for some lenses."

George looked pained. "Aw, c'mon Jake. You're not gonna use that ancient Leica of yours, are you? It's never been the same since they fished it outta the Nile."

"Nonsense," Jake retorted. "You cleaned it up as good as new. Better, actually, since you replaced the old lenses with multicoated glass."

George shrugged. "All modesty aside, you got a point. But, still, the Leica just doesn't have the metering system you're gonna need. Exposures are tricky at those altitudes." George squinted. "The sunlight up there is *intense.*"

"Thanks for the advice. I'll be sure to slather the lens with sunscreen. Now, what do you have in a 500–800 AiAF zoom?"

"Depends," George said slyly, "on just what sort of a body you're gonna be using . . ."

Jake chuckled. "OK. You win. It's an F3."

George shrank away in mock horror. "An F3? You gotta be kiddin'! You're not putting any of my lenses on a relic like that!"

"A brand-new prototype, *based* on an F3," Jake finished patiently, trying not to laugh.

The equipment manager's horror was replaced instantly with indignation. "An F3-based proto?" He peered at Jake suspiciously. "Where'd you get it?"

"It's a unit I'm being asked to evaluate," Jake prevaricated.

The short, round man stared up at Jake. "You got it from Pat Mayekawa over at Nikon, right?" He smacked his fist against his palm. "I knew it! The bum! Sending my photographers equipment without letting me know. I'll murder her the next time I see her!" George looked at Jake eagerly. "Does it have standard bayonet mounts?"

"Sure does."

"Great!" George bustled off across the equipment room.

"Lookit this, Jake!" he called. "Just got it in! A large-aperture 300-mm AF Nikkor ED-IF telephoto that'll make your eyes water!"

Lee tipped the pizza-delivery boy a dollar and a big smile, then carried the pizza into Anne's living room. She scooted a stack of videos out of the way with her foot, set the box on the carpet, and plopped down cross-legged next to it.

Anne followed, carrying sodas and paper napkins. "How elegant," she observed. "If I'd known it was going to be a formal occasion, I would have dressed."

Lee opened the box and wrinkled her nose as a cloud of steam enveloped her. "Ugh! I simply do not understand why you insist on ruining a good pizza with anchovies."

"I got to like them in Peru. They use them in *ceviche*." Anne sat down on the other side of the box.

"That's where they serve them raw, mixed with lime juice, right?" Lee shuddered. "Gross." She peered at the pizza, then turned the box around. "*That* half is yours."

Anne held out her hands. "You pray."

Lee took her hands, and Anne closed her eyes. After a long moment of silence, Anne looked at Lee's bowed head. As she watched, a tear fell, then another. She squeezed Lee's hands. "I've seen you cry during prayer, but *before?* Must be some grace you thought of to say."

Lee wiped her eyes with a napkin. "Sorry," she sniffled. "It's just that—"

"It's just that he really got to you, didn't he?" Lee nodded. "That explains the tears," Anne observed. "But why now?"

Lee smiled ruefully. "It was the other night, at dinner in Freeport. I wasn't thinking, and after the food arrived I waited for Randy to say grace—like you do when you're out with a man." Lee winced. "He was nice about it. He deferred to me, but it was *really* awkward. I should have realized right then that something was wrong." She toyed with a string of cheese, then looked at her best friend. "I think I *did* realize that it wasn't right, but I let it go on anyway." Lee shook her head miserably.

"Zzt-zzt."

Lee looked up. "Huh?"

"Zzt-zzt," Anne repeated. "That's what Mama uses in her notes for 'love at first sight,' 'that certain spark,' or 'electricity.' It means that someone's fallen head-over-heels in love with a handsome, charming, extroverted hunk." Anne took a slice of pizza out of the box. "Like Randy."

Lee looked sharply at Anne. "Or Jake."

"Or Jake." *As long as we add 'insensitive lout' to the list.* "Only after she's married him," Anne continued, "does Mama's client find out that her perfect man drinks too much, can't hold a job, or is a philanderer. She's frightened, confused, and disillusioned, and her pastor sends her to Mama for help. You," Anne added gently, "got off easy."

"It sure doesn't feel like it. Randy's so *nice.*"

"Was what he asked you to do this morning nice?"

"No."

"Was he nice about it when you refused?"

Lee's shoulders slumped. "OK. I get the point. Did he pull this kind of stunt when you went out with him?"

Anne laughed. "When I 'went out' with Randy, I was seventeen and he was twenty-four. We went out twice. Once to a movie—a matinee—and once to a crafts fair. He bought me popcorn at the movie and ice cream at the fair, and in both cases he had me home in time for dinner. And each time Mama came up to my room at bedtime and we talked about the day." Anne bit off the end of her slice of pizza. "Randy Cavanaugh is an honest, ethical man."

"Not today he wasn't!"

"But he was," Anne replied. "By his standards he was. Randy, like most men, would never proposition a teenage girl.

But, by *his* standards, asking a grown, single woman to do the same thing is a really good idea."

"That doesn't make sense."

"You're right, it doesn't. Not by *our* standards. That's why *he*—whoever *he* is—has got to share our standards. Our faith, our beliefs, our love of God."

"You're lucky," Lee said quietly. "Jake shares those things with you."

"So he does," Anne replied bitterly. "When he's around."

Anne's tone caused Lee to look up sharply. Their eyes met, and the two young women laughed.

"Fine pair we are," Anne said reprovingly. "Here it is, a Friday night, and we're moping over a pizza." She picked up the box and headed toward her kitchen. "I'll pop it in the oven, and while it's warming we can pray."

Anne returned to find Lee holding one of the videos they had rented. "Should we pray before or after the movie?" Lee asked.

"Who's in it?"

"Harrison Ford."

"After. Definitely *after.*"

Jake pressed the shutter button lightly, and the whitish blur in his viewfinder became the apron of a man scattering cheese on a pizza in the window of the restaurant across the street from his SoHo apartment. He moved the camera upwards, and a red-neon GIORGIO'S sign snapped into focus.

Sure wish this thing would bring my life into focus, Jake thought as he disassembled the camera Greg had given him. *Here I am, about to leave on the assignment of a lifetime—the one I've worked for, the one I've always wanted. This is the one that's gonna get me into the galleries and museums, right there beside Robert Capa and Ansel Adams.*

He stuffed a tripod into a nylon sack and pulled the

drawstring tight. *I should be dancing in the streets instead of feeling like elderly roadkill.* Jake shook his head. *What's with you, Mac?* He picked up the big telephoto he had been peering through and reached for its lens cap. As he moved the lens a white rectangle appeared in its depths. Jake frowned, then looked up. Anne looked out at him from the source of the reflection, a large portrait of her that hung above Jake's fireplace. . . .

"Miss Dryden?"

Annoyed at the interruption to her effort to finish the welter of last-day-of-school paperwork that littered her desk, she looked up sharply to find him leaning against the door to her first-grade classroom.

"May I," he inquired politely, "accost you?"

Over her laughing protests he had locked her classroom and escorted her to his car. "Ten minutes," he informed her when they pulled up in front of her apartment. "Then I'm outta here." She made a face at him as she got out.

Eight minutes later she came out to find him lounging insolently against his MG, his arms folded, watching her as she walked toward him. He brought his eyes to hers as she neared, then held something out to her. Her eyes widened at the sight of the MG's keyring. She fought back the near-irresistible desire to say, "Well, it's better than no ring at all," and instead affected a Southern drawl. "Why, Mistuh MacIntyre, you're gonna let little ol' me drive your cah?" She pressed the back of her hand to her forehead. "I do believe that ah'm a-gonna faint right heah."

"Then try not to dent a fender on your way down, OK?" He tossed the keys into the air. She caught them neatly and walked around to the driver's side.

"Where'd you learn to drive like this?" he shouted over the wind an hour later as she snaked the car around a curve cut into the face of a cliff. On the other side of the blurred guardrail, the Atlantic washed against the rocks far below.

"Peru," she shouted back. "One of the Marine guards at the embassy had an old Camaro he worked on. Sometimes on his day off, he'd teach me how to drive it." She downshifted expertly and swung into a straightaway.

He looked over at her. "What else did he teach you?"

Not taking her eyes from the road, she just smiled and stepped on the accelerator. The little car leaped forward, snapping his head back against the headrest. Jake laughed quietly and slid a Mark Knopfler CD into the player mounted in the dashboard.

From their table on the patio of the little Bar Harbor restaurant, they ate lobster salad and watched the nightly flotilla of pleasure boats jostle for berths in Frenchman's Bay.

When they had finished, he studied the sky, then stood. "Let's go."

She stretched and closed her eyes. "Must we? It's so peaceful here."

"You've had your fun," he said with a grin. "Now, it's my turn."

He drove southward, around the eastern bulge of Mount Desert Island to a sweeping expanse of white sand beach. Hand in hand they walked, laughing and talking, tossing oyster crackers from the restaurant into the wind to be snapped up by the teeming, raucous gulls.

He reached into the daypack she had brought along and handed her the bulky, white alpaca sweater they both knew was his favorite. She pulled it on, glad she had thought of it. When her head emerged he was holding his Leica.

"My hair!" she protested as the stiff onshore wind trailed it out behind her.

"Your hair," he replied, smiling.

She had never seen him before at his work. With the comfortable, confident authority that accompanies the mastery of a craft, he photographed her.

"Sit," he told her after a while.

They sat a few feet apart. Sand Beach trailed away behind her, the forested slopes of Otter Cliffs hazy in the distance. They said nothing. Arms wrapped around her knees, she felt him watching her. He smiled at her, with a light in his eyes that was more than the sunset. Then, just as she fell a bit more in love with him, he took the picture. . . .

"I wish you were in that kind of mood every day, lady," Jake told the picture. "I don't know what's gotten into you lately." He sighed. "Well, maybe we'll work it out when I get back, and maybe we won't." He paused, as if listening to the part of him that knew that "maybe we won't" was no longer an option. Then he capped the lens and put it into its compartment in the case he always carried with him.

Rain rattled against the windows of New York's Kennedy International Airport. Jake waved to the beckoning gate agent and finished dialing Anne's number. Ten seconds into her answering-machine message, as the agent began to walk toward him, Jake hung up. He shouldered his camera bag and trotted toward the gate.

19

"Lhasa tower, China Southern thirty-three-oh-three, with you level at ten thousand."

"Thirty-three-oh-three, Lhasa tower," the reply came over the pilot's headphones. "Radar contact. Descend and maintain five thousand meters."

Captain Corey O'Toole looked over at the copilot of the Boeing 757. "OK, Chuck, let's set her up for the approach."

Zhong Xiue glanced at O'Toole and nodded seriously. Unable to pronounce either of the copilot's names, O'Toole had nicknamed Xiue "Chuck" after the Chinese pilot's hero, General Chuck Yeager.

"Engines to 75 percent," the pilot ordered. The muted roar of the 757's engines descended in tone as Xiue pulled back on the throttles. "Twenty degrees flaps." The airliner pitched back slightly and started to descend. "Butts and belts, Chuck." Xiue flipped the switches that illuminated the No Smoking and Fasten Seat Belt signs in the cabin.

"Lhasa tower," the copilot said into his headset, "China Southern thirty-three-oh-three out of ten thousand for five."

O'Toole glanced at the 757's Instrument Landing System.

The aircraft was headed right for the runway, tracking exactly the ideal glide slope displayed on the ILS. "We're right in the groove," O'Toole told the copilot. "Nice job setting her up."

The pilot's blonde ponytail bobbed as she nodded in satisfaction. O'Toole leaned back in her seat. Feeling a headache coming on, she closed her eyes and massaged her temples. *Just another week, max,* she thought tiredly, *and I'll be back in the civilized world of deep-dish pizza and iced decaf lattes.* O'Toole smiled as she thought of her Siamese kitten, Chocks, so named because the kitten's crossed, slanting eyes had reminded the young woman irresistibly of the thumbs-inward signal used by ground crews to tell a pilot that the aircraft's wheels had been secured.

It had been seventeen days since the senior contract pilot had lifted the 757 off from the airfield at the Boeing plant in Everett, Washington. China Southern Airlines had purchased two 757s and had also contracted with Boeing to train its pilots and fly the jets until the Chinese airline's captains were certified on the new aircraft. With its fuselage loaded with extended-range fuel tanks, O'Toole had flown the aircraft nonstop to Shanghai. There she had met up with Xiue, who had just graduated from Boeing's ground school. After the plane was outfitted with its interior, the two had ferried the 757 to its base in Chengdu, where it would be placed in regular service on China Southern's Chengdu-to-Lhasa run.

Half a mile to the north, a man knelt on the crest of a ridge. Below him lay the Lhasa valley. He watched as the blue-and-white 757 broke through the thin clouds overhead.

Her eyes still closed, O'Toole listened to the engines and noted the aircraft's altitude and rate of descent. *Right on the money. A few more days,* the pilot decided. *A couple of instrument landings and a bad-weather approach or two, and Chuck'll be ready to solo.*

The voice of the Lhasa air traffic controller crackled in her headset. "Thirty three-oh-three, cleared to land, runway two-five. Wind one-seven-zero at eight. Altimeter two-niner-niner-six." Not for the first time, O'Toole was glad that English was the universal language of air traffic control.

O'Toole opened her eyes and glanced at the altimeter, which was just indicating five thousand meters. *They're on the ball this morning*, she thought gratefully. *Must have put on the first string for a change.*

"Cleared to land, China Southern thirty-three-oh-three," Xiue replied.

O'Toole sat up and grasped the aircraft's steering yoke. *Feels a little logy*, she decided. *Not surprising, since we've got twice the fuel we need just in case we'd had to divert because of bad weather.* "I've got it, Chuck." Xiue nodded and placed his hands in his lap. O'Toole grinned. *Time to grease this puppy onto the runway. Wouldn't want to slop any champagne on the VIPs in back.* This was the inaugural flight of the 757 into Lhasa. Aboard was the American consul from Guangzhou, as well as Chinese government officials, and executives from both the airline and Boeing.

The aircraft was now level with the man on the ridge. As it passed in front of him, he brought something to his shoulder.

"Ten klicks out," Xiue told O'Toole. O'Toole pushed her intercom button. "Ladies and gentlemen, this is Captain O'Toole. We'll be landing at Lhasa shortly." She was careful to use her "professional" voice. "On behalf of the entire flight crew, I'd like to thank you for flying the inaugural flight of China Southern's brand-new Boeing 757." She released the button and started to laugh. *I'd love to see their faces now that they know a woman is herding this thing.*

"Full flaps," O'Toole ordered.

"Full flaps," Xiue replied. "Airspeed two-oh-five."

"Gear down."

Xiue lifted up a protective cover and flipped three

switches. "Gear coming down." He paused. "Three green lights—gear shows down and locked."

Sunlight glinted off a silver emblem on the 757's starboard engine cowling. The man on the ridge spotted the reflection in the open sight through which he was peering and turned slightly to his right.

"Runway in sight," O'Toole reported. "Seat the cabin crew." Xiue pressed a button three times. At the sound of the chimes, the flight attendants hastily finished filling champagne glasses and scurried to their seats. "Air brakes," she ordered.

Xiue flipped switches. "Airspeed now one-eight-five. Six klicks out—passing through forty-five hundred."

The glow from the tailpipe of the 757's starboard engine appeared in the man's field of view. His right forefinger tightened slightly, and a red light came on in the sight.

"One-seven-oh, through forty-four."

The man on the ridge tightened his hold on the grip. The red light turned green.

O'Toole swept the instrument panel with her eyes. All normal.

The man pulled down hard on the trigger.

O'Toole smiled. *Commander of the first flight of a 757 into Tibet. Corey, old girl, that's an entry in your logbook that the airlines back home* won't *be able to ignore.*

The booster charge of the Soviet-made SA-7 GRAIL kicked the surface-to-air missile out of its launching tube. Half a second later the sustainer ignited, accelerating the missile to Mach 1.5.

"Five out, through forty-two." Xiue pressed his headset against his ear. "Cabin crew reports ready to land."

The SA-7 was fifteen years old and hadn't received regular maintenance. Two seconds into its flight moisture inside the uncooled PbS IR seeker shorted it out, and the missile lost its lock on the 757's engine. As the SA-7 dipped toward the ground, the man on the ridge came to his feet. The GRAIL's launcher slipped unnoticed from his hands.

"Four klicks out," Xiue reported. "Through four thousand."

Then the SA-7's backup seeker took over. The missile arced upward, traveling at over seven hundred knots.

O'Toole pulled the 757 up into "slow-flight" mode. "Throttles fifty."

Xiue brought the throttles back to 50 percent power. "Airspeed one-six-five," the copilot reported. He reached down, ready to activate the thrust reversers after touchdown. They were now less than five hundred feet above the valley floor.

The GRAIL impacted just above the 757's starboard engine, and the SA-7's graze fuse detonated the warhead. Pieces of the warhead's fragmentation casing tore through the Rolls-Royce RB211-535E4 engine, which began to disintegrate.

A panel of lights flashed red in front of O'Toole, and an angry buzzer began to sound.

"Fire in Two!" Xiue barked.

"Kill it," O'Toole ordered instantly. Xiue slapped the switches that cut the flow of fuel to the engine, then pulled the red lever that activated the 535E4's fire extinguisher.

"Full power to One," O'Toole snapped. The copilot slammed the throttle levers to the port engine wide open.

Through her seat, O'Toole felt a growing vibration. She pressed her microphone button. "Lhasa tower, China Southern thirty-three-oh-three calling MAYDAY. Repeat, MAYDAY. We've lost our starboard engine."

"Thirty three-oh-three, MAYDAY acknowledged. Land any runway, your discretion. Crash trucks are rolling."

O'Toole felt the unbalanced thrust begin to push the plane to the right. She savagely slammed her foot down on the left rudder pedal, and the aircraft's nose straightened out. "Crash positions," she ordered. Xiue began speaking into his microphone in rapid Chinese. O'Toole glanced at the altimeter. *Four hundred feet to go. Hang tough, sweetheart,* she coaxed the aircraft.

The damaged engine's titanium-honeycomb turbofan was still spinning at twenty-two-thousand RPM. Loosened by the explosion, one of the turbofan's blades tore loose. The 535E4's Kevlar containment casing shattered, its shards tearing through the wing like shrapnel. The almost-full fuel tank exploded, and the starboard wing of the 757 disappeared.

The aircraft shuddered, then bucked violently, throwing O'Toole against her shoulder harness. As the 757 began a slow roll to starboard, O'Toole threw the controls hard to port in an attempt to right the plane. *Get it level. Get it level and pancake in.*

Transfixed with horror, the Lhasa tower controllers watched the jet's steepening roll. Through their headphones, they could hear a recorded voice in the 757's cockpit shouting, "PULL UP! PULL UP!"

Corey O'Toole looked up. The ground flashed by through the eyebrow windows over her head. *We're too low. We're not gonna—*

The echoing boom briefly interrupted the prayers of the pilgrims at the Jokhang Temple in downtown Lhasa. As they resumed their prostrations, Kailas Barabise began the long walk down to the valley floor.

20

Hua Chen snatched the jangling phone from its cradle. *"Whey?* This is Chen. What is it?" The inspector fished around in his desk drawer for a box of matches. "Yes, I heard the explosion. I was over by the Jokhang. A group of Australian tourists asked me what it was, and I told them it was blasting down at the cement plant by the river. Why?"

The match Chen had lit burned toward his fingers as the inspector listened, aghast, to the news of the crash. "I'll be right there." Chen blew out the match and ran from his office.

The guard at the entrance to the cordoned-off area saluted respectfully as the inspector got out of his car. A gust of wind reached him, and Chen grimaced. *Smells like a haunch of yak that's been left too long in the sun.* He spat superstitiously, to clear from his throat the evil spirits the wind had carried.

His hands in the pockets of his overcoat, Chen walked around the blackened landscape. Every fifty feet around the perimeter was an armed soldier, keeping the growing throng of curious onlookers at bay. Everywhere, it seemed, small red flags were sticking up from the ground. Each flag was numbered. The number on the flag matched the number on the bag into which the body part found at that spot had been placed. *It looks*, Chen thought, *like a field of poppies*. More PLA soldiers were loading personal effects into the large orange bags that dotted the site.

Chen paused in the shade of the twisted and burned tail assembly to light a cigarette. "How many?" he asked the constable who had joined him on his grisly stroll.

"One hundred forty-seven, including crew." The constable checked his notepad. "One hundred thirty Chinese, and seventeen Americans. Including the American consul from Canton."

Chen swore. The death of Americans, especially American bureaucrats, insured the arrival of the foreign press. It would be up to him to make certain that they saw and found out only what the government in Beijing wanted them to see and find out.

"Did the pilot report any trouble?"

The constable nodded. "According to the controllers, just before the crash she issued a MAYDAY call."

Chen frowned at the constable. "Did you say 'she'?"

"That's right. The pilot was a *quai loh* female. An American." Originally an insult, the reference to foreigners as *quai loh*, or "foreign devils," had long since ceased to be a pejorative.

Shaking his head, Chen hawked and spit again. "Did *she* say what was wrong?"

"Only that they had lost their starboard engine. No transmission after that."

Chen ground out his cigarette. "Very well, Constable. Keep me informed of any new developments." A squabble broke out among the onlookers, and the policeman hurried away.

After another look around, the inspector decided that there was nothing more to be learned right away. *Besides*, Chen thought dryly, *the sooner I get back to my office, the sooner I can find a clerk to start in on the paperwork*.

A gleam caught his eye. Chen bent over and scooped up a

small heart-shaped locket. He opened it with a thumbnail. Inside was a picture of a cross-eyed Siamese cat. Chen tossed the locket into the nearest orange bag and walked on.

✧ ✧ ✧

"Has something changed?" Cathy asked from her end of the couch.

Greg stared at the urban nondarkness of Cathy's apartment, the pictures and paintings black shapes against gray walls. "If by that you mean, 'Do you still want to get married?'" he said quietly, "the answer is yes, I do."

"Then, can't we at least talk about it?"

"Talk about what?"

Cathy glared at him through the gloom. "About our wedding. We've been engaged for almost a year, and we haven't even set a date yet." *And all my friends are starting to think I've fallen into the same trap they have: That you slept with me until I threatened to throw you out, so you proposed and just like the rest of them we've embarked on an endless live-in engagement. It might not be so bad if we really were sleeping together, but only Lee really believes that we're not.*

"We've tried to set a date," Greg reminded her.

"And each time your research was going to be at a critical stage, a new satellite was going to be launched, or you had been invited to give a paper at an important conference in Burkina Faso or someplace like that. What's wrong?"

"Nothing's wrong."

"How can you say that? Everything's so different now that we're engaged. When we were going together we used to go places and do things. We spent time with our friends and alone together. Now I hardly see you anymore." Cathy looked at his profile. She wondered if he was listening. "We used to have fun," she said plaintively. "Please don't tell me nothing's wrong."

"Nothing's wrong. Nothing's changed. It's just that I'm

not ready to get married yet." *I want you and need you. I love you. I just can't be married to you.*

"Then, why did you propose?" Cathy fought back her growing exasperation.

Because I can't imagine a life without you in it. "Because I do want to get married."

"Then, why aren't we at least talking about it?" Cathy chose an emotionless monotone over the alternative scream.

Greg stared out the window as the silence lengthened. *Because when I think of marriage I'm four again, cowering in bed with my younger brother. I hear the front door slam, and I hear dad bank off the walls as he staggers down the hall and into his bedroom. Then I hear the shouts, the blows, and my mother crying. Night after night.* "Because I look at our married friends, and they all seem to be getting divorced so they can marry the person they've been having an affair with."

Cathy stared at him. "Are you saying that's going to happen to us?"

Feeling trapped and confused, Greg avoided looking at her. "No. But we can't say that it won't, can we?"

"Maybe you can't," Cathy replied angrily, "but I can!" A terrifying thought occurred to her. "Are you seeing someone else?"

Shocked, Greg turned to look at her. "Of course not. What possible reason would you have to ask a question like that?"

"You'd know better than I would," she snapped back.

Greg stood. "Look, I don't want to have to deal with this any more right now. I'll call you tomorrow, when you've calmed down."

"When I've calmed down?" Cathy shouted. "You're the one who's behaving like a lunatic!" Hurt and frustration boiled over within her. "Go on—go home!"

Just before Greg closed the front door behind him, he heard something clatter against the wall across from Cathy's apartment door. He looked down. Then, feeling very tired, he bent over and picked up her engagement ring. Greg knocked once, then again. Exhausted, he leaned against the door. From the other side came muffled sobbing.

The boulder against which they huddled provided some shelter against the biting wind. Tenzig stood beside Ganden, scanning the horizon with binoculars.

"Truck coming!" Tenzig whispered excitedly.

Barabise looked at Ganden. "You ready?"

Wires ran down to the road from the box Ganden held. He placed his thumb on a red button, then nodded.

Tenzing ducked down behind the rock. "Any second now."

Barabise leaned out to see the road. The truck crested a small hill in front of them.

"NOW!" he shouted.

Ganden pressed the button. With a muffled *crump* a flash of light appeared beneath the front of the truck. One wheel came off and went rolling across the rocky steppe. The truck listed over and slewed around in a cloud of dust, coming to a stop perpendicular to the road.

Barabise leaped up. With a roar he raced toward the truck, getting to the passenger's side just as the door opened. Barabise reached in and hauled the soldier out, holding the man at arm's length. With his other hand he removed his *thupta* from its sheath. He showed the dagger to the squirming man, the blade glittering as he held it up in front of the terrified face. The soldier's eyes went wide, then closed as Barabise plunged the *thupta* into his heart.

"This one's dead," Tenzig called from the other side of the truck. "Shrapnel must have got him."

Ganden, who had been carefully rolling up the precious detonating wire, met them at the back of the truck. Barabise took a crowbar out of the truck's toolbox. He inserted it into the lock on the truck's back doors and snapped the lock off. Instantly the doors flew open. Men jumped out and, shouting and laughing, began pummeling Barabise.

"My friends," the nomad explained, "and our fellow warriors. They were being transported to labor camps in Chengdu." Barabise looked into the truck. "Come out!" he called. A small figure peered hesitantly out of the truck, spotted Ganden, and threw herself into his arms.

"You said she was dead!" Ganden exclaimed as he held the sobbing Puzhen against him.

The nomad shrugged. "I needed to test you. You needed a reason to fight." He grinned. "Enjoy her while you can. Consider this a reward for your faithfulness."

21

Ganden came into the room behind Barabise's shop. The nomad sat behind his desk, talking to a man in the corner of the room. Upon reaching Lhasa, Barabise had ordered Ganden to report to him immediately after seeing Puzhen safely to his apartment.

"You can claim your reward later, boy," Barabise had said, obviously enjoying Puzhen's displeasure with the way he looked at her.

Barabise shoved a stack of paper across the desk. "Can you understand this?"

Ganden sat down. He picked up the sheaf and found himself looking at a complex electrical diagram. After running his finger along the schematic for a few minutes, he looked up at Barabise. "I recognize only a little of this," Ganden said helplessly. "Most of it uses symbols I've never seen before."

The chieftain frowned. "How much does he need to understand?" Barabise asked the man in the corner.

"The circuitry is unimportant," Yousef Bey replied. "What he needs to understand is the arming sequence." Bey looked at Ganden. "Do you understand the rest of the pages?"

167

Ganden set the schematic aside. On the remaining three sheets was a list of numbered steps. While Ganden couldn't read the original Russian, he could read the Chinese characters that had been printed above the Russian words. The men watched as Ganden, lips moving silently, ran down the list of steps.

"I can do this," Ganden said when he was finished. "This is very much like programming the sequencing timers at work."

Barabise nodded. "Good. Learn it perfectly. You'll need it tomorrow."

Ganden looked at the sheets he held. "If I'm going to understand this perfectly, I'll need to know what I'm going to be programming."

"I'll show you," Barabise replied. He got up and unlocked the cabinet that stood against one wall of the office. "See this?" the Khampa asked, pointing inside the cabinet. "*This* is the key to the liberation of Tibet."

Jake pulled out a chair, turned it around, and sat down. Sheila Atherton, a deeply tanned middle-aged woman with short gray hair, glared at him from across the table at the Flower Garden Snack Bar in Chengdu.

"About time you got back," she groused. "I couldn't face another cup of green tea."

Jake grinned, used to Atherton's crusty facade. "Did you order the Phoenix and Dragon soup like I told you to? Specialty of the house."

"I most certainly did," Atherton replied tartly, "and what I got was peach custard. Why the Chinese can't give their dishes sensible names I'll never know." She smiled. "It was, however, delicious."

"Awfully kind of you," Geoff Sheffield rumbled. A mountainous man with a flamboyantly bushy beard, he reminded Jake of a cross between Lawrence of Arabia and Captain Kidd.

Jake frowned. "You're more than welcome. What did I do?"

"I am assuming, from the amount of time you were gone, that you walked to Lhasa to reconfirm our flight there tomorrow. Quite decent of you."

Jake took a sip from the cup of the Dragon Well tea the hostess had brought. "I wish it were that simple. A China Southern flight crashed this morning just short of the runway at Lhasa. Until they get the mess cleaned up and sorted out, the airport's closed."

"That does it!" Atherton declared. "I am *not* setting foot in a Chinese aircraft again. After that barbaric flight yesterday from Shanghai in that Russian Tulip—"

"Tupolev," Sheffield corrected. "It was a Tupolev TU-154."

"Whatever it was called, it had no lights in the lavatories and no locks on the lavatory doors. And when I leaned back, my seat collapsed and I ended up with my head in Geoff's lap."

"Delightful," Sheffield murmured.

"Maybe for *you*. To top it all off, the ceiling fell down when we landed. Never again," Atherton finished firmly.

"If it's any consolation to you," Jake replied, "it wasn't a Tupolev that crashed at Lhasa."

"Too bad."

"It was a Boeing 757. Brand-new, and piloted by an American."

The table creaked as Sheffield leaned forward. "Do they have any idea why it went down?"

"The locals don't, and the investigative teams from the airline, the FAA, and Boeing are still in transit." Jake took another sip of tea. "The wreckage will still be in place when we get to Lhasa. Let's make sure to get some shots of it."

"Won't it be old news by then?" Atherton asked.

"Not in the U.S. They will have heard about it, but they won't have seen it, since pictures of domestic air disasters are not high on Beijing's export list."

"Now that the airport's closed, how *are* we getting to Lhasa?" Sheffield inquired. "If we will, indeed, be walking, then I shall need time to buy a new pair of shoes."

Jake threw a bundle of tickets onto the table. "Hope you're still packed. In an hour we leave on the Sichuan Air flight to Kunming. Then, after a restful night in the airport terminal, we catch the morning Dragonair flight to Kathmandu. From there it's overland to Lhasa."

Atherton peered suspiciously at Jake. "This Sichuan Air doesn't fly Tupolevs, does it?"

"Absolutely not." Jake waited until Atherton had relaxed. "Tupolevs are too new for Sichuan Air. They fly the other Chinese airlines' Soviet-made hand-me-downs. The Anotovs and Ilyushins." Jake smiled reassuringly. "Khrushchev flew in them, if that helps."

Atherton closed her eyes. "Have you flown Sichuan Air before?"

"Many times. They've been responsible for some of my most memorable flights."

From between slitted eyelids, Atherton peered at Jake. "And just what, exactly, do you mean by 'memorable'?"

Jake finished his tea. "Well, there was the time when, just after takeoff, the pilot came out to use the lavatory. When he tried to get back into the cockpit, the door wouldn't open. After the pilot had jiggled the latch for a while, to no avail, he beat on the door until the copilot opened it. The copilot then came out with some tools to help fix it. In order to better work on the door the copilot slammed it behind him, thus locking the flight crew out of the cockpit."

"Fascinating," Sheffield murmured. "I presume you crashed?"

"Sichuan Air pilots are nothing if not resourceful," Jake continued. "The pilot and copilot took turns using a fire axe on the door—fire axes are standard equipment on all Sichuan Air flights—until they hacked it open. Then they went back to flying the plane."

Jake grinned at the bug-eyed Atherton. "Time to pack, Sheila. We leave in half an hour."

"Why I'm bothering to pack I don't know," Atherton declared as she stood up, "since I'm obviously never going to need any of the clothes again." She walked off, muttering, *"Ave Imperator! Nos morituri. . . ."*

"You shouldn't do that to her," Sheffield chuckled.

"Sheila can take it." Jake rested his chin on his fist. "I first met her at a field hospital in Nam. She was photographing for AP, and I was recovering from a close encounter with some VC machine-gun bullets. One day, while Sheila watched, one of our air strikes went astray. She picked up a little girl who had been napalmed and ran to the hospital with her in her arms. When the medics said there was nothing they could do for the girl, Sheila sat down, right in the middle of the compound, and held that little girl until she died. She quit AP the next day and started photographing the 'other side' of the war." Jake looked at Sheffield. "She's tough."

"I know," Sheffield replied. "That's why I say you shouldn't do that to her." The big man smiled. "She-bear baiting is dangerous sport."

22

From his table beneath the dropping-spattered awning of the Blue Bird Restaurant, Markov stared moodily at the throngs hurrying down Pyaphal Street toward Kathmandu's Durbar Square. Two days of threats and bribes had brought him no closer to finding Yousef Bey. He watched as a Hindu procession, all gongs, cymbals, and incense, wended along the street on its way to the temple of Khaila Bhairab, the god of terror.

"Another Iceberg, sir?" the waiter asked.

Markov shook his head. He rubbed his hands together. "Where can I get a hat and some gloves? It's getting cold at night." *And you are getting old, Grigory Ivanovich. There was a time when you thought nothing of sleeping in the snow. Now, the slightest chill causes you to bundle up like it was February in Siberia.*

"The shops on Tridevi Marg have the best selection," the young Nepalese suggested.

Markov looked at the waiter skeptically. "And if I am not a naive tourist aching to be fleeced?" A twenty-rupee note appeared on the table.

The waiter smiled. "Try the Jawalakhel. It's just down Pyaphal, across Durbar, on the left. Top-quality Western goods left behind by the mountaineers."

Markov drained his bottle of Iceberg beer, then started shoving his way through the masses worshiping prostrate before Kumari Chowk—the house of the Kumari Devi, the prepubescent girl currently serving as Nepal's living goddess.

❖ ❖ ❖

Ganden steered with his knees as he wiped his hands on his pants legs. The man sitting next to him saw the motion and grinned. Hands again on the wheel, Ganden brought the panel truck to a sudden stop in front of the gate to the Red Star power plant. The guard, caught by surprise, stepped out of his small booth.

"I didn't expect you back with the spare parts so soon, Ganden." He stopped trying to hide the cigarette he had been smoking.

Ganden smiled. "I want to get out of here early tonight. A group of Americans is coming in, and there's fifty *waihui* in it for English-speaking tour guides." He winked at the guard. "Don't mention my leaving early, and I won't mention your cigarette."

"Who's that?" the guard asked, looking at the other man in the truck.

"Warehouseman. He's going to help me unload, then I'll take him back to Lhasa."

"Does he have a pass?"

The man reached into a shirt pocket. He took out an unopened pack of cigarettes and tossed them to the guard. "My pass," he said with a grin. The guard pulled open the gate and waved them through.

"You did well, Ganden," Barabise said as they neared the dirty-gray concrete dome of the nuclear reactor's containment facility. "You kept your head and knew when to let me take over." Barabise slid his pistol out from under the clipboard that rested on his knees. It disappeared into his jacket.

"Why not here?" Barabise asked as Ganden drove the truck past the dome.

"Not with the prevailing winds as strong as they are," Ganden explained. "You may want to do to Lhasa what the Han have done to the rest of Tibet, but I don't."

The young Tibetan stopped the truck at the base of the plant's enormous, hourglass-shaped cooling tower. "Here will achieve the effect you desire. And there will be fewer casualties."

"Why are you worried about killing people, boy?" Barabise demanded to know.

"I have many friends, and *we* have many countrymen, who work here. I don't want to endanger them unnecessarily. In addition, this will cripple the plant but not destroy it. We'll need to bring it back on line quickly once Tibet is free." Ganden regarded him evenly. "Did you take me on as a killer, or as a technician?"

Barabise stared back at him, then broke into an approving smile. "Well said, Ganden. I like a man who stands up to me." He threw open his door and jumped out of the truck.

Ganden opened the truck's rear doors. The only cargo was a canvas-wrapped object about the size and shape of an expedition backpack. He tugged on it, struggling until Barabise reached in with one arm and picked it up. "Only about thirty kilos," he muttered, holding it in front of him. "Can't see how this will do the job."

"It will," Ganden assured him. He opened a gate in a rickety board fence, and they stepped into an enclosed area at the tower's base. Blue-painted metal drums, rusting and leaking, were piled high inside the enclosure.

"Watch it," Ganden warned. He pointed at a thick, yellowish sludge that was puddled at the foot of the pile. "That's radioactive." The nomad jumped back, and walked carefully around the pool. Ganden chuckled. "Now who's nervous?" He pointed at the base of the tower. "Put it there." Barabise leaned the backpack against the concrete.

Ganden knelt and pulled open a flap in the canvas, revealing stainless steel. He took cut a small screwdriver and opened a hatch in the gleaming metal skin, then reached into his jacket pocket and took out a diagram, which he compared against the array of lights and color-coded switches uncovered by the opened hatch. After a moment's study, he began flipping the switches. Lights came on, and numbers began to appear on an LED panel.

"Sure you know what you're doing, boy?" Barabise asked warily.

Ganden's eyes flicked from the diagram to the panel. "Disturb me now, Kailas," he said softly, "and I'll be both your technician *and* your killer." Barabise backed off a step. Ganden's fingers ran over an alphanumeric keypad. "Safing off . . . Begin pre-arm sequence." He ran a finger down a checklist under the diagram. As he flipped switches, a row of lights began to change from green to red. "Disable implosion interlocks . . ." More lights went to red. "Initiate arming sequence . . ."

Moments later a single light remained green. Ganden looked at the light, then at the nomad chieftain. Suddenly he stood up. "I can't do this."

Barabise frowned. "Something is wrong?"

"Yes," Ganden replied. "Something is very wrong. You're asking me to kill innocent people. I will not do that. It's against everything I believe."

Barabise whipped out his pistol and pointed it at the young Tibetan's head.

Ganden felt a rivulet of sweat run down his back and knew that it was not from the stress of the arming sequence. "Go ahead, Kailas," he said, more calmly than he would have thought possible. "Shoot me. Then *you* can finish activating the bomb." Ganden smiled grimly as he held out the operations manual. "Be sure to read the procedure carefully, because only one switch is the right one."

Barabise's face purpled with rage. His finger tightened on the trigger. Ganden closed his eyes, then opened them when the expected shot wasn't fired. With a visible effort the nomad brought himself under control. He holstered his pistol and stared at Ganden.

"You are right. I *do* need you." *But when I no longer do, I will kill you myself.* "And you are also right that innocent people will die. But, which innocent people will die is up to you." Barabise grinned at Ganden's puzzled frown. "You finish, and soon people here will die. The dead will be the Han overseers, our sworn enemies, and Tibetans who have sold themselves to the occupationists." Ganden knew that Barabise considered him one of the latter. "Or," Barabise continued, "we can pack up and leave, and no one here will die." His tone became conversational. "Then, when we get back to Lhasa, we stop and get Tali."

Ganden stiffened at the mention of his youngest sister. "What do you want with her?" he whispered.

Barabise stifled a laugh. "You're as innocent as you are educated, boy." *So innocent that you do not realize that I turned in your house church and paid that lieutenant well to make you appear to be an informer.* "The men you helped rescue are more than a little jealous of my gift of Puzhen to you. They've been in prison a long time and have spent the day drinking *chang.*" Barabise waited.

Ganden thought of his baby sister, just twelve. Tali had been cut from her dying mother's womb. Raised by her sisters, she had been the only one of Ganden's siblings who had still been small when he had come home for good, and the two had become inseparable. She adored Puzhen, who had become a second mother to her. Ganden remembered how Tali and Puzhen had laughed as his fiancée had braided the girl's hair for the first time.

You said that the poor will always be with us, Lord, Ganden reasoned. *Doesn't that mean that some will always die unnecessarily?*

You also told us to honor our father and mother. I loved my parents. Tali is the last of their union, and for her to die horribly would do their memory a great dishonor. Just as you died for us, some must die that she might live. Ganden took a deep breath. *If I am wrong, Lord, may it be upon my head.*

He bent over and flipped a switch. The last light turned green. Ganden closed up the backpack. They hid the ADM beneath a pile of drums, then started toward the truck.

✧ ✧ ✧

The Jawalakhel Surplus Shop was a dimly lit jumble of foodstuffs, outdoor equipment, and clothing. A counter ran along one wall of the store, with pots and pans hanging on hooks from a wire stretched above it. Each gust of wind that entered the store caused them to clatter together, producing a dissonant wind chime that rippled the length of the shop. Hat and gloves in hand, Markov waited while the only other person in the store, a young European, sold the proprietor his backpack.

"Anything else, today, *sthi?*" the tall, scrawny shopkeeper asked. He held up a pair of grimy wool knickers. "A nice pair of plus fours, perhaps?"

Markov scowled and held up his selections. "How much?"

"Ten rupees, my friend?" The Russian threw a bill on the counter. He turned to go. Amazed at his good fortune, and wishing he had asked twenty, the shopkeeper scooped up the bill. "Wait!" he called, not wishing to let this mother lode escape unmined.

Markov stopped. He looked back slowly over his shoulder at the Nepalese.

The proprietor pulled back a blanket hanging on the wall. "Overcoat, *sáthi?*" he asked. "Best quality stuff. Go well with your hat and gloves." Markov's expression caused him to hurriedly cover up the topcoat. "How about this?" the shopkeeper persevered, reaching under the counter. Markov watched as he pulled something out. "Only one like it in all Nepal! Just meant for a *sthi* like you!"

Something glinted as the man set the object on the counter. Markov frowned, then stepped back to the counter as the shopkeeper continued his spiel. The Russian picked up the leather briefcase. The gleam that had caught his eye came from a silver monogram: YB.

Markov's left hand caught the Nepalese just under the chin. Thumb and forefinger around the thin neck, he lifted the man over the counter. "Where did you get this?" he asked, his voice a deadly whisper.

"Please, *sthi*," the bug-eyed man gasped.

With his right hand, Markov touched the point of his bayonet to the terrified man's Adam's apple. "Answer me, *doorük*. Now."

"It was a foreigner," the shopkeeper squeaked. "Sold me the coat, too. Take them both, but let me live!"

Markov released his hold, and the man slumped to the counter. "Where was he going?"

The Nepalese looked into Markov's eyes. He saw that his life depended on the truth, instantly. "Tibet."

"You are sure of this?"

"I am sure, *sthi*. He was with a Tibetan friend of mine." The shopkeeper coughed and took a deep breath. When he looked up, Markov was nowhere to be seen.

23

"Now *that* flight," Sheila Atherton remarked happily as they crossed the tarmac of Kathmandu's Tribhuvan International Airport, "was a decided improvement. What kind of plane was that?"

"757," Jake called over his shoulder.

Atherton looked stricken. "A 757. Wasn't that the kind of plane that—"

"Identical."

Atherton stopped and looked down. "If the ground was just a teensy bit cleaner, I'd kiss it."

Geoff Sheffield peered amiably at his colleague. "Frightfully annoying, isn't it?"

"What's annoying, Geoff?" Atherton asked.·

"Just how dirty dirt can be." After accepting their laughter with a graceful bow, he turned and lumbered on toward the terminal.

❖ ❖ ❖

Puzhen glared at her fiancé from across Ganden's tiny apartment. Her tears of relief at seeing him had been followed by tears of sorrow at the news of the executions. Now they were replaced by incredulous fury.

"How could you even consider such a thing?" she asked angrily.

Ganden folded his arms and glared back. "*You* didn't have to watch them die. *You* didn't have to watch the Han officer laughing as he pulled the trigger."

"Yes, they died. But they died singing a song of praise." Puzhen paused. "They didn't fear death—the way you seem to."

Ganden grabbed his pillow and flung it across the room. "I fear nothing!" Puzhen didn't move as he strode toward her. "If I was afraid," he said, staring down at her uplifted face, "then a prison full of men in Chengdu would now be being passing you around." The young woman lowered her eyes, and Ganden put his arms around her. "Please try to understand, *ajala*. When Kailas talked about a new generation of leaders, I realized that he was talking about *me*. I remembered what is written in Corinthians: 'The old has gone, the new has come!'" He held her tightly. "It is time for a new day. It is time for the new—Tenzig, me, and you—to sweep away the old, the legacy of brutality and oppression inflicted upon us by the Han." Ganden sat down on his bed and pulled Puzhen into his lap.

"Yes, *chola*," Puzhen said, returning his endearment. "Things must change. The new must come, but not this way." She lifted her head from his shoulder. "On the eve of another, much brighter dawn, when our Lord faced those who were about to arrest him, he said, 'Put your sword away!' Shouldn't you do the same?"

"Christ also told his disciples that two swords were enough to defend themselves. Two swords will defend *Per La*," Ganden declared, using the Tibetan name for his homeland. "Kailas is one, and Tigers and Dragons the other."

The door banged open. Barabise stood in the doorway. "Finished with her?" he asked Ganden. His lascivious grin engulfed Puzhen's glare of defiance. *After I feed your boyfriend to the vultures, I'll tame you. Then I'll train you, slowly and thoroughly.* "Come along. We have work to do."

"Staring at it's not going to help, Jake," Atherton chided quietly.

The three photographers were sitting in the bar of the Rum Doodle Restaurant, all the cash they could come up with in a heap before them on their table.

"It's not your fault," she continued, "that the last bus to Lhasa this week left yesterday. And it's not your fault we don't have enough cash to hire a Landrover." She patted his hand. "I think it's a wonder you got us this far. Now we'll just have to hope that our boss-man Stevenson ponies up enough money to get us there." Across the bar an all-girl combo finished "My Way" and swung into "Runaround Sue."

"What'll it be, folks?" the long-haired American waiter inquired. Sheffield and Atherton looked to Jake for guidance.

"Since it looks like this is the end of the trail, folks," Jake told them, "let's live it up." He turned to the waiter. "*Buff, gurr,* and Golden Eagle all around." The waiter nodded and left.

"Is that one dish, or three?" Atherton asked as Jake stuffed the cash into his pocket.

"Three. *Buff* is steak—"

"Wait a minute," Atherton interrupted. "Nepal is a Hindu country. I thought eating cow was taboo."

Jake nodded. "It is—officially, at least. *Buff* is short for 'water buffalo', the acceptable local substitute." He grinned. "Two inches thick here, cooked medium rare."

"That's fine for you two carnivores," Atherton said dryly, "but is there anything on the menu that's a little less macho?"

"You'll like the *gurr,*" Jake promised her. "It's a Sherpa concoction. Sort of like spiced hash browns smothered in cheese."

Atherton brightened. "Sounds more like it."

"Goes really well with Golden Eagle, too."

Sheila waited for Jake to continue, then frowned suspiciously at him. "You don't mean that . . . You wouldn't!" An ardent conservationist, she stared at Jake in horror. "I am positively *not* eating Golden Eagle!"

"You are absolutely correct, Sheila," Sheffield rumbled. "I won't be eating Golden Eagle, either." Atherton shot him an appreciative smile. "I will, however," he continued, "be *drinking* it." Atherton's smile evaporated as Sheffield winked. "Golden Eagle, you see, just happens to be the best of the local beers." The Yorkshireman's frame vibrated with his subsonic chuckle.

Atherton glared at Jake, then looked around. "I must admit this place is uniquely decorated. Just what are those things on the walls?"

"Yeti footprints," Jake replied. "Autographed by members of the Rum Doodle assault teams."

Atherton sighed. "I know that a 'Yeti' is the Abominable Snowman, but who or what is a 'Rum Doodle'?"

Jake looked pointedly at Geoff Sheffield.

"As any Englishman worth his salt knows," Sheffield explained, "Rum Doodle is the world's highest mountain."

"Then it's a local name for Mount Everest?"

"Not at all. At exactly forty thousand and one-half feet high, Rum Doodle towers a good three thousand meters over puny Everest." Sheffield ignored Atherton's look of exasperated disbelief. "Its heroic conquest was first accomplished, I'm proud to say, in 1956 by a team of British mountaineers led by the redoubtable Binder himself."

As the waiter arrived with a laden tray, Atherton shook her head. "I'm glad the food's here, since it's painfully obvious that I'm going to get no sense out of you two tonight. Let's eat."

❖ ❖ ❖

The all-girl band finished "Wooly Bully" as the waiter cleared the dishes.

"What's on the agenda for tomorrow?" Atherton asked.

"Keep calling New York." Jake replied bleakly. "If Dave can wire us the money tomorrow, we'll just be able to make it. But, given that the Nepalese banking system seems to have been designed by the Marx Brothers, it doesn't look like we're going to get to Lhasa anytime soon."

The scraping of a chair caused the trio to look up. From the next table, a man the size of Geoff Sheffield was looking at them.

"Did I hear you say you were going to Lhasa?" he asked in heavily accented English.

Jake spread his hands. "We *were.*"

"There is a difficulty?"

Jake explained their situation, ending with "We can get a Toyota Land Cruiser in Zhangmu, the Tibetan town just across the border. Barring landslides, if we take turns driving we can make it to Lhasa in around eighteen hours, which will get us there in time. But the best price I can get for a one-way to Lhasa is five hundred dollars cash, and all we have is just under four hundred."

The man frowned. "These Toyotas," he asked, pronouncing the Japanese name with difficulty, "how many passengers do they carry?"

"Seven," Jake replied.

"And it is just you three?" Jake nodded.

The man's shaggy brows beetled, and he stared past them. Then he nodded abruptly. "I am on my way to Lhasa, too. If you would let me accompany you, I would be more than happy to pay my way." He produced a thick wad of bills.

Jake grinned. *All right, God! Nice going.* "Pull up a chair, Mister . . . ?"

The stranger frowned at Jake, then smiled as he understood. "Markov. Grigory Markov."

"Are you going to Tibet on business, Mr. Markov?" Atherton asked after introductions had been made.

Markov gazed at the roaring fire in the fireplace across the room. "No," he said after a long moment. "I am a—how do you say it?—a hunter." He smiled broadly. "Yes. That is correct. I am going to Tibet to hunt."

✧ ✧ ✧

"Did you get that job guiding the American?" Barabise asked. Ganden nodded. "Good. Tenzig will guide the other man, and Thupten the woman."

"But Thupten doesn't know a thing about photography!" Ganden protested.

Barabise smiled. "Exactly. In a moment, I'll explain what I want you three to do. But first, tell me how to work this." He reached into a desk drawer, took out a small metal box, and handed it to Ganden.

Ganden took the remote detonator gingerly, as if afraid that dropping it would set off the ADM. "First," he told the nomad, "flip this switch on the back." A small light on the front of the detonator glowed green. Ganden looked at Barabise. "Do you have the combination?" The Khampa nodded. "Next, use these thumbwheels to set the combination, like this." Ganden demonstrated, setting the display to 666. "Finally, push both of these buttons at *exactly* the same time."

Ganden placed his thumbs on the buttons, held out the detonator, and squeezed. Barabise went rigid, then snatched the detonator away from the laughing Ganden.

"Don't worry, Kailas. I knew that wasn't the real combination."

The glowering nomad forced himself to laugh. "A good joke, boy." *And a better joke will be when I drag you to death behind my horse, with your woman tied naked to the back of my saddle.*

Barabise got up and shouted into the hall. Tenzig came in and joined them. he was followed by Thupten, a muscular giant whose face was puckered with scowls and ragged scars.

"It's time," he told the trio, "to reclaim our homeland."

24

"You know," Cathy said as she sat down across the formica-topped table from Anne, "I always have wondered what the inside of a teacher's lounge looked like." She surveyed the room. Microwave, refrigerator, couch, phone. "Not too bad."

"This one's nice," Anne agreed. "I've seen some that, if they had been classrooms, Child Protective Services would've condemned the school and hauled us away."

Cathy took a plastic container out of a paper bag and held it out. "Thanks for letting me impose on you for lunch. I got us chef's salads. Hope that's OK."

"Perfect. And it's no imposition." Anne tore open her packet of dressing. "What brings you to Portland?"

"The presidential lecture this weekend. I'm part of the advance team, making sure that the site's securable."

"Enjoying your new job?"

Cathy smiled. "Love it. I'm really grateful to your dad for recommending me for the Secret Service."

"Give yourself credit," Anne replied. "Daddy knows talent when he sees it. Besides, you're much too adventurous to be cooped up in the stuffy old State Department. Especially after the way they treated you." Anne used the blade of her knife to pop the top on her can of soda.

After a moment of silence, Anne looked up to find Cathy toying with her salad. "Maybe that's it," she said quietly. "Maybe I'm too 'adventurous.'" Without taking her eyes from her lunch, Cathy held up her left hand.

"Oops," Anne said when she saw the engagement ring missing. "What happened?"

Shrieks of laughter drifted in from the playground as Cathy related her argument with Greg. "So," she finished, "that's why I think I was too adventurous. Maybe it was all my fault for bringing it up in the first place."

"If it was, then you're better off not wearing that ring."

Cathy frowned. "Huh? Why do you say that?"

"Because communication is everything in a marriage. If Greg is going to storm out every time you bring up something that the two of you need to talk about your marriage would never get off the ground. Isn't it better to find that out now?"

"I suppose so," Cathy agreed glumly. "But it sure doesn't feel better."

Anne nodded sympathetically. "Hard work never does." She brightened. "Are you busy tonight?"

"No. We'll be done this afternoon. We're flying back to D.C. at six."

"How about staying over, instead? Mama will be here tomorrow. It's her consulting day at the hospital. You can ask her what to do. And Lee's coming in tonight. We can go to dinner and then rent a movie."

"How's Lee doing?"

"I'll let her tell you about it."

"Oh. That bad, huh?" Cathy stuffed the remnants of her salad into the bag. "But aren't you going out with Jake?"

"Actually, no. He's halfway around the world at the moment. In Tibet."

Anne's tone caused Cathy to peer at her. "You mad at him?"

"Furious. If he walked through that door this very minute I'd ignore him."

Cathy frowned. "Hold it. Who just said 'communication is everything'?"

Anne bit her lip. "True. OK, first I'd tell him I was furious at him, *then* I'd ignore him. How's that?" She glanced at the clock, then stood up. "I've got to go. My apartment, at five?"

"It's a deal. I wouldn't miss this evening for anything."

"DEFCON Three?" Mike O'Brien exclaimed. "Don't you think that's a little premature, General?"

Rodriguez mentally ran through a career's worth of military curses, then mustered every ounce of the patience for which he was famous. "No, I do not." The omission of the customary "sir" was lost on no one. "General Petersen, commander of our forces in the European Theater, has just reported that the Chinese have begun a massive mobilization of troops along their western border. Command appears to be centered with the Second Artillery Corps in Jinxi. This has been confirmed by the various NATO intelligence agencies. Apparently, the Chinese have grown tired of the Russian bear lurking in the woods just across their common frontier."

"Just what do you have in mind, Roddy?" the president asked.

"Fighters and bombers will be brought out of hangars and deployed on flightlines with armament nearby. The Sixth Fleet will deploy some additional AWACS aircraft and fly some extra Barrier Combat Air Patrol. Back here, our rapid deployment forces will lose a little sleep." Rodriguez smiled. "Not much more, really, than an exercise. Just enough to let them know we're watching. We'll stay in our own front yard, but we'll be sure to let the Hatfields and McCoys know that our gun is loaded."

The president looked around at his cabinet and the rest of the chiefs of staff.

The air force chief spoke up. "I, for one, could use the readiness, Mr. President. Ever since we lost Clark, I've been spread real thin. My supply lines are a lot longer than I'd like them to be." The rest of the general officers at the table smiled. General Winthrop had adamantly opposed the return of Clark Air Force Base in the Philippines. When Mount Pinatubo had erupted and destroyed the air base, Winthrop had considered the volcano's actions a personal affront.

The president looked to the end of the table. "Admiral Harrison?"

The navy chief of staff nodded. "The Sixth Fleet hasn't had much to do since the Gulf War. We're getting ready for our annual PERSIAN CARPET exercise down there, anyway. We'll just heat things up a little more."

O'Brien leaned over and whispered to the president. Rodriguez waited, contenting himself as he did with the image that he was once again a drill instructor and it was O'Brien's first day of basic training.

The president nodded, then looked at Rodriguez. "No forces will be deployed?"

The chairman understood the question. "No, sir. Not in any way that would require you to notify Congress."

"Very well, then. Go to DEFCON Three."

"Dear God," Atherton breathed as Jake brought the Land Cruiser to a halt. Just across the Kyichu, twisted metal glinted in the midday sunlight. The acrid stench of burned jet fuel still hung in the thin, dry air. "After thirty years, I'm still not used to it." She shaded her eyes with her hand. "It's a long way away, but I think we can get some usable shots."

Sheffield looked up from locking a long telephoto onto the body of his Canon AF-EOS-RT. "That's better. You had me worried there for a minute." Atherton peered at him. "After all these years of photographing disasters," he explained, "I was afraid you were losing your ghoulish figure."

"There is a difficulty?" Markov asked after the groans had subsided.

"Just Western decadence in action," Atherton reassured him. "Do you happen to know if any of those labor camps in Siberia are still open?"

Markov blinked. "No. Our new president had them all closed."

Atherton looked at Sheffield. "Pity."

Sheffield finished bolting a small tripod to a socket on the telephoto lens. Then he climbed out of the Land Cruiser and set the tripod and camera on its roof, joining them shortly. "Perfect," he murmured, and started taking pictures.

"We've got company, boys," Atherton announced. Another Land Cruiser, its blue lights flashing, skidded to a dusty halt behind them. A tall Chinese and a uniformed sergeant got out.

"I am Inspector Chen of the PSB," the tall man announced. "Your passports, please."

Chen flipped through the proffered documents. "You three are the Americans I was notified to expect. How did you get to Tibet?" Chen nodded approvingly as Jake explained. "Most resourceful. Now," he asked Markov in fluent Russian, "just who are you?"

"I am traveling alone. I joined these Americans in Nepal." Markov held Chen's eyes. "Your Russian is quite good, comrade."

Chen stared back. "I am not a Party member." He held up Markov's passport. "You are military?"

Markov shook his head. "Retired." *Except for the pension, the dacha in the woods, and any hope of going home, that's the truth.*

"Then why the army passport?"

"The bureaucracy in Moscow is not what it once was—as I am sure you are well aware. My visa was issued in Kathmandu. I believe you'll find that it is in order."

Intimidated by Markov, and not wishing to lose more face in front of the Americans, Chen turned back to Jake. "Photography is prohibited in this area."

Jake handed Chen a sheet of paper. "This is our permission from the Ministry of Culture in Beijing to photograph anything we wish."

The inspector studied the paper. "This is not valid until tomorrow. Tomorrow you may take pictures here, but it is forbidden today. I'm afraid," Chen told them, "that I must confiscate your film."

"What kind of logic is that?" Atherton bristled. "Of all the nonsense I've ever heard!"

Jake held up a hand. "Quite all right, Inspector Chen. We understand perfectly. Geoff?"

Sheffield opened his camera, pulled out the half-used roll of film and handed it to the sergeant.

Chen looked at the snout of Jake's camera, which was protruding over the door of the Land Cruiser. "Yours, too, Mr. MacIntyre. If you please."

Jake opened the back of his Nikon. "No film. I was just testing a new lens."

The inspector nodded. "Very well. Now, please follow us to your hotel."

"You two," Atherton groused as Jake swung the Land Cruiser around, "are the last I'd expect to roll over and play dead like that."

"Have no fear," Sheffield chuckled. "We've got our shots."

"If by that you mean that we'll come back tomorrow, by then the Chinese will probably have carted away the wreckage and paved the crash site over."

"I mean just what I said. We've got our shots. Jake's using a new digital system. Showed it to me while you were packing in Chengdu. Absolutely smashing."

"So all the images are on disk."

"Exactly."

Jake grinned at Atherton in the rearview mirror, then frowned as he noticed that she was making a great show of looking out her window. "Is the Chinese Air Force after us now?" he asked.

"No. I'm just watching for the lightning."

"What lightning? There's not a cloud in the sky."

"The lightning bolt that God's going to strike you down with. I want to see it coming so I can duck."

Jake peered over his shoulder at Atherton. "What on earth are you talking about?"

"Well, if I understand these newfound Christian ethics of yours, lying is a sin, right?"

"Depends."

"On what?"

"On what you're saying and why you're saying it."

"Well, since I think you lied to that policeman, I'm waiting for God to go *zap!* and charbroil you for sinning."

Jake laughed. "It doesn't quite work that way. First, I didn't lie to Inspector Chen. I told him I had no film in my camera, which was the truth."

"That's a copout. You were being deceptive." Atherton leaned out the window again.

Jake thought about it. "Guilty as charged," he replied. "But the world has a right to see what happened here, whether the Chinese government wants it to or not." Atherton and Sheffield nodded their agreement. "I'm just part of a long line of smugglers of the truth," Jake went on. "The apostle Paul was smuggled out of Damascus, and missionaries have been smuggling Bibles for hundreds of years. Even today there are people who carry the entire

Bible around in their heads because carrying it in their hands would mean instant death." Jake looked out his window, then grinned at Sheila. "Still not a cloud in sight. Try the New Testament some time. There's a lot less lightning and a lot more Light."

✧ ✧ ✧

Sheila's shriek brought Jake running into her room. He found her backed against a wall, pointing at something.

Geoff Sheffield crowded in behind Jake. "Wasn't going to disturb you two 'til I saw the door open," he remarked. "What on earth is amiss?"

"*That*," Sheila said acidly, "is what is amiss." She pointed to the brown, dusty skull of a goat, which was attached to a triangular willow-branch frame and nailed to the wall above her bed. The hanging was festooned with brightly colored yarn, bits of straw, and small bells.

Geoff looked toward where she was pointing. "Fascinating," he murmured. "What is it?"

"It's a spirit trap," Jake explained. "It's supposed to protect you against demons. The tinkling of the bells attracts evil spirits, which then get tangled up in the yarn. When the trap is full, it's burned, destroying the bogeymen."

Sheffield walked across Sheila's room and peered at the object. "It would appear that the goat succumbed to a particularly virulent strain of leprosy and was then mounted by a demented taxidermist." He turned to Sheila. "I don't have one in *my* room. How did you arrange for such unique decor? Friends with the manager?" The Yorkshireman smiled benignly at Atherton's glare.

"I don't care if it's a fragment of the True Cross," Sheila snapped. "I want it out of my room. Now."

Sheffield reached up and tugged on the spirit trap. The tiny brass bells chimed melodically, and dust rained down onto her pillow. "Won't come off."

"You're sure?"

"Quite."

Sheila relaxed. "Well, I've woken up to worse looking things than that. Just as long as it doesn't fall down on me during the night."

Jake pulled back the curtains of his third-floor room. Above a line of trees, the Potala Palace loomed in the eastern distance. Somewhere over and beyond it, Jake knew, the relay satellite waited.

He opened a black nylon case, took out the laptop PC Greg had given him, and set it next to his camera on the desk beneath the window. A short cable, retrieved from a pouch inside the case, plugged into both the camera and the laptop.

"OK," Jake said as he pressed the laptop's on button. "I lugged you halfway around the world. Now earn your keep." He grinned. "Even Dave'll be willing to cough up big bucks for an exclusive shot of a major air disaster."

Once the machine had booted, he used the PC's built-in trackball to move the cursor to an icon labeled SLIDE SHOW. Jake double-clicked the trackball button. A small green LED on the camera came on, and he heard the tiny hard drive in the Nikon's base spin up. A few seconds later the first of his photos of the wreckage of the 757 appeared on the laptop's color LCD screen. Jake whistled softly. *Sharp color and great resolution. Not to mention the depth of field. Looks like it's time to give up on film.* He riffled back and forth through the images until he had decided on the one to send.

Jake pulled the transmitter dish from its pocket in his camera bag. He had practiced assembling and attaching the transmitter on the long plane flight to Shanghai, and a few seconds after he clicked on UPLOAD, the WAITING prompt Greg had told him about appeared.

Jake reached for the dish, then stopped. He strode across his room and flipped the door's security lock into place, then wedged a chair under the doorknob for good measure. Sitting at the desk, Jake moved the dish antenna back and forth across the air until a warbling was heard from the PC's speaker and AOS was displayed on the screen. *Acquisition of signal, just like the man said*, he thought approvingly. Jake paused to run down his mental list of instructions, then clicked on SELECT. Twenty-eight seconds after Jake clicked on OK, TX COMPLETED appeared.

"Not too shabby," Jake decided. "I could get used to this real quick." He shut off the PC, then unhooked everything and put it away. He stretched out on his bed with a copy of the *International Herald-Tribune*, then sat up suddenly. *There is*, he realized, *the minor problem of getting Greg to forward the photo to Dave.*

Jake thought for a minute. Then, remembering something he had seen in the hotel lobby, he grinned.

25

Pat Dryden smiled at her husband as he came into the kitchen. Joel took the mug of coffee she held out as he went by and sat down at the breakfast table.

"It must be the altitude," he said. "That's the only logical explanation." Pat stopped stirring the pitcher of orange juice she was preparing for their breakfast and raised an eyebrow at Joel. "Fax from Jake," he explained, holding up the piece of paper he had brought with him. "The cover sheet says it was sent from the business center at the Lhasa Holiday Inn. Came in at 5:03 this morning."

"What does it say?"

Joel held the paper at arm's length and squinted. "Quote: 'Tell Greg to send it to Dave Stevenson ASAP.' Unquote."

Pat came over and stood behind Joel. She reread the fax over his shoulder. "He doesn't say what 'it' is, does he? Do you have any idea?"

"None whatsoever. I've left messages at Greg's home and work numbers, as well as the Global office in New York." Joel shook his head. "It makes so little sense, even for one of Jake's communiqués, that I figure he must not be getting enough oxygen." He tilted his head back and looked up at his wife. "Your professional opinion of this morning's activities, doctor?"

Frowning, Pat put on her "physician" face. "Well, I'm not current on the latest research in high-altitude medicine, but it would seem that someone as physically fit as Jake is—"

Joel, still looking up at her, reached up and pulled her face to his. A kiss effectively silenced her diagnosis. "I wasn't," he said with a roguish smile, "referring to Jake's activities."

Pat smiled down at him. Tenderly, she smoothed the gray hair at his temples behind his ears. "In my 'professional opinion,'" she said with feigned asperity, "*you* are getting more than enough oxygen."

The phone interrupted their second kiss. With a muttered *darn*, Joel reached out and took the phone from its cradle on the wall.

"Hello? Hi, Greg . . . No, Alzheimer's didn't set in overnight. That's exactly what Jake's fax says. Does it make any sense to you?" Joel listened for a moment, then nodded in surprise. "Very interesting. Will you see that Dave Stevenson gets it? And fax me a copy, too, OK? Thanks, Greg. Bye."

Joel hung up and turned to Pat, who had gone to check on the bran muffins she had in the oven. "Seems that when Greg got in this morning, there was a satellite image waiting. When he downloaded the image, it turned out to be a photo of the tail section of a 757. Must be the one that crashed outside Lhasa the other day." Joel nodded his approval. "Smart thinking on Jake's part. There's big money in an exclusive like that."

The timer on the stove went off. Pat pulled the tin of muffins out of the oven, then came over and sat down next to Joel. "I have wondered, sometimes, if Jake will be able to provide for them after he and Annie are married." She watched an oriole breakfasting at the feeder in the tree outside the kitchen window.

"'*After* he and Annie are married'?" Joel chuckled.

"Matchmaking, it would seem, is an avocation universal to all women old enough to talk." He smiled at the face she made, pleased to be getting a rise out of his psychiatrist wife. "It's their decision, love, not ours, however much we may want it to be."

"I know," Pat sighed. "But, can you really envision them *not* getting married at this point?"

"No. And that's exactly why we need to stay out of it. Remember all the 'good advice' our parents gave us when we were courting?"

Pat smiled, thinking of summer nights on Hunter's Point in San Francisco. Sitting on a park bench, watching the lights on the bay, held tightly in the arms of a raffish young man of whom her Beacon Hill parents thoroughly disapproved. "Good point," she admitted. "Still, it hurts me to see Annie so distressed."

"That's because you're afflicted with an acute case of motherhood. Still incurable, if I'm 'current on the latest research.'" Joel winked. "How about some bacon and eggs to go with those muffins of yours?" he suggested as Pat turned the muffins out onto the breadboard.

"How about a pacemaker to go with those nitroglycerin pills of yours?" Pat replied with a withering look.

Joel winced. "*Touché.*"

"You know," he added pensively as Pat set breakfast in front of him, "when our Lord said, 'Man does not live by bread alone,' he *must* have been eating a bran muffin."

A constable stuck his head in Chen's door. "Someone to see you, Inspector. A *dopka.*"

Chen looked up from his desk as the constable brought in a tiny, wizened, nomad woman. Once seated, she smiled toothlessly at the inspector.

"*Toshi dili, mola,*" Chen said in greeting. The nomad's smile broadened at Chen's use of the honorific due an older woman. "May I offer you some *chang?*" The woman slurped noisily at the bowl of beer Chen gave her. He followed the beer with a cigarette filled with what the Lhasa PSB office, in reports to Beijing, euphemistically termed "local tobacco."

Chen fished a Mild Seven out of its pack. He smoked quietly, waiting patiently both as manners dictated and to let the beer and the coarse marijuana take effect.

"What may I do for you, Grandmother?" he asked when she had finished.

The old woman belched politely. "I found something. Something I think belongs to you." She reached over her shoulder and rummaged around in the baggy shawl Tibetan women use to carry everything from barley to babies.

Chen's patient composure disappeared when he found himself staring down the muzzle of a large-caliber weapon. As he tensed to dive out of the line of fire, the woman, after much struggling and cursing, freed the weapon from her shawl and threw it onto his desk.

"What is it?" she asked breathlessly.

"I don't know," Chen told her, breathing just as hard. He stared at the device. "Where did you find it?"

"Near where I take my flock down to the river to water. On the cliffs above Gonggar."

"Could you find the place again?"

"Of course," the woman answered scornfully. She stood and reached for the weapon.

Chen placed his hand on it. "This is mine."

The old nomad glared at the inspector. She sat back down, and the bargaining began.

The interior of the teahouse was gloomy. Light filtered through a single, dirty window, reluctantly illuminating the once-red pillars that supported the smoke-blackened ceiling. Waitresses carrying large thermoses scurried across the earthen floor, flirting with their all-male clientele and pouring milky, sweetened tea into chipped glasses. At a table in a corner Grigory Markov waited, very much at home in a place like this.

Earlier in the day Markov had walked into the PLA head-quarters in downtown Lhasa. With the practiced ease of a career soldier he had used the little Chinese he knew to ingra-tiate himself with the bored contingent of men staffing the office. As Markov expected, it hadn't taken long for one of the men to reveal that he had trained in the Soviet Union and spoke a little Russian. Lured by the promise of tea followed by vodka, the man eagerly agreed to meet Markov when he got off duty.

Markov took a photo out of his jacket pocket and laid it on the battered table in front of him. He stared at it as he waited.

Chen shifted his weight slightly to brace himself against the gusting wind. Heights had always made him nervous, and it was a sheer drop to the valley floor below. After an hour's drive along the river, the nomad had told Chen to stop. It had taken them another hour to make their way up the cliff, the young Chinese struggling up the narrow track behind the nimble *dopka*.

A mile away, straight across the valley, the golden roof of the Jokhang gleamed in the afternoon light. Dust devils eddied around his feet as Chen surveyed the valley floor. Slightly to the west, in the middle of a patch of blackened earth, the tail section of the ruined 757 was being winched onto a flatbed truck.

"You found it here?" Chen asked. The old woman nodded. "Has there been anyone else around here recently?"

The nomad cursed fluently. "Soldiers. Two days ago. They shot one of my sheep!"

Chen nodded. That explains it, then. *Probably lost during a training exercise. I'll drop it off at the base on my way back to town. I pity the poor private who set it down and forgot to pick it up.* Unwilling to waste any more time on this, Chen turned to the nomad. "Take me back to my car, *mola*. It's been a busy day."

"Mr. MacIntyre?"

Jake looked up to find a young Tibetan man looking earnestly at him. "Yes?"

"I am Ganden Nesang. Your assistant."

Jake motioned for Ganden to sit down next to him on the couch in the lobby of the Lhasa Holiday Inn, "Call me Jake," he said. "It's a lot easier to pronounce than MacIntyre."

Ganden handed Jake a folder. "This all your work?" Jake asked as he leafed through the photographs.

"Yes, sir. I take pictures on my days off and on vacation."

Jake laughed to himself. *That's how you tell the professionals from the amateurs*, he thought. *Days off and vacations are the only time I* don't *take pictures.* He finished inspecting Ganden's portfolio and nodded approvingly. "My compliments. These are quite good."

Ganden grinned happily. "Thank you, sir. My favorite work of yours, if I may say, is your photo essay on the Great Rift Valley in Africa."

I haven't thought of that assignment in years, Jake realized. He looked out the lobby window to where the westering sun was disappearing behind a series of jagged peaks, and his mind drifted. . . .

In the evening, after a day's shoot, Johnson Mutuula and Jake sat on his bougainvillea-draped porch and watched the sun disappear behind the escarpment across the valley. The equatorial light vanished from the sky as if switched off. Lamps were being lit, and Jeddi Mutuula brought out a pitcher of lemonade and a small plate of chopped bananas and set them near Johnson. As they talked and drank lemonade, Johnson took a piece, and reached up toward the bougainvillea just above his head. A small, wizened hand reached slowly down from the vine, took the banana, and vanished.

The first time it happened, Johnson began laughing uproariously at Jake's expression, as did his family, who had been watching from the doorway to see how Jake reacted. When the laughter had ceased echoing, he repeated the performance. This time the hand was accompanied by the face of a galago, complete with enormous eyes and a huge bristling white mustache that made it look like an elderly and indignant Greek fisherman. They spent the rest of the evening feeding the galagos, and Jake could to this day feel the gentle tug on the banana as it was snatched from his hand. . . .

Jake shook his head wistfully. The Mutuulas were believers, and they paid for their faith with their lives a few years later in one of the purges that swept Kenya. *I hope Johnson knows that the seeds he so gently planted have taken deep root.*

Jake turned back to his assistant. "How did you get copies of my photos? Western magazines aren't available here."

"When I was going to college in Beijing, I had a girlfriend who was a housekeeper at the Great Wall Sheraton. She collected the magazines the tourists threw away and brought them to me." Embarrassed, Ganden looked away. "I always cut your photos out and saved them."

Jake smiled. *The Jake MacIntyre Fan Club, Beijing Branch, is now in session.* . . . "Down to business, Ganden. When do we have to leave to be at Chomolungma by sunrise?"

The young Tibetan's face fell. "There is a problem with that, sir. I'm afraid that getting to Everest is going to be impossible."

Jake, a veteran of third-world snafus, took a deep breath. "Why?" he asked quietly. "I thought that, through CITS, my agency had rented a helicopter for us to use to get to Everest Base Camp."

"That's right, sir," Ganden agreed. "But it was rented from the army, who took it back after the plane crash."

Jake didn't bother to ask if the army had refunded Global's money. *Well, at least I can hope that Dave doesn't find out until I get*

203

back. That way, I can tell him myself and see the look on his face. Disappointed, Jake scrubbed his face with his hand. *Maybe I can team up with Geoff. He takes the buildings, and I take the temples. . . .*

"Might I make a suggestion, sir? There is another mountain—"

Jake looked inquiringly at Ganden.

"Mount Kula Gangri. Almost eight thousand meters high. It's near Kangmar, where I grew up."

"Anything special about it?" Jake asked. "If I can't photograph Everest, why should I bother to take pictures of this mountain?"

"I remember something you once wrote," Ganden replied, "in *Popular Photography*. You said that good photographs were either a familiar representation of something unusual, or an unusual representation of something familiar. Right?" Ganden grinned at Jake's nod of recollection. "Well, since you can't take an unusual picture of a familiar mountain, how about taking some straightforward shots of a mountain few Westerners have seen?"

"What is it you do for a living, Ganden?"

"I'm an electrical technician. Why?"

Jake shook his head. "You're wasted there. Back in the states, you could be either a salesman or an attorney. Or maybe both. OK, I'm sold. How do we get there?"

"Your Land Cruiser, if you don't mind. I can gather our supplies Thursday morning, and we can leave in the afternoon. We'll camp out partway there, then have plenty of time the next day to get to Kula Gangri by sunset."

"Best light then?" Jake asked.

Ganden nodded. "The mountain faces northwest, so the sun sets right across its face."

"Sounds good to me," Jake said with a grin.

Ganden stood. "Could I ask a favor of you, sir?" he asked diffidently.

"Sure. What is it?"

"Would you take a picture of my fiancée for me tomorrow? I can't afford color film."

"You bet, Ganden." Jake shook hands with the Tibetan. "And if these pictures of Kula Gangri turn out, I'll make sure that you have all the film you need."

Markov's new friend sat down at his table. Three more men stood behind him. The Russian held up the picture he had been staring at. "Ask them if they have seen this man."

Each man shook his head as he examined the picture of Yousef Bey that Markov had ripped from a frame on the wall of the house in Taldy Kurgan.

"Who is he?" the PLA man asked.

"A friend of a friend," Markov replied. He smiled at the irony of it all and again roundly cursed Pyotr Tallin's memory.

The Chinese looked impassively at the Russian. "There are many foreigners in Lhasa. . . ."

Markov nodded, amused by the blatant lie. "So there are. And there is *this* for the man who finds the one I'm looking for." He opened his fist, and something clattered onto the table.

The Tibetans gasped as the gold Imperial stopped spinning. Their excited whisperings brought the rest of the teahouse's patrons, fluttering moths drawn to the small, gold sun that rested on the tabletop.

His hands in his pockets, Jake wandered out of the Hard Yak Cafe. He had eaten alone, altitude sickness brought on by Lhasa's two-and-a-half-mile elevation having driven both Sheila Atherton and Geoff Sheffield to their beds.

This was one of the nights when the streetlights would be on until nine, and the way back to the Lhasa Hotel was alive with people. Thick cakes of the bread called *kabtse* sizzled on oil-drum griddles. A grinning Muslim stood waving a yak-tail fly whisk over grilling kebobs.

As Jake detoured around a cloth-walled *chang* shop that jutted out into the sidewalk, a noisy fight broke out inside. The commotion inside the portable bar caused two of the skinny mongrels that infested the city to look up from their foraging in one of the overflowing dumpsters lining the streets.

"Old stuff, mister," the man hissed. Jake watched as one of the street vendors sitting near the gate to the hotel opened his jacket to reveal a statue of Buddha encrusted with obviously fake jewels. Jake shook his head and went on, passing the Lhasa branch of the Nice Daily Use Chemical Shop.

The glint of polished brass caught his eye. The small shop was well kept. Copper-and-brass kettles hung from hooks, with smaller items neatly arranged in glass cases. A leathery old man with short gray hair got up from a stool and bowed.

"*Inji-gay shing-ghi dugay?*" Jake asked.

The old man smiled. "Yes, *sahib*. I speak English." Jake did a double take at the man's precise, lilting Indian accent. "I learned it while living in Calcutta," he explained.

"When was that, *pola?*" Jake asked, using the civility due an older acquaintance.

"Long ago." The shopkeeper reached into a case. "You would be interested, perhaps, in a prayer wheel?" He showed Jake an ornate, revolving brass cylinder set on a wooden handle. A small brass weight attached to one side of the cylinder caused it to rotate when the handle was moved. "We fill the cylinder with copies of our mantras. Each time the cylinder goes around the mantras go up to heaven and earn us merit."

A brass thunderbolt was set next to the prayer wheel. "Or perhaps a *dorje?* This is the symbol of our protector god Drakden. It will keep you safe from evil spirits and the powers of darkness."

Jake shook his head. "I'll pass on the amulets, thanks. What else do you have?"

A tray of jewelry appeared. The ancient proprietor watched as Jake sifted through the broken pocket watches, old compasses, cheap brass *chome*, and strings of beads. Jake thanked the man and turned to go.

"Wait!"

Jake stopped.

"You are indeed a *sahib*," the old man said happily, "to not be fooled by these trinkets. These I sell to the tourists who come to *Per La* to see the 'Tea-beeshans.' Please wait a moment." The shopkeeper disappeared behind a curtain in the back of the store. He emerged a moment later holding a small chamois sack.

"Look at these, *sahib*." He upended the sack, and a gleaming array of rings clattered onto the counter.

One glance told Jake that these were a cut above the rest of the merchandise. He picked up a silver ring whose setting was a delicately twisting vine that held turquoise and coral carved into flowers.

"My sons make these in Kathmandu," the old man said proudly. "They send them here for me to sell."

"Why don't they live here, with you?"

The man shook his head sadly. "It's very hard here. Artisans like my sons fled during the Cultural Revolution. Even if they came back, the Han would confiscate their work. That's why I keep these in the back."

"Then, why don't you go live with them?"

"*Per La* is my home. I could not be close to the clouds in Nepal. Here, I am near the light."

A gust of wind swung the bare bulb that dangled overhead at the end of a knotted, frayed wire. A flash in the shifting shadows caught Jake's eye. The ring he picked up was gold—heavy, yet delicate. Into each shank was carved an ornate, detailed Byzantine cross set beneath crossed shepherd's crooks. Jake held the ring near the light, captivated by the magnificent, flawless emerald that glittered with verdant fire.

"Your sons do good work," Jake said quietly.

The jeweler smiled at the look on Jake's face. "No man living made that ring, *sahib*. It is said that the ring you hold was a gift to his bride from the hand of Prester John."

Jake turned the ring under the light. "Who is Prester John?" he asked absently, lost in the emerald fire.

The old man laughed quietly. "If a *pukka sahib* such as you does not know the tale of John the Presbyter, then perhaps at last the search for him is truly over." He settled onto a stool. "It is said that Prester John ruled these parts a thousand years ago. He was called the Ruler of the Three Indies and Lord of the Kingdom of the East. His realm extended into the sunrise, bounded only by the walls put up around the Christian Paradise. Rivers of precious gems flowed through his hands, as did the Fountain of Youth. Seventy-two kings paid him homage and dined in his palace each night at tables of gold, amethyst, and ivory. His clothes were spun from the silk of the salamander, a worm that lived in fire. In his palace garden grew trees that blossomed at sunrise, fruited at noon, and by sunset had disappeared once more into the earth. A mighty warrior was he, who routed the Persians and Selucids and did battle with the khan named Gengis on the plains of Tenduc, not too far from here."

Out in the dark Tibetan night, a dog howled.

Fascinated, Jake listened as the old jeweler wove a tale of a land filled with lakes of fire and turbulent seas of sand, and populated by phoenixes and hippogriffs. Jake held up the ring. "What about this?" he asked, pointing to the cross on the shank.

The old man searched Jake's face. "The Prester was a Christian king. He adhered to the true faith, as did all those he ruled. According to legend, he was a descendent of one of the magi who visited the Christ child in his manger. Prester John would ride to war preceded by thirteen crosses of gold and gems, each cross followed by ten thousand soldiers on horseback and a multitude of infantrymen.

"When the day came that Prester John wished to marry, he had made a wedding ring without a stone in its setting, representing the earthly life of a man without a wife. The Prester then had arrayed before him all the maidens of his land. As each was brought before him, with bowed head she held up the ring and Prester John touched it with the emerald set in the end of his scepter. If nothing happened, the girl was led away.

"Then, as all but Prester John were beginning to despair of finding a wife for him, a maiden was brought before the king. She did not cast her eyes down, but instead gazed serenely into the eyes of Prester John. Much smitten by her beauty, the Prester lowered his scepter and touched this ring, which she held before her. When he raised his scepter, the ring's setting had been filled with the stone you see, and the top of the emerald in his scepter was no longer smooth. He slipped the ring onto her finger, and they were forthwith married. The girl's name was Eleni, and she was to be a ruler both fair and wise. Legend has it that the Greeks were so taken by the beauty of this queen they called Helen that they went to war over her, a woman they would never see." The Tibetan glanced at the ring and smiled. "It would seem that Prester John was a man of valor when it came to the battlefield of the heart, as well."

Seeing Anne's eyes in the emerald's fiery depths, Jake slipped the ring onto his little finger. It fit perfectly, which meant that it would also fit perfectly on Anne's ring finger. For a moment he imagined the ring on her hand. Then, reluctantly, he took it off and handed it back. "Thanks for showing it to me. And for telling me the story."

The old man thrust out a palm. "No. It is yours."

Jake shook his head. The Land Cruiser rental had used up all his cash, and there were no *American Express Cards Welcome Here* signs in sight. "I can't afford it," he said simply. As Jake held out the ring the moss-green stone glittered once more.

"It is not for sale. It is yours."

Dumbfounded, Jake stared at the jeweler. "But, why? If you don't want it, shouldn't you send it to your sons?"

The brown, lined face looked up at Jake. "If I send it to them, they will melt it down and make new jewelry from it. And so, the last relic of the kingdom of Prester John will be lost. They are young and do not understand. My sons are good men, but they are not *sahibs*." The old man looked out into the night. "I will die soon, and before my spirit flies, I want to know the ring is in good hands. That it's cared for by a *sahib*." The old man looked at the ring, then at Jake. "Prester John was a *sahib*, and so are you."

26

Jake paid off the driver of the fringed pedicab that had brought him to the base of Chagpori, the "Iron Mountain" on the southwest corner of Lhasa. Ganden had suggested it as a fine place from which to photograph the city. He shouldered his camera gear and began a slow trudge up the trail that wound around the hill, being careful not to overexert himself in the thin mountain air. Halfway up the hill, the monks of a small temple set into the mountainside returned Jake's wave.

Ganden was right on the money, Jake thought as he set up his camera on Chagpori's summit. *You can see the whole city from here.* Half a mile away, the Potala gleamed white in the bright morning sun. Realizing that he was squinting, Jake got out his mountaineering sunglasses and bush hat and put them on. He then looked around carefully. Seeing that he was unobserved, Jake reached into his camera bag. He took out a copy of the *Lonely Planet* guidebook to Tibet, which he opened to page 128.

"It's really quite simple," Greg had explained as he opened the guidebook to the same page. "What we want you to do is get to the top of Chagpori." Greg circled the mountain. "From that vantage point we want you to take a series of pictures of

Lhasa. Start with a wide-angle, overall shot of the city, then go to maximum zoom."

Greg drew Xs at four locations throughout the city. "These are spots where fissionable material might be located. I stress the might because the detector in the satellite just doesn't have the resolution to find out for sure." The physicist picked up the Nikon. "Since your camera doesn't use it, I've replaced the regular light meter with a miniaturized version of the detector aboard the Keyhole. It's a lot less powerful, but you'll be a lot closer."

"How will I know if anything's there?" Jake asked, looking at the map of Lhasa with growing reluctance.

"For your protection, you won't. If the detector senses anything, an intensity reading will be overlaid on the appropriate spot on the digital image. We'll pick it up back here after you transmit it and then focus the satellite detector on that spot. If that doesn't do it, we'll ask you to get closer if you can and take another reading."

✦　✦　✦

Jake found that he was humming the "James Bond" theme as he fastened the F3 to his tripod. He grinned and shook his head. *You're not cut out for this cloak-and-dagger stuff, Mac. Time for you to settle down.* He lightly pressed the shutter button, and the Potala snapped into crisp focus. The brown and white, thousand-room winter home of every Dalai Lama since the seventeenth century filled the viewfinder. Jake watched awestruck, as cloud shadows raced across its multitiered face. He was looking at something that no modern European had seen until 1903, when Sir Francis Younghusband had led a British expeditionary force into Lhasa.

Of course, his inner debate continued, *if you do settle down, the closest you'll ever again come to seeing something like this is at Disney World. . . .*

Jake shook his head again. Then, consulting Greg's map, he started taking pictures.

✧ ✧ ✧

"And so, after eating my camera case, that bear kept me up in the tree until a park ranger came along and shooed him away."

Across the table, Ganden and Puzhen laughed as Jake regaled them with tales of his misadventures around the world. Ganden had suggested to Jake that he meet them for lunch at the restaurant owned by Puzhen's parents.

Puzhen's father brought out a tray laden with dishes and covered the table with food. When he had disappeared back into the kitchen, Ganden and Puzhen joined hands and bowed their heads. When they had finished their hurried grace, Ganden glanced anxiously at Jake.

"You're Christians," Jake said gently, "and Puzhen's parents don't understand why." Relief filled the eyes of the two young Tibetans. "How about if we say grace again, and this time I'll join you."

When they had finished, Jake leaned over and inhaled the appetizing aromas. "What's on the menu?" he asked Puzhen.

She pointed at each dish in turn. "That's *chemdu*, raw yak meat minced with onion and spices; that's *shoko pali*, deep-fried meat and potato dumplings; and that's *shogo dori*, a thick lamb and turnip stew."

Smiling happily at Jake's anticipation, Puzhen served them. While in Tibet Jake, naturally left-handed, had had to concentrate on eating only with his right hand, following the ancient custom of a land where toilet paper was a recent, exotic import.

"How did you come to believe?" Jake asked, wielding his chopsticks deftly.

"We've had teachers over the years," Ganden replied. "Some American, some Indian, and a few Chinese. After they got to know us, they'd ask a few of us, very cautiously, if we had ever heard of Jesus." He picked up a dumpling and bit it in two. "One of our favorite teachers was Miss Wagner. She got to be very good friends with us, especially with Puzhen. Then the Chinese decided that she had stayed too long and ordered her to leave. The night before she had to go she invited a few of us to her apartment—to say good-bye, and to ask us again if we wanted to believe." Ganden smiled at the memory. "She told us once more about heaven, and about whom we had to trust in order to get there. I asked her why I should believe in her heaven when I had Shambhala."

Jake's eyebrows went up. "Shambhala?"

"An American once told me that you call it Shangri-La." Puzhen replied. "It's an ancient kingdom in the north surrounded by impenetrable mountains and hidden by mist. All evil, including death, is unknown there. In its capital city of Kalapa is a shining palace, and in the palace are kept the sacred writings of Kalachakra, which contain all the world's wisdom.

"One day, when all is in chaos and Lhasa lies beneath the sea, a *feringy*—a foreigner—will claim to have conquered the world. It is then that Shambhala will be revealed, and its king will ride forth to defeat the *feringy*. Once he has defeated evil, the king of Shambhala will establish a kingdom that will last a thousand years."

"What did Miss Wagner say when you told her about Shambhala?" Jake asked.

Ganden grinned. "She told me that I was right. I couldn't believe it. Then she told me that I had the wrong source for my information. Miss Wagner took out her Bible and read to us from the book of Revelation about a holy city coming down from heaven, prepared as a bride beautifully dressed for her husband. She read about how there will be no more death or mourning or crying or pain, and how the old order of things will pass away. Then she read to us about the white horse whose rider is called Faithful and True. His eyes are like blazing fire," Ganden recited, "and on his head are many crowns. He has a name written on him that no one but himself knows. He is dressed in a robe dipped in blood, and his name is the Word of God."

Ganden looked thoughtfully at Jake. "That did it for me. I realized that if it was true that the real name of the king of Shambhala was the Word of God, then everything else she had been telling us about the Bible must be true, too." Ganden took Puzhen's hand. "Miss Wagner baptized us that night before she left. I wish we could see her again," he finished wistfully.

"Write down what you know about her," Jake said, taking his photo log out of his jacket pocket. "I'll see what I can do."

"Could we do it now, Jake?" Ganden asked eagerly when he had finished writing.

Jake nodded, grinning at the expression on the young man's face. He looked around the small restaurant. In one corner, a skylight threw a shaft of light onto the floor a few feet from the dark brown interior wall.

"Put a stool down over there, in the light," Jake directed, pointing to the corner. Ganden placed the stool, then beckoned to Puzhen.

The young woman frowned suspiciously. "What's going on?" she asked.

"Jake has agreed to take your picture for me," Ganden replied. His excited smile was infectious, and with a laugh Puzhen acquiesced. As Jake posed Puzhen, Ganden called out in Tibetan, and her parents came out of their kitchen to watch. Jake picked up the F3. He knelt, noting with satisfaction how the single light source highlighted Puzhen's high cheekbones and long, shining braids.

"What will you do with the pictures of our daughter?" Puzhen's father asked as Ganden translated.

Jake answered between shots. "I intend to show them to my friends in America. Puzhen's beauty will make both American men and women very jealous. Of course," he added with a wink to Ganden, "they will be jealous for very different reasons."

❖ ❖ ❖

At Ganden's suggestion, Jake's postlunch walk took him along the Barkhor Bazaar, the beehive of shops, markets, and hawkers that lined the octagonal pilgrim circuit that encompassed the Jokhang Temple.

The brass yak-butter votive lamps called *chome* were for sale everywhere. Itinerant monks clad in black, yak-wool robes pushed past him, twirling their prayer wheels as they pressed on toward the Jokhang. Prostrating pilgrims covered in leather shields scraped their way along the cobblestones at Jake's feet. A stall filled with brightly colored skeins of yarn caught his eye, as did a group of men hunched intently over a pool table set out on the street in an open-air parlor.

Jake turned at the sound of music. Down one of the narrow alleyways that crisscrossed the Tibetan section of Lhasa, a circle of nomads was dancing. As Jake approached, camera ready, several of the burly, rough-looking men watching the dance turned toward him. An enormous man, his dark, leathery face contrasting sharply with the bright red yarn that was twisted into his hair, folded his arms and shook his head. Jake nodded, waved, and turned to go, only to find three more men blocking the alleyway.

"Excuse me," Jake said and attempted to push his way past the men.

One of the men shoved Jake in the chest, sending him reeling backward. The first group of men ran up, caught Jake, and spun him around. They pushed Jake back toward the other group.

This time Jake was ready. As he neared one man in the second group, the knifelike edge of Jake's hand lashed out, catching the man in the side of the neck. As he crumpled to the cobblestones the rest of the men swarmed over Jake. Grabbing his arms, they slammed him up against one of the buildings. Jake's head cracked painfully against the stone wall.

When his vision cleared, Jake saw a wicked, curve-bladed knife glittering in front of his eyes. Behind it was the face of the man with the red yarn in his hair, grinning evilly.

"You hit us," he hissed, "we cut you." The man brought the knife toward Jake's eyes. As he closed them reflexively Jake felt the man hook the point of the knife inside his nostril.

Just as the man began to pull, a shot rang out. Jake heard the clatter of metal on stone and the sound of running feet. He opened his eyes to find Hua Chen standing in front of him, smoking pistol held aloft.

"Perhaps, Mr. MacIntyre," Chen said urbanely as he scooped up the knife that lay at Jake's feet, "you'll allow me to suggest that from now on you frequent only the better parts of town."

Grigory Markov peered through the midnight gloom at his guide. "Here?" he whispered. The man who had approached him that afternoon in the teahouse nodded vigorously. The Russian handed the man a wad of bills, then grabbed the man's arm. Markov's bayonet appeared in front of the man's eyes. "If you lie—," Markov hissed. He released the man, who scuttled off into the darkness.

Markov surveyed his surroundings. The man had led him up into the hills above Lhasa, to the encampment of a Khampa family on pilgrimage to the Jokhang. Firelight streamed from chinks in the yak-hide walls of the nomad tent called a *yurt*. With the tip of his bayonet Markov slit one of the rawhide thongs which held the skins to their supporting poles and peered through the widened crack.

Inside the smoky *yurt* a woman stirred a bubbling pot suspended over a crackling fire, while to one side a young girl played with an infant on a yak-wool blanket. A man sat cross-legged on the floor, his back to Markov, facing the door. Markov carefully cut the rest of the thongs holding up the skin.

When it dangled loosely, he gathered himself, then sprang into the tent.

Yousef Bey was fast, but Markov was faster. As the Afghan whirled, Markov was upon him. One massive fist smashed the pistol from Bey's hand, the other sank the tip of the bayonet into the arms merchant's neck.

"Freeze, Afghan," Markov growled. The Khampa women watched from their terrified huddle in the corner of the tent. "Do you know who I am?" The trembling Yousef Bey nodded. Markov grinned wickedly. "Good. Then I'm sure you won't mind coming along with me."

The Russian placed the thumb and forefinger of his free hand on either side of Bey's neck. He squeezed, cutting off the flow of blood to the Afghan's brain. When Bey passed out, Markov slung him over his shoulder. He tore open the door to the *yurt* and stalked out.

✧ ✧ ✧

A light rain began to fall on the earthen roof as Ganden stared across Barabise's desk at the nomad.

"I don't understand why that had to happen," Ganden exclaimed angrily. "MacIntyre is a good man. Why did you send Thupten and the others after him?"

Barabise glared back at the young man. "While he may be a good man, he is also *feringy*. The fact that he is a foreigner is reason enough."

"To almost kill him? They say that MacIntyre's alive only because Inspector Chen intervened in time."

Barabise roared with laughter. "You, boy, are as gullible as the old women and children we carefully arranged as witnesses! Your precious *feringy* would not have been killed. At most, Thupten would have given him a small souvenir of Tibet with which to impress the girls at home."

"But, why assault him at all? He is our guest!"

Barabise slammed his fist against the table. "*Our*

guest?" he thundered. "Who invited him? You? Tenzig?" Barabise pointed at the young man who was sitting quietly in a corner. Then he smiled. "Perhaps it was Puzhen who invited him."

Ganden frowned. "Why would you think Puzhen invited MacIntyre?"

"To get from him," the chieftain said sardonically, "that which you seem unwilling or unable to provide."

Infuriated, Ganden started to get up.

Instantly, Barabise's *thupta* was out of its scabbard. "If you so much as twitch, boy," Barabise growled, "Puzhen *will* have to turn to the *feringy*." The *thupta*'s wicked point glittered cobralike just in front of Ganden's eyes.

Breathing hard, Ganden stared at the Khampa for a long moment. Then, very carefully, he sat back down.

Barabise's dagger disappeared. He folded his arms and stared at Ganden. "Why do I always have to explain things to you, boy? Every foreigner in Tibet, from the teachers of English at the Academy down to the wretches sleeping in the courtyard of the Yak Hotel, is a guest—*of the Han!* Every cent they spend in our country—to get here, stay here, eat here, and leave here—goes to subsidize our Han overlords! Even the fake *thangkas* they buy from the vendors in the Barkhor are brought from Kathmandu by Chinese trucks." The chieftain spread his hands. "We must make their stays here unpleasant. If they do not come, neither does their money."

"Isn't there another reason?" Tenzig asked. Barabise looked over at the young man sitting in the corner. "Our people are like the explosive we use down at the cement plant," Tenzig said intently. "Jostle them too hard, and they will blow up." He peered up at Barabise. "You *wanted* the American to fight back, didn't you?"

"See, boy?" Barabise asked, pointing at Tenzig. "He understands. I've seen your *feringy* friend, Ganden. He's a fighter.

That's why I picked him. Knocking out that first man was exactly what I wanted him to do. But then, after Thupten had cut him, I wanted the *feringy*, mad with pain, to assault a few more of us. The people of the neighborhood would have attacked him. Then they would have turned on the PSB when it responded in force, thus bringing on the insurrection." Barabise snorted. "As it was, that cursed Chen intervened. Now, I shall have to use other means."

"Is there no peaceful way, Kailas?" Ganden asked.

"Go to your family's home and ask yourself that question," Barabise responded quietly.

"You know I can't do that," Ganden replied irritably. "The house is gone."

"Exactly. The home where you grew up, bulldozed into rubble by a Chinese tank on its way to assault our people during the last riots. Your parents' bodies, flung into the river to rot. Our children, torn screaming from their mothers' wombs. Is that a peaceful way, boy?" Barabise turned away. "Think about it. Now go."

✧ ✧ ✧

"WAKE UP!" Markov roared. He backhanded the unconscious Bey again. The combination of the stinging slaps and the bitter cold of the Tibetan night brought the Afghan back to shivering consciousness. "Again, Afghan. Do you remember me?"

The bound Bey looked up at his captor. "I can make you wealthy, Colonel. Anything you want. Just release me."

Markov buried the steel toe of his boot in Bey's ribs, cutting off his blandishments. "Quiet, *zudnicta*. You are quite right. You *will* provide me with what I want."

Markov bent over. He grabbed Bey's hands, which he had bound in front of him. The Russian pulled Bey to his feet. "See where you are?" Far below them, the lights of Lhasa spread out from the base of the cliff upon whose edge they stood.

"Colonel, please," the terrified Bey gibbered. "We'll be partners. Half of all I have is yours. Just let me go."

"Half?" Markov scoffed. "Only half? You offered Christ everything when you tempted him. No, Afghan, there is only one thing I want from you." Markov grabbed Bey's hands. He stepped forward, leaning Bey out over the abyss.

"Colonel, *please.*" The Afghan scrabbled to maintain a toehold on the edge of the precipice.

Markov reached into his pocket. He held out his hand. "Recognize these, peddler?"

Markov opened his fist and saw Bey's eyes go wide.

Markov nodded. "Now you know the price I claim from you, and for whom I claim it." He stared at Bey for a long moment. "And now, Afghan, I grant your wish. I release you." Markov opened his hand.

✧ ✧ ✧

"So," Cathy asked, "how *did* you finally get Joel to start leaving his muddy boots outside?"

Curled up in an overstuffed chair in her daughter's apartment, Pat Dryden smiled at the memory. "It actually turned out to be quite simple. One cold, rainy fall night, after he'd tracked mud into the house about seven times, Joel pulled back the covers on his side of the bed—"

Wide-eyed, Anne stared at her mother. "You didn't!"

She nodded. "There they were, still dripping. *That* got his attention." Pat looked archly at the trio of young women seated at her feet. "And *he* had to change the sheets, too."

"You never told me about that!" Anne said accusingly.

Pat smiled. "Your father and I have done quite a few things together that we've never told you about." She looked at Cathy. "But, from what you tell me about Greg's behavior, it's going to take more than a little negative reinforcement to get him to face up to his problem. Do you think he'd be open to professional counseling?" Cathy stared at the floor. "Not with me," Pat added. "I'm

221

too far away, and besides, it wouldn't surprise me if Greg had difficulty opening up to a *haole*." Cathy looked up, surprised at Pat's usage of the Hawaiian creole term for anyone not born in the Islands.

Pat glanced at her watch. "I've got to run. I've got a consultation at one-thirty." She took a business card from her purse and wrote on the back of it. "Here's the number of a young Asian colleague of mine who practices in Washington. He's really quite good."

Cathy took the card. "Brian Ichikawa!" she exclaimed. "We know him. He and Greg sometimes play handball together at the CIA club."

Pat smiled. "That's good. If it's all right with you, I'll call Brian this afternoon and fill him in."

Cathy's nod was both eager and grateful.

Markov made his way to the base of the cliff. *Neither of us took delight in killing the enemy, Pyotr,* he thought as he stood over Bey's shattered body. *But, since you could not have the military funeral you so richly deserved, this is the best I can do for you, my old friend. No taps, no salute fired over your coffin, no folded flag handed to the weeping Natalia. Just an honor guard of one—an old ex-soldier who served long and well with you—and these.*

Markov took out of his pocket the two gold Imperials he had shown Yousef Bey. Leaning over, he placed them on the Afghan's eyes. Then he began the long trek back to Lhasa.

27

Jake filled his plate from the lunch buffet in the Everest Room of the Lhasa Hotel, then joined Geoff Sheffield and Sheila Atherton at a table.

"Dratted shame your not getting to shoot Everest," Sheffield rumbled sympathetically.

Jake shrugged. "At least this way I don't have to worry about outdoing Galen Rowell." His two companions nodded at the mention of the world-famous nature photographer. "Hardly anyone's seen Kula Gangri, so if I can get a couple of good shots I'll be fine. You two ready to go?"

Atherton frowned, then nodded. "Can't say much for my 'assistant.' Don't think he's ever seen a camera before." Her face lit up. "I won't need him, though. You should see the faces around here! And the kids!" Both men smiled at Atherton's anticipation of photographing children, her special passion.

"My guide's all right," Sheffield said. "We're going to start with sunrise over the spires of the Jokhang, do the whitewashed façades of the Tibetan quarter in the full brilliance of the noonday sun, and finish with long shots of the Potala at sunset. Not to mention every alleyway, nook, and cranny I can find."

"When do you leave?" Atherton asked Jake.

"After lunch. Kula Gangri's about twelve hours away. Since it's a really bad idea to drive in Tibet at night, Ganden and I are improvising. We'll get as far as we can before sundown tonight and camp out. Then leave at sunrise tomorrow and drive like a bat to get to the mountain well before sunset. Ganden has relatives nearby, so after the shoot we'll spend the night at their house before returning the day after tomorrow."

"Pretty hectic," Atherton observed.

Jake grinned. "Sounds like it could be a lot of fun."

Ganden stared at Barabise in disbelief. "MacIntyre a spy? I don't believe it!"

The nomad chieftain nudged the small, scrawny man who sat huddled in a chair beside him. "Tell him."

Xongnu looked up at Ganden. "It is true, *chola*. Two nights ago, I saw your friend in Namche's shop."

Ganden frowned. "Old Namche? The jeweler over on Beijing Xilu? He's been there forever. How does that make MacIntyre a spy?"

"Namche once lived in Calcutta," Barabise explained. "While he was there he worked as a translator for the India Office of the British government. The same office that sent the spies called 'pundits' to survey our land for invasion. The government of the country that itself invaded us in 1903, and then three years later handed Tibet over to the Han."

"All that happened years ago. That doesn't mean that Namche is a spy."

Xongnu glanced nervously at Barabise, who nodded. "He and your friend talked for a long time," the little man said rapidly. "Then Namche gave your friend something, and he left."

"Namche has been dealing with foreigners ever since he returned to Tibet," Barabise added.

"Of course he deals with foreigners!" Ganden shouted. "The man is a shopkeeper!"

"The man is a spy!" Barabise roared. "Both he and your *feringy* friend are in collusion with the Han!" The Khampa took a deep breath. "You will find out the truth about your friend in time, Ganden. And, when that time comes, I trust you will know what to do."

Ganden shook his head. "Are we finished? The 'spy' and I are leaving for Kula Gangri in an hour."

Barabise nodded. "Go. And take Xongnu here with you. Tenzig and I have some planning to do."

"Wait!" Tenzig called.

Ganden stopped as his friend came across the room. His eyes widened when he saw what Tenzig was holding out.

"Take this," Tenzig urged.

Ganden shook his head vigorously. "No. I couldn't."

"The Word calls us to be 'wise as serpents,' Ganden. If you are going to be dealing with a *feringy* who may be a spy, you'll need this."

"Listen to him, boy," Barabise added.

After a long moment Ganden took Tenzig's offering. He slipped it into a pocket as he left with Xongnu.

"How should I know?" Chen groused to his superintendent. He pointed to the two gold Imperials that lay glittering on his desk. "If it wasn't for these, I'd figure he was some idiot tourist out for a midnight stroll." The inspector ground out his cigarette irritably and immediately lit another. "You know," he told his boss, "between the plane crash, that band of photographers, and now this, I'm getting to hate foreigners almost as much as the Tibetans do."

Chen's superintendent handed him a piece of paper. "That's not all. I want to know where this came from," he said grimly.

Chen looked at the sheet. Dominating the page was a grainy, black-and-white photograph. It showed a headless, business-suited corpse still sitting upright in a seat of the 757. The rest of the page was filled with rows of large Tibetan characters.

"Hundreds of these were flung at dawn from all four sides of the roof of the Jokhang," the superintendent explained. "By the time we found out about it most of them had been scooped up. Now they're all over town."

Chen looked up at his boss. "Any trouble?"

"Not so far. Can you make out what it says?" the superintendent asked. Chen shook his head. "Then go find your little snitch Xongnu and get him in here."

Chen snapped his fingers. "Speaking of my little snitch, he sold me a photo the other day when you were over in Shigatse. Said you'd know who it was." The inspector rummaged around in his pockets, then shrugged. "I must have left it in my other coat."

"Could the Americans have taken this photo of the crash?"

Chen shook his head. "I intercepted them when they were photographing the wreckage and confiscated their film. Besides, their equipment is much too sophisticated for this. This looks like it was done in one of the cheap photo shops over by the Nepalese consulate." An idea hovered at the edge of the inspector's mind, then disappeared before he could grab it. Chen got up. "I'll go find Xongnu."

Dust swirled around the Land Cruiser as it shuddered to a stop.

"We're not going any farther?" Jake asked. "We've only come about forty kilometers."

From behind the wheel, Ganden grinned at him. "This is where we leave the road," he explained. "Kula Gangri is only about a hundred kilometers due south of here. We'll have plenty of time to get there tomorrow." The young Tibetan got out and opened the back of the Land Cruiser.

After insuring that Ganden was busy unloading their gear, Jake got out his guidebook. Inside the front cover Greg had taped a list of dates and times when they would be expecting Jake to transmit anything he had for them. Next to today's date was 1830. Jake looked at his watch. It read 5:00 P.M., which gave him an hour and a half.

Jake got out of the Land Cruiser and stretched. They had climbed steadily after leaving Lhasa, and the Chumbi Valley stretched before him. The plateau on which he stood was barren and arid, with the cold wind flinging up a fine dust that clogged his nose and caused his eyes to water. *The Israelites must've wandered through a whole lot of this kind of terrain on their way to Canaan,* Jake decided as he fished around for his handkerchief.

"I need your help," Jake told Ganden after he had blown his nose.

"With photography?" the wide-eyed young man asked.

Jake grinned. "In a minute." He handed Ganden a sheet of paper and a felt-tipped marker. "First, I need a hand with my spelling. Then you can take my picture."

Standing in Chen's office, Xongnu shifted uneasily from foot to foot. "Can we make it quick please, *genla?*" he pleaded, upset with himself for having been collared by Chen just down the street from Barabise's hideout.

Chen grinned. "Ashamed to be seen with us, Xongnu?" He picked up the flyer. "There's twenty *waihui* if you translate this for us."

The Tibetan stared at the paper. He said nothing.

"Well?" Chen prodded. He took a bill out of his wallet and held it where Xongnu could see it.

The informant took a deep breath. "It says, *genla,* 'People of *Per La,* arise! As promised long ago, those who dared to fly over our holy city and look down upon the home of our Dalai Lama have died. The clawed hand of Gonpo reached out and tore the symbol of our hated *feringy* overlords from the sky. Gonpo hurled it to its death, and from a severed skull he now drinks the blood of our oppressors. Arise and strike down the Han! Gonpo has spoken—the time for blood is now!'" Xongnu stopped, and mopped his brow with his sleeve.

"Is that all?" Chen asked. Pale, the Tibetan nodded. The name of Gonpo, defeater of hostile demons in the pantheon of Tibetan gods, had brought an uncontrollable shudder from Xongnu.

When the informant reached for the twenty-*waihui* bill, the much taller Chen held it out of his reach. "Who wrote this?" he asked.

The informant shook his head. "I don't know."

"Who took the picture? Where was the flyer produced?"

"Please, *genla*," Xongnu gasped. "I don't know. Please let me go."

Seeing that the man was truly terrified, Chen handed him the bill. "Find out, Xongnu," he called as the Tibetan scurried out of his office.

Xongnu looked both ways before darting from the police station. He ran down the street, unaware that Tenzig had come around the corner. The young man watched for a long moment, then trotted off in a direction of his own.

From the ridge above their camp, Jake watched through the viewfinder as the ice-blue shadows of twilight crept up the length of the Chumbi Valley. As the valley floor was consumed by night, Ganden heard Jake speak:

> **In the evening light this country can be beautiful, snow mountains and all: the harshness becomes subdued; shadows soften the hillsides; there is a blending of lines**

and folds until the last light, so that one comes to bless the absolute bareness, feeling that here is pure beauty of form, a kind of absolute harmony.

Ganden looked at Jake. "That's wonderful."

"It was written seventy years ago by an Englishman named George Mallory, in a letter to his wife, Ruth, a few weeks before he disappeared while climbing Mount Everest. He was last seen less than eight hundred feet from the summit. Some think he made it, thirty years before Tenzig Norgay and Sir Edmund Hillary, and then died on the way down."

"He was very brave to take on Chomolungma."

Jake zipped up his jacket against the freshening breeze. "In his last letter home he wrote, 'We are going to sail to the top this time, and God with us.'" The two men watched as the sky filled with stars.

Jake rose, wincing as his knees cracked and popped, and shouldered the heavy camera and tripod.

Ganden heard Jake's exclamation of pain. "Do you want me to carry that for you?" he offered. "My mother always told me that I have Sherpa blood in my veins."

Jake smiled at the pride in the young man's voice. "Thanks, but I can manage."

They made their way down the trail by the light of a rising full moon. Jake watched as slivers of silver appeared between the spires of the Himalayas and found himself thinking of harvest moons rising behind the pines and cedars of Maine.

"Are you a colporteur?" Ganden asked.

"Yeah, I guess so," Jake replied absently. In his mind he was sitting in the Dryden's porch swing, his feet up on the rail, with Anne next to him. Her head was on his shoulder as they watched the moonlight ripple across the cold waters of Somes Sound.

"Really?" Ganden said brightly. "That is wonderful!"

"I agree. *Anything Goes* is probably my favorite musical of his."

Ganden frowned. "I'm sorry. I do not understand."

Jake tore his mind from Anne and forced himself to pay attention. "Didn't you ask me if I like Cole Porter?"

"No sir. I asked you if you are a colporteur."

"A *what?*"

"A colporteur. They taught us about them in college."

Jake shrugged. "Well, who knows? Maybe I am one. What is it?"

"Someone," Ganden recited studiously, "employed to travel about distributing Bibles, religious tracts, and other literature, gratuitously or at a low price."

"Afraid not. I'm just a semi-itinerant photojournalist." Ganden's face fell. "Why do you want to know?" Jake asked, seeing the young man's obvious disappointment.

Ganden instinctively lowered his voice. "I was hoping that, if you were a colporteur, you might have a Bible you could give to me."

Jake looked at him closely. "Don't you have a Bible of your own?"

The young Tibetan shook his head. "I had the one Miss Wagner gave me, but it was taken from me by Public Security. And before it was broken up by the Han, my house church was assembling one in Tibetan." Jake saw the flash of pain in his eyes.

Jake reached into his shirt pocket. The Bible he took out was worn, its lower margin stained a dark red-brown. "Take this one." He handed Ganden the Bible that Alex Stratton, his best friend, had given him just before the young Englishman had died in the Egyptian desert.

"A friend of mine gave it to me not too far from where Moses watched the Israelites enter the Promised Land," Jake explained. *The work goes on, Brit*, Jake thought as Ganden thanked him profusely. *The work goes on.*

230

28

"Talk!" Barabise roared. The back of his hand crashed again into the face of the man he held writhing at arm's length.

"Please, *genla*," Xongnu whimpered. "I've already told you—"

The nomad backhanded the small man again. Xongnu spit out a tooth. His eyes closed, and his head lolled to one side. Barabise opened his hand, and the informant crashed to the floor.

"Now," Barabise said calmly when Xongnu's eyes fluttered open. "The truth. Why did Tenzig see you coming out of the police station?"

"I have told you, *genla*," Xongnu whispered. "Chen grabbed me on my way back from the Jokhang. He asked me who had produced the flyer. I told him I didn't know."

"Is that all you told him?"

"Yes," the informant lied.

"Then get out of my sight. You disgust me."

Xongnu got to his feet and hobbled to the door. As he reached for the doorknob there was a *thunk*. The small man squealed as the edge of Barabise's *thupta* grazed his hand, an inch of its point embedded into the door by the force of the nomad's throw.

"If you talk to the Han again," Barabise growled, "the next time it will be the back of your neck."

"How long 'til dinner?" Jake called down.

Ganden looked up from the small camping stove he was tending. "No more than five minutes."

Jake waved. He knelt and extracted his PC from his backpack and set it on an upended water can. *Five minutes is just enough time to get this thing fired up. Treat the folks back home to a slide show while we eat.*

Jake faced away from the remnants of sunset and moved the dish antenna back and forth across the sky until a warbling was heard from the PC's speaker and AOS was displayed on the screen. A few seconds later the first of his photos, a picture of a wizened old woman selling the prayer scarves called *khatas*, appeared on the screen.

Jake started transmitting the photos to the satellite. The next image appeared—a string of colorful, pennantlike prayer flags against a dark-blue sky. Jake nodded approvingly. From below, Ganden's shout announced dinner. Jake rose and, careful not to walk in front of the antenna, began to backtrack along the enticing aroma that drifted up the trail.

"What happened to you?" Chen asked as Xongnu peered up at him through blackened eyes.

"I have the information you seek," the little man croaked. "The print shop is over on Linkuo Liu. The warehouse next to the People's Hospital." He peered at Chen. "You know the one?"

"I know it," Chen assured him. He reached for his wallet. "How much?"

Xongnu shook his head. "No money," he said as he gingerly touched a split lip. "Not for this."

Barabise strode brazenly past the PSB station on his way to the print shop that fronted the barracks where he kept his men. As he neared the front of the station he spotted a small Tibetan man ducking furtively out of the station house door. Barabise pressed forward. Xongnu saw him. He grabbed the sleeve of a PSB officer and pointed at Barabise. The officer barked at the small man and shoved him away roughly. As the man fled, Barabise changed course, flinging people aside as he bulldozed along the crowded street.

The Khampa chieftain caught the small man at the end of the block. Barabise dragged the struggling man into a fetid alley. Holding him at arm's length, Barabise smiled.

"Were you offering to enlist in the PSB, Xongnu?" Barabise asked. "Or did you merely provide your usual impeccable information?"

"*Genla*, I—," the informer stammered.

"Save your excuses," the nomad ordered. "I'm going to do you a favor. I know that you've been worried that you wouldn't be able to afford a sky burial, so I'm going to provide you with one." Barabise pulled the terrified Xongnu's face to within inches of his. "Only, in your case, you're not going to be dead before the flesh is stripped from your bones."

Barabise encircled the weeping man's neck with his free hand. He slowly squeezed until the thrashing Xongnu lost conciousness. Then Barabise slung him over his shoulder and continued down the alley.

Anne fingered the white plastic card that hung on the end of the chain around her neck. The number 018 was the only writing on it. As a schoolteacher whose life revolved around bulletin boards, colorful visuals, and students' artwork, she found CIA headquarters to be depressingly sterile. *It's as blank as this tag,* she thought. *You'd think that they'd at least put up a calendar on the wall or something. And the rooms aren't even numbered. How do they remember which is the bathroom?* She noticed Greg beckoning to her and hurried over from where she had been trying to stay out of the way.

Greg pointed to something incomprehensible on the screen. "The satellite's picked up Jake's carrier wave," he announced. "We should see the first picture in a minute." Greg glanced at his watch. "Eighteen-thirty, Tibet time." He grinned at Anne. "Jake's a punctual man."

Anne nodded agreement. *When he bothers to show up at all . . .*

Greg, Cathy, Susan, and Anne watched as the pictures appeared.

"Hold it!" Greg exclaimed. "Check out number four." The photo was one of a panoramic series of Lhasa that Jake had taken from the top of Changpori. On one side they could see a string of red digits.

Susan peered at the numbers, then whistled softly. "Pretty high readings. Is that one of the coordinates you gave him?"

Greg glanced at the screen as he flipped through a looseleaf notebook. "No." He snapped his fingers. "You know, I bet that's their secret nuke."

"Huh?" Cathy exclaimed. "How could a nuclear power plant be kept a secret?"

"Easy, if you're the Chinese government. You just claim that it doesn't exist. Like the Tienanmen Square incident. The government decided that nobody died in the massacre. Therefore nobody did, and all reports to the contrary are false." Greg thought for a moment. "If they just brought it on line, that could explain the readings we've been getting from around there."

"Why would China have a nuclear power plant some-where as remote as Tibet?" Anne asked.

"To provide power for the huge PLA garrison there," Greg replied. "But also, more importantly, to process and enrich the plutonium mined from Tibet's abundant reserves."

"The presence of a nuke would explain some of those sensor readings," Susan observed. "But not all of them."

Greg nodded. "That's why we're going to ask Jake for some close-ups. Retransmit the photo to him, in case he's erased it. Circle the area in question, and ask him to get close-ups from as many angles as possible. Maybe a stronger reading will provide us with more information."

As Susan typed at her console, Cathy nudged Anne. "I bet they'd let you add a P.S. if you want. Here's your chance to tell him off."

Anne looked at Cathy out of the corner of her eye. "I *could* tell him I'm eloping with Randy."

Cathy tried hard to keep a straight face. "Now *that* would get his undivided attention." By the time the two women had stopped laughing, Susan had punched the TRANSMIT button.

The seventh photo showed a grinning Jake, unshaven and disreputable standing on a hill with a range of jagged peaks looming over his shoulder. He was wearing mountaineering sunglasses, and his battered bush hat was pushed back on his head. Just below his stubbly chin he held a white piece of cardboard.

Cathy squinted at the screen. "Is there lettering on that?"

Susan moved her mouse, and a box appeared around Jake and the sign. With a click of a mouse button the enclosed area appeared on an adjacent screen, magnified greatly. A chorus of *Awww*s went up as the group read the untidy hand lettering: HAPPY BIRTHDAY, LADY! With a smile Susan punched a button labeled PRINT. In the corner of the lab, a color laser printer whirred into life.

Susan fetched the photo. "That's quite a corsair you've got there, lassie," she told Anne as she handed her the print.

Anne looked at the picture, feeling Jake's roguish smile more than seeing it. Exasperation, worry, and desire all welled up inside her once again. *You come back to me soon, you big oaf,* she told the picture, giving it a small shake as she did so.

Cathy peered at the photo. "What's that stuff under the 'Happy Birthday'?"

Anne brought the print closer. Long, jagged lines extended down the rest of the sign. She showed it to Susan, who made an enlargement of the area.

"Looks like Sanskrit to me," Susan pronounced after scrutinizing the lettering. "I'll get the Linguistics folks on it in the morning." She looked up at Anne. "Maybe your pirate's proposing." Anne felt her cheeks burn as laughter filled the room.

Greg whistled. The women turned and saw Puzhen staring regally out at them from the monitor. Her braids glistened in a shaft of sunlight, and the dark background highlighted the red and yellow of her nomad dress. A sliver necklace studded with amber, coral, and turquoise gleamed at her throat.

"And just what are you whistling at?" Cathy asked.

Greg smiled innocently down at her. "At Jake's consummate skill. He's got an excellent eye."

Cathy wrinkled her nose at him. "Humph."

Without realizing it, Anne gave the picture another shake.

Shouts brought Barabise out of the office at the back of the print shop. Twelve armed PSB policemen were clubbing their way through the front door. As he watched unnoticed, they surrounded the men who had been printing the next batch of flyers.

Enraged, the nomad grabbed an AKS-74 assault rifle lying just inside the doorway. He whirled and opened fire on the nearest policeman at point-blank range. The fusillade of bullets from the Russian-made weapon cut the man down. The rest of the PSB officers opened fire in response. The shouts of his men became screams as Barabise threw down the AKS-74. He dove out the back door of the office, pausing just long enough at the room behind his cobbler's shop to snatch open his desk drawer, then he escaped down the alley.

29

Jake finished the last of the dumpling soup. "What did you call this?" he asked Ganden.

"*Momo.* Yak meat in barley flour, boiled in yak broth."

Jake set down his bowl and rested his arms on his knees. "Are there many others beside you and Puzhen who read the Bible?" he asked quietly.

Ganden looked at Jake narrowly. *Kailas says he is a spy. But why would a spy want to know such things? And why would a spy talk about the evening light? And why would a spy give me his Bible?* "A few who do," he answered cautiously, watching Jake closely.

"It must be very hard for you."

Startled by the simple compassion of the statement, Ganden found himself telling Jake about the eradication of his house church. "Sometimes," he concluded glumly, "even though Puzhen's there, I feel like I'm the only one left."

Jake nodded understandingly. "So did Elijah."

"Who?"

"Elijah," Jake repeated. "The Old Testament prophet. In the book of First Kings he says, 'I am the only one left, and now they are trying to kill me too.'"

Ganden sighed. "I've never read the Old Testament. I've heard stories from it, but I've never even seen one."

"You've got one now."

Ganden smiled happily and touched his pocket.

"You'll enjoy it," Jake went on. "It tells about thousands of people over thousands of years. Most of them tried hard to do what God wanted. Sometimes they did really well, and sometimes they really blew it. But God always honored their efforts and always forgave their mistakes."

Ganden smiled tentatively. "They sound like us."

Jake grinned. "Just like us."

From a nearby mountaintop, Barabise gazed down at the "Peoples' Glory" power plant. A semicircle of blood-red sun sat on the horizon, its horizontal rays sweeping across the steppe.

Now, the nomad decided. *It must be now. I can endure no further atrocities against my people and my way of life. The weaklings among us have pleaded with you to leave, and those you have pacified have asked politely to be permitted to live in groveling coexistence.*

Barabise reached into his pocket.

But no more. The time for civility has passed, as has the time for scratching the truth timidly on pieces of paper and the walls of our temple. It is time now to do something of which my Mongol forefathers would be proud.

The Khampa chieftain took out the detonator he had retrieved from his desk drawer. Carefully, as Ganden had shown him, he dialed in the combination.

My ancestors wanted nothing of yours. Genghis, the first khan, leveled your proud city of Beijing. Upon its ashes his grandson Kublai built Khan-baliq, a city of his own. They would have nothing to do with you. They drove you out of your comfortable decadence and into the wastelands to die. As shall we.

240

Barabise raised the detonator. With both hands he pointed it straight at the heart of the dying sun.

They turned their backs on the degenerate pleasures in which you revel. You offered them your so-called civilization, and they flung it back in your face. As I do now.

With both thumbs he slammed home the detonator buttons.

A torrent of light and sound threw him to the ground. He was bathed by intolerable heat, as if hell itself had for an instant enveloped him. The earth writhed beneath him. When his vision cleared, Barabise pulled himself slowly to his feet. His hand went to his forehead and came away sticky and wet. Below him, illuminated by scarlet twilight, chaos reigned. Barabise raised a bloody fist. He roared with triumph as the flames surged upward.

✧ ✧ ✧

Jake got up and stretched, eager to put the PC away. Halfway up the path, a flash of light to the north made him blink. He looked back. Ganden was staring northward.

"Lightning?"

Ganden shook his head. "Not at this time of year."

Jake took another step. Then the ground heaved beneath him, and a giant invisible hand knocked him over. Just as he struggled to his knees, a dull, echoing roar rolled past them toward the south.

Ganden reached the plateau above camp just after Jake. As they watched, a spot on the northern horizon faded from white to dull red, then vanished.

"You're right," Jake said quietly. "That wasn't lightning." He nudged something with his toe. Jake looked down to find his PC lying at his feet, knocked off the water can by the concussion. Jake glanced at Ganden, then bent over and picked it up. Jake straightened up to find Ganden pointing a small revolver at him.

"Then it's true," Ganden exclaimed, his tone desolate. "Kailas was right. You *are* a spy."

"What's going on?" Jake asked sharply.

"I have an advanced degree in electronics, Mr. MacIntyre," Ganden answered calmly. "I know a satellite transmitter when I see one."

Jake stared back at Ganden. "I suppose you also know what caused that explosion."

Ganden nodded. "It is time for us to return to Lhasa." He motioned with the revolver. "This time, you'll drive."

❖ ❖ ❖

Marcus Connor, pilot of the shuttle *Discovery*, nudged the man next to him. "Did you see that?"

"Nope," Colonel Bruce Ellis murmured. "I'm busy inspecting the inside of my eyelids." Ellis, eyes closed, floated just above his commander's couch, tethered loosely to it by a seat belt. "If it's a little green man, tell him we gave at the office." Ellis turned over.

"Nothin' that excitin', Colonel," Connor replied casually. "Just a little flash of light bright enough to be seen up here." Connor glanced out the shuttle's flight deck windows at the full Earth suspended two hundred miles below *Discovery's* nose.

Ellis opened one eye. "Did you get it on tape?"

"Sure did. It's now a permanent part of USGS Topological Survey tape number 9220–4375."

Ellis sat up and stretched as Connor rewound the tape. Both men turned their attention to the overhead monitor and watched as the flash winked an actinic white, then died away slowly.

"OK," Ellis admitted. "This wasn't one of your hot flashes."

Connor grinned at the reference to the mysterious flashes of light sometimes seen by astronauts. The pilot was particularly susceptible to the phenomenon, which had made him the butt of an unending stream of jokes.

The shuttle commander watched the flash again. "Looks like our Chinese comrades are celebrating *Gung Hay Fat Choy* in a big way."

"Say what?"

"*Gung Hay Fat Choy*," Ellis repeated. "The Chinese New Year. You know, firecrackers, banquets, and so on."

Connor shook his head. "Can't say I do know. Didn't go in much for that sort of thing when I was growing up in Tuscaloosa. We had firecrackers, but nothin' like this." He thought for a moment. "The explosion was kinda close to the coordinates we were supposed to keep an eye on, wasn't it?"

"Maybe," Ellis agreed. "But I doubt anyone's started shooting. If World War III just started, there'd be more than one flash. I bet the Chinese just popped a big one up at their Lop Nur testing ground," the commander speculated. "Ship the video down via the relay system with a note that the DIA boys might want to check it out."

Connor nodded, knowing that the Defense Intelligence Agency would probably be very interested, indeed. "Think we should download it priority?"

"Nah. They're getting the seismic reports about now, and if they're interested in our august opinions, they'll call. Let's get some sack time—tomorrow's a busy day."

The image of Puzhen was still staring out of Greg's monitor when the alarms went off. At that instant she disappeared, to be replaced by an insistently blinking UNEXPECTED LOS. Greg turned to a console where a message was flashing.

"EOSAT-3's picked up something," he announced. With a few clicks of a mouse, he picked out some items from the menu displayed on the EOSAT's console. Greg typed a command and then muttered a curse.

He turned to the women. "Susan," he ordered, "call

NORAD and see if they know what's happening. Cathy, you and Anne have to leave."

Susan glanced at the EOSAT console, then at Greg. "If you don't tell her, laddie," she said quietly, looking at Anne, "then I will." She picked up the phone and began dialing.

"Tell me what?" Anne asked.

Greg took a deep breath. "EOSAT-3, one of our Earth observation satellites, has just picked up evidence of an enormous explosion in Asia."

"*Where* in Asia?"

"South-central China. Tibet."

The color fled from Anne's face. "*Where* in Tibet?" she whispered.

"I don't know. We'll have to triangulate with SAC before we can pinpoint it exactly."

Anne pointed at the message on the screen that had displayed Jake's pictures. "Does this explosion have anything to do with that?"

Greg spread his hands. "I just don't know," he said helplessly. "They do a lot of weapons testing up near there. It's probably no more than that. We should know in a couple of hours."

"I'll wait."

"I can't let you do that." He glanced at Cathy for help as Anne started to bristle.

Cathy nodded. "We've got to go, Anne. It's gotten really Top Secret in here really fast." She looked up at her friend. "I've gone to enough parties with the security types around here, and personally, I don't think that now is the time to get to know them better." Cathy turned to her fiancé. "But, Gregory J. Miahara, if you don't call us at my apartment absolutely as soon as you know anything . . ." Her voice trailed off menacingly.

"I will. Promise." He motioned with his head toward the door.

In his three decades in the marines, Roddy Rodriguez had seen many things, but this was the first time he had seen a president in his bathrobe. As the president yawned and stretched, a door to the Oval Office opened and Mike O'Brien came in, brisk and efficient in a starched white shirt, tie, and expensive suit.

Maybe he never sleeps, Rodriguez mused as O'Brien rang for coffee. *Maybe they just stand him up in a closet somewhere.*

"What's up, Roddy?" The president blinked and stifled another yawn.

"Sorry to get you up, sir, but seventeen minutes ago we registered a possible nuclear detonation."

Sleep vanished from the president's eyes. He sat down behind his desk, his hand near the phone that provided a direct line to SAC headquarters. "Where?"

"South central China. Outside Lhasa, Tibet. At oh-four-fifty-two everything we had looking at the region went nuts. NORAD reported it immediately. Right behind them was some hotshot spook over at the IPF at Langley. How *he* detected it, I don't want to know. Even *Discovery* reported it, although it was at the extreme limit of their range."

"You said a *possible* nuclear explosion?" the president asked.

Rodriguez nodded. "We're not sure because the coordinates of the blast match exactly those of the People's Glory nuclear power plant. Also, the radiation released is consonant with the amount of fuel in a reactor of that size."

"So one of their reactors blew up," O'Brian ventured.

"Maybe," Rodriguez replied. "But the detonation of a small tactical nuke will also release that amount of radiation. It could be a real life China Syndrome, but we just don't know yet." Rodriguez smiled at O'Brien's frown. "*China Syndrome* is a term for the ultimate meltdown. Remember the movie a few years ago? Starred Jack Lemmon."

The president rubbed the stubble on his chin. "Anything happen since?"

"No. And that's the weird part. Everyone's just sitting tight. That's what makes us think that some Chinese pushed the wrong button." The chairman pointed to a map. "If the Russkys were invading, we'd expect to see strikes all along here," his arm swept along the Sino-Soviet border, "followed by massive troop movements. Instead, we've got *nothing*. On either side. Everyone must know about it, but nobody's reacting." Rodriguez scratched his head. "And that's what worries me. I'd almost be happier if the Chinese *were* going ape. At least then I'd know what was going on."

"What's the analysis of the North American Air Defense Command?" The president asked.

"NORAD didn't pick up any ignitions, nor did they detect the heat signature of a missile in flight."

"Then nothing was launched," O'Brien interjected.

"Not necessarily," Rodriguez responded. "Lhasa is about fifteen hundred kilometers from the nearest point on the Russian border. That's well within the range of one of their SS-24s."

"But NORAD didn't detect anything," the president objected.

"Their job is to detect the strategic stuff—high flying and fast. The SS-24 is a tactical missile. It flies low and slow, down in the muck where it's hard to sort out from mountains, water, and all the other stuff that drives radar nuts."

The president poured himself another mug of coffee. "Recommendations, General?"

"Watch and wait, sir."

"Why?" O'Brien asked sharply.

"Two reasons, O'Brien." Rodriguez replied, his voice as calm as his eyes were hard. "First, that's what everyone else is doing. Second, we're not involved in this, and there's no reason we should be. If anybody's going to make the first move, it sure shouldn't be us."

The president nodded agreement, then looked at his watch. "I've just got time to look respectable for our briefing."

"One more thing, sir."

"Yes, Roddy?"

"I'd like to see if I can find that CIA superspy and get him in here. He might know something useful."

The president shrugged. "Fine with me." He grinned. "Elliot's out on the Cape, isn't he? Give him a call and get him on it. Seeing a sunrise will do him good."

Cathy came out of her apartment's kitchen to find Anne staring out the living room window at the Washington skyline. She set down the mugs of tea and put her hand on Anne's arm.

"You know," she said softly, "when you were missing in Peru last year, your dad spent a lot of time praying for you. All of us did." Anne turned a tear-streaked face toward her. "It worked then," Cathy continued, "so maybe it'll work now. But I'm not very good at it, and I could use some help." Anne took her hand.

30

Jake's head slammed against the roof of the cab as the Land Cruiser hit yet another pothole. Driving with one hand, he rubbed the top of his aching skull. Ganden sat beside him, his pistol trained unerringly at Jake.

"One thing I don't understand," Jake said, trying to sound conversational. "A while ago you told me that you believe in the Bible. But just where in the Bible does it tell us to go around pointing guns at each other?"

Ganden stared at Jake. "The Bible warns us about people who 'claim to know God but by their actions they deny him.' You claim to believe, Mr. MacIntyre, but your actions reveal you to be in the service of those who enslave us."

Gotta admit that it sure does look that way, Jake thought glumly.

"Paul warned the Ephesians," Ganden continued, "to watch out for those who would try to deceive them with empty words. He also said to have nothing to do with them."

Hearing the finality in those words, Jake glanced at Ganden. "Where are you taking me?"

"To the leader of our group. Kailas warned me that you were a spy. Now he will know what to do with you."

A cold wind flung dust into the headlights' beams as they headed north toward Lhasa.

Elliot French's polo shirt and wrinkled chinos stood in stark contrast to the dress blues of the marine corporal who escorted him. Picked up from his Cape Cod vacation home by two FBI agents, he had been driven to the Air Force station at Buzzards Bay and from there helicoptered to the White House east lawn. Greg and another Marine were waiting for him under the east portico.

"Figured it was you as soon as General Rodriguez explained what was going on," French remarked as the elevator descended to the Situation Room. "You just stick to the techie stuff," he cautioned. "I'll handle any policy questions that come along."

Greg nervously tried to comb his hair with his hands. "OK by me. First I'm rousted out of my lab by a pack of feds with guns, and now I'm about to play Mr. Wizard to a bunch of politicians. Some day this is turning out to be."

French smiled. "Don't worry about it. Until they've had their morning coffee, the pillars of our government are a pretty sorry sight."

A covey of suits and uniforms surrounded the Situation Room's mahogany conference table. Greg stood inconspicuously in a corner until French motioned him over to a chair.

"Coffee?" French asked.

Greg surveyed the sideboard. "I'd prefer a beer."

"Not unreasonable, considering the night you've had."

As Jake and Ganden approached in the Land Cruiser, a PLA sentry carrying a submachine gun blocked the entrance to the bridge across the Kyichu River.

"Your papers," the guard ordered. Seeing Ganden hand over his identity folder, Jake surrendered his passport. *I can't even tell the guy I'm being kidnapped,* Jake thought, heaving a sign of resignation, *since he doesn't speak English.*

Tucking his flashlight under his arm, the guard studied Jake's passport, then spoke at length to Ganden. "We're to turn around and take the other road," Ganden explained to Jake. "We're to go to the airport. All foreigners are being evacuated." Jake looked at the guard, who brought up the muzzle of his gun. "We'd better go, Mr. MacIntyre," Ganden suggested. Jake spun the Land Cruiser around. They headed east toward Gonggar Airport, along the opposite side of the Kyichu from Lhasa.

Conversation ceased as the president came in and sat down. Following his boss's lead, Greg remained standing. The president nodded at French.

"This is Dr. Gregory Miahara of our image processing facility," the DDO began. "Dr. Miahara was the senior imaging officer on duty at the time of the incident. I've asked him here to see if any additional light can be shed on the explosion. In addition to being an imaging specialist, Dr. Miahara is an authority on particle radiation. Please bear in mind that Dr. Miahara hasn't had time to prepare any formal notes." All eyes turned toward him, and Greg felt very alone as French sat down.

Roddy Rodriguez broke the ice. "How did you detect the blast, Doctor?"

Greg nodded, grateful to start on familiar ground. "Actually, I didn't. We regularly monitor the Earth observation satellites, and it was one of them that first registered the explosion. Since then, however, we've had all available sensors trained on the site."

"Do you know yet if the reactor blew up or was bombed?" the president asked.

"Not yet, sir. We still don't have enough data." *He looks like he knows I didn't vote for him.*

Mike O'Brien studied Greg skeptically. *"Could* it have blown up?"

"Lord knows it could happen—they build their reactors out of the world's spare parts. And their engineering's none too swift. For example, only after the foundation of the Daya Bay power plant near Hong Kong was laid did the Chinese find out that the workmen had been reading the blueprints *upside down.*" Greg wished he had something to hold. "We regularly get unconfirmed horror stories about their nuclear program. The Lhasa reactor is—was—in the twelve-thousand megawatt range, so enough fuel was present. Also, it was a graphite-modulated, boiling-water plant, which is old technology."

"Like Chernobyl?" the secretary of energy asked.

"Like Chernobyl."

"What are you doing to find out?" O'Brien interjected.

"As I said, we've got all available sensors trained on the area." Greg hesitated. He glanced at French, who nodded. "Also, we've got some new stuff just coming on line that should help a lot."

"But, you don't know yet."

"No," Greg replied tersely, irritated by O'Brien's combativeness. "And I don't know when we will know." Greg didn't see the wink that Rodriguez slipped him.

"Try to make it as soon as possible, Doctor," the president said. "Thank you for your briefing. Please keep us informed." He glanced at French. "Elliot, will you see Dr. Miahara out?"

Greg took a deep breath as they walked toward the elevator. "Who was that Grand Inquisitor in there?"

"Mike O'Brien, the president's hatchet man. Don't worry about standing up to him—it earned you the respect of everyone in the room. Except O'Brien, but he doesn't count."

The Secret Service agent at the end of the corridor opened the elevator doors. "Take the doctor anywhere he wants to go, Watkins," French instructed. "And, while you're at it, find him a beer."

✧ ✧ ✧

"Let me go, Ganden," Jake urged as they sped along the airport road. "When we get to the airport, my friends and I will get on the first flight out of here." *Assuming we're still alive by then*, Jake added mentally. "I may disapprove of your methods, but I'm no threat to you." Jake divided his attention between keeping the winding road in the headlights and the struggle apparent on the young Tibetan's face.

"I wish I could believe you," Ganden said at length. "But after this—" He gestured at Jake's laptop, which he was cradling on his knees. His face and his tone hardened. "Kailas will know what to do with you. Perhaps he will let you go."

From your description of this Atilla the Hun of yours, Jake thought, *I doubt it.* "How do you propose to get us back into Lhasa?" Jake asked.

Ganden pointed. "See that culvert ahead? Pull off the road when we get to it."

Dust swirled around the Land Cruiser as Jake brought it to a stop. The dry wash cut across the road on its way to the Kyichu. At Ganden's orders, Jake pointed the Land Cruiser's headlights down the culvert. They got out of the Land Cruiser and walked toward the short overpass that spanned the wash.

As they passed under the road, Jake bumped into something. He looked down. In front of him was a small coracle, a boat no more than eight feet long, made of dried yak hide stretched over a wooden frame.

"Pick it up," Ganden ordered. Jake shouldered the small boat easily. "Bring it to the river. Kailas keeps this here in case we want to cross the river unobserved by the sentries." *Careful, Mac*, Jake warned himself. *If Atilla is this prepared, he must be smarter than he sounds.*

With the boat on his back, Jake crunched along the gravelly beach toward the river. The headlights spotlighted small, spiky plants with purple, thistlelike flowers dotting the shore.

"Now we hide your truck," Ganden ordered as Jake set the boat at the water's edge. "Kailas will be able to make use of it."

Once they had hidden the Land Cruiser in the culvert, they went back to the water's edge. Ganden pointed across the river, toward where a black hump blotted out the lights of Lhasa. "See that island? That's Jarmalinka. From there, we'll walk." He handed Jake the paddle he had picked up from beneath the overpass. "You'll paddle. Careful getting into the boat. Keep your feet on the wood. The hide is brittle—if you step on it, you'll put your foot right through it."

Jake looked at the cold, fast-flowing river and balanced himself carefully on the thwarts. Ganden shoved off, and beneath the midnight stars they made their way toward Jarmalinka Island.

✧ ✧ ✧

"Package for you, Inspector." The sergeant set the lumpy parcel, wrapped in brown paper and string, on Chen's desk. Chen yawned, finished his morning cup of tea, and lit his first cigarette of the day.

Chen peered at the package. The only markings on it were HUA CHEN, PSB, written in brown ink. Interested, Chen found a pair of scissors and slit the parcel open, then pulled the paper back. His astonished bellow brought half the station rushing into his office.

✧ ✧ ✧

The president waited calmly in front of his desk as the Chinese ambassador was ushered in. Mike O'Brien flanked the president on one side. On the other was Melinda Cunningham, the secretary of state.

"You wished to see me, Ambassador Liu?" the president asked.

Liu stopped halfway across the small room and surveyed the trio in front of him. He noted O'Brien's usual latent hostility. He could read nothing in Cunningham's face, enhancing her already considerable reputation for inscrutability.

"Mr. President, it is with deep regret that I must bring a most unfortunate matter to your attention." All three Americans were instantly on guard. Straightforwardness from an official of the Chinese government meant that a crisis was both imminent and severe. "At 5:00 A.M. eastern time, as you undoubtedly know, there was a tremendous explosion in my country."

The president frowned. "We noted what appeared to be a nuclear detonation in your country last night. It was assumed that the blast was yet another test of which you had failed to inform us." He looked sharply at Liu. "I must reiterate my insistence that your government adhere to the terms of our prenotification treaty."

"The blast was entirely unscheduled, Mr. President," Liu replied slowly.

"You're saying that it wasn't a test?" O'Brien interjected.

Liu smiled thinly. "Quite right, Mr. O'Brien. A power-generating plant and a satellite tracking station in the province of Xizang were destroyed by a tremendous explosion."

The president relaxed slightly. "I'm sorry to hear that. I hope that the loss of life was minimal."

The Chinese ambassador paused for a long moment. "I find it odd that you should wish such a thing, Mr. President."

"Why is that?" the president asked with a puzzled frown.

The ambassador's eyes hardened. "Is not one of the objectives of war to maximize the enemy's casualties?"

"And just precisely what do you mean by that?" Melinda Cunningham snapped.

Liu looked up at her. "I mean precisely that, in the eyes of my government, the United States of America has committed an unprovoked act of war against the People's Republic of China."

A stunned silence enveloped the Oval Office.

The president was the first to recover. "Mr. Ambassador," he replied evenly, "*war* is not a term to be used lightly in this room. I must insist that you provide us with full particulars as to this alleged act of war."

Liu opened his briefcase and took out a sealed envelope. "This letter from Premier Wing details the incident." He handed the envelope to the president. "It also states that if an explanation satisfactory to my government is not received within forty-eight hours, this private letter will turn into a public declaration." Liu snapped his briefcase shut. "Of war."

The ambassador walked back toward the door to the Oval Office. He paused with his hand on the doorknob. "I do hope this situation is resolved, Mr. President."

"I am sure it will be, Ambassador Liu."

"I would dislike being recalled to Beijing," Liu replied. "You see, while I've been posted here, I've grown quite fond of that American cuisine called . . ." Liu frowned, then smiled. "Ah, yes. Tex-Mex."

❖ ❖ ❖

A chorus of superstitious curses swept the knot of people gathered in Chen's office. Sitting on brown paper in the middle of his desk was an amputated hand, fingers and thumb drawn up into a fist.

The superintendent was the first to recover. "Where did this come from?" he demanded to know.

"Pedicab," the sergeant who had delivered it to Chen replied. "I was on the front desk when this driver came in, handed it to me, and trotted out."

"Did you recognize him?"

"Never seen him before."

"Find him," the superintendent ordered. The sergeant hurried out. The superintendent bent over the hand. "Looks like it's wearing a ring," he observed. Gingerly, Chen used a letter opener to flip the hand over. His grunt of recognition caused his boss to look up.

"Xongnu," Chen muttered. "One of our informants."

"Who," the superintendent asked, "didn't like him?"

"Nobody likes snitches," Chen replied dryly. "But Xongnu was a small-time operator. I can't imagine what he'd know that'd make him worth killing."

Unwilling to spend too much time on the death of a Tibetan, Chen's boss turned to go. "Ask around. Find out if he annoyed anybody recently."

Jake woke from an uneasy doze. Footsteps echoed in the hall outside the storage room in which Ganden had imprisoned him.

Jake got up as the door opened. A man surveyed him coldly from the entrance to the cell. *I'm half a foot taller than he is,* Jake decided. *But I bet I don't outweigh him. This guy looks like an escapee from the cover of one of the body-building magazines.*

"You are the man called Kailas?" Jake asked. Ganden withered under the look Barabise gave him.

Barabise stared arrogantly up at Jake. "Talk, spy," the nomad commanded. "Tell us who you work for, and I'll give you back to the Han."

Jake shook his head. "I'm not a spy. I'm a professional photojournalist here by invitation of the Chinese government."

"Which is not here in Tibet by *our* invitation!" Barabise thundered. He thrust his face up toward Jake's. "You, spy, are in league with those who ravish and plunder our homeland." The Khampa grabbed Jake's laptop and thrust it under his nose. "With this you were gathering data to enable the Han and your CIA to more efficiently rape *Per La.*" The computer exploded as Barabise flung it against the far wall of the cell.

Jake winced. *So much for my insurance premiums . . .*

Barabise stared at Jake. *This feringy is just like the other CIA spy. The one who so long ago recruited us and then deserted us when we needed him most.* His anger exploded, and he arced his massive left fist toward Jake's head.

Reflexively, Jake's hand came up and caught Barabise's fist. He swayed as he absorbed the force of the swing, then his muscles knotted as he steeled himself. Eyes locked, sweat beaded the men's foreheads as their silent struggle intensified. Ganden watched as, with clenched teeth, Jake slowly forced Barabise's arm to his side. Jake let go abruptly of Barabise's fist, then sidestepped as the off-balance nomad staggered past him.

As Jake crouched, ready to strike, Barabise whirled. Sunlight glittered from his *thupta*. Keeping the dagger between himself and Jake, the Khampa chieftain circled toward the door.

"In time, *feringy*," Barabise growled. "In time. When I have reclaimed my land, I will return for you." He pointed at the shattered laptop. "That, for you. In time."

31

As Randy Cavanaugh took off his dripping raincoat, Gil Markham rose from behind his desk in an office on the third floor of the U.S. embassy in Manila. He stuck out his hand. "Good to see you again, Cavanaugh," Markham said with a grin. "You lost as usual, or just here for the beer?" The CIA station chief shared his old friend's fondness for San Miguel, the Philippines' national brew.

Randy shook hands and pulled up a chair. "I don't know what I'm doing here. I was hanging around Kiev, minding other people's business as usual, when I get a FLASH to come see you." He looked inquiringly at Markham. "So you tell me; am I here for the beer, or did you just need someone to beat you at cribbage?"

"Wish it was both. Unfortunately, it's neither." Markham pulled a folder from a desk drawer. "You know about Russian troops massing along the Chinese border."

"That's why I was nosing around up there."

"Here's what you don't know: Six days ago, a 757 plowed in on its final approach to Lhasa." Markham handed Randy a copy of the *New York Times* article.

Randy glanced at the clipping. "How'd they get a photo of the wreckage?"

"Some hotshot smuggled it out. Beats me how he managed it."

"Don't tell me that this is why I'm here."

"Nope. This is. *This* happened yesterday."

Randy opened the folder Markham handed him. He scanned the two-page report. Then he sat upright and read it again, slowly.

"Let me see if I've got this straight," Randy said incredulously. "The Chinese are accusing us of using the space shuttle to blow up a nuclear power plant that they deny exists."

"You got it." Markham rested his elbows on his desk. "It's starting to get out of hand. The old men in Beijing are going ape. The Chinese ambassador's been crawling all over the president, accusing him of everything from collusion with the Russians to belching in church."

He grinned at Randy. "And you get to be our man on the scene."

"What about Eddie Kwan?" Randy asked. "Wasn't he just posted to that part of China?"

"He was. Unfortunately his cover was interpreter for the consul in Guangzhou, which means that he—"

"He was on that 757," Randy finished. He sighed. "Well, I *was* getting tired of borscht and potatoes." Randy put his feet up on Markham's desk. "You got my stuff?"

The CIA station chief nodded. He held up an envelope. "It's all here. Australian passport, Nepalese and Chinese visas, airline ticket to Kathmandu, and big bucks in both rupees and yuan."

"Kathmandu? Not Lhasa?"

"Nope. The crash closed Lhasa airport."

Randy grimaced, then flipped through the well-worn passport. "Nice stuff. But why Australian? And why did I have to come here to get it?"

"Australian because Americans are *persona non grata* in

China right now. And here because our New Delhi office doesn't have the equipment to do the job. Without a PC and a color laser printer, that full-page multicolor Nepalese visa would take a week to forge. Our documents officer did it in five minutes." Randy smiled at the pride in his friend's voice. "Finally, Vicki's looking forward to having you over for dinner. And you've never seen the twins."

Randy smiled again. He had introduced Vicki Lambert to Gil when the two men were roommates at Bowdoin. "Cribbage afterwards?" Randy asked.

"You got it."

From atop the Chagpori, Ganden and Tenzig surveyed the devastation. Smoke billowed from the fires that still burned furiously in the middle of the huge crater that had been the People's Glory Power Plant. Knots of people were huddled in front of the apartment buildings on the edge of Lhasa that had been knocked off their foundations by the force of the blast. Sirens and flashing lights were everywhere.

"Look at it!" Tenzig exulted. "The Han can't ignore us now."

"Look at what?" Ganden replied, appalled at the carnage in front of him. "At the full hospitals where the dead are piled outside? At the ruined homes? At the children blinded by the heat and radiation? Over three hundred of our people are dead, with more to follow." Ganden shook his head. "It wasn't supposed to be like this."

"Radical changes require radical measures," Tenzig replied. "That's what Kailas says."

Ganden glared at his friend. "So now you are quoting Kailas. Will you tomorrow be compiling his thoughts into your own version of Chairman Mao's *Little Red Book?*"

Tenzig put his arm around Ganden's shoulders. "Calm

down, Ganden. I understand your anger—I'd be upset too if I had discovered the American I was supposed to escort was a spy."

Distracted by this change of topic, Ganden looked at his friend. "You know about that?"

"Kailas told me all about it after you got in last night. He says you did exactly the right thing." Tenzig beamed, his adulation of the Khampa chieftain showing clearly on his face. "Do you know what he's going to do with the American? Kailas is going to hand him over to the Han and tell them that he is a CIA spy responsible for the blast. At the same time, Kailas is going to start telling our people that it was Han mismanagement and corruption that caused the deaths of their friends and relatives. That way the Han are distracted, the people are stirred up, and we are free to strike again." Tenzig pulled Ganden toward the path. "Let's go back to our base. Puzhen and your sister Tali are there, and I bet they'll both be glad to see you."

"Absolutely not, Mr. President," Chief of Staff Rodriguez was saying as French took his seat at the emergency session of the National Security Council. "The shuttle mission had nothing to do with the destruction of the power plant." Melinda Cunningham, seated next to French, handed him a scarlet folder marked TOP SECRET.

French reached the bottom of his copy of Premier Wing's letter. He looked up in disbelief. "They must be joking!"

"They're dead serious," Rodriguez replied. "Our latest satellite photos show increased troop redeployment, and all of their Han-class attack submarines and Xia-class boomers have left their berths at Guangzhou and Huludao."

French grimaced. "Both the attack and the missile subs have bugged out, eh? Don't like that very much. I guess that explains why Admiral Harrison isn't here."

"Right," Rodriguez confirmed. "He's enroute to Hawaii

to confer with CINCPAC, the commander in chief of the Pacific."

"If I read this letter correctly," French continued, "the Chinese are claiming that *Discovery* was responsible for the destruction of that tracking station." The DDO shook his head. "General Rodriguez is right. No way *Discovery* was involved."

A phone chimed quietly. Mike O'Brien answered it, listened for a moment, then hung up. He pointed at a tall and slender rod atop a short, squat box that jutted up from the table like an architect's nightmare. A green light in the base came on.

"Can you hear me, Colonel Ellis?" the president said into the conference phone's omnidirectional microphone.

"Five-by-five, sir," the commander of the shuttle *Discovery* replied.

"Have you had time to review the information sent up to you?"

"Yes sir, I have." Ellis stared at the sheet that hung, suspended in zero-gravity, in front of his eyes. *And for this sort of grief I gave up the command of a whole squadron of F-17As.*

"The Chinese claim that a particle-beam type of weapon was fired from *Discovery* just before the explosion. Is that true?"

"No sir. It is not."

"Could any activity aboard the shuttle have triggered the blast?"

"None that I know of, Mr. President. We were in powerdown mode at the time—our version of night. Most of us were asleep."

"Were there any sort of transmissions at all from *Discovery?*"

"The communications log shows none that were initiated here, sir."

Melinda Cunningham spoke up. "Colonel Ellis, this is the secretary of state. Are you saying that, at the time of the explosion, *Discovery* was transmitting?"

"Were almost always transmitting something, ma'am.

Telemetry, flight dynamics data, that sort of thing. At the time of the explosion, we were acting as a relay station."

Cunningham's reply was interrupted by O'Brien's up-raised hand. "Thirty seconds until we lose our secure uplink," he told the president.

"Thank you, Colonel," the president concluded. "You've corroborated nicely what we already know. I just wanted your personal verification. Happy landings."

"Thanks, Mr. President. *Discovery* out." Ellis stared out the flight deck windows at the clouded Earth below. *Sure hope there's something left to land on. . . .*

"So the shuttle *was* transmitting," Cunningham said accusingly.

"Ellis was telling the truth," French replied. "No transmissions were being *generated* aboard the shuttle. We were using *Discovery* as a relay. That's one of the reasons its course was changed."

"What sort of a relay?" the president asked.

"We were downloading some information."

"How was it being transmitted?" the secretary of state inquired.

"Via short-pulse laser."

Melinda Cunningham frowned. "A laser? Is this related to Star Wars?" French smiled. "No, ma'am. This was not an SDI weapon. The laser in question was an argon laser, in the milliwatt range." He caught the secretary's eye. "Much less powerful than the one your dermatologist used to remove that birthmark last year." All present studiously ignored Cunningham's incredulous blush.

"To whom was the information transmitted?" the president asked. "One of your agents?" When French hesitated, the president glowered at the DDO. "Cut to the chase, Elliot. I'm your boss, not some freshman congressman out to make a name for himself."

"No sir. Not to a CIA operative. The recipient of the information was a civilian photojournalist, cooperating with us on this one assignment."

"And where is he operating?"

"Lhasa, Tibet."

"Which is where the tracking station and power plant were."

French nodded.

"What was the nature of the information we were transmitting to him?" the vice president asked.

"We were telling him what to take pictures of. However, given the relative transmissivity of the carrier—"

The president cut French off with a gesture. "Save the details for later. If there *is* a later." He leaned forward. "Let me get this straight. China is about to declare war on us because we were suggesting photo ops to some hack photographer? Elliot, this time you've really done it. If we live through this I'll have you guarding Elvis's grave until you're old and gray."

The president lightly banged a knuckle against his chin, a sign to all who knew him that he was worried. "How do we prove to the Chinese that the signal they accurately detected as coming from the shuttle had nothing to do with the sudden destruction of their tracking station?"

"A good question," French responded. "How *do* you prove a negative?"

"*That*, Elliot, is exactly what you have to figure out. Forget the Graceland duty—if you don't come up with an answer in less than forty-six hours, I'm staking you out at ground zero." The president's face became grim. "All joking aside, people, we've got work to do."

After a quick survey of his fellow chiefs of staff, Roddy Rodriguez spoke up from the far end of the table. "Mr. President?"

"What is it, Roddy?"

"We need to begin to shift to a war footing." The Situation Room was dead quiet. "It'll take the better part of a day to deploy our forces according to plan and get all our subs out to sea. We also need to begin shifting some of our assets to secondary bases."

Everyone in the room knew the rationale behind the redeployment. If the country's prime military installations were taken out in a preemptive nuclear strike, an effective retaliation could be launched from forces that had been hidden at civilian and commercial airfields.

The president straightened up. "Very well, General. I'm declaring DEFCON Two. Deploy your forces for combat." Rodriguez grabbed a phone.

The president glanced at the Situation Room door. On the other side, a uniformed air force captain sat with a briefcase resting on his knees. Called the "football," it held the codes for arming and firing the nation's nuclear weapons as well as the means for transmitting the firing order. *I don't know the captain's name*, the president thought, *and I hope I don't have to find out.*

"Mr. President," the secretary of the interior said quietly, "I should authorize FEMA to begin preparing Mount Weather."

The president nodded. "Do it."

The secretary grabbed another of the phones in the room. At his command, the bunker to which top government officials would retreat in event of war was begun to be brought on line.

Built in 1958, the "Special Facility" was a massive underground complex located forty-eight air miles west of Washington in the Virginia hills. Designed to survive a direct nuclear hit, it was the cornerstone of the Federal Emergency Management Agency's "Continuity of Government" plan. If evacuation of the capital became necessary, those government officials holding special, electronically encoded evacuee cards would assemble at predesignated sites, where they would be helicoptered to Mount Weather. Once there, they would run the country from their small, subterranean city. Completely self-sustaining, Mount Weather would provide them for weeks with the sustenance and technology to begin dealing with the specter of post-nuclear-war America.

At the mention of Mount Weather, Melinda Cunningham looked up sharply. Because the secretary of state was fourth in the order of presidential succession, she had been issued an evacuee card. Cunningham kept it in her wallet, tucked between pictures of her husband and her daughter, son-in-law, and grandson. None of them had cards.

"Melinda," the president ordered, "start calling our NATO allies. Begin with Prime Minister Wakefield. Tell them that I'll call each of them personally within the next twelve hours." He paused, measuring each of them with his eyes. "We'll meet back here every four hours until the crisis is resolved." The president stood, bringing all of the others to their feet. "Let's go, and may God be with us."

Chen walked into the office of the Chinese doctor who doubled as the PSB pathologist in Lhasa. On the back of the surgery door a chart pinpointed on a human figure the two thousand locations used in acupuncture. Wooden drawers filled with herbal medicines lined the walls. Atop one of the cabinets a knot of preserved snakes glared balefully from within their jar of alcohol.

"Thought you might want to see this," the pathologist told Chen. "I was having difficulty folding back the fingers until I noticed this." The doctor pointed with a pair of forceps to the one finger he had pried open. "See the flesh missing from the fingertip? Now look at this." He pointed to the palm.

Chen bent over and peered at the hand. The missing flesh was secured to the palm by a thread that came out of the palm, looped over it, and disappeared into the hand on the other side. "It looks like someone sewed the hand up."

"Very neatly, too," the pathologist concurred. "I couldn't make better sutures myself. When I noticed this, I wanted you to be here for the rest of the procedure."

As Chen watched, the physician reached underneath each fingertip with a pair of long-nosed scissors and snipped the thread. When he was finished, he pulled the fingers back.

"*Waah!*" both men exclaimed.

The doctor examined the dark, jagged lines that covered the informant's palm. He probed one with his scissors, then looked at Chen. "Burned in."

Chen stared at the lines. "Looks like writing."

"Nonsense!" the pathologist snorted. "Those aren't Chinese characters."

"Not Chinese. Tibetan."

"Do you know what it says?"

"No. I speak the language, but I don't read it." Chen took out his notebook and began carefully copying the letters. "Please have the thread sent to Beijing for analysis," he asked when he was through.

The doctor gazed at the lines. "What kind of person would burn a message into a man's palm?"

"I don't know," Chen replied grimly. "But I intend to find out. Thank you, Doctor."

"One more thing, Inspector."

Chen turned back from the surgery door. "Yes?"

"This man was mutilated before his hand was chopped off."

Chen frowned. "How do you know?"

"See this webbing here?" The doctor pointed between Xongnu's fingers. "See how it's torn? Such tearing can occur when the filaments of the palmar branch of the median nerve, which run through the palm, are overstimulated and spread the fingers too far apart."

"'Overstimulated' like in being burned?"

The pathologist nodded. "This wouldn't have happened if the hand had been amputated first." He looked at Chen. "Take care, Inspector. When you find your man, you'll also find a madman."

32

Tears glistened in the corners of Puzhen's eyes. "I don't know who you are, Ganden Nesang, but you're not the man I fell in love with. Look at you! You stand there, stone-faced, telling me how the incinerated bodies of your coworkers' children will further the cause of Tibetan liberation. But what about them? Their only crime was to be children, playing next to the plant while their parents worked. What have you done for them? What have you done *to* them? The Ganden I love would have wept over their little bodies, not used a weapon on them and then used them as weapons." She stared at him in anguish. "Where is your sorrow? Where are your tears? Cry, Ganden. *Please* cry. Jesus wept—and I cannot marry a man who won't." Puzhen's hand went to her throat, and Ganden's engagement necklace tore apart as she ripped it from her neck. Turquoise and coral beads clattered at his feet as she fled.

✧ ✧ ✧

"Did she say anything after you picked her up at the airport?" Pat asked.

Joel shook his head. "I tried, and she was nice about it, but mostly she just stared out the window. Did you talk with her?"

JON HENDERSON

Pat leaned against the island in the middle of her kitchen. "I didn't have the chance. She was out walking all afternoon."

"So, now what?"

"We let her be."

"But—"

Pat smiled at her husband's frustration. "I know, love. When Annie was little, sulking was against our rules. But she's not little any more, and she's not sulking. She's going through something completely new and foreign to her, and she deserves time alone to work through it."

"She wasn't like this after she was abducted last year."

"Different circumstances. You and I both know that Annie cares much less about herself than she does about others. If you remember, she told us after you and Jake rescued her that the hardest thing about her time being held captive in Peru was not knowing how Jake and Lee were. Plus, she was only enamored of Jake then; she's in love with him now." Pat paused. "I often wondered how she'd take it if something tragic happened to someone dear to her—one of us, Lee or Jake, or one of her first graders. Now, in a way, we'll get to see how she handles it."

Seeing Joel grimace and shift restlessly, Pat walked over and sat down beside him. "You don't get to fix it this time, love," she said with gentle firmness. "You have a passion for helping others—and most of the time that's positive. You rescued the Ashaninka Indians years ago, and you went back to Peru to get Annie. You even saved me from a life as an old maid." Joel returned Pat's smile and laid his hand on hers. "But sometimes being a rescuer can be an interference. God is using this to teach both Jake and Annie something, and all we can do is wait." Pat squeezed Joel's hand. "There's nothing worse you can do to others than to rescue them from God's difficult training ground."

One corner of Joel's mouth twitched his grudging acquiescence. Prescribing a quick change of subject, she asked. "Have you found out anything?"

Joel sat up. "Not a thing. Elliot says that embassy row in Beijing has been practically marching *en masse* daily to the Great Hall of the People to try and find out what's happened to their nationals. And, as usual, the Chinese profess quiet astonishment and claim that nothing has happened. The officials in Lhasa are probably tearing their hair out because a disaster of this magnitude had the temerity to occur while a bunch of foreign photojournalists are on hand to document it." Joel smiled wryly. "The Chinese government knows that hard evidence has an annoying tendency to wreak havoc with their policy of 'tinker with the facts until they fit the party line.' What's probably going on is that Jake and company are locked down tight in the Lhasa Hotel, beating their guards at poker and waiting to be evicted to Chengdu. Everyone who might find anything out knows to call me ASAP." Joel looked toward Anne's room. "Until then, we wait."

"I take it you're here to offer your profound thanks for my getting you off the hook once again," Chen said as the PLA lieutenant sat down across the desk from the inspector. Chen tossed a pack of cigarettes to his old friend. "An evening at the Lotus Blossom will do nicely by way of way of compensation."

"I'd gladly stand you to a night of drinking *maotai* if there was anything to celebrate. Trouble is, there isn't." The soldier lit his cigarette before continuing. "You're in a pretty good mood, considering what's happened around here recently."

Chen shrugged. "Actually, my part in it is almost over. Other than supervise the evacuation of the foreigners to Chengdu, most of the load is now on the Internal Division. Needless to say, Beijing wants an acceptable explanation very soon."

"Aren't you still working on the crash?"

"Not really. The next of kin have been notified, and the site cleaned up. Now, the only thing left is to wait for the report of the investigating board."

The lieutenant, wise in the ways of the Chinese bureaucracy, smiled thinly. "A matter, I presume, of rendering the report suitably 'acceptable'?"

"No chance of that. The flight recorder was damaged too badly for our people, so the Americans shoved them aside and took over." Chen laughed. "Like it or not, the truth will come out."

The lieutenant nodded understandingly. "I hope the truth also comes out about that piece of equipment you dropped off."

"It's not yours?" Chen asked.

"Not only is it not ours, it isn't even PLA issue."

"Then, whose is it?"

"That's what I was really hoping you'd be able to tell me. I had to send it to Beijing for identification—that's why it's taken me so long to get back to you. Turns out that it's Soviet made." The lieutenant nodded seriously as Chen stared at him. "And the powers-that-be in Beijing are climbing up my back to find out just exactly how it got onto Chinese soil. Especially *Tibetan* Chinese soil." Twin streams of smoke shot from the soldier's nostrils as he exhaled.

"I wish I knew," Chen confessed. "A *dopka* found it and brought it to me." The inspector leaned back in his chair and smoked as he told his friend the story. "Then," Chen finished, "the old hag dragged me up the cliffs above Gonggar to show me where she had found it. Cost me—"

Chen stopped suddenly as his friend came up out of his chair. "Where did she find it?" the lieutenant asked intently.

"Up above the airport. About two kilometers east. Why?"

The soldier's eyes narrowed as he thought. "It can't be. But it *must* be."

"What?" Chen demanded to know.

"What you dropped off is a Soviet missile launcher. A Soviet *surface-to-air* missile launcher."

Chen's eyes became as narrow as his friend's. "Are you trying to tell me that—"

"Exactly. *Our* airliners may suddenly fall from the sky, but brand-new American planes piloted by experienced American pilots do not. That 757 was shot down by someone using your old woman's little toy." The soldier watched Chen's face as the truth sank in.

"But," Chen asked slowly, "who around here could use such a thing?"

The lieutenant laughed. "That's the rub. The Soviet soldier is stupid, and his weapons are designed accordingly. Anyone with five minute's training—even your drunken old *dopka*—could have pointed the launcher and pulled the trigger." He stood to go. "Let me know when you get the report from the investigative team; for once, the truth may serve us well. Until then no *maotai* for either of us, as much as we may need it."

For the twentieth time, Jake tested the lock on his cell door and found it sturdy as ever. Frustrated, he resumed his pacing. *OK,* he thought, his hands flexing as he planned, *if I can just overpower the next guy to come through that door and get out of here, then I can—* Jake stopped. *Then I can what? I'm smack dab in the middle of a mountainous, inhospitable police state two miles in the air. I don't speak the language, I can't disappear into a crowd, and everybody is on the lookout for me anyway. Get a grip, Mac.*

Jake tripped over the demolished PC and sent it skittering across the floor. He eyed its remains. *Joel always says that stealth is stronger than steel. So let's dismantle this stealth computer of his and see if we can find anything to prove him right.*

He sat down and began disassembling the PC, arranging the ruined machine's components around him in a semicircle.

The first thing he picked up was the PC's battery, a brick about the size and weight of a bar of soap. *It's a lithium-hydride battery that hasn't been used all that much, so it should be still almost fully charged. I hope.*

Jake pulled the laptop's motherboard from its case. *Now for part number two. If this thing breaks, I'm sunk.* Jake carefully applied pressure to a small black box on the motherboard, pushing on alternate sides until it snapped off into his hand. He held it up, smiling at the four fine wires it trailed.

Last, but certainly not least, is the heart of this hi-tech knuckle duster. Jake popped open the screw-on base of the "flash unit" that had served as the satellite transmitter for his now defunct PC. A fat blue cylinder the size of two D batteries slid out of the transmitter and into his hand. *Greg said that this was one of those new carbon-metal supercapacitors developed by the SDI folks. Maybe that means it'll hold enough juice to do the trick.* Holding the two wires it trailed close to where they were attached to the cylinder, Jake tugged gently until they came loose from inside the transmitter. *Now for the fun part.*

Jake twisted the cylinder's two wires together with two of the wires from the black box. Gingerly he touched the box's other two wires to the battery's terminals. When nothing happened, Jake relaxed. *Sure am glad I paid attention during all those field electronics classes in Ranger OCS.* He looked at his construction. *If I'm doing this right, six volts are flowing out of the battery, being stepped up to three hundred volts by the DC-to-DC converter, and then charging the hundred-millifarad capacitor that used to power the laser pump in the transmitter.*

Twenty minutes later he removed the wires from the battery's terminals. *Only one way to find out if that's enough of a charge.* Jake detached the capacitor from the converter. *Time to field-test this contraption.* He went over to the door and began to pound on it thunderously.

✧ ✧ ✧

"It figures," Susan Kirkcaldy muttered. "Makes sense that this'd be my lot."

"Huh?" Greg replied absently, his eyes fixed on the screen in front of him. "A lot of what?"

"After a lifetime of advancing the frontiers of particle physics, it figures that my doom would come in the form of a nuclear missile. And a Chinese one at that." She shook her head. "It'll probably be the only one of the bunch that actually works, too." Susan looked pensively at Greg. "But that's not what really worries me."

"Sounds good enough to me," Greg replied.

"No what really terrifies me is that I, a loyal subject of Her Britannic Majesty Queen Elizabeth II, will be blown to kingdom come surrounded by Yanks. When the good Saint Peter sees that it's a bunch of you Americans, he will probably relegate the lot of us to the inferno out of hand, without ever giving me a chance to plead for clemency by reason of place of birth." Her exaggerated sigh filled the room. "Oh well. Such are the 'slings and arrows of outrageous fortune.'"

Greg hit the ENTER key on his keyboard. "Let's see if this works. We need a lot of data, and we need it *fast*. So, since we can't go up and down quickly enough, let's try going sideways." He leaned back in his chair. "Is there anything you don't talk with Jeremy about?" Greg asked diffidently.

"Quite a few things, actually," Susan admitted.

"Like?"

"Like how much suet to put in the Christmas pudding, or what type of nappies are best for our youngest granddaughter. Things about which he neither knows nor cares. But—" Susan waited until she had Greg's eye. "If it's something of import that concerns the two of us, then it's brought out in the open at the earliest appropriate moment. If you can't talk about something with your spouse, then you need to talk with someone about why you can't."

Greg's hand went to his shirt pocket. His fingers closed around a phone message from Brian Ichikawa, M.D., suggesting a game of handball followed by lunch. "Keep an eye on it for me, will you?" he asked Susan. "I've got a phone call to make."

"It uploaded clean," Greg said happily when he returned from his office. "Now let's beta-test it using the TDRSS. If it works, we can call Elliot and tell him that we're back on the air."

❖ ❖ ❖

With a curse the guard unlocked the door to Jake's cell. He shoved it open and interrogated Jake with a grunt.

"*Kalak!*" Jake demanded, pointing to his mouth and rubbing his stomach. "*Kalak!*" With another curse the man slammed the door behind him.

Jake took the capacitor from his shirt pocket. With his teeth he stripped more of the insulation from the wires attached to the capacitor. Jake wound one wire around the iron door handle. The other he bent carefully out of the way. Then he stepped back and waited.

A few minutes later the guard's key grated in the lock. He shoved the door open with his foot and motioned threateningly with his automatic rifle. Jake obediently backed into a corner of the cell, watching the swinging capacitor anxiously as he did so. *If that free wire contacts anything metal, I've had it.* The guard set a bowl of barley gruel on the floor just inside the door, then backed out of the cell.

Jake darted toward the closing door. He grabbed the capacitor by its blue plastic covering. Jake ran his fingers down the free wire, careful to keep them on the insulation. When he heard the grating of the key in the lock, Jake touched the bare end of the wire he was holding to the door handle. There was a *snap* and a blue-white spark as the capacitor discharged its accumulated voltage into the lock.

Jake heard a gasp from the other side of the door, followed by a muffled *thump.*

He opened the door and dragged the body of the unconscious guard into the cell. He stepped into the hallway. No one was in sight.

Chen opened his notebook and laid it on the counter of the CITS office. "Can someone tell me what this means?" he asked.

Several of the Tibetan tour guides clustered around the counter. "His writing is terrible!" one of them, new to Lhasa, laughed.

"You're right, it is," Chen replied in flawless Tibetan. "Now tell me what it means." Dumbfounded, the new guide stared at Chen as the rest roared with laughter.

The senior guide spoke up. "It says, 'Forest of Razors,' *genla.*"

Chen frowned. "What does that mean?"

"In our faith," the man explained, "there are eighteen hells. Eight are fiery, and eight are freezing. Those who fail to attain Nirvana are consigned to one or more of them. But the last two are special hells, reserved for those who incur the wrath of the gods. Of the two special hells, the Forest of Razors is by far the worst." A collective shudder ran through the Tibetans.

"Why did you tell him that?" the new guide asked after Chen had left.

The older guide merely smiled as he put on his jacket. "I'll be back."

He looks tired, Rodriguez thought as he assessed his commander from across the Oval Office. The president hadn't shaved, and his tie hung loosely at his unbuttoned collar. *Can't really blame him for being beat, seeing what he's going through, but tired men make mistakes.*

"Any news from that amateur agent of yours?" the president asked Elliot French.

"MacIntyre's not due to report in until 9:00 A.M., our time."

"We've already used *Discovery* once to drop him a line," Mike O'Brien observed. "Why don't we just get hold of him and tell him to phone home?"

"Two reasons. First, MacIntyre's operating from a prearranged transmission schedule. Until his next report, it's impossible to reach him. Next, you can bet that the Chinese have every satellite dish they own trained on the shuttle, just waiting for it to transmit again." The DDO looked bleakly at the chief of staff. "We don't know of anything they have that could knock *Discovery* out of the sky, but are you willing to find out the hard way that we're wrong?"

The president drummed his fingers on his desk. "We need to know what's going on over there. Is there any way to contact MacIntyre?"

French nodded. "Tonight is one time when his transmit and receive schedules coincide."

Melinda Cunningham looked worried. "But I thought you just said that we can't use the shuttle to communicate with him."

French grinned. "We won't. Greg Miahara, that hotshot optophysicist who was here today, just checked in with a way around this. The Chinese will be listening to the shuttle, not the TDRSS satellite that we tried to use initially. It can transmit short amounts of data quite adequately. So, while *Discovery* keeps them busy, we'll sneak an electronic note to MacIntyre via the TDRSS. If PHONE HOME appears on his screen, he'll know what to do."

"This cannot endanger the shuttle crew in any way," the president stated.

"It won't, sir," French replied. "We'll be delivering our

news via the paperboy while the Chinese are watching for Federal Express."

The president looked at his secretary of state. "We'll have thirty-three hours after we talk to MacIntyre, Melinda. How are you going to manage to come up with something that'll at least get the Chinese to talk?"

Cunningham smiled grimly. "Easy. As long as I don't tell my staff that we've been asked to do the impossible, they should have no problem."

A red light on the president's phone began blinking. O'Brien answered it, then handed the phone to Cunningham. All present watched the Secretary's face fall as she listened. Cunningham spoke briefly, then hung up.

"What's up?" the president asked his old friend. "Lose this week's lottery?"

Cunningham sat back down. "That was Ambassador Liu. He was calling to inform me officially that Beijing has recalled him for 'consultations.' He's to leave immediately."

"So?" O'Brien interjected. "That's routine in situations like this."

"So it is," Cunningham agreed. "What *isn't* routine is what he really called about. Seems that Beijing also told him to inform us, officially, that they aren't going to accept any evidence that we present unless Liu brings it back with him."

The president shook his head. "That makes no sense at all. Any idea what they're up to?"

"Liu's sure that it's an attempt to force us into preemptive action. By putting the squeeze on us, they hope to get us to do something rash."

"Why do they think we'd fall for a stunt like that?" O'Brien muttered.

Roddy Rodriguez looked up. "Because they're used to snookering the Soviets," he explained quietly. "For whom rash actions are the order of the day."

"Can we trust him?" Elliot French asked.

Cunningham nodded. "I do. He's tough and absolutely loyal to his government, but Liu and I have been friends since we were acting deputy assistant undersecretaries together. He really loves both countries."

The president looked up at Cunningham. "How much time do we have?"

"Not enough. Liu's leaving on American's 11:00 A.M. out of Dulles. An Air China 747 will be waiting for him at San Francisco."

"Then we can't wait to talk to MacIntyre." They waited as the president, eyes closed, decided what to do. "Mike, lean on American. See if that flight can develop mechanical difficulties. Melinda, call our ambassador to the U.N. I want an emergency meeting of the Security Council, and I want to make sure that the Chinese representative is there. We're not going to let them turn this into a back alley mugging. Elliot, I want everything there is on this MacIntyre." When French didn't move, the president slammed the flat of his hand against his desk. "I mean it, Elliot! I want everything, from his birth certificate up to and including schematics of the communication device he's using. We're going to give it all to Ambassador Liu, along with a note from me disclaiming any official sanction of his actions."

The two men exchanged stares. "When he checks in, may I at least inform him of your decision to expose him? He is after all," French added quietly, "a private citizen doing us a favor."

"You will do no such thing!" the president thundered. He took a deep breath and removed his glasses. "Cripes, Elliot, I don't like turning him over any better to that bunch of ex–Red Guards than you do. But if some jail time for him keeps us out of a war, it'll be a cheap price to pay." Unnoticed by the president, French and Rodriguez exchanged a long look. "At the same time that you're getting MacIntyre's dossier together," the president continued, "be thinking about who we can trade him for. Figure out which Chinese agent is worth most to them, and we'll have the FBI nail him. Hard. Then we'll cut a deal. We should have MacIntyre back in six months, tops."

Rodriguez sat silently, thinking of stories about Chinese prisons told him by veterans of the Korean War. *Bad mistake, man. Six months in the Chinese gulag is going to be way too long, even for a Ranger like MacIntyre.*

French stood. "Yes, Mr. President," he said with cold formality. "There is, however, one act which you will have to take care of personally."

"And that is?"

"You, sir, will have to be the one to call Joel Dryden and explain that you've just dropped a dime on his future son-in-law."

33

The windows across the hall from Jake's makeshift cell looked east over a moonscape of earthen roofs toward a line of snow-capped foothills. Jake paused just long enough to orient himself before trotting down the staircase at the end of the hall.

The door at the bottom of the stairs opened onto a court-yard. Flattening himself against the doorframe, Jake opened the door a crack and peeked out. When he saw that the courtyard was deserted, he slipped out through the door and ran toward the front gate.

"Plans, General?" the president asked after Cunningham and French had left.

Rodriguez got up. Hands behind his back, he began to pace. "What worries both me and Admiral Harrison out at CINCPAC HQ in Honolulu is that the Chinese have already emptied their submarine pens at Guangzhou and Huludao." The general walked over to the huge globe that dominated one corner of the Oval Office. "Admiral Harrison figures, and I agree, that they're not going to try and sneak up on us, given the amount of ocean they have to cover. With a top sustainable speed of eighteen knots for a Xia-class boomer, and in light of their head start, we figure them to be somewhere around *here.*" Rodriguez traced a line through the arc formed by Wake Island, the Marshall Islands, and Kiribati. "There's nothing left in the Philippines for them to attack, so they must be heading east—"

The president, studying the globe, interrupted, "Toward Hawaii."

Rodriguez nodded. "I'm afraid so. Our big base at Yokosuka in Japan is a sitting duck, but it's a sure bet that the Chinese don't want to give their old friends in Tokyo an excuse to get in on this. They already know that the Japanese are champing at the bit for an excuse to unload on them." The chairman resumed pacing. "Based on this analysis, CINCPAC and I have decided to clear as much hardware as possible out of Pearl Harbor. Under the guise of a surprise drill, code-named OPERATION BELSHAZZAR, everything that can get up steam will head west at flank speed. Shortly thereafter, all available P3 Orion sub-hunters will take to the air. Once they rendezvous with the fleet at 160° west longitude, a major antisubmarine warfare exercise will be put on."

"And that's just about where you expect the Chinese subs to be."

"Exactly right, sir."

"And if you find them?"

"Then we lash them with sonar hard enough to make their eardrums bleed. We hope that if they know that we know just where they are, they'll turn tail and run."

"And if they don't?"

"Then the ASW part of the fleet—the land-based P3s and the baby carriers—continue to harass the Chinese Xias while our strike force heads west." The four-star general looked at his commanding officer. "After that, Mr. President, it's up to you. If the Xias cross 160° west, we'll want your authorization to order our 688-class attack subs to hunt the Xias down and destroy them. While that operation is underway, long range F/A-18 Hornets from the carriers *Nimitz* and *Kennedy* will conduct a raid on the Xias' home base at Huludao. Once the Chinese realize they have no more missile submarines and no more missile submarine base, we're hoping they'll quit the field of battle quietly."

"And if they *still* don't get the hint?"

"Then, you hold a press conference that goes on a global satellite TV net. You describe how much we regret having to take action against the innocent citizens of the People's Republic of China." Rodriguez grinned. "Then you announce the date and time of the next air strike: the mining of Guangzhou Harbor. If and only if the Chinese cease hostilities immediately will the strike be cancelled."

"You want me to *announce* the strike?" The president looked at his old friend. "Your collar's too tight, General— you're not getting enough air."

"Tim Harrison over at CINCPAC gets the credit for this idea, not me. The whole point is for the Chinese to find out they're unable to stop us even when we announce our intentions at every turn."

"Can we realistically expect to be able to do that?"

"Even if the Chinese air force wasn't the joke that it is, by the time we're ready to lay this on, the strike force will be in place, and we'll have full operational capabilities. If mining Canton Harbor isn't enough for 'em, we move north to Shanghai. No country can function with all of its principal ports blockaded." Rodriguez paused. "By the way, sir, at the press conference after the mining of Guangzhou Harbor—if there is one—we're going to have someone ask you if nuclear mines were used. We'd appreciate it if you'd answer, 'No comment.' It'll add considerably to the Chinese FUD."

"FUD, General?"

"Fear, Uncertainty, and Doubt. A concept pioneered by

the marketing folks at IBM. Keep 'em guessing. They'll be looking out at a harbor full of mines, wondering if one or more of those mines is capable of taking out their city if they whang it too hard. Ultimate FUD. Should do the trick."

Gasping for breath in the thin air, Jake slumped against a wrought-iron fence. Ahead of him, he spotted a policeman patrolling an intersection. With a silent *hallelujah!* Jake stumbled toward the officer.

Another drunkard from the chang tents, the policeman thought as from the corner of his eye he saw a figure stumbling toward him. *The blast has unnerved these superstitious peasants, and those who aren't flocking to the temples are drowning their fears.* The patrolman pulled his billy club from the ring on his belt. *Let's just make an example of this one.* He raised the club to strike, then let it drop in amazement when he realized he was looking at a foreigner.

"Please, help me," Jake rasped.

The officer started to sheath his nightstick. Then, remembering something, he stopped. "Your passport," he demanded.

Jake swayed, dizzy from his exertions. "Stolen," he croaked, trying to stay upright.

With his free hand the policeman unbuttoned the breast pocket of his uniform. He pulled out a folded piece of paper and shook it open. Jake watched as the man's eyes flitted from him to the paper.

It's him! the patrolman realized, unable to believe his good fortune. *It's the* quai loh *spy!* Just to be sure he looked once more at the face on the paper. He had been told at the briefing that it had been faxed from Washington to Beijing and from there to Lhasa. He also knew that catching the spy could mean a ticket home to Hangzhou. *Can't let him get away!* The patrolman raised his eyes and his billy club at the same time.

Jake had seen that look in the eyes of policemen before.

288

Instinctively, he shoved the patrolman and sent him sprawling. Then he turned and ran. As the shriek of the police whistle filled his ears, Jake stumbled, got up, and kept running.

The president gave the Oval Office globe a gentle spin. "You're making this sound way too easy, Roddy. What's the downside?"

"If we miss even one of their boomers, we've had it. It sneaks up off Hawaii and starts flipping missiles. Oahu is a few seconds away for a nuclear-tipped cruise missile; twenty minutes later their ICBMs hit Seattle, San Francisco, San Diego, and L.A."

The president looked out the window behind his desk. The brilliant light of a full moon was sweeping across the east lawn. Almost two centuries ago Thomas Jefferson had planted the trees whose shadows were etched on the close-cropped turf. *Mr. Jefferson*, the president thought as he gazed out at the magnificent old elms, *I wish you were here right now. I'd ask you what you'd do. But, knowing you, you'd stare back at me and say,* 'You're *the president,* you *decide.*' "Conventional weapons only, General," the commander in chief ordered. "Even the mines."

"Yes, sir. We stay conventional as long as they do."

"Has the operation already begun?"

"The 'exercise' has. The recall order went out to all active-duty personnel at Pearl Harbor four hours ago."

The president nodded. "Proceed as planned." He frowned. "By the way, why 'BELSHAZZAR' as a code name?"

Rodriguez smiled. "It's for my dad."

"Your father? His name was Philip."

"It's from my dad's favorite Bible story. In the book of Daniel. Belshazzar was the king who was feasting when a mysterious hand appeared and wrote, 'MENE, MENE, TEKEL, PARSIN' on Belshazzar's wall. The Good Book says that the king was so frightened that 'his knees knocked together and his legs gave way.' After that, old Belshazzar shaped right up."

Rodriguez laughed quietly. "My dad loved to tell my brothers and me that story—especially when trying to get *us* to shape up. When he got to the part of the story about the hand, he'd point a trembling finger at our bedroom wall. Then, with his eyes bulging out, dad would clutch his throat and pretend to fall over dead. Sometimes he'd scare us so bad it'd take our mama two hours to get us to sleep." The two men smiled. "Anyway, I named the operation BELSHAZ-ZAR because I hope the Chinese will shape up when they see the handwriting on their wall." Rodriguez glanced at his watch. "If you'll excuse me, Mr. President, I need to check in with Admiral Harrison."

Alone, the president spun the globe again, watching as the countries swept by. He turned abruptly, punched a button on his intercom, and spoke. Seconds later the door to the Oval Office opened, and a young air force officer hurried in.

"You called for me, sir?" the officer asked as he came to attention and saluted.

The president smiled. "At ease, Captain. And you can put down the 'football.'"

"Yes sir." The captain didn't put it down.

"What's your name, son?"

"Sir?"

"It suddenly occurred to me that you've been bird-dog-ging me for years now, and I don't even know your name."

"Kellin, sir. Captain Nathaniel Kellin."

"Your family call you Nate?"

Kellin nodded happily. "Yes, sir."

"How long has it been since you called your mother, Nate?"

Taken aback, Kellin hesitated. "I don't exactly recall, sir."

"Then you call her. Right now. Yes, I know it's two in the

290

morning. Use that phone over there." The president pointed across the Oval Office. "That," he said with mock severity, "is an order, Captain."

Kellin looked at the phone, then at the president. "Yes sir," he said quietly.

"Take all the time you want."

Then the president went for a long walk on the East Lawn, leaving a bewildered air force officer to phone home.

Joel came out onto the sun porch. "Phone call for you."

Anne looked up dispiritedly from her reading. "Who is it?"

"Susan Kirkcaldy."

Worry clouded Anne's face. "Have they found something out?"

Joel smiled. "Yes, but not what you expect. Come on," he said gently.

Susan waved to Anne from the screen of the TV set in Joel's study. "Hi, Anne. No, we haven't heard anything yet." She smiled sympathetically at the look on Anne's face. "Dinna worry yourself t' death, lassie. That pirate of yours looks perfectly capable of taking care of himself, and besides you'll want to be looking your prettiest when his masthead appears on the horizon." Anne found herself smiling at Susan's nautical allusions. "Anyway," Susan went on, "I'm taking advantage of the fact that we had to set up a videoconference with Joel to tell you about my big discovery. It's taken a good deal of effort, but we finally found someone who can translate Jake's little note." Joel handed Anne a fax, then left the room. The letterhead on the fax read:

Lynn Bartee, Ph.D.
Summer Institute of Linguistics
University of Texas, Dallas

Anne glanced at Susan, then read the note.

Dear Mrs. Kirkcaldy:
The quotation shown in the photo you sent me is
in Tibetan, not Vedic Sanskrit as you suggested. It
is written in the most common of the four Tibetan
alphabets, and the characters are quite well
formed. The translation is, quite simply, "I LOVE
YOU."

Anne saw Susan smile, and she felt a blush creep up her cheeks.

"Look at the estimable Dr. Bartee's postscript," Susan suggested. Anne looked at the bottom of the note:

P.S. Who is he? He's *really* cute.

"What's the matter, lassie?" Susan asked when she saw Anne cloud up. "If I had a corsair like yours telling me that he loved me, I'd be dancing a jig instead of looking like the North Sea in February."

"He's never said that to me before," Anne explained quietly. "And now he's halfway around the world when he tells me for the first time."

Susan smiled in understanding. "Some lads are like that," she replied gently. "Put them on the other side of the earth, or even down at the local pub after a wee dram, and they'll confess to all around their undying devotion to you. But put them across a table from you, and it's like talking to the walls of Castle Glenarvon." Susan looked up at Anne. "That doesn't mean that he doesn't really love you. He does, and he's trying to tell you as best he can."

Anne smiled. "You sound just like Mama."

"Then your mother's a wise woman, indeed." Susan smiled again. "*Slandie vaugh*, lassie."

Anne frowned. "Slandya vaw?"

"Aye. Where I come from, that's what we wish all young couples just starting out. It means, 'God go with you.'"

"Don't you mean, 'Go with God'?"

Susan laughed. "Others do. But we in the Highlands have been Christian for almost two thousand years. Legend has it 'twas Joseph of Arimathea himself who brought the faith to our clans. So, since we know who we believe in, we invite the Good Lord to accompany his children on their new life together rather than the other way 'round. I see that faith in the two of you." Susan looked at the picture, then back at Anne. "Does your pirate express his beliefs with far greater ease than he does his feelings for you?"

Laughing, Anne nodded. "Will you keep Jake in your prayers?" she asked.

"The two of you already are, lassie." Susan winked. *"Slandie vaugh."*

34

Chen picked his way through the sleeping tourists stretched out on the floor of the waiting room at Gonggar Airport. As he stepped over flight bags and suitcases, he brusquely fended off the irritable questions of the Chinese tour group leaders.

The inspector stopped beside a large man sprawled on a wooden bench. "Colonel Markov?" Chen said quietly. When no response was forthcoming, Chen nudged Markov with his toe. The Russian was instantly awake and alert.

"Yes?" he growled in Russian. "What is it?"

"Could we perhaps speak English, Colonel?" Chen asked politely.

"Very well. First, tell me when we are going to get out of this dump."

"Tomorrow," Chen replied soothingly. "The military has allocated enough transport planes tomorrow to evacuate you all to Chengdu." He smiled. "You carry a military passport, Colonel. You know how these things work."

Markov rose, towering over the slender Chen. "I presume, Inspector," he rumbled, "that you didn't come all the way here just to update my itinerary."

"No, Colonel, I did not. May I ask if you are an infantry-man?"

"Why do you want to know?" Markov asked warily.

"If you are, we have need of your expertise. You could do us a great service."

"I am retired. But I once commanded a division of rifle," Markov replied, a hint of pride in his voice. *Now that that doorük Bey is dead, I am truly retired.*

"I suspected as much," Chen said disarmingly. "You carry yourself like a tank commander." *Arrogant, overconfident, and full of yourself.* "We could use your assistance in identifying a weapon we believe is of Soviet manufacture. I assure you that this will in no way compromise your oath to your country."

"What sort of weapon?"

Chen spread his hands. "I am a simple policeman, Colonel. That is why I need your help. The weapon was brought to us by a peasant, and we need to know what it is." The inspector gestured at the waiting room. "A few minutes of your time tomorrow morning will earn you a night and a meal at the Lhasa Hotel, where the accommodations are considerably less Spartan." *And, with luck, you will tell me what else I want to know. Then you will also earn a jail cell followed by one of my bullets in the back of your thick skull.*

"And I will be back here in time for the flight to Chengdu?"

Chen nodded. "Guaranteed."

Markov swept the duffel bag containing his Kalashnikov to his shoulder. He shook Geoff Sheffield, who opened one eye. "Glad to hear they've reopened the guest wing, old man," Sheffield replied sleepily when Markov had explained. "Now, if you see MacIntyre, tell him to put a cork in the bottle of whatever he's drinking and get over here." The Yorkshireman closed his eye. "And don't the two of you be goin' and drinking all the rest of it on the way here, either."

The flickering of dozens of yak-butter *chome* served as a beacon to a hungry and exhausted Jake MacIntyre. Leaning against a building, he peered down the alleyway from which their yellow glow emanated. The *chome* sat in ranks on one side of the alley, their light reflecting off a dozen, man-sized prayer wheels made of gleaming, hammered brass. As Jake watched, a pair of Tibetans entered the far end of the alley. As they made their way down the lane they dragged their hands along the prayer wheels, setting them spinning. When they reached the end of the walk-through temple, each one dropped a coin in the bowl of the monk who sat by its exit.

Knowing he couldn't go much farther, Jake crept toward the alleyway. He dropped the only change he had left into the monk's bowl, ready to run if the monk shouted for help.

Hearing the American quarters hit the wood of his bowl, the monk turned eyes clouded with cataracts toward Jake. "*To duo chay,*" the monk said in thanks.

Seeing that the monk was blind, Jake relaxed slightly. He walked halfway down the alley, then stopped. Silently he stretched out underneath the lowest shelf of *chome*, offering a quick prayer that their light would keep him from being seen in the darkness below. Before he finished the prayer, he was asleep.

As a servant cleared the dinner dishes, Chen's superintendent handed him the cigarette box. "That informer's body washed ashore near Qüxu," he remarked. "His hand wasn't all he was missing."

Chen exhaled a plume of smoke and told his boss about the writing on Xongnu's palm. He got out his notebook, opened it, and handed it to his boss. "I showed it to the guides at CITS, and they told me the most preposterous story about a Forest of Razors. To top that off, Beijing reports that the hand was sewn up with bootmaker's thread." Chen shook his head. "Figure that one out."

The older man took the notebook. He looked at the lettering, then barked, "Tri!"

A young woman got up from the corner of the room where she had been sitting. Pregnant with the superintendent's third child, she made her way ponderously across the dining room. Promising to marry her, he had bought the fifteen-year-old girl from her nomad family when he had arrived in Tibet four years ago. Chen watched her with sadness, knowing that for years Chinese officials posted to Tibet had been quietly encouraged to father as many children as they could by Tibetan women in order to dilute the minority's bloodline. He also knew that she'd be abandoned when the superintendent returned next year to Beijing. Her family would refuse to take her back in, and Chen again wondered what would become of her.

The girl knelt beside the superintendent. "Yes, Husband?"

"What can you tell us about this Forest of Razors?" He pointed to Chen's transcription.

Tri looked at the notebook. "But, Husband," she said with a frown. "That does not say, 'Forest of Razors.'"

The superintendent looked sharply at the Tibetan girl. "What does it say?"

"It says, 'Tigers and Dragons.'"

Through a veil of smoke, the two men stared at each other across the table.

"Think this'll work, son?" Roddy Rodriguez asked.

Greg looked over his shoulder at the general. "It should, sir. It worked just fine the other day, using the TDRSS. *Discovery* will just provide us with more bandwidth." Rodriguez turned to greet the vice president, who had just arrived with the secretary of defense.

Acutely aware of the small crowd gathering behind him,

Greg turned back to his console. *Oh well*, he thought resignedly. *I did promise Cathy that I'd get more visibility.*

Susan spoke into the headset she was wearing, then looked at Greg. "*Discovery* has acquisition of signal on the satellite and reports ready to relay."

"You ready to go, Ken?" Greg called.

Across the lab a young man, feet propped up on his console, looked up from the copy of *PC Magazine* he was reading. Ken Sumrall, chief system administrator for the IPF's Cray YMP, surveyed his status lights. He nodded lazily and went back to his reading.

Greg glanced at Susan, who returned his nod. He typed a command on his keyboard, then stood up. *It's showtime.*

"Both the satellite and *Discovery* are in position," Greg began, "and we've started our scan."

Rodriguez frowned at the console's screen. "Nothing's showing up."

"We won't see anything for about twelve minutes, sir," Greg replied. "Perhaps I can use the time to explain the process we're using." He walked over to where a whiteboard was mounted on one wall of his lab. Greg picked up a marker and began to draw, grateful for something to do. "The computers onboard the Indigo-Lacrosse will preprocess the data, sorting out the background interference from what we want to see. Then the satellite will relay the data to *Discovery*, who will download it via microwave to us."

"Doesn't the TDRSS system use microwave downlinks?" the secretary asked. Greg nodded. "Then why the need for the shuttle?"

"Bandwidth, sir," Greg replied. "*Discovery* has a much higher-powered microwave linkup than the TDRSS satellites. It has to do with how much data can be transmitted in a given time." Greg started drawing. "The Indigo-Lacrosse-TDRSS hookup works fine for stationary targets. It'll send down all the data it can during a pass, then pick up where it left off the next time the target is visible. That is, as long as the target hasn't moved in the interim. If it has, then we have to start over. That's been our problem with these Chinese nukes—they just haven't sat still long enough for us to have a peek at them."

"Can't the satellite store the data it creates and then transmit it later?" the vice president asked.

"Good question. Unfortunately, no. To do what you suggested would require a great deal more storage than we were able to fit into the bird. Hence the need for the shuttle, which has more than enough bandwidth to transmit all the data during a single pass."

Rodriguez scratched his head. "By 'bandwidth,' I presume you don't mean the number of tubas playing, 'The Stars and Stripes Forever' on the parade ground."

Greg laughed with the others. He liked the old soldier. "Think of bandwidth as a combination of power and frequency. Power is like the *diameter* of a pipe: the higher the power, the wider the diameter of the pipe and the more information that can pass through. Frequency is like water *pressure*. The higher the frequency, the 'denser' the information passing through the pipe. Put them together, and you've got bandwidth." Greg pointed to the diagram he had drawn on the whiteboard. "The TDRSS's low-powered transmitter normally has to transmit data relatively slowly. But since the shuttle is only a few miles away in space, not hundreds of miles away on the ground, the I-L can transmit at a much higher frequency. *Discovery* has more than enough juice to take the data it receives and punch it at high frequency through the ionosphere and then down to us."

Rodriguez shook his head. "Frankly, I'll stick with the tubas."

"Data coming in," Susan announced. They clustered around her console, where columns of large numbers were being displayed. "Each of these numbers is a data point," she explained. "And each is a number from 0 to 2^{32}-1, which is around four billion possible values." Susan pointed across the room. "It's the job of the computer being baby-sat by that young laddie over there to see if each value matches up with an entry in our database of nuclear signatures. If enough of them correspond, we've identified what we're looking at."

The secretary glanced at his watch. "How long will this take?"

"Depends," Greg replied. "How certain do you want to be?"

"Can you do '100 percent sure'?"

"No. But we *can* manage 'almost positive.'" Greg looked at Ken. The system administrator reached over to his console.

"Twenty-seven minutes for a SWAG," he called. "For 98 percent certainty—," Ken said as he typed again, "just over four hours."

"A SWAG?" the vice president asked.

Greg began to answer, but was interrupted by Susan. "A Scientific, Wildly Approximate Guess. It means that we're not really sure." Rodriguez laughed quietly in the background.

The secretary looked at Greg. "Can you be 98 percent ready for the meeting tonight at nine?"

Greg glanced at the clock, then nodded.

"General," the secretary said to Rodriguez, "I want a marine guard outside this door and an escort for Dr. Miahara."

Great, Greg thought as the group left. *And I burned my draft card. . . .*

✧ ✧ ✧

The scuffling feet of passing worshipers awakened Jake. When no one was in sight, he rolled to his feet and made his way out of the alley. He stopped in a secluded patch of sunlight, both to collect his wits and to try and massage the meager solar warmth into his stiff muscles.

I'm beginning to get some idea of how David felt when he was on the lam from King Saul, Jake thought as he rubbed his legs.

But I must admit this 'every man's hand against me' bit wears real thin real fast. Where now? I can't phone for help with the PC in pieces. No pay phones in this town, either. Not a Denny's in sight, so I guess breakfast is out. And after my little run-in with that Keystone Cop yesterday, I'll assume the police aren't driving the welcome wagon. Jake took a deep breath. *I gotta get back to the hotel. Geoff and Sheila are my only chance.* Thanks to his Ranger training, the Lonely Planet map shone clearly in his head. Jake traced out his route, then headed west.

With a groan the dilapidated truck shuddered to a stop in front of the No. 6 truck depot on the outskirts of Lhasa, dust swirling in the thin, early morning light. As he painfully uncoiled himself from the truck's cramped interior, Randy groaned almost as loudly as the truck had. *This was a lot more fun back when I was in college*, he thought as he stretched and rubbed the kinks out.

Randy had wandered out of Tribhuvan International Airport in Kathmandu with only a vague notion of how he was going to make the overland journey to Tibet. As he walked past the airport's loading docks, he looked up at the sound of splintering glass. A case of San Miguel beer had fallen from an overloaded cart being manhandled by the driver of one of the ancient Chinese trucks called a *Jiefang*. Randy sprinted over and steadied the beer, then helped the driver load the cases into the truck. The assistance, along with the promise of a carton of Marlboros, earned him a ride to Lhasa.

He spent the next thirty hours wedged into the cab of the ancient vehicle, one knee pressed against the glove box and the other against the gearshift. Randy soon found that his driver, in order to save gas, would shut off the engine and coast downhill. This treated him, on several occasions, to a view out his window straight over the edge of the road to the valley floor a thousand feet below. The ordeal had soon descended into a nightmarish routine of feeding the driver cigarettes, singing loudly to keep him awake, and trying to avoid emasculation when the driver shifted into low.

Randy walked around the snout of the dinosaur-green vehicle. Fastened to the front bumper was a much-painted-over plate on which was stencilled 23. Randy knew that the figure indicated the number of times the truck had traveled ten thousand kilometers. He did some mental arithmetic, then shook his head. *One hundred forty thousand miles, and I feel like I've ridden every one of them. On the axle . . .*

Randy waved to the driver and tossed him the promised cigarettes. Then he pulled his hat down over his eyes and headed into downtown Lhasa.

Jake swallowed the last segment of an orange he had traded his Swiss army knife for. Knowing the surge of energy from the water and sugar wouldn't last long, he strode purposefully along. *Whenever you're someplace you're not supposed to be*, he reminded himself, *look and act as important as possible.*

The clutter of downtown thinned as Jake headed westward along Beijing Xilu. A nomad woman hurried by in the opposite direction, whirling her prayer wheel. Pedicab drivers jostled for position in the street, shouting at each other and thumbing their bicycle bells. Ahead, a group of men were playing pool on a battered table blocking the sidewalk. They looked up disinterestedly as Jake approached, then resumed their game. Jake stepped off the curb, intending to give them a wide berth.

But as Jake passed, one of the pool players swung around and kicked him savagely in the stomach, doubling him over. Someone grabbed his hair. Retching, Jake blindly drove his fist upward into his assailant's jaw. As the man staggered back, Jake felt himself seized from behind. Jake grabbed the arm that gripped his shoulder and threw the man over his hip. Waves of nausea swept over him. He tried to run, staggered, then twisted violently as both of his arms were pinned behind him.

The man he had punched struggled to his feet. Jake recognized the hate-filled face that turned toward him as the man with the red yarn in his hair. The one who had assaulted him in the alley. Grinning evilly, Thupten grabbed a pool cue and walked toward him.

❖   ❖   ❖

Joel hung up, then looked at Anne. He shook his head. "No news. That was Elliot French. He just got off the phone with our consulate people in Chengdu. The last batch of tourists was just processed at Gonggar Airport. All foreigners have been accounted for."

"Except Jake?"

"Except Jake. The other photographers say they haven't seen him since the day they split up. The situation in Lhasa is deteriorating rapidly. Martial law has been imposed, and anyone out after curfew is being shot on sight." Joel saw the tears glittering in the corners of his daughter's eyes. "I'm sorry, honey. Everyone I know is doing all they can."

Pat, carrying an envelope, came into the den. She held it out to Anne. "This just arrived. It was sent from Kathmandu five days ago."

Anne tore the envelope open and upended it. A folded piece of paper and a set of car keys on a worn keyring slid into her hand.

Anne looked at the paper. Then, sobbing, she buried her face against her mother's shoulder. Pat put her arms around her daughter. Joel came over, took the note from Anne, and held it where he and Pat could read it:

> **Keep the MG limbered up for me.**
> **I'll be back,**
> **Jake**

35

Through his pair of small Swarovski binoculars Randy could see the crater clearly. *About the size of a football field and fifteen feet deep.* Randy whistled. *Gotta be a nuke—nothing conventional could vaporize that much rock. But was it deliberate, or did somebody drop the baby?* He swept the binoculars slowly over the site of the demolished power plant. Suddenly, he stopped. *Wait a minute,* he mused. He lowered the binoculars, then put them back to his eyes in order to get a better look at what had attracted his attention. *If* that's *still there, then . . .* Randy slipped the binoculars back into their pouch and stuffed them in a pocket. *Then I've found out what I came here to find out, and I don't like it one bit. Now it's time to bug out of here. Fast.*

Don't think it's broken, Jake decided as he gingerly rubbed his cheekbone. He waggled his jaw experimentally. *But, then again . . .* He took a deep breath and nearly gagged on the stench of the rotting yak meat in the darkened storeroom.

The rusty iron door opened. Ganden entered, carrying a bowl. "My hemlock, I presume?" Jake asked, unsurprised when the young Tibetan frowned at him in confusion.

"I thought you might like some water," Ganden explained, offering Jake the bowl.

Jake drank deeply, then asked, "Does Kailas know you're doing this?"

Ganden hesitated. "No . . ."

"Then," Jake snapped, "if you've placed yourself under his authority, why are you acting without orders?" When Ganden said nothing, Jake stared at him. "Could it be because you really do know that Barabise is out of his mind? Listen to me, Ganden, Barabise is going to kill us all. Me first, but you won't be far behind."

"Kailas has promised to help us free Tibet—"

"How? By turning it into an uninhabitable wasteland? Are you better off now than you were a week ago? When I got here, you had power, water, uncontaminated food, and a whole bunch of people, who are now dead from radiation poisoning, were still alive."

"But, the Han—"

"There are more Chinese here now than ever before!" Jake pressed his fingertips to his throbbing temples.

Ganden retrieved the bowl. "I must go."

"You haven't read it yet," Jake said as Ganden unlocked the cell door, "but the book of Acts talks about someone a lot like Kailas." Ganden stopped. "According to some historians," Jake continued, "this guy led four thousand of the fanatics called Assassins out into the desert in order to start an uprising against the Romans. Know how many of them came back?" Ganden shook his head. "*None.* They were *all* killed or captured, while their alleged leader quietly disappeared when the going got rough. Think about it. Barabise is leading you off into a waste-land to die. And at the rate you're blowing up your city, the trip's going to be a short one."

As the door clanged shut behind Ganden, Jake leaned back against the wall, exhausted.

✧ ✧ ✧

Markov handed the photograph back to Chen. "Your intelligence is quite accurate. That is the launcher component of an SA-7 surface-to-air missile launcher."

"Do you have any speculations as to how it might have arrived on Chinese soil, Colonel?"

Markov shook his head. "None whatsoever. GRAILs are the Uzi of the missile world. They are cheap and easy to make, and are manufactured widely. We probably left more behind in Afghanistan than we used while we were there. And besides, I am merely a retired foot soldier on holiday."

Chen smiled. "Of course. You've been most helpful. But there is one more thing—" Chen opened his outstretched hand. In it were the two Imperials. "These too are Soviet, are they not?" Chen saw the slight narrowing of Markov's eyes.

The colonel made a show of bending over and examining the coins. "May I?" he asked as he picked one up. "Actually they're Russian, not Soviet. No Imperials were minted after the Revolution." He smiled innocently at Chen. "Thank you for showing them to me. I haven't seen one since I was a boy. Might I buy them from you?"

"I'm afraid not. They're evidence in another case." Chen stared at Markov. "A homicide."

"A pity. Terrible thing, murder. Might I be taken back to the airport now?"

Chen smiled. "The car that will take you to the airport will be here shortly. We'll have you there in plenty of time. The last flight out doesn't leave for five hours." He pressed a button on his intercom, and a sergeant showed up in his office doorway. "Show the colonel to the waiting room."

The sergeant saluted. "By the way, sir, a foreigner just showed up out front. An Australian. Claims he's been trekking for the past two weeks. Do you want to talk to him?"

Exasperated, Chen nodded. *How many more are there? Perhaps we should set traps for them, like we do for the rats.* "Bring him in."

Chen glared at the large man the sergeant showed in. "All foreigners were to have reported here two days ago. Where have you been?"

The man grinned fatuously. "Out in the bush, mate. Just havin' me a bit o' a walkabout."

Incomprehension glazed the inspector's countenance. "What?"

"You know. Loadin' up your cut lunch in your tuckerbag 'n' headin' into the back of Bourke to find a corroboree." The man's grin brightened as Chen's frown deepened. "Trekkin's what you call it, mate."

Chen nodded. "Ahh, trekking." He leafed through the man's passport. "Then, where is your trekking permit?"

The man looked puzzled. "Me *what?* Wot's all this about a permit? 'Ay, mate," the man called out to Markov, who was watching the proceedings from the other side of the room, "we don't need no stinkin' permits, do we?" Somewhat nonplussed by his sudden inclusion in the exchange, Markov nonetheless managed to shake his head vigorously. The man turned back to the bemused Chen. "Now, matey," he wheedled, "be a dinkum cobber 'n' let me go 'ome t' Alice Springs, 'ay?"

Shaking his head in disbelief, Chen handed back the man's passport. He spat copiously on the floor near the man's left shoe, then motioned to the sergeant. "He can wait with Colonel Markov."

"Xongnu's brother is here, too," the sergeant added.

"Wonderful. Bring him in. When the Dalai Lama shows up, send him in, as well."

Once out of the inspector's sight, the trekker mopped his forehead with his sleeve. "That was close," he told Markov. "Thanks for picking up your cue."

Markov stared at him. "You sound different now. Not Australian."

"That's because I'm not an Aussie. I'm American." The man saw Markov glance at his forged passport.

"But," the Russian rumbled, "all that back there—"

"Was learned from a series of beer commercials, a movie that was a big hit a few years ago, and a song called 'Waltzing Matilda.'" He looked Markov over. "You're Colonel Grigory Markov of the 165th Motorized Rifle Division?" Markov nodded increduously. The man stuck out a hand. "I'm Randy Cavanaugh. I've wanted to meet you ever since I read your dossier."

"You have something for us, Dr. Miahara?" the secretary of defense asked.

Sure wouldn't be here at ground zero if I didn't, Greg thought as he stood up. "Thanks to the *Discovery* linkup, we had time to collect data on three targets. I've brought along the raw data if anyone would like to examine it." He held up a thick computer printout, then lowered it slowly when no one showed the least interest. "Right. Anyway, the hyperon signature of the fissionable material we examined matched that of warheads known to have been produced at the Red Sickle Enrichment Facility located at Troitsk in the Ural Mountains."

"You're sure of that, Doctor?" the president asked.

"Yes sir. The signature match is almost exact. Well within the limits of error."

"So you're telling me that Russian nuclear weapons have suddenly shown up in Tibet."

Greg nodded gravely. "Yes sir." The president looked grimly around the table.

"Got a handle on what kind of stuff the Chinese have got their hands on?" Rodriguez asked.

"I can venture a good guess, General," Greg replied. "The masses of plutonium involved are very small. So small, in fact, that I can think of only one type of weapon that could utilize them. ADMs."

Rodriguez swore. All eyes flicked to the general as he glanced apologetically at Melinda Cunningham.

Cunningham smiled understandingly. "I take it you don't like these 'ADMs,' General?"

"No, ma'am. I do not."

"What, then, is an ADM?"

"Atomic Demolition Munitions. The only atomic bomb whose operator's manual includes instructions on what to do if it's a dud." Cunningham stared at Rodriguez, who nodded. "The 1980 edition of the manual for the U.S. version of the ADM includes a section on how to retrieve and disarm the warhead if it fails to fire." The general smiled wryly. "That section also mentions in passing that the emergency disarm procedures have been known to cause the weapon to detonate."

"You said 'the U.S. version of the ADM.' That means that we're using them, too?"

"Yes, ma'am. Where do you think the Sovs got the technology from?" Scowls ringed the Situation Room table. "Right now," Rodriguez continued, "ADMs constitute about 3 percent of our arsenal, or around a thousand warheads."

Mike O'Brien looked up from his notes. "Does it make sense that this type of weapon could turn up in Tibet?"

"Absolutely. We haven't been sure if the Russians had any." Rodriguez glanced at Greg. "At least we haven't been sure until now. Getting them to Tibet wouldn't be a problem—portability is the name of the game for ADMs. They come in two sizes: medium and special." Rodriguez looked inquiringly at Greg.

"Based on the amount of fissionable material involved, I'd say they have to be specials," Greg replied.

"Then it makes even more sense. Mediums are big things—four hundred pounds—and ride in the back of a truck. Specials are the commando weapon. Small, and weigh about sixty pounds. Can be easily transported by one man. We call them 'nuclear backpacks.'"

"Just how powerful are they?" the president asked.

"If the Soviet versions are like ours, the medium has a yield of around 12 kilotons of TNT and the special a yield of around 250 tons."

Melinda Cunningham took a deep breath. "One man can carry the equivalent of 250 tons of TNT?"

Rodriguez nodded. "Easily."

The president rested his chin on his fist. "Any ideas why these things are in Tibet?"

Elliot French spoke up. "Terrorism."

The president sighed. "I don't think I want to hear what you're about to tell me, Elliot."

"It's the only answer, sir. We know that the weapons in Tibet are of Russian manufacture, and we know that Russia and China aren't on speaking terms about much of anything, least of all nuclear weapons. So, they must have been transported to Tibet clandestinely. We also know that Special ADMs are a terrorist's dream come true. They're small, portable, and easy to use."

"I thought that only trained specialists handled ADMs," the secretary of defense interjected.

"That's right," Rodriguez answered. "But most of their training goes into maintenance and effective placement of the munitions."

"Aren't there safeguards against accidental detonation?" Cunningham asked.

"Even though both Russian and American ADMs use Category F Permissive Action Links—twelve-digit, multiply encoded combination locks that destroy the detonating circuitry after a limited number of incorrect attempts at arming— their detonation sequence is designed to be simple and quick to initiate. Anyone with a degree in electronics would have no problem with their operator's manual."

The president took off his glasses and scrubbed his face with his hand. "You're telling us, Elliot, that Tibetan terrorists have acquired a bunch of mini-nukes?"

French nodded slowly. "It would appear so. And it seems entirely plausible. General Rodriguez described the Special as a 'commando weapon.' I agree with him. I would also add that the only difference between a commando and a terrorist is the presence or lack of a uniform."

"Can you get word to Cavanaugh?"

"Maybe. I'll send FLASH messages to our Calcutta and New Delhi station chiefs."

"He's smack in the middle of a nuclear minefield. What are you going to tell him?"

The DDO smiled grimly. "Try not to tap dance."

✧ ✧ ✧

"And what did our little friend have for us this time?" Chen's superintendent asked as Xongnu's brother hurried out of Chen's office.

"He claims to know where the headquarters of Tigers and Dragons is. Says that they both killed his brother and blew up People's Glory."

The superintendent looked skeptical. "How much did he want?"

"That's the strange part. Nothing."

"Then that's probably exactly what the tip is worth. Let's detail a couple of patrolmen to go over and check it out. Did he say why he's suddenly being so philanthropic?"

"Seems that the dismemberment of his brother has caused him to develop something of a grudge against the *tai-pan* of the group." Chen snapped his fingers. "That reminds me. He said that the man in charge of Tigers and Dragons is the same one as in the picture Xongnu sold me. I finally remembered to bring it in. It's of some bootmaker." The inspector fished around in his jacket pocket. He pulled out the photo and handed it to his boss. "Xongnu said you'd recognize—"

"*Tar mar the!*" The superintendent's epithet cut Chen off short. "Forget the patrolmen. Call your PLA friend, and have him send over a platoon of his best troops."

Chen stared at his boss. "OK, but he's going to want to know who's invading."

"Tell him that we're under attack by the Hun." The superintendent pointed at the photo. "This is Kailas Barabise. It was he who helped that miserable dog Zhou defend the Potala when we were about to take it in '59. After we finally routed him, he fled over the border, joined up with the American CIA, and harassed us continually. Until a few years ago." The policeman glared at the picture. "I thought he was dead at last, and here he's posing as a cobbler right under our noses."

Chen frowned, then his eyebrows shot up in realization. "Xongnu's hand was sewn up neatly with bootmaker's thread!" He stared at his boss. "Do you think this Barabise could be responsible for the shooting down of the 757 and all the rest of the agitation?" The superintendent nodded grimly.

"Didn't you say Barabise worked for the CIA?" Chen asked.

"*With* them is probably closer to the truth. I can't imagine that madman working *for* anybody. Rumor has it they trained his band of thugs and then supplied them until they grew tired of their sport. Why?"

Chen picked up a fax. "This came in from Beijing this morning."

The superintendent scanned the sheet. "This MacIntyre is our only officially missing *quai loh*, right?" Chen nodded. "Which makes sense," the superintendent continued, "if he's Barabise's CIA contact. Keep an eye out for him during the raid.

Try and take him alive—Beijing will want to parade him around like a circus animal."

"And if he resists?"

"Then we'll be forced to inform his embassy that his mutilated remains were found in the ruins of a collapsed building near the power plant."

"What would an American tourist have been doing in that part of town?"

The superintendent smiled sardonically. "Didn't you know? The building in which he will be found was the home of Lhasa's most notorious bordello." He gestured at Chen's phone. "Call your army friend. Tell him to meet us in half an hour at the address Xongnu's brother gave you."

36

"You look good in fatigues and a flak jacket," the PLA lieutenant told Chen as he spread out a map on the hood of his jeep. "We should organize more hunts like this one."

Chen smiled thinly. "Perhaps, but not for this particular type of game. I prefer our regular expeditions—you don't need a bulletproof vest to stalk the waitresses at the Lotus Blossom."

The narrow side street in the Tibetan district of Lhasa filled quickly as soldiers and policemen jumped out of two trucks. They talked quietly, small knots of men whose automatic rifles glinted coldly in the noonday sun.

"We've got buildings abutting the objective on two sides," the lieutenant pointed out. "Let's put teams on the rooftops *here* and *here*." He jabbed at two spots on the map. "My men and I will take the main floor, while you and your people secure the second story."

Chen studied a blueprint of the building Xongnu's brother had identified. "I'll divide my force. Half goes with my sergeant up the stairway at the far end of the building, while I take the rest up the near stairs." He pointed to the map. "I'll put my less experienced men on this rooftop." The inspector looked at his friend for approval.

The PLA officer beamed. "Excellent! You should be in the PLA. You're wasting your life in the PSB. No excitement."

Chen merely fingered his bulletproof vest in reply.

There was a knock at the door. "Who is it?" Ganden called in reply to the muffled call of "*ulay, ulay!*"

"Tenzig. I must speak with you."

Ganden opened his door to find his friend sweating and breathing hard. Puzhen was beside him, looking scared. "What's going on?" Ganden asked. "And why do you have Puzhen with you?"

"You two must go," Tenzig whispered. "You must leave now."

"Why?"

Tenzig pointed toward the window. Puzhen, who was closest, pulled back the curtain and gasped, then ran across the room to Ganden, who put his arm around her.

"What is it, little one?" he asked.

She looked up at him, her eyes clouded with worry. "The street is full of soldiers."

"What's going on?"

Tenzig shook his head. "No time. Take Puzhen and go. Now."

Ganden frowned. "But, if we're going to fight the Han, I should go with you."

Tenzig put his hands on Ganden's shoulders. "No. I'm the fighter, Ganden, not you. You've already done your part. I've got nothing to offer Kailas except my right arm and my *thupta.*" He smiled at Puzhen. "Give my friend here many sons, and name the first one after me." Before they could protest, he turned and ran from the room.

Ganden went to the window. "It must be a raid. I've got to be with Kailas." He turned to find Puzhen blocking the doorway.

316

"Please," she begged, "take Tenzig's advice. Let's go." His face grim, Ganden walked slowly toward her.

Crying, she watched as he approached. When he loomed over her, she saw his hand come up, and turned her face from the expected blow. Her eyes opened as she felt instead the soft caress of a forefinger wiping away a tear.

"You go," he said gently.

Puzhen threw her arms around him and pressed her face against his chest. After a moment, she turned her tear-stained face to his. "No," she whispered, her mouth quivering. "I will *not*. I will live with you and die with you, but I will not be separated from you." She touched his cheek. "I was going to tell you that as part of our wedding vows. Now I'll have to think of something else." Ganden smiled as he saw the familiar stubbornness ignite in her dark eyes. "You told me that Jake asked if you wanted to be an assassin. Do you? You don't look like one. And try as you might, you don't act much like one. And I won't be married to one." She clung more tightly to him. "The angel God sent to warn us to leave this place has come and gone. Please, let's go."

Ganden held her, watching the curtains drift in the breeze. *Who can I trust? Kailas says Jake is a spy, and Jake says that Kailas is going to kill us all. I wish I could ask you, Pastor Ling. What was it you used to say when someone asked you what they should do? You'd smile and tell them, 'Choose life, so that you and your children may live, so that you may love the LORD your God, listen to his voice, and hold fast to him.' You always reminded us that the Lord is our life.*

He took Puzhen by the hand, and they ran.

Crouched on the upstairs landing, Chen waited tensely. One hand held his Type 59, a Chinese copy of the Soviet 9-mm Pistolet Makarova. The other held the doorknob of the stairwell door, ready to go when the shooting started downstairs. He glanced at the faces of his men. *Should I be as eager as they look,*

Chen wondered, *or should they be as scared as I am?* Through the stairwell window he watched as a contingent of PLA soldiers dashed across the courtyard and into the shadow of the building. Chen tightened his grip on the doorknob. *I think I'll go with scared. . . .*

A single shot echoed, followed instantly by a staccato roar of gunfire. Chen threw open the door. Keeping low, he ran along the corridor. Behind him, a pair of his men jumped into each room along the hallway. "Keep down, fool!" he shouted at the young soldier next to him.

The sound of the shooting brought Barabise to his feet. The door to his office opened. Seeing the khaki of a PSB uniform appear in the doorway, Barabise shoved his desk across the small room. The heavy piece of teakwood slammed into the door, pinning the screaming policeman between the door and the frame.

Barabise turned to the window. Two uniformed men stood on the roof of a single-story building across a narrow alleyway from Barabise's window. They were watching the melee in the street below. The desk blocking the doorway began inching backward as the policemen in the hall threw their weight against it. Barabise silently slid the window open and drew his *thupta*. Behind him, the banging against the door grew louder. The Khampa pulled himself onto the sill. As the door splintered and flew open, Barabise hurled his dagger. Then, feet first, he followed it as Chen flung himself across the room.

Barabise's dagger buried itself in the chest of one of the policemen on the roof. The other constable started as his partner collapsed, then looked up. Barabise's boots caught him in the face. The nomad hit, rolled, and retrieved his *thupta*. Puffs of dust kicked up around Barabise as Chen emptied his pistol from the window. The Khampa ran to the far side of the building and disappeared over the edge. At the window Chen watched for a moment, panting, then went back into the hall. He found that his two groups of men had mistakenly opened fire on each other, killing his sergeant and four others. Chen ordered the bodies removed, then went to find his friend in the PLA.

✧ ✧ ✧

"It could have been worse," the PLA lieutenant consoled Chen. "At least we seem to have put them out of business pretty thoroughly." He pulled aside the canvas covering the back of an army truck. "And look at all this stuff. There's enough here to outfit a small army."

"Where do you think they got it?" Chen wondered.

The lieutenant held up a grenade launcher. "Stuff like this they probably got from the Afghans, who got it from the American CIA. But most of the stuff is of Soviet manufacture. How they got their hands on it I don't know."

"Soviet, you say?" Chen asked. The lieutenant nodded, and Chen smiled to himself. He hadn't yet released Markov.

"By the way," the lieutenant added, "we found something else locked in one of the rooms." He pulled aside the canvas on another truck. "Someone, I should say. He's a *quai loh*, so I figure he should be your headache."

Jake blinked as daylight flooded the back of the truck. He spotted Chen and grinned. "A familiar face at last. I sure am glad to see you, Inspector."

"And I am glad to see you, too, Mr. MacIntyre," Chen replied. He didn't return Jake's smile. Chen looked at his friend. "It would appear you were right about their getting the American weapons from the CIA," he said in Chinese. "This man is their supplier."

Chen switched back to English. "Mr. MacIntyre, you are under arrest."

"*What?*"

"The charge is espionage."

37

"We must get him to Beijing immediately," Chen's superintendent remarked. He glanced at Jake, who sat on a hard wooden bench, flanked on each side by a PSB constable.

"I've got an idea," Chen replied. "Let's put him in with the Russian. I think it's no coincidence that both a large cache of Soviet arms and an allegedly retired army colonel showed up here at the same time. Perhaps Markov is serving his government in the same capacity as MacIntyre."

"But the Americans claim that MacIntyre is acting entirely on his own."

Chen shrugged. "Either they are lying and MacIntyre is working for the CIA, or he is the mercenary they claim him to be. Does it make a difference? By putting them together, perhaps we can get them to say something incriminating." Chen smiled. "In any event, we have enough circumstantial evidence for Beijing to embarrass Russia as well as the U.S. And delivering two spies instead of one can only help our careers."

Avarice gleamed in the superintendent's eyes. "What about the Australian?"

"He's an idiot," Chen said derisively. "Far too stupid to be connected with a covert organization. There's just enough time to get him on the last plane out of Gonggar."

The superintendent nodded. "Take the Australian to the airport," he ordered a constable.

Muddy water flew as Barabise pelted down Yak Alley. The nomad ducked into the back of his shop and bolted the door behind him. Breathing hard, he leaned against the doorframe. Chiding himself for his weakness, Barabise took an ornate Tibetan key out of his pocket and unlocked the large cabinet that stood against one wall of his office. Fists clenched, he surveyed its contents. *This generation of Han is a more formidable opponent than I imagined. Since I cannot persuade them to leave* Per La, *I will instead persuade them never to return.* The chieftain pulled an olive-drab aluminum case from a shelf in the cabinet.

"It's about blinkin' time!" The outburst of indignance caused Jake to look up. Shocked amazement washed over him as he watched a protesting Randy Cavanaugh escorted across the lobby of the station house. "Wot's the idea o' keepin' me locked up 'ere in the back of beyond like a drunken abo, ay?" he demanded of Chen.

Playing to the galleries, Randy looked around the station. He barely suppressed his start of surprise when he saw Jake gaping at him. *What is* he *doing* here?

As Jake started to speak, Randy preempted him roughly. "Don' go givin' me yer sob story, cobber. Belt up 'n' save it for the wallopers, 'ere." Randy stared at Jake. "Let on that we're mates 'n' we'll never get outta this flamin' Never Never together, clear?" Jake barely nodded.

"What's he saying?" the superintendent asked.

"I don't know," Chen replied irritably. "I speak English, not this gibberish."

"Does he know the American?"

"Obviously not," Chen hissed when Jake turned away with a seemingly disinterested shrug. "I told you the Australian was an idiot." He gestured to the constable. "Get him out of here."

"I want to speak to an official of my embassy," Jake told Chen when the protesting Cavanaugh had been led out of the station.

"Of course, Mr. MacIntyre. All that will be taken care of in Beijing. My job is merely to keep you comfortable until such time as transport can be arranged."

As Jake started to come to his feet, the constables on each side of him pulled him roughly back down onto the bench. "With what acts of espionage am I charged?" he asked angrily.

"That is not my concern," Chen replied calmly. "I am merely acting on orders from Beijing." He smiled thinly. "Beijing, it would seem, is merely acting on information supplied by your government."

Jake frowned. "What do you mean by that?"

Chen took some sheets of paper from his jacket pocket. "Here is a note from your State Department, along with its Chinese translation. In the note your government denounces you as an independent mercenary and disavows any complicity in your actions."

"I don't believe it!" Jake replied indignantly.

Chen handed him the papers. "I believe you'll find this to be interesting reading. As I said, my job is to make your stay with us comfortable." He switched to Chinese. "Lock him up with the other spy," Chen ordered the constables.

"Ganden!"

The shout brought Ganden and Puzhen to a halt just outside the refuge of Ganden's apartment. The young couple turned to find a filthy Kailas Barabise grinning at them.

"It's good to see that you escaped too, boy. Let's go; we've still got work to do."

"Where's Tenzig?" Ganden asked immediately.

Barabise's eyes hardened. "Dead. The Han cut him in two with their machine guns." Puzhen put her arm on her fiancé's shoulder. "He died well, boy," the nomad continued. "Took four of them along to serve him in hell."

Ganden paled when he recognized what the nomad was carrying. "You have another?" he gasped.

Barabise nodded grimly. "Since we seem to be unable to persuade our people to rise up against their oppressors, we must eradicate them ourselves."

"But not this way," Ganden protested. He gestured at the ADM. "Not with another of these. Hundreds of our people are dead, and more are dying each day. People unhurt by the blast are wasting away. *Our* people, not just the Han."

"They are casualties of war. However, we will next destroy someplace where no one lives." The nomad staggered slightly, then shook his head to clear it. *You are getting old, Kailas*, he thought. *Time for the job to be finished.*

"Where?" Ganden asked.

"The Potala."

Dust swirled in through the windows of the police car as it rattled along the road to Gonggar Airport. Randy stared out the window, the landscape passing unseen as he tried to figure out why Jake MacIntyre would be under guard in a police station in Tibet.

"Practice English?" the driver asked. "I take class."

Just like everyone else in China, Randy thought. He settled into his seat and closed his eyes, answering the driver's unending stream of questions with the small part of his brain that wasn't thinking about Jake. *MacIntyre's a big boy*, Randy decided. *He can get himself out of whatever he's gotten into. Yeah, and try explaining that to Anne if he doesn't come back.* He grimaced mentally. *Oh well—'Once more into the breach.'*

Randy sat up. "Your English is *tai hao la*." The driver beamed at Randy's use of the superlative. "Who was the foreigner at the station?" he asked casually, handing the driver a cigarette.

The driver frowned through a cloud of tobacco smoke. "Furrinah?"

"You know—" Randy searched for the Chinese "—the *quai loh.*"

"Ah!" the driver replied with a nod of understanding. "He from 'merica." The driver frowned. "Where you from?"

"Australia," Randy replied, realizing that he had inadvertently dropped his accent.

The driver nodded again. "Good thing you not 'merican. Beijing say the 'merican a big spy for CIA."

Just after the car rounded a bend in the road, Randy tapped the driver on the shoulder. When the policeman glanced in the rearview mirror Randy used a series of graphic gestures to indicate what he needed to do. The driver grinned and pulled over. Randy climbed out of the car, followed by the policeman, then turned suddenly and rammed his massive fist into the policeman's jaw. The driver spun around and collapsed by the roadside. Randy took the pistol from the policeman's holster and pocketed it, along with the officer's ammunition case.

He looked down at the inert form. "Sorry, matey." He got back into the police car, spun it around, and headed back toward Lhasa.

Ganden recoiled. "You wouldn't!"

"Why not, boy?" Barabise asked contemptuously. "Since bringing down the Han aircraft and destroying their power plant didn't stir up our people, perhaps the destruction of their national shrine will."

"*You* shot down that airplane?" Puzhen asked, horrified.

Barabise ignored her. "Tomorrow, a leaflet will appear that will explain that the Han have retaliated for the destruction of their power plant by blowing up the Potala. It will go on to tell the superstitious peasants that unless they drive the Han out of *Per La*, Gonpo will lead all the demons of the fiery and icy hells in the destruction of Lhasa."

Ganden shook his head. "I'll have nothing to do with this, Kailas. I've helped you once too often already."

The Khampa chieftain smiled sardonically. "You just need some incentive." He whistled, and Thupten stepped out of the shadows. Barabise gestured, and Thupten grabbed Puzhen.

Ganden's charge at Thupten was interrupted by Barabise's fingers closing around his neck. "I find it interesting that the weakest and strongest of my men were the ones who survived the raid. But you have talents I need." *For now*, he thought. Ganden and Puzhen reached out to each other, their fingertips missing by inches. "How touching," Barabise said contemptuously. He looked at Thupten. "If we're not back by sundown, start in on her." Thupten dragged the squirming Puzhen into Ganden's apartment.

Barabise loosened his grip on Ganden's neck. "Do we have an agreement, boy?" Desolate, Ganden nodded. Barabise picked up the ADM and motioned for Ganden to follow him.

The constables shoved Jake into the holding cell and locked the door behind him. Markov held his finger to his lips when Jake started to speak. The Russian leaned over and pointed underneath the wooden bench that he was sitting on. Jake knelt down. Fastened to the underside of the bench seat was a primitive listening device. Jake looked at Markov and nodded.

"Have you ever heard of the song 'Waltzing Matilda,' MacIntyre?" Markov asked. When Jake stared at him in confusion, the Russian pointed elaborately at the listening device.

"Sure I have," Jake responded enthusiastically, picking up his cue. "Do you sing it a lot in Russia?"

"Never. But the Australian who was in here told me about it. Do you know the words?"

"Yep. Would you like me to teach them to you?"

"Please."

"OK. 'Once a jolly swagman sat beside a billabong . . .'"

In the next room, Chen took off his headphones and buried his face in his hands.

The air in the dark corridor was heavy with the fumes of burning yak butter. Ganden trotted along in front of Barabise, past the endless rows of shrines. In front of each shrine a monk sat impassively on a stool, tending the rows of butterlamps. Each niche that held a gilded, jeweled statue of a Buddha was fronted with chicken wire installed during the Cultural Revolution as a precaution against the depredations of the Red Guards. The floor of each shrine was littered with paper money pushed through the wire. At the Buddha's feet, dozens of the silk prayer scarves called *khata*s lay crumpled in pools of grease. In and out of the patches of eerie, flickering lamplight the two silently ran.

"Wait, boy!" Barabise called. Ganden stopped and watched as Barabise, breathing heavily, shifted the ADM from one hand to the other. *That's the third time he's had to do that,* Ganden noted.

"Do you know where the Chamber of the Dharma King is?" the nomad asked as he picked up the bomb.

"Yes," Ganden replied curtly. He trotted on, deliberately setting a punishing pace. At the end of the corridor he turned right, then abruptly left. At the end of a short, low corridor, six steps led up through a small door into the shrine called the Chamber of the Dharma King. This was the heart of the Potala Palace, a meditation cell established by King Songsten Gampo in the seventh century.

They burst into the natural grotto that formed the shrine. Its walls were lined with gilded, gaudily painted statues draped in silks. The monk tending the butterlamps came to his feet, protesting the invasion. His angry invective ended in a gurgling cry as Barabise's *thupta* tore through his throat.

"Get to work, boy," Barabise growled. He held the dripping dagger where Ganden could see it.

Ganden unsnapped the latches on the ADM's shipping container. He threw back the cover, and high-tech death gleamed in the ancient butterlight.

He held out a hand to Barabise. "Let me have the detonator."

Barabise coughed. "Don't have it. Lost it in the last explosion."

Ganden looked up at the Khampa. "Then there's nothing I can do."

"You lie!" Barabise thundered. "I read the manual. This can be detonated by a timer as well as a detonator." His hand flickered out. Ganden gasped as the edge of the *thupta* scored his cheek. "One more attempt at treachery, and I'll make you watch as Thupten and I have our way with your woman." Greasy sweat dripped from the nomad's chin.

"If I'm going to set the timer, I'll need the operation manual." Ganden's attempt to stall failed as Barabise pulled the sweat-stained booklet from inside his shirt, handing it to Ganden. He opened the manual. "How long?"

The nomad sat down heavily. "Two hours. Just at sunset."

Ganden squinted at the manual in the dim light, flipping switches with shaking fingers. Barabise leaned over his shoulder, watching closely. Ganden tapped the keypad, and 2:00:00.00 appeared in the display. A single light remained green. Ganden felt the nomad reach around him.

As Barabise's finger neared the final switch, Ganden threw himself violently backward. The nomad went sprawling, rolled, and sprang to his feet. With a bestial roar he rushed Ganden, his dagger outstretched. Ganden scuttled backward, trying to circle toward the door. He tripped over the body of the monk and went down. Instantly, Barabise was upon him.

The nomad's teeth bared in a grimace, and his breath hissed between his teeth. "I kill you now, boy." He raised his arm. The steel of the *thupta*'s blade flickered white in the lamplight. Barabise's arm came down, and the dagger's tip descended in an arc toward Ganden's eye.

The projected display glowed on the Situation Room screen. Generated by a PC hooked into the Tracking and Data Relay Satellite System, it updated the display every thirty seconds. Those seated around the table saw a map of the western Pacific. On either side of a yellow line, a cluster of green rectangles faced a smaller cluster of red triangles.

"The green is our carrier force," Roddy Rodriguez was explaining. "The red represents all known Chinese subs."

Mike O'Brien looked up. "All *known* subs? Surely you've had enough time to find them all."

Rodriguez took a deep breath. "It's a big ocean. Our P3-Orion subchasers have been harassing them for hours. Sonobouys, active sonar dips; nothing subtle about it. We still have fixes on six subs—the same number we started with. Either we've found them all, or there's one that's nowhere near the others."

"I sure hope we've found them all, Roddy," the president said.

"So do I, sir. My family's in San Diego."

Eight green triangles appeared very close to the yellow line. Rodriguez turned from the screen. "Our 688s just checked in. That means they're just this side of 160° west." The chief of staff tapped the yellow line.

"What are they doing?" Melinda Cunningham asked.

"Waiting."

"For?"

"For the president to issue a 'GO' command. Once their weapons are released to them, the 688 commanders will destroy any Chinese sub that crosses 160° west longitude."

The president tapped a knuckle against his teeth as he stared at the screen. "How long do I have?"

"If the Chinese maintain flank speed, at most three hours."

"I wonder," the president said quietly, "if it took three hours for God to decide to destroy Sodom and Gomorrah."

The *thupta* stopped, the messenger of death hovering just above Ganden's face. "I have a better idea, boy," Barabise rasped. "The *thupta* would be too quick." His hand around Ganden's throat, the Khampa dragged the young man across the floor of the shrine.

"Watch," Barabise ordered. With the tip of the dagger he flipped the final switch. Scarlet numbers began racing across the ADM's LED panel. "First I tie you to the bomb, then I hamstring you so that even if you do get free, you will not be able to crawl away." Barabise held his dagger between his teeth. With his free hand he pulled one of the silk *khata*s from the shrine. Pinned by the throat, Ganden struggled as Barabise reached for his hands.

Suddenly, the nomad's eyes bulged. He retched violently. Ganden watched the slow motion brought on by terror as Barabise toppled over and fell across him.

Ganden scrambled out from under the nomad and ran to the far side of the grotto. Barabise lay unmoving. Slowly, his eyes never leaving the Khampa's body, Ganden made his way to the ADM. He picked up the operation manual. Ganden opened it and riffled through its pages. Then, heedless of Barabise, he ran headlong out the door.

38

Light streamed from beneath her daughter's bedroom door as Pat Dryden walked softly along the upstairs hall. She knocked gently, then opened the door. Anne looked up. She was sitting cross-legged on her bed, her Bible in her lap. Pat crossed the room and held out a porcelain mug.

The steam from the mug enveloped Anne. "Chamomile tea!" she exclaimed. "I haven't had any in years." Anne looked up at her mother. "You used to bring it to me when I had those awful earaches. It always helped me get to sleep." Understanding swept across Anne's face, and Pat nodded.

"How are you doing?" Pat asked.

Anguish replaced understanding. "I'm worried about him, Mama, and it hurts so much not knowing if he's all right." She bit her lip. "I'm scared for him—," Anne paused, finding strength in the wise gaze of a woman who was both mother and doctor. "And I'm scared for me, too," she admitted. Anne dropped her eyes, and tears stained the pages of the book of Jeremiah.

"Let's take a walk."

Anne raised her head to find her mother holding out her bathrobe. "Now?"

Pat nodded. "Now."

Anne followed her mother up to the attic, and they spi-raled their way up a small staircase set in its corner. A low door led them out onto a narrow, railed gallery. Below them, the night wind sped with a soft roar through the tops of the cedars. Anne tied her robe shut. She watched as a late-rising full moon scattered its light across the restless waters of Somes Sound. Anne leaned on the wrought-iron railing next to her mother.

"Do you know where we are?" Pat asked.

"I don't know what it's called, but I do remember the spanking I got for sneaking up here without permission."

Pat smiled. "This is a widow's walk. A lot of the houses along the coast have them. This house was built in 1833 by a man named Micah McCain. Since he was a proper sea captain, Mr. McCain made sure that his home had one. There's a picture of him in the attic. He was a tall, handsome man, the master of a clipper ship on the trade route between Portland and Glasgow.

"On one trip he brought back a very precious cargo— Abigail McCain, his young Scottish bride. Abigail soon learned that being a captain's wife meant spending a good deal of time right here—awaiting her husband's return, watching for his ship to crest the horizon.

"Then came the day when he didn't return. Abigail waited and wept and donned the black dress called widow's weeds. When her mourning was over, other young captains came courting. They found her still clad in black, and she turned them away. For the next sixty years she could be seen up here on nights like this, gripping the rail, always looking to the east."

Anne shivered. "I'm glad you didn't tell me that story when I was little and couldn't get to sleep." She turned to look at her mother. "Why now?"

"To remind you that you have what Abigail McCain lacked—a choice. Abigail predicated her life on her husband. When he vanished, so did her reason for living. You, my love, predicate your life on Someone who will *never* vanish, who promised us that 'I will never leave you.'"

"Jake *may*"—Pat made sure that Anne caught her emphasis—"not come back." She put her arm around Anne's shaking shoulders. "But, whether he does or not, the foundation of your life is still intact. If you choose to let it be.

"You were reading from Jeremiah just now. Remember where Jeremiah is told to 'stand at the crossroads and look'? The Lord tells him to 'ask where the good way is, and walk in it, and you will find rest for your soul.'"

"That's Jake's favorite verse," Anne whispered.

"Then apply it," Pat suggested gently. "Which way are you going to take? The walk of life, down there with the rest of us, grieving, growing, and going on? Or the widow's walk, up here with Abigail, rejecting life and gazing into nothingness?"

The wrought-iron railing was cold beneath Anne's hands. She tightened her fingers around it, as if to squeeze the chill from the metal. Anne watched as a covey of ragged clouds streamed across the face of the moon. Far below her, a comber boomed against the granite cliffs.

"I've never had trouble praying before," she said at last. "But now, I just can't find the words."

"Then let's do what your father and I do when one of us doesn't know what to say. The other one of us starts, and pretty soon the words come." Pat hugged her daughter. "Let's pray."

✧   ✧   ✧

"You must believe me!" Ganden shouted as he struggled in the grasp of a huge, saffron-robed monk. "Unless I can get help, the Potala will be destroyed!"

An abbot surveyed him skeptically. "I've seen you here before. You work for the Han, putting lights where they have no place being. Why, then, should I believe you?"

Ganden stopped struggling. "I don't work for them anymore. I'm sorry I ever did. But go look for yourself. In the Chamber of the Dharma King. It can destroy the entire palace."

Just then, a young initiate ran up. "There are bodies in the Chamber of the Dharma King," he gasped. "Some sort of mechanical device, too." Concerned murmurs swept over the assembled monks.

The abbot gazed at an enormous altar dedicated to the thousand-armed Avalokiteshvara, the patron god of Tibet. *Where is the immortal happiness you are supposed to provide us?* he wondered. He turned to the monk who held Ganden. "Let him go. He can bring no worse than that which has already befallen us."

Ganden sprinted out the door and onto the wide marble steps that led to the front of the Potala. He stopped, torn between two equally urgent priorities. Lhasa lay before him, the towers of the Jokhang Temple golden in a patch of sunlight. Ganden quivered with the intensity of his mental struggle. Then he decided. Taking the worn marble steps three at a time, he raced down the steps of the Potala and disappeared into the alleyways of the city called The Place of God.

Markov and Jake looked up when the door to the holding room slammed open. Chen strode in, followed by two enormous constables. "Enough of your nonsense!" the inspector barked. He gestured, and the policemen flanked Jake. "Come, Mr. MacIntyre, and we'll see just how long you can last before you start spouting the truth instead of foolishness."

Coffee slopped from the president's mug as he slammed it down on the Situation Room table. "What do you mean I only have an hour to issue a 'GO'? Thirty minutes ago I had three hours!"

"That's before our communications satellite went on the fritz," Rodriguez explained. "Our 688s are waiting at a depth of thirty meters, which is shallow enough for the krypton-argon laser aboard the satellite to reach them with a message. This gives us instantaneous communication with shallow-running subs. Until the satellite disappeared, that is."

The president threw away the paper napkins he had mopped up the spilled coffee with. "It just disappeared? Could the Chinese have done it?"

Rodriguez shrugged. "I doubt it. But we don't know."

"So, how *do* I talk with my subs?"

"ELF."

"Sure, why not?" the president said resignedly. "Elves, leprechauns, banshees; let's throw in a few hobbits for good measure."

The chief of staff grinned. "ELF stands for Extra-Low Frequency. ELF radio waves cycle three hundred times per second. Compare that with your favorite FM station, which broadcasts at around a hundred million cycles per second. The good thing about ELF transmissions is that they can penetrate the ocean for up to a hundred meters."

"So we can talk to even our deep-running subs."

"Exactly. The downside is that since bandwidth—the amount of information that can be transmitted in a given time—is determined by frequency, ELF takes a long time to transmit even single characters."

"Sounds like you've been having lunch with that Miahara kid, Roddy. What's the bottom line?"

"We'll use the ELF facility outside Clam Lake, Wisconsin, to broadcast to the 688s a three-symbol order to surface. Once they get to the surface, their captains will lock onto one of our SSIX communications satellites. We can then communicate normally with them."

The president frowned. "If the order to surface is only three characters long, how come I only have—" He stopped to check his watch. "—fifty-two minutes?"

"It takes ELF twenty seconds to broadcast a character. While the three-character order to surface will only take a minute to transmit, to it we have to add an eleven-character key to the cipher the subs will be using, as well as routing information. Add in the time for them to decode the message and get to the surface, and we'll have only a minute or so to give them the GO and still leave enough time for them to get back down to firing depth."

The president drummed his fingers on the polished wood. His daughter Allison was honeymooning at a friend's estate on the island of Molokai, and he grimaced at the notion of a Chinese attack sub prowling the waters near his daughter and her new husband. He considered having them evacuated, but decided against interrupting her bliss. *If the balloon does go up, Allie, I hope the airburst catches you in Brad's arms. Of course*, he thought with a fatherly smile, *where else would you be on your honeymoon?*

"Issue the order to surface." The chief of staff grabbed a phone. The president picked up another. "Wake up the Speaker, the Senate majority and minority leaders, and the chairs of the Foreign Affairs and Armed Services committees," he ordered. "I want them here in thirty minutes. And start preparations for a joint session of Congress at 9:00 A.M."

The president hung up. *Time to figure out how to tell the people who elected me that soon more than a few of them may be dead.* He looked across the table at his old friend. "You went to West Point. Did the bookstore there carry any Cliffs Notes on how to declare war?"

Thupten finished his cigarette. He flipped the butt toward Puzhen, who sat huddled on a corner of Ganden's cot. The scars on his face were etched deeply by the lengthening light. His face twisted into a grotesque leer, Thupten got up and walked across the room to reach for the cowering Puzhen.

Ganden heard the screams as he sprinted up the steps to his apartment. The cheap lock shattered as he kicked the door open. Grabbing a chair, he slammed it down across Thupten's broad back. The giant pulled himself off Puzhen and lunged at Ganden. With both hands Ganden swung the fragment of chair he held. A wooden bulb on the end of the post caught Thupten on the temple, and the huge nomad crashed to the floor at Ganden's feet.

Sobbing, Puzhen fell into his arms. "Are you all right?" He felt her nod. Ganden reached into a drawer and slipped a pistol into his jacket pocket. "Then come," he said urgently, taking her hand. "We must find Jake, or we will die."

Feigning indolence, Randy leaned against the wall of a building across the street from the police station. He had hidden the police car in a nearby alley. Then he had circled the PSB building, searching for a way to free Jake. Seeing no unbarred windows or back doors, he decided to wait until sundown. Not wishing to become conspicuous in his loitering, Randy went back to the police car. A few minutes later, with the collar of his jacket turned up, he began wandering the streets of Lhasa.

Randy walked down Jianshe Lu. The street formed the northern part of the Lingkhor, the outer circuit taken by pilgrims earning merit as they circled the Jokhang. A tiny woman bustled by him, swinging her prayer wheel and muttering mantras. Puffs of wind blew dead leaves onto the rippled surface of the Dragon King Pool. The Lukhang Temple sat deserted and brooding on an island in the small lake.

As Randy rounded the corner of Jeifang Beilu, he was sent reeling against the door of a Tibetan pharmacy. "Watch it!" he barked. Randy glared at the young couple who had collided with him.

The young man's eyes went wide. "You speak English!"

"So do you," Randy replied, amused by the man's amazement.

"I am Ganden Nesang. I need your help." Ganden pulled something out of his jacket. "Can you read this?"

Randy took the booklet. He glanced at it and frowned. "This is in Russian."

"Please, can you read it?"

Cavanaugh opened the manual. He blurted out an expletive as he read the title page. "Where did you get this?"

Randy leaned back against the pharmacy wall for support as Ganden hurriedly explained. He glanced up at the Potala, seeing only the death ticking away within its bowels.

"Can you help?" Ganden asked pleadingly.

Randy flipped through the operations manual. "I can make out most of this, but if you only get one chance and no practice, you want to be absolutely sure." He looked at his watch. "And that's going to take more time than we have." Sweat beaded Randy's brow as he studied the intensely technical Russian. Suddenly, he snapped his fingers. "C'mon, kids," he said with a grin. "I've got just the man for this job, but I'm going to need your help getting to him."

39

Looks like an electric chair, Jake thought as he was shoved roughly into the sturdy wooden chair that occupied the center of the interrogation room. *Feels like one, too,* he decided as the viselike hands of the two burly constables gripped his shoulders against the back of the chair's back. Two more policemen pinioned his wrists to the chair arms.

Chen stood in front of Jake, surveying him contemptuously. *How much your face looks like the face of that U.S. Navy captain who refused my mother and me asylum and so consigned us to this living hell.*

"You are worth much to me, *quai loh,*" the PSB officer explained. "More than you are apparently worth to your country." Jake grimaced as Chen held the fax where he could see it.

"Since your government has disavowed any complicity in your actions, I'm sure they won't care what happens to you. Because of that, I can use my own methods to extract a confession from you. One which I will be able to barter in Beijing for a posting far away from this pesthole."

Chen zipped open the small leather kit he was holding. He set it on a battered wooden table. Glass and metal gleamed in the harsh fluorescent light. The inspector pulled an old-fashioned syringe from the kit and screwed a needle onto its end. From his coat pocket he took out five small vials, which he meticulously arranged in a line along the table's edge. Between thumb and forefinger he held a sixth vial in front of Jake's eyes. Its label read:

HYDROCYANIC ACID
0.001 MOLAL SOLUTION

"Can you read the label, Mr. MacIntyre?" Chen asked. When Jake didn't answer, Chen plunged the needle into the rubber insert in the vial's cap. He filled the syringe, withdrew the needle from the vial, and carefully purged the air from the syringe's barrel. "Perhaps you know this better by its common name," Chen suggested. "Prussic acid."

The cords in Jake's neck stood out tautly as he strained against the constables' grip.

Holding the hypodermic needle in front of him, Chen advanced slowly toward Jake. "This is a very diluted solution. Just strong enough to make you unable to stand. That way we won't need my associates here, and you and I can chat undisturbed." The inspector waved at the line of vials. "Each solution is ten times stronger than its predecessor. Everyone has confessed after the second vial, and no one yet has lasted past the fourth." The constables' grip tightened as the point of the hypodermic needle touched Jake's neck. Chen smiled. "Now, a cocktail before we talk."

The door to the interrogation room flew open. "Inspector Chen!" a voice yelled.

Chen turned. "What is it?" he snarled in Chinese. An increasingly strident commotion could be heard out in the station's foyer.

"Two Tibetans. They claim the Potala is about to be blown up."

"Tell them to wait. Take down a transcription of this fairy tale of theirs," the inspector ordered. "I'll see them in a moment." *To order their deportation to the labor camps in Chengdu.*

"But," the sergeant protested, "they asked for you by name."

"Tell them to wait!" Chen shouted. He turned back to Jake.

"FREEZE!" A commanding voice filled the room.

Chen whirled. The point of the needle grazed the skin of Jake's neck. The PSB inspector stopped dead when he realized he was staring down the barrel of a large-caliber pistol. "The Australian!" he gasped.

Jake looked past Chen. His eyebrows shot up. "I thought," he said conversationally, "that if we're dueling over Anne, then I was supposed to get a gun, too."

Chen studied the face behind the gun. "Who *are* you?" he asked increduously.

The intruder stared at Chen. "Never mind. And if you don't all want to be blown to kingdom come, you'd better let him go."

Someone tackled Randy from behind. As he went sprawling, the pistol flew from his hand. The man who had hit him dove for the gun. On his back, Randy put his boot in the pit of the sergeant's stomach. He pushed, and the policeman slammed against a wall.

In one lithe motion Randy came to his feet, pulled back hard on the pistol's slide, and raised the weapon. "Now, MacIntyre!" Randy shouted as the pistol roared.

Jake heard bullets whistle past his ear. The hands gripping him went slack. Jake hurled himself out of the chair and barreled into Chen, throwing the inspector to the ground. With the knifelike edge of his hand Jake chopped at the man's wrist, knocking the syringe from his hand. Jake grabbed the hypodermic needle and held it menacingly in front of Chen's eyes.

The burly policemen rushed Randy. He stepped against the far wall and put a round into the ceiling. The three policemen froze as plaster dust rained around them. Randy gestured sharply toward the floor with his pistol, and the constables hit the dirt.

Randy waved Jake out through the interrogation room door. Keeping his pistol trained on Chen, Randy backed through the door. He kicked it shut, then wedged a chair under the doorknob.

"Hi, Jake," a voice called out. Jake turned to find Ganden holding a group of constables at bay with the Type 57 pistol he had once trained on Jake. "Sorry about you missing your flight. Some assistant I turned out to be."

Markov stood next to the PSB officers, all of whom were staring fixedly at the muzzle of his Kalashnikov.

"All is forgiven, Ganden," Randy interrupted, "*if* we get out of here unatomized."

Jake frowned at Randy. "Unatomized? Does this have anything to do with the 'blown to kingdom come' part of your little speech to Chen?"

Behind them someone began hurling himself against the interrogation room door. They heard muffled shouting, and Randy backed toward the entrance to the station house. "Later. Let's hit the bricks, troops."

The four men ran out of the station house. Following Ganden and Randy, Jake and Markov sprinted down the crowded street as PSB officers boiled out of the station. Excited voices shouted in Tibetan. Shots were fired, and the shouts turned into screams.

They ducked into the alley where Randy had left the police cruiser. Puzhen sat in the driver's seat, ready to drive the car off if anyone else approached. She slid over, and Ganden leaped in behind the wheel.

"Punch it, Ganden," Randy ordered.

The young Tibetan barreled the car out of the alley.

"Hang on!" Ganden shouted. Tires screaming, he whipped the cruiser into a right turn. Khaki uniforms scattered as they tore past the PSB station.

"Down!" Randy yelled just as a bullet shattered the rear window.

"The local motor pool is not going to be at all happy about that," Jake remarked as he shook the glass from his hair. "Now, what's going on?"

Jake and Markov listened with growing horror as Randy explained about the ADM. "So that's why I had to come get you first," he finished. "The colonel's the only one who can accurately translate the operations manual. I could mostly make it out, but this is definitely *not* the time for guesses."

Randy gave the manual to Markov. Bracing himself against the front seat with one hand, the Russian began reading as Ganden sent the cruiser hurtling through the streets of Lhasa.

✧　✧　✧

Randy rummaged around in the flight bag at his feet. "Item one," he said as he tossed a shaving kit to Jake. "You'll need this."

Frowning, Jake glanced at Randy, then opened the kit. Inside were a razor, a blow dryer, what appeared to be two large butane cartridges, and various smaller items. "It's very nice," Jake commented. "But I thought the 'poise and appearance' phase of the beauty pageant was tomorrow."

Randy pointed at the case. "That's your weapon."

Staring at Randy in confusion, Jake picked up the twin-blade razor. "Well," he mused, "I suppose I could nick someone to death. If he holds still long enough, that is." He looked sharply at Randy.

"This is how the Company gets weapons into a country where we don't have a station. First, the indispensable butane-powered hair dryer." Dumbfounded, Jake watched as Randy pulled off the circular barrel of the dryer, leaving its grip in his hand. "Your handy-dandy one-piece sliding receiver," Randy narrated.

Randy then took the razor and removed its blade assembly. "The handle of the razor becomes the barrel. It *has* to be metal, but nobody minds a metal razor handle." He laid the metal handle of the razor along a groove in the top of the dryer's handle. "Next you take the blow dryer's heating element—that's your recoil spring—and put it in place." Snapping open the body of the blow dryer, Randy took out a strong steel coil. He put it in its place on top of the pistol's grip.

The CIA agent then tugged on the handle of the shaving kit. It came apart, a long metal piece sliding off two leather thongs that were tucked into a groove in its base. Randy carefully set it on top of the other pieces, then shoved it with the heel of his hand. It clicked decisively into place. "The shaving kit's handle becomes your slide, and presto! You're done."

Randy tossed the assembly to Jake. "A Glock Model 19." Jake peered suspiciously at the pistol, turning it over in his hands. "That's right," Randy confirmed. "It's not metal. The Glock's grip is molded from a high-impact composite resin that shows up just like plastic on an airport X-ray machine."

Jake glanced at Randy. "How accurate is it?"

"Don't worry about accuracy," Randy assured him. "It's got a Colt-Browning cam-controlled dropping barrel. Locks down tight when you cock it."

Jake nodded approvingly. "OK," he admitted. "I'm impressed. But only semi-impressed. What about the minor details of a magazine and some ammunition to put in it?"

"That's why the blow dryer is butane-powered," Randy said triumphantly. He snapped plastic caps off both ends of one of the butane cartridges and handed Jake a magazine for the Glock.

Jake whistled appreciatively. "Nine-millimeter?" he asked as he examined the magazine.

"Uh-huh. Nineteen NATO standard rounds. That's where the 'Model 19' comes from." Randy reached into the flight bag. "As for ammo—" He tossed Jake a clear, plastic zip-seal bag.

Jake inspected the contents. "Kodachrome 25. Great film. Terrible ammunition, however. Too slow. No stopping power." He looked quizzically at Randy.

The CIA agent grinned. "One of the tech-types over in Ordnance thought this up. He's a shutterbug who carries a lot of film around, and on his honeymoon he figured out a way we could get ammo through airport security."

Wonder if he figured out how to do anything else on his honeymoon, Jake thought sardonically.

"Open up one of the canisters," Randy told Jake.

Jake took a film cartridge out of the bag. Holding the canister with the flange pointing down, he rapped it smartly against the side window. When nothing happened, Jake frowned and tried it again.

"HOLD IT!" came a muffled shout. Jake looked down to find Randy peering at him from where he was crouched behind the front seat. "What are you doing?" Randy demanded to know.

"Opening the canister," Jake explained patiently, "like you told me to. Anyone who develops their own film knows that the fastest way to open a canister is to bang on the flange. That presses the film spool against the lid on the other end of the canister, and off it pops."

Randy crawled back into his seat. "Right," he said, taking a deep breath. "It may be a tad slower, but just pry the lid off, OK?"

Jake borrowed Randy's Swiss army knife and used its bottle opener to pop off the lid of the canister he was holding. "Oops," he said quietly, as he stared into the cassette.

Randy grinned. "Now you can see why I thought for a minute that you had suddenly developed a death wish."

Jake upended the canister, and his ammunition tumbled into his hand.

"Three rounds per film canister," Randy explained. "Twelve canisters gives us almost enough to fully load two of the Glock's magazines." They got to work opening the cartridges. "Glasers or Hardballs?" Randy asked when they were done.

Markov looked up from the manual. "What are those?" he asked Randy. He pointed at the ammunition, which Jake and Randy had sorted into two piles in their laps. Half the bullets had little blue caps on their tips.

"Glaser Safety Slugs," Randy explained. "They were originally developed for Israel's air marshals to use in shootouts aboard aircraft." He picked up one of the blue-tipped slugs. "Inside the Glaser's hollowed-out bullet are dozens of tiny pellets. When the round impacts, the pellets spray out through the plastic-capped hole in the end of the slug, acting like a miniature shotgun shell. This causes extensive damage with little penetration. That way, the air marshals can concentrate on putting holes in their targets without having to worry about putting holes in the aircraft."

Jake's other choice were the Hardballs, the full-metal-jacket slugs mandated by the Geneva Convention for use in wartime. "I'll take the Hardballs," Jake decided. He knew these rounds passed through the target cleanly, inflicting minimal injury if they didn't kill.

"Great," Randy said happily. "Makes sense—you're a lot better shot than I am. I like the Glasers, because wherever I manage to pop someone they go down and stay down." Randy picked up one of Jake's magazines. "Careful with the feed lips on these," he cautioned, pointing to two small metal tabs at the end of the magazine. "They're real delicate. Bend one of them, and the pistol will jam right up on you."

Jake nodded and started sliding cartridges into his magazines. "Never heard of Glock," he admitted. "German outfit?"

"Nope. They're headquartered in Austria. But these little honeys were manufactured in Smyrna, Georgia."

Finished with his loading, Jake held the pistol at arm's length and sighted along the barrel. He smiled, then softly started whistling "Dixie."

40

"What on earth?" Jake muttered as they came to a halt on the landing that led into the Potala.

A line of monks blocked the entrance to the palace. The horizontal light of the setting sun bathed in scarlet their silver chain mail and breastplates. Each monk also wore a silver-and-leather helmet topped with an embroidered, peacock-feathered fan whose plumes stirred restlessly in the evening breeze.

Jake heard Randy's disbelieving chuckle. "It'd be funnier if they didn't have those pieces of field artillery pointed at us," he whispered. Jake motioned with his head at the rank of ancient muzzle-loaders the monks had leveled at them.

Ganden shouted in Tibetan at the monks. One of them shook his head. Ganden shouted again and pointed at the palace. The monk barked an order, and another of the defenders disappeared into the Potala.

"These are warrior monks from the monastery at Litang," Ganden explained when the monk had left, "who have vowed to defend the Potala with their lives. They have agreed to get the abbot who let me go earlier."

As the tense standoff wore on, Jake studied the pathetic,

yet potentially deadly, row of militia. "Why do they look like something out of the Crusades?" he wondered aloud.

"Hundreds of years ago," Ganden answered, "a Muslim army marching on Lhasa perished in a blizzard. When the bodies were discovered, their arms and armor were divided up between the Tibetan army and the warrior monks. The Han confiscated the army's equipment in 1959, but the monks hid theirs."

The monks broke ranks to admit the abbot. "Why have you returned?" the wizened, gray-haired old man asked Ganden.

"To help, *khenpo*," Ganden replied, according the abbot his traditional title. He pointed at the rest. "These men can save the Potala."

The abbot's shrewd eyes surveyed Jake and the rest. "No *feringy* may enter the Chamber of the Dharma King," he told Ganden. "To do so would desecrate the shrine." Dismay swept over them as the abbot shook his head. "It is forbidden."

"Does he realize that he's about to die?" Jake asked Ganden.

"He does. And he views this as a chance to go straight to Nirvana."

They watched as Ganden, thinking hard, stared at the ground. The prayer bells atop the Jokhang began to toll the call to sunset prayers.

Ganden's head came up suddenly. "I think I've found a way he can let us in."

Randy checked his watch. "Make it quick, man. Short and persuasive."

"Cannot that which has been desecrated be once again made holy, *khenpo?*" Ganden asked. The abbot's eyes narrowed. "Cannot a special ceremony of *rab-ne* be held to reconsecrate the shrine once the *feringy* have finished?"

They waited as the abbot considered this. "How long?"

Jake whispered to Randy. His watch had been stolen by one of his guards.

"Seven minutes," Randy replied. Under his breath he started whistling "We'll All Go Together When We Go."

The abbot spoke to his men. Four of them trotted to the entrance to the Potala. Then he turned to Ganden and spoke sharply.

"Let's go!" Ganden shouted as he started to run. "Those monks are going to clear the way for us."

Preceded by their Byzantine honor guard, they disappeared into the mouth of the Potala.

"How long does it take to disarm one of your ADMs?" Randy asked Markov as they ran.

"My best recruits could safe one in three minutes," Markov replied. "The poorer ones took eight."

Randy grimaced. "Then you two had better do at least B+ work, or we all flunk out in a big way."

The ADM sat where Ganden had left it, the numbers on its LED panel clicking downward. Barabise lay huddled in a corner. Ganden and Markov knelt next to the bomb. Ganden opened the access panel as Markov reached into his jacket.

"*Nichevo!*" Markov exclaimed. "The manual is missing! It must have fallen from my jacket when I got out of the car." The three men waited, motionless, as the Russian mopped his face. He closed his eyes and began muttering in Russian.

"You know," Jake whispered to Randy. "Dmitry may be on to something. Praying right now is probably a great idea."

Markov opened his eyes. "Step one," he said in English. "Reset exclusion region surge capacitors." Ganden's fingers flew over the keypad as Markov alternated between Russian and English.

Jake saw the LED timer drop below four minutes. "Just how do you feel about Anne?" he whispered to Randy. "I know

351

that you've dated her a couple of times—not that you seem the type to kiss and tell."

Randy glanced at Jake. "I never kissed her, so there's not much to tell."

Three minutes.

"First off," Randy continued. "I wouldn't exactly call what we did 'dating.' I was going to school at Bowdoin. After I got to know Joel, he invited me to his place a few times for the weekend. The Drydens were just back from Peru, and Anne didn't know anyone. So, as a favor to them, I took Anne to see *National Velvet.* I got to check out Elizabeth Taylor, and Anne cried the whole time because Velvet reminded her of some horse she'd had to leave behind in Lima." Randy grinned at the memory. *"Not* my idea of a hot date." His hair shimmered in the butter light as he shook his head. "She'll be a tough nut to crack. Probably even tougher than that friend of hers." Randy looked pointedly at Jake. "Any guy Anne gives an inch to had better take all he can get."

Two minutes. Ganden whispered urgently to Markov, who repeated himself.

"Then why was she so glad to see you at Pat's party?" Jake asked obstinately.

Randy smiled. "My," he said disparagingly, "we are para-noid, aren't we? She's a *friend*, see, and we hadn't seen each other in a while. Do you know why she was so glad to see me? Because she hadn't had a chance to tell me about this guy she had met."

One minute.

"She loves you, man, and that's something you *don't* take for granted." Randy turned and watched the flickering *chome.*

Markov spoke emphatically to Ganden, who flipped a switch. The bank of green lights below the keypad changed to red. The two men sank to the floor.

"Weapon disarmed," Markov gasped.

Randy glanced at the timer. "Thirty-seven seconds. Heck, we could've walked."

"There is one more thing to do," Markov said. "Enter three incorrect combinations into the Permissive Action Link," he ordered Ganden.

Ganden used the keypad to type three twelve-digit numbers. The LEDs flashed, then went dark.

"The weapon has now been disabled," Markov explained. "And certain critical components have been destroyed. In order to restore the weapon to operational readiness, the Chinese will have to return it to the factory." He smiled wryly. "Since that factory is located in Siberia at Novosibirsk, I don't think they'll bother."

A movement in the shadows attracted their attention. Barabise had struggled to his knees and was fumbling for his *thupta*. Jake walked over, snatched the dagger from Barabise's hand, and stuck it in his own belt.

Behind him, Jake heard an outburst of Tibetan and whirled around. Ganden had pulled his pistol from his jacket. He stared down at Barabise. "I thought you were already dead," he whispered in English. The muzzle of his Type 57 quivered with the intensity of the young Tibetan's hatred.

"Ganden, don't," Jake said urgently. "It's not worth it. I know."

"What do you know of killing?" Ganden retorted. "You live in America, not Tibet."

"About the time you were born I spent two years killing men your age—in a place called Vietnam."

Ganden looked at Jake out of the corner of his eye. "And you call yourself a Christian!"

"I do," Jake replied quietly. "Now." Ganden continued to stare at him. "God helped me get over what I did and what happened to me. He'll help you get over what's happened to you, too. If you let him. But shooting Barabise will only make it a lot worse and a lot harder."

Ganden shook his head. "No! I must have my vengeance!" He screamed in Tibetan at Barabise, who stiffened. The nomad watched as Ganden's finger tightened on the trigger. Jake tensed as he prepared to knock Ganden's arm aside.

"You're about to kill a dead man, Ganden." Randy's voice came out of the shadows.

He pointed at Barabise. "See those blisters on his face? And see how much he's bled from that small cut? This guy's suffering from radiation poisoning." Randy looked at Ganden. "Ask him how close he was to that nuke he detonated."

Barabise's eyes flicked to Randy as Ganden spoke to him. "About a kilometer," Ganden told Randy.

Randy shook his head. "That's about half a mile. I'm surprised he's alive at all. If the warhead he corked off is similar in yield to our W54-2, then he got dosed with well over two hundred rads. That's the equivalent of over two thousand chest X-rays."

"Then are we fried from the fallout?" Jake asked.

Randy shook his head. "ADMs are 'clean' weapons. Very little fallout and almost no residual radiation. This guy's in a bad way only because he was so close to the blast."

"What does that mean?" Ganden asked.

Randy leaned over and tugged on a strand of Barabise's mustache. The nomad winced as the hair pulled free, leaving a raw, red patch on his upper lip. "It means he'll be dead within a week. Shooting him would be a kindness—dying of radiation sickness is a miserable way to go."

Ganden wavered.

"Vengeance *isn't* ours, Ganden," Jake said quietly. "No matter how much we may want it to be."

The young Tibetan stared at Barabise for a long moment,

then lowered the pistol. As Ganden spoke to Barabise at length the Khampa went rigid, then collapsed.

"What did you tell him?" Jake asked.

"The truth," Ganden replied grimly. "That he was dying. That he will soon be at the mercy of his old enemy the Han. And that because his flesh was poisoned, the monks will deny him a sky burial and will instead bury him in the ground. Which, in his faith, means that instead of being a blessing to his land he will be a curse." Ganden looked at Barabise once more, then turned away.

✦ ✦ ✦

Puzhen ran into the grotto from where Ganden had posted her as lookout. "The PSB!" she whispered. "They just came in through the north entrance!" Puzhen looked at Barabise. "What about him?"

"We're leaving him for the Han," Ganden replied.

Puzhen gazed down at the nomad chieftain. Barabise tried to return her stare, then dropped his eyes.

Ganden beckoned from the doorway to the shrine. "Come. Quickly."

He led them back the way they came, the *chome* still flickering before the gilded statues. Faintly, they heard the sound of running feet. Ganden paused at the top of a steep, wooden stairway.

"You go out the east entrance," he told Puzhen. "I'll meet you at your parents' house."

Puzhen hesitated, one hand on the time-polished banister. "But—"

"Go! I must help those who helped us." *And, if we are captured, I don't want you with me when the torturing starts.* Puzhen flitted down the stairs and was gone.

"This way," Ganden told Markov, Jake, and Randy. He led them into a huge assembly hall whose smoke-blackened ceiling was supported by 108 wooden columns, each studded with a fortune in agate and coral. Dusty light streamed down from high windows set into the western wall.

The four men weaved among the columns, their footsteps silent on the earthen floor. Jake stared at the far wall of the hall, which was covered by a grotesque fresco.

"The tantric protector god Hayagriva," Ganden explained as they trotted across the vast hall. "He's embracing his consort Vishvamati, and they're standing on the corpses of lesser deities." Hayagriva fingered his massive sword as he glared down at them from over the shoulder of his mistress.

"Hayagriva protects the riches of this place," Ganden added. "It is said that if anyone pries one of the stones from a column, Hayagriva will leap down and lop off the hand that holds the jewel."

"He must get a cut of the souvenir shop business," Randy remarked.

A door in the base of the fresco opened into a long hall painted orange and green. A line of bare lightbulbs ran down the center of the ceiling, suspended at intervals by hooks.

"How do you know your way around this place so well?" Jake asked. "It's not as if you came here every Sunday."

Ganden grinned. "The electricity in this part of the Potala is my responsibility." He pointed at the string of lights. "This wiring is more than fifty years old. Ever since a short circuit in 1984 started a huge fire that destroyed the Hall of the Buddha Maitreya, we've conducted monthly inspections. Still, it was almost a year before I could find my way around on my own."

The hallway ended in a door that led out onto a tiny landing. Lhasa stretched westward before them. Across the river, storm clouds, suffused with orange and silver by the setting sun, loomed over the mountains.

Ganden pointed at a small cluster of whitewashed buildings huddled at the foot of the palace. "That is all that is left of our ancient village of Chö. The Han bulldozed the rest so as to bring their tanks within shelling range of the Potala. There are people there who will give you shelter, and the PSB does not dare to patrol at night." Jake, Markov, and Randy followed Ganden down a stairway that jutted out from the towering west face of the palace. The marble steps had been polished and hollowed-out by countless pilgrim feet, and all four men kept their hands on the scalloped stone and plaster railing as they trotted down the stairs.

The stairway emptied into a flagstone plaza. Across the square, lanterns in shop windows winked invitingly. Ganden waved them on. As the last vestiges of light vanished from the evening sky, they ran across the plaza and into the alleyway.

"*Toshi dili, chola!*" Ganden called to a man who was picking up large copper and brass tubs from in front of a shop and carrying them inside. The man set down the stack of tubs he was carrying and waved. As Ganden spoke rapidly in Tibetan, the shopkeeper eyed Jake, Randy, and Markov. After Ganden had finished what was obviously a question, the man spoke briefly, then nodded.

Ganden turned to the three. "This used to be my parents' shop," he explained. "And this is Delag, an old friend of my family. He has agreed to hide you until we can figure how best to smuggle you out of the country."

"*Tujaychay,*" Jake said.

The merchant smiled at Jake's thanks and led them inside. Polished brass gleamed in the warm lantern light. Kernels of barley leaked from burlap sacks stacked along the wall and crunched underfoot. A middle-aged woman smiled nervously at them from behind the counter. Delag spoke to Ganden, then went back outside.

"Delag said that after he's closed up the shop for the night we'll have dinner."

"Good," Markov murmured. "I could eat a horse."

"We probably will," Randy replied.

Outside, they heard the roar of a powerful engine and the squealing of brakes. The soft yellow glow of the shop's lanterns was replaced suddenly by harsh white light that streamed in the open door and leaked through the closed shutters. Delag shouted; angry voices shouted back. The woman behind the counter whispered urgently to Ganden.

"This way. Quickly," Ganden ordered.

The four men squeezed into a small storage room at the back of the shop. The woman slammed the closet door behind them. Jake heard a scraping as she pulled something in front of the door.

"I thought you said the PSB never patrolled here at night," Jake said to Ganden.

"Doesn't sound like a patrol to me," Randy remarked. "Sounds more like an all-out raid."

Breaking glass and the clattering of metal on concrete were added to the angry voices. There was a frantic knocking on the door, followed by the woman's voice.

"They must have seen us," Ganden said. "They know we are here."

Randy looked at Markov. "So much for a leisurely dinner."

"Can you open that window?" Ganden asked Jake. "It's our only chance."

Jake reached up to the rectangular window set high in the back wall of the closet. He turned the latch, then pushed against the window. It opened slightly, then stopped. Jake reached out and placed the palm of his hand against the closet wall opposite the window. Stretched across the storage room, he pushed again. With a sudden groan of metal the window flew open. It shattered, raining shards of glass down on Jake's hand.

"Just call me Samson," Jake said as he shook the glass off.

"I'll go first," Ganden said. "The soldiers won't notice me. If it's clear, I'll throw a rock back through the window." He reached up to the windowsill and pulled himself up and through.

The three men waited tensely in the darkness. Behind them, the sounds of the store's ransacking grew nearer.

"If they try to get in," Jake whispered, "you two get out while I hold the door shut."

"Thanks very much, Horatius," Randy replied.

A rock clattered against the wall above their heads. They all looked at each other. Then Markov shrugged, shouldered his Kalashnikov, and clambered through the window. Randy followed and waited with Ganden and Markov until Jake dropped silently to the ground beside them. Keeping low, they scuttled down an alleyway that ran along the side of the building.

Ganden peered cautiously around the corner of the storefront. "Wait here," he whispered. He darted across the street and disappeared into the shadows. Jake and Randy waited motionlessly. Ganden's hand appeared in a pool of street light, beckoning. Markov joined him. At the next summons Jake shoved Randy, who sprinted over to where Ganden and the Russian were hiding. Jake held his breath as shots were fired inside the store.

When Ganden waved, Jake came to his feet. Halfway across the street, a cat darted between his legs. The animal's squeal echoed as Jake stepped on it. Jake tripped and went sprawling. A powerful flashlight came on in the doorway of the store. It swept up and down the street, inches above where Jake lay flattened against the dusty cobblestones. The beam passed over him twice, then went out. Slowly Jake crawled the rest of the way on knees and elbows. Breathing hard, he pulled himself into the shadows next to his three friends.

"Since you didn't get us captured," Randy whispered, "I won't turn you in to the ASPCA for trashing that cat."

"Where now?" Jake asked.

Ganden's eyes glinted in the light. "We must make our way down to the river. To the island called Thieves' Park."

41

The reassembled National Security Council watched the shapes crawling across the projected map.

"All our 688s have surfaced, Mr. President," Rodriguez reported. "They're awaiting your orders."

The president studied the screen. "Have the Chinese crossed our line?"

"No sir. They've stopped just the other side of it. Seems like they're waiting for something to happen, just like us."

The president rubbed his chin. "Put the subs back on patrol. If any of the Chinese subs cross our line, or if any of our assets are fired upon, they may fire at will." As Rodriguez passed the orders along, the president turned to the group of civilians seated at the far end of the table. "Gentlemen, I have just ordered our attack submarines into a situation that very well may lead to war. You've been briefed on the events that led up to this. If it comes to a declaration of war, I hope I'll have your support."

The Speaker of the House and the Senate majority leader nodded. "You will, Mr. President."

The phone in front of Air Force Chief Winthrop warbled.

The general picked it up, listened, and turned to the president. "It's the Pentagon Command Post, sir. The A-3 is asking for the release of his weapons."

An air force general, one of three who rotated eight-hour shifts manning the post, had just received a call from SAC Headquarters at Offut Field in Omaha. The caller, identified as "A-3," was actually Lieutenant General Barry Mathewson, commander in chief of the Strategic Air Command.

Legally, the president had technical ownership of the nation's nuclear arsenal. Hence, the air force could fire its weapons only with his permission. Mathewson's call meant that SAC felt that the situation was now serious enough to warrant asking for that permission. The president frowned. "We're still at DEFCON Two," he reminded General Winthrop.

"Yes sir. But if we go to One and start shooting, SAC might need that release right quick."

Roddy Rodriguez looked out at the Rose Garden lawn. *Wonder if there'll be an Easter for my grandkids to hunt eggs out there.*

The president knew Barry Mathewson to be a level-headed, conservative man. He took a deep breath. "Weapons free." *Yea, though I walk through the valley of the shadow of death.*

"Weapons free," Winthrop repeated into the phone. He looked at his watch. "Time is oh-nine-oh-four Zulu. Will confirm electronically." The old general looked at his commanding officer. "Thank you, sir. Better to be safe than sorry."

The president laughed. "Glad this makes *you* feel safe, General, because it makes me feel nothing of the sort."

They waited beside the road, crouched in a copse of scraggly rhododendron, until a three-truck convoy roared past.

"Do I hear water?" Markov asked.

"The Kyichu," Ganden whispered. "We must cross it to get you to safety."

The four trotted across Yanhe Xilu, where Ganden's outstretched arm brought them to a halt. Ahead of them, a bridge arced away into the night.

"Is it moving?" Randy asked, squinting to see better.

"It is covered with prayer flags," Ganden explained. "The steady wind causes them to flutter, and each flutter of a flag gains merit in heaven for the one who placed it there. We must be very quiet," he cautioned. "The old woman who collects the bridge toll sleeps in a hut on this side."

One by one they crept onto the bridge, finding that the sound of their footsteps was masked by the resonant snores that emanated from within the tollbooth. On either side of them the red, yellow, and white of thousands of ragged, triangular prayer flags was visible in the brilliant moonlight. The wooden planking of the bridge swayed beneath them, its creaking lost in the gurgle of the Kyichu.

"Are we going back to the Land Cruiser?" Jake asked when the four had safely crossed the river.

"We will drive it to my home village of Kangmar," Ganden confirmed. "From there friends of mine will help you across the border to Nepal."

"Are you going to be all right?"

Ganden smiled, a white crescent against the blackness. "I won't be able to return here, so instead I will send for Puzhen. There are worse places to raise a family than where I grew up."

Ganden led them past a cluster of shuttered buildings, stark and barren in the light from a single gooseneck lamp. As they circled a grove of mountain ashes, a startled exclamation from Markov was followed by a feminine squeal and a guttural oath.

"As crowded here as Gorky Park in Moscow on a July night," the Russian muttered as he came to his feet.

As they trotted through a clearing at the end of the small pond that occupied the center of Jarmalinka Island, Ganden scooped up several long, sturdy branches.

"The PLA around here must be armed with quarterstaffs," Randy whispered to Jake.

"I think I know what he's up to," Jake replied. "Glad it's a nice night for punting."

✧ ✧ ✧

They watched as Ganden dragged the yak-hide coracle out of the thicket of bulrushes and lowered it into the river.

"Must be nice to have a private berth," Randy commented. "How'd he know it was there?"

"Ganden hid it there the night he kidnapped me," Jake replied.

"Kidnapped you? I thought he was on our side."

"He is. He just forgot for a while who he's really working for."

When Ganden beckoned, they hurried across the shingle beach to the river's edge.

"Here," Ganden said, handing each of them one of the branches he had gathered. "Have you ever poled a boat before?"

"Sure," Randy replied. "I was on a four-man shell crew at Bowdoin." He looked at Markov. "You know the words to 'The Song of the Vulgar Boatmen?'"

The Russian frowned. "You mean the *Volga* boatmen, don't you?"

"Not the way we sang it at Bowdoin, I don't."

"When you get in," Ganden cautioned, "be very careful to step only on the thwarts. Otherwise your foot will go right through the yak hide and into the river."

"Something is wrong?" Markov asked.

"No," Ganden replied. "Why?"

"Didn't you just say we were thwarted? And doesn't that mean we are frustrated or stopped?"

Ganden stared at Markov. He pointed to the pair of wooden seats fastened to the coracle's hull. "*These* are thwarts. At least, that's what an American rafter I guided told me." The two turned to Jake.

"You're both right. *Thwart* means both to frustrate and a boatman's seat."

"*Nichevo*," Markov muttered as he stepped carefully into the boat. "The American language is a far more formidable weapon than your ICBMs ever were."

Fifteen minutes of poling ended with the scrape of the coracle's hull against the far bank of the Kyuchi.

"The culvert in which we hid your car is straight ahead," Ganden whispered. "Wait here while I get it." He trotted up the beach.

The Tibetan's startled cry brought the three men running.

"It's gone!" he exclaimed, emerging from the black mouth of the overpass. "The army must have found it and towed it away."

"Did you leave my camera in the backseat?" Jake asked. Ganden nodded. *Wonder who's going to be more upset*, Jake thought. *The PLA guy who tries to take pictures with that F3 or my insurance agent when he gets a fifty-grand claim from the CIA.* "Can we take the coracle downriver?"

Ganden shook his head. "The river soon gets very shallow. Besides, the guards on the bridge at Qüxu have machine guns."

"Down!" Randy snapped. The four men hit the ground. Looking up, Jake could see that a light had come on in a small, cinder-block building about a hundred yards upstream.

"Somebody just pulled a curtain aside," Randy explained. "Don't know if he heard us or not."

"That's wonderful!" Ganden exclaimed.

"It is?" three voices asked in unison.

"Yes. The building is a small PLA outpost that is supposed to protect the road leading to the airport. It is unmanned except in emergencies like—"

"Like this little one we've whipped up," Randy finished. "Think they might have a car?"

"Maybe," Ganden replied. "If they weren't dropped off."
He motioned them forward. "Let's find out."

Four shadows blotted out the starlight dancing on the
Kyuchi as they crept up the beach.

The door to the outpost flew open. The four men froze,
trapped in the narrow strip of shore between the water and the
light from the open door. As they watched, a figure was silhou-
etted in the doorway. Jake held his breath, ready to dive into the
river if the figure approached. Voices called loudly from inside.
The figure turned, and the red spark of a cigarette butt arced
into the water. Jake relaxed as the door closed.

Silently, following Ganden, they worked their way past
the outpost to the far side of the building. Ganden pointed.
Parked beneath a light mounted to the rear of the outpost was
a Jiefang. A red star mounted prominently above the cab
marked it as a Red Army truck. They ran toward it. Raucous
laughter and the clatter of *mah jongg* tiles drifted from inside the
building as they circled the front of the truck.

"No keys," Ganden reported from inside the cab.

"Too heavy to push-start," Randy reported. "And besides,
the way we want to go is slightly uphill." He motioned to Jake
and Markov. "You two in back. Ganden, you get ready to drive."
Jake and Markov scrambled into the back of the truck as Randy
eased up the hood and disappeared beneath it.

Ganden leaped into the driver's seat as the truck rumbled
into life.

Randy, smiling triumphantly, appeared on the passenger's
side. "GO!"

He scrambled in as Ganden threw the Jiefang into gear. A
Red Army cap was lying on the dash. Randy jerked it down low
over his eyes as Ganden pulled onto the road. The Jiefang
moved eastward, gaining speed.

"Did the CIA teach you to hot-wire vehicles?" Markov

asked through the partition that separated the cargo area from the truck's cab.

Randy wiped his greasy hands on his pants. "Nope. Learned as a member of the South Side Dukes, growing up in Detroit."

"South Side Dukes?"

"Yeah. It was a sort of youth program."

Markov nodded. "Ah! Like our Young Pioneers." He disappeared into the back of the truck.

Randy frowned at Ganden. "I'll be a little conspicuous up here with you, won't I?"

Ganden shrugged. "Since even those soldiers weren't drunk enough not to notice the theft of their truck, it is a chance we'll have to take. They will report it, which means we'll be pursued. Besides, these Jiefangs always stall." He looked at Randy, his face pale in the reflected headlights. "If it stops, you'll have to get it restarted. Quickly."

Rodriguez hung up his red phone. "That was Admiral Harrison. The BARSTUR listening station on Kauai is monitoring a long ELF message being transmitted to the Chinese subs."

"BARSTUR?" O'Brien interjected.

"Barking Sands Tactical Underwater Range. The Pacific Fleet's network of bottom-mounted hydrophones and three-dimensional range tracking instrumentation. It's our principal line of defense in ASW. That's Anti-Submarine Warfare," Rodriguez added, knowing that it would cause the civilian O'Brien to smolder. "Hopefully any Chinese subs, stray or otherwise, won't be able to cross it without our knowing."

"Do we know what they're being ordered to do?" Melinda Cunningham asked.

The chairman shook his head. "That's the problem with ciphers. Since they're not a code, they can't be decoded. But the NSA boys and girls at OMEGA seem to think it's an ops order."

"Ops?"

"Operations. The subs are being told to go somewhere." All eyes in the Situation Room went to the projected TDRSS image.

"What action is Admiral Harrison taking?" the president asked.

"Everything still at Pearl is being sent to sea, and all aircraft at Hickam have been scrambled."

"What next?"

"We watch, wait, and above all, listen."

Everyone in the room watched as the president placed his hand on the phone that, when used, would plunge them into nuclear war.

❖ ❖ ❖

Feeling the truck stop suddenly, Jake looked through the partition. "What's up?" Grinning, Randy pointed out his window. "Why," Jake asked, "are you whistling 'Ticket to Ride?'" He scrambled out of the truck. Markov followed, Kalashnikov on his back. The Russian crept to the edge of the cliff.

It sat fifty feet below them, bathed in spotlights. "F-70-CT Blackhawk," Randy whispered. "Sikorsky sold twenty-four of them to the Chinese back in '84." Randy shook his head. "When I opposed the sale, I never dreamed that one of them would turn out to be our ticket out of here."

"You know how to fly that, Cavanaugh?" Markov asked doubtfully.

Randy nodded. "I cut my helicoptering teeth on its first cousin, the S-67."

The helicopter sat in a large courtyard, surrounded on three sides by buildings, with the cliff on which the men stood forming the fourth side of the compound.

"Know anything about this place?" Jake asked Ganden.

"They use that helicopter for crowd control," Ganden replied. "During the last uprising it was used to spray the crowds with gas. Many people died." Ganden stared at the dark green machine. "I do not know how many troops are stationed here."

Markov returned. "The cliff face is vertical and smooth as a *tsarina*'s skin."

Ganden nodded. "That is why they built here."

Randy swore. "Great. So that means that it's two pistols and one semiautomatic against the Chinese army." He took a deep breath and turned to Ganden. "OK, here's what we'll do. You drive the truck up to the gate and honk. Maybe the grunt that's pulled tonight's sentry duty will think it's the pizza he ordered and open up. If he does, then we'll—"

"Hang on a sec, General Custer," Jake interrupted. "Let's save the Last Stand for later."

"You got a better idea?" Randy asked irritably.

Jake vanished into the back of the truck. He emerged a moment later, carrying something. In the light reflected from the courtyard below he unrolled a yard of gauzy blue material from the bolt he was holding. "I was sitting on this."

Randy stared at Jake. "I must admit," he finally said, "that it's your color. But don't you think it's a little sheer for this weather?"

Markov frowned. "I don't understand, MacIntyre. How will this negligee material help us?"

Jake swapped grins with Ganden. "*Khata* cloth," Ganden explained. "They sell it by the yard to pilgrims as prayer scarves. It's silk. Very strong. The soldiers use it to buy favors from the barmaids."

"Just a moment, MacIntyre," Markov ordered. He crawled forward and reconnoitered. "One sentry, almost directly below us," he reported. "Too close to the cliff to have heard us coming." The Russian unslung his Kalashnikov and aimed carefully. The rifle barked once.

Jake tied one end of the bolt to a ring welded to the truck's frame. He walked to the edge of the cliff, trailing the cloth behind him, and flung the bolt into the night. It arced outward, unrolling as it went. The material settled against the cliff face as it came off the cardboard tube. The tube clattered against the courtyard's floor, and the four men dropped to the ground.

Jake crept forward cautiously, peered over the edge, then stood up. "We're about eight feet short, gentlemen," he announced. "So watch out for that last step."

"OK," Randy said. "You guys are the rough-and-tumble types. Just how are we going to pull this off?"

The two infantrymen looked at each other. Jake instinctively deferred to his superior officer. Markov walked to the edge, beckoning for them to follow.

"How long will it take you to get ready?" he asked Randy.

"After engine start, it takes them about a minute to warmup until we're able to lift."

"Then I'll go down first," Markov explained, happy to at last be doing something familiar, "and position myself *there.*" The colonel pointed to one corner of the compound. "MacIntyre, you'll be over there in the other corner. After the enemy is alerted by the noise of the engines, we'll set up a crossfire that should provide Cavanaugh with cover. When he signals, we board the helicopter." Markov slung his Kalashnikov over his shoulder and walked to the edge of the cliff. He grabbed the cloth, and after a solemn salute, began his descent.

"Me next," Randy volunteered. "Some spy I am. Never have been able to stand waiting." When the cloth went slack, Randy followed Markov over the edge.

Jake looked at Ganden. "As soon as I hit dirt, you beat it." He cut off Ganden's protests. "There's nothing you can do for us once we're down there, and I don't want you to be connected with this in any way." Ganden returned Jake's gaze for a moment, then nodded. Jake stuck out his hand. "Fight the good fight, brother."

Ganden returned Jake's grasp. *"Kâli pay,* my friend. Go slowly."

Jake grinned. *"Kâli shu,* my friend. Stay slowly," he replied to the traditional Tibetan farewell. He grabbed the cloth and leaned out over the cliff. "Let me know when your first child is born. I'll be back for the christening."

Ganden waved and walked to the truck. When he looked back, Jake was gone.

✧ ✧ ✧

Jake hung from the end of the cloth, then dropped lightly to the ground beside Randy. A soft rustling above him told Jake that Ganden had pulled up their makeshift rope. *Only one way out now.*

"As soon as you're in position, I'll break for the chopper," Randy whispered. Jake nodded. Keeping low, he trotted over to his corner of the compound. Jake pulled his Glock from his jacket pocket, then gave Randy a "thumbs-up." Randy looked over at Markov, who nodded.

Randy ran up to the Blackhawk. He reached into a recessed compartment, and the helicopter's Plexiglas canopy rose silently on hydraulic pistons. Markov and Jake watched as Randy jumped into the cockpit and settled into the pilot's seat.

So far, so good, Jake thought as he swept the compound with his eyes. A low hum filled the courtyard. *Sounds like it's showtime.* He pulled back the slide on his Glock, feeling a round slide into the chamber. Out of the corner of his eye Jake saw Markov bring up the muzzle of the Kalashnikov.

Randy ignited the Blackhawk's twin T58-GE-5 turboshaft engines, and the hum became a roar that rattled the buildings. Across the compound a head popped out of the sentry booth near the front gate. Markov sprayed the gate with a burst from the Kalashnikov, and the head disappeared.

A door opened on Jake's side of the barracks. Jake snapped off three shots in quick succession, bracketing the doorway.

The Blackhawk's five-bladed rotor began to turn slowly. Jake ducked as a bullet ricocheted off the wall inches above his head. *Talk about life's longest minute,* he thought as he looked around for the shooter. The whine of the two 1500-horsepower jet engines rose in pitch.

Doors began flying open all over the compound. Markov was on his feet, directing a withering fire anywhere a face appeared. Several bodies lay sprawled across doorsteps. The *whop-whop* of the rotor blade tips breaking the sound barrier began. Jake fired on an empty chamber, ripped the magazine from the Glock, and slammed home his only spare. *C'mon, man,* he urged Randy. *Time for a little action.*

Markov looked up from his reloading just as a PLA soldier jumped out of a doorway right in front of him. As the soldier brought up his rifle, Jake turned. With the Glock held in both hands he squeezed off a shot. The soldier spun to the ground and began to crawl away.

Randy's beckoning arm came out of the cockpit. Jake waved to Markov, then began his dash to the helicopter. Halfway there, Jake noticed that Markov was still standing in his corner. He waved again, but the Russian didn't move. Jake changed course, sprinting around the Blackhawk's tail rotor. Bullets cratered the ground around him as he ducked and swerved. Markov's Kalashnikov cleared a path for Jake as he approached.

"Go, fool!" Markov shouted. He pointed at his left ankle. "Twisted it when I fell from the rope. I think it's sprained. I'll cover you. Now move!"

Jake threw his right arm around the Russian. "I've never missed a pickup on a mate yet, and I'm not about to start now."

A guard appeared on the wall above them. Jake fired, and the man spun out of sight. Markov put his arm over Jake's shoulders. He braced the Kalashnikov against his hip. Firing as they went, the pair began their three-legged race across the compound.

Halfway there, Jake winced as a bullet creased his arm. He snapped off a shot, then flung away the empty Glock. They could see Randy looking out of the cockpit. The roar of the turbines increased.

"He's leaving!" Markov bellowed.

If he is, Jake thought, *I hope I live so he can live to regret it.*

Clouds of dust began to fill the compound as the tornadolike winds created by the rotor picked up force. Jake threw his free arm in front of his face to shield his eyes. The dust swirled up over the walls, completely enveloping the barracks. Blinded, the two men hobbled on.

The grit ceased to sting his face, and Jake opened his eyes. The area under the rotor had been swept clear of dust, and they could see the Blackhawk hovering about a foot off the ground.

"It's a smokescreen!" Jake shouted. "He laid down cover for us!"

Jake threw the cargo door of the Blackhawk open, and Markov clambered in. He could see Randy pointing at the seat directly behind him in the S-67's tandem cockpit. Jake slammed the cargo door and lunged toward the cockpit. He was halfway in when Randy slammed the throttles home and hurled the Blackhawk into the sky.

Half a mile away, Randy brought the S-67 to a hover. He twisted around and pointed to a helmet hanging on a hook beside Jake's head. "Glad you could make it," he said over the intercom when Jake had the helmet on. "If I'd known you were going to take the scenic route, I'd have charged you for waiting time." Randy lowered the cockpit canopy, and the Blackhawk picked up speed.

"Appreciate your waiting around," Jake replied. "Since I think a bullet hole through your visa probably invalidates it."

"You there, Colonel?" Randy asked.

"I am," Markov answered. "Thanks to MacIntyre." The Russian paused. "You called me a 'mate' back there, MacIntyre. I do not know this word. What does it mean?"

"It's a U.S. Army term," Jake replied quietly. "It's what you call someone you trust—someone who's proven himself, who you'd be willing to have at your back in a fight."

"Ah," Markov replied. "What we call a comrade." He paused again. "MacIntyre, you are a comrade, mate."

Randy put the Blackhawk into a sweeping turn. "Nepal's our only hope," he said. "And that's not saying much. It's about five hundred klicks from here. Which means that, if this S-67 is like the others I've flown, the Nepalese border is right at the extreme limit of its range."

"What are our chances?" Jake asked.

"Hard to say. We'll be flying higher, which is good. We'll also be flying faster, which is bad."

"Go for it," Jake replied. "Pedal to the metal. Forced landing is the worst that can happen to us."

"I'm afraid not, MacIntyre," Markov interjected. "I've been monitoring the radio traffic. The air base at Chengdu has just scrambled its fighter squadron in response to Lhasa's call for help."

"That does it," Randy muttered. "I'm charging you guys double."

"What is our top speed, Cavanaugh?" Markov asked.

"Around 170 knots," Randy replied. "Maybe 200 at this altitude. Why?"

"The fighter squadron at Chengdu consists entirely of F-4s. That's the Chinese copy of our old MiG-17 from the late fifties. They have a top speed of about six hundred knots."

Randy picked up the calculation. "Chengdu is about a thousand klicks from Lhasa and around fifteen hundred from

Kathmandu. That means they're about ninety minutes from the border, just like we are."

"So," Jake added, "we have a chance of getting into Nepalese airspace before they find us."

"We have a chance of *reaching* Nepalese airspace," Randy agreed, "but probably not before they find us. See that little light on your console that's been blinking every eighteen seconds? It's our passive radar detector, telling us that we've just been swept by the radar at Lhasa airport. You can bet they've been tracking us since we lifted off. So from here on it's a simple speed run." The Blackhawk nosed down as Randy applied full throttle. "Sit back, gents, and enjoy the ride. We'll see who gets there first."

✧ ✧ ✧

Rodriguez said nothing as he hung up the phone again. He just pointed at the TDRSS display.

"I don't believe it," Melinda Cunningham breathed.

The president watched, then thumped his fist on the table. "Yes!" The display clearly indicated that the Chinese subs were turning around. "Do we know why, Roddy?"

"Pacific Command doesn't," Rodriguez replied, "but this must've been what the ops order was all about." He shrugged. "For all we know, they just got bored."

"Resume peacetime operations," the president ordered. "But I want them to know that we still care."

The chairman nodded. "Walt Harrison and I agree with you, sir. The sub-chasers will continue to hound the Chinese until they're out of range."

"They're not the only ones we're going to hound," the president added. He turned to his secretary of state. "Melinda, you and I are going to draft a letter to Premier Wing as hot as that allegedly 'Tex-Mex' chili his ambassador whips up." Everyone rose as the president came to his feet. "But first, folks, let's have breakfast."

42

"MACINTYRE!"

Amplified as it was by the headset inside his helmet, Randy's shout jolted Jake out of the doze into which he had been lulled by the whickering rotor just overhead.

"Do you always snore like a buzzsaw?" Randy asked.

Still half asleep, Jake rubbed his eyes. "How should I know? I'm the one doing the sleeping."

"True," Randy agreed. "When we get back, I'll ask Anne."

Jake bristled at the implication. "What makes you think she'd know?"

"Well," Randy replied nonchalantly, "if you usually spend as much time sacked out on the Drydens' couch as you did when I was there, Anne must've had ample exposure to your dulcet tones."

Taken aback by Randy's reasonable explanation, Jake found himself wanting to change the subject. "Tell me how to shut off the intercom so I can go back to sleep."

"Sorry to interrupt your recital, Caruso, but I need your help. We're about half an hour from the border, and I'm expecting bogeys any time now."

"What do you want me to do?"

"You've just been appointed our intercept officer, by virtue of your sterling character, rakish good looks, and the fact that you're riding backseat. That means that you're in charge of spotting the bad guys, while I steer us around mountains and other such trivia."

"Are they going to be flying low and slow and trailing a banner that reads Bad Guys, like they do at football games?" Jake asked hopefully.

"I'm afraid not. They'll be coming in high, fast, and from behind us."

"That's gonna make it tough."

"You'll have help. See the two switches under the display in the center of your console?"

"The ones under the plastic cover?" Jake asked.

"The very same. Lift up the cover and flip the lefthand switch."

"I've got what looks like a topography map, with a red cross in the center and some figures down in the lower lefthand corner."

"Are the figures changing?"

"Every five seconds."

Jake heard Randy's sigh of relief. "That's good news. I was worried that it might not work out here in the middle of nowhere. The figures are latitude and longitude from our GPS."

"What is this GPS, Cavanaugh?" Markov asked.

"You mean you don't know?" Randy asked in mock surprise. "I thought you Russians invented it, too—" Randy was interrupted by Markov's derisive snort of laughter.

"GPS," Randy continued, "stands for Global Positioning System. A receiver picks up signals from three of the GPS satellites in geostationary orbit. It sends the signals to the computer onboard this bucket, which uses them to determine our position by triangulation."

"But, is it accurate?" Markov asked skeptically.

"Within about fifty meters," Randy told him. "This baby has a three-channel GPS. Some of the newer five-channel models are accurate to within a meter or two."

Markov whistled appreciatively.

"The topographical map Jake's seeing," Randy continued, "is generated in real time, based on our position, from a stored database of coordinates."

"Any way of telling how much farther we have to go?" Jake asked.

"Sure thing. See that panel marked FCS? That's your Fire Control System."

"You know," Jake commented, "we've already stolen one of their choppers. If we shoot down their air force, too, they're not going to like us very much."

"Unfortunately," Randy replied, "we don't have anything to shoot with if we wanted to. This is the civilian model of the S-67. That means it came without the luxury option package of Sidewinder missiles, rocket pods, and a 20-mm multibarrel cannon." Jake saw Randy shift uncomfortably. "No leather upholstery, either."

"So what do I do with the FCS?" Jake asked.

"On the left of the panel is a switch marked CIV and MIL. Flip it to CIV."

"The map's been overlaid with a yellow line."

"Right. You told the computer to display civilian boundaries. That yellow line is the border between Tibet and Nepal."

"OK. So now we know where we are. Any way of knowing where *they* are?"

"This is where it gets fun. Push the button marked SEARCH."

"I've got a radar display overlaid on top of everything else."

"You just fired up our active radar. Until now we've been passive. That is, we've only been listening. Now we're on the air and looking around. While that means that we'll see 'em coming, it also means that we're lighting up the radar sky like the Goodyear blimp. So heads up, chum."

As Jake watched the display, he felt an old, familiar tension reawaken within him. He was again a young second lieutenant, sitting in the back of a Bell UH-1D Huey attack helicopter as it flitted over the Vietnam treetops in the dead of night. In the glow from the instrument lights sweat glistened on the camouflage-painted faces of his scared, young platoon. Jake looked out into the Himalayan night, remembering once more those of his men who had charged into the midnight jungle and never returned.

"You're right, Cavanaugh," he found himself saying. "It is the waiting that gets to you."

"Huh?"

"I was thinking of what you said on the top of the cliff above the PLA base." *Time to change the subject. Too many ghosts.* "You called this bird an S-67. I thought that the Black Hawk was designated the UH-60A."

"You're thinking of the two-word *Black Hawk*. This little honey is the one-word *Blackhawk*."

"Never heard of it."

"Not surprising. Officially, Sikorsky only built one prototype, which crashed during a test run in 1974."

Jake laughed to himself. *Sheila, you should be here now.* "'Officially,' you say?"

"Yeah. That Blackhawk proto caught the Company's eye during its army flight tests. They were looking for something that was versatile, maneuverable, and above all, *fast*. They got all three in this baby. At one time she held the world helicopter speed record. So when the army lost interest, the CIA, through a network of dummy companies, encouraged Sikorsky to go into private, very secret production. They build a few every year, and we buy all they make. In fact, it was one of those dummy outfits that sold the Chinese this very machine." Jake heard Randy chuckle. "I'll have to buy some stock in that firm."

"Did the CIA teach you how to fly?"

"Helicopters, yes. I moved up from fixed-wing aircraft just before we invaded Grenada. Flew there and in Panama, too." Randy banked the Blackhawk slightly to the right. "Panama was plenty hairy. The night before the invasion I was bringing in a team of SEALs who were going to do a little preliminary demolition work."

"Seals, Cavanaugh?" Markov asked in amazement. "How could animals blow anything up?"

"SEAL means Sea, Air, Land. It's a elite force. Like your Thirteenth Division."

"I was at Stalingrad," Markov interjected. "The Thirteenth was my division." Randy whistled appreciatively, remembering the Thirteenth's heroic defense of Stalingrad against the Seventy-ninth Panzer Grenadiers in World War II.

"Anyway," Randy continued, "there we were, a quarter mile out, when right smack in the middle of our landing zone a firefight like you wouldn't believe broke out. By the time I got us stopped we were right over the LZ, a hundred feet above what looked like World War III. Nothing but machine-gun tracers below us. If any of those jokers had bothered to look up, we'd have been toast. For lack of anything better to do, I let off a few bursts of the thirty-millimeter, and they faded. I found out later it was a bunch of government troops settling a little dispute over turf."

It was growing light outside, and Jake could see that they were following a river of ice. On either side of them sheer cliffs vanished upward into the still-dark sky.

"How far to the border?" Randy asked Jake.

"About thirty klicks."

"I wanted us to be closer than this at moonrise. The Chinese are miserable night fighters, but in full moonlight we're going to have our hands full." Randy dropped the Black-hawk closer to the blue-white ice.

A soft *ping!* sounded in Jake's earphones. A glance at his radar screen showed a blob of light that had just appeared on its edge. The blob was heading toward them rapidly. "Company," Jake told Randy. "Fifty klicks out and closing fast."

"Roger," Randy acknowledged. "We're flying through the Rongbuk valley. If I remember my geography, the valley flattens out into a plateau about twenty klicks from the border. We're going to sneak along the valley floor, low and slow, and hope that they can't pick us out from the radar clutter generated by all the rocks and ice. Then, when we run out of ravine, it's a speed run for the border and hope they aren't looking our way."

Randy tucked the S-67 against the valley wall, weaving his way around cliffs and outcroppings. "What sort of toys will those boys have to play with, Colonel?" he asked Markov.

"I assume you mean weapons, Cavanaugh," Markov replied. "The F-4 can be outfitted with either three 30-mm cannons, four pods of eight 55-mm rockets, or four air-to-air missiles."

"Those the missiles we call 'Alkali'?" Randy asked.

"Yes." Markov chuckled. "The names your NATO came up with for our armament! We didn't mind when you named our MiG-25 the 'Foxbat,' but when you called our beautiful new Su-11 night fighter the 'Fishpot,' you almost started another world war."

"Thirty klicks," Jake reported. "Bearing zero-four-zero." The men listened as Jake counted down the kilometers.

"Visual!" Markov shouted. A second later Jake and Randy saw three shapes, glinting in the brittle moonlight, sweep by far overhead.

"Looks like at least one of them has Alkalis fitted," Randy observed. The helicopter skimmed along, twenty feet above the ice. "OK," he said quietly, "ain't nobody down here but us chickens."

"They're in front of us now," Jake reported. "Looks like they missed us." His tone sharpened. "I spoke too soon. They're coming around."

"Guess somebody clucked," Randy muttered. He brought the S-67 out into the middle of the valley to give himself maneuvering room.

"Now heading straight for us," Jake said. The *beep, beep* of the threat-detection system filled their headphones. "Missile fired!" Jake shouted.

Randy savagely yanked up on the Blackhawk's collective control. The men were pressed into their seats as the helicopter shot upward. A small shape flashed by below them. Just as Randy brought the S-67 to a sudden hover, the F-4 that had fired the missile rocketed by overhead. The turbulence generated by seventeen thousand pounds of jet-engine thrust caught the helicopter and flung it toward the ice below.

The three men were tossed around as Randy fought the controls of the tumbling S-67. A crazy quilt of ice, rocks, and sky filled Jake's vision as the helicopter fell. With a final, fierce pull on the collective, Randy brought the Blackhawk to a standstill. Jake could see that they were twenty feet above the jagged ice of the Rongbuk valley.

"*That*," Randy said breathlessly, "was close."

"You just earned that tip, Cavanaugh," Markov remarked.

"We aim to please." Randy pushed the cyclic control forward and shoved the throttles home with his feet. The Blackhawk shot ahead.

"Any sign of our other two playmates?" Randy asked.

"Entirely too much," Jake replied. "Coming up fast on our six." Randy knew that Jake meant the fighters were approaching from behind.

The distinctive sound of a magazine being slammed into a Kalashnikov was heard over the intercom.

"Colonel," Randy remarked, "if you're going to shoot at them, do remember to open the cabin door, OK?"

Markov laughed. "Have no fear, Cavanaugh. I am just getting ready. If they do force us down, I want to try and take at least one of them with us."

Visions of Markov blazing away at supersonic fighters filled Randy's mind. "Good luck," he muttered.

"Don't laugh," Jake interjected. "More than one F-111 was shot down in Nam with a bow and arrow."

"Are the Alkalis infrared or beam-riders?" Randy asked.

"We made both," Markov replied.

The cliffs on either side of them dwindled as the valley rose to meet the Rongbuk plateau. Randy began swinging the S-67 back and forth across the widening expanse. "If the guy flying the F-4 has to guide the Alkali with a radio beam, this should keep him from getting a fix on us," Randy reasoned. "But if the Alkalis are guided by infrared, we've had it."

"Missile!" Jake shouted.

Randy jinked the Blackhawk into a ninety-degree bank. As he leveled out, a cloud of snow mushroomed upward from an icefield ahead of them as the Alkali impacted.

"Beam-rider," Randy decided. "Can't keep a lock on us." Traveling at almost two hundred knots, the S-67 continued to seesaw thirty feet above the frozen Tibetan wasteland.

"They're still behind us," Jake reported. "Must've slowed down. No sign of any more—"

The canopy in front of Jake exploded, filling the cockpit with Plexiglas shards. He heard a series of dull *thunk*s. The Blackhawk bucked violently. Over Randy's shoulder Jake saw the S-67's control panel light up red. Randy flipped switches as the helicopter's turbines changed in pitch. Cold wind whistled around them.

"You still there, MacIntyre?" Randy asked. "Somebody caught us with a burst from his thirty-millimeter."

"Still here," Jake replied. "That was the guy who shot at us head-on. He must've circled around and come in from the east." He heard a grinding sound begin overhead. "How bad is it?" Jake saw a drop of blood soaked into his pantsleg. He reached up, then winced as he pulled a Plexiglas splinter out of his cheek.

"We took a shot in the port gearbox," Randy told him. "It's holding together, but we're losing oil fast. You all right back there in the cheap seats, Colonel?"

When he received no reply Randy repeated his call. Markov still didn't answer.

The Chinese F-4s were close enough for Jake to have three distinct targets on his screen. "They've linked up," he told Randy. "Coming in on our six for another run."

Only a small range of hills to their left broke up the arid expanse of the Rongbuk valley. The remains of the ruined Rongbuk monastery slid by below them as Randy nudged the Blackhawk toward the slight protection of the hills.

"Almost no maneuverability," Randy noted. "Now there ain't nobody down here but us sitting ducks."

Jake watched the radar. "They've turned in on us." The three dots closed on the center of his screen. "Here they come!"

The men waited silently. Randy shook his fist in helpless frustration. As Jake tensed, expecting the rending explosion of an Alkali's impact, he saw once more a pair of emerald eyes, a cloud of auburn hair, and a brilliant smile. *Take good care of her, God.*

With a deafening roar the three fighters blazed past the Blackhawk. In a delta formation, they banked left and quickly disappeared eastward into the clouds.

"Some fist you've got there," Jake remarked when he had recovered from his astonishment.

"Don't I wish," Randy replied, relief evident in his voice. "Actually, the Chinese broke off because they had to. See those hills up ahead? They're in Nepal. Another few seconds, and our friends would've violated Nepalese airspace."

Exhausted, Jake leaned against the shattered canopy. "Home, James."

✧ ✧ ✧

The Blackhawk limped toward the border. "By the way," Randy told Jake, "as we come around this last hill, you should be able to get a great view of the source of the Rongbuk glacier." Randy pointed to his right. *"Now."*

Just as Jake looked to his right, the rising moon bathed the summit of Mount Everest in icy light. A nimbus wreathed the mountain; an ethereal banner of snow was torn from Chomolungma's upper slopes by hurricane winds and flung across an indigo sky. The mountain towered above them, the moonlight seeming to run down its rugged, triangular face in rivulets of molten silver.

A soft *"Nichevo!"* filled their earphones.

"Quite a sight, isn't it Colonel?" Randy asked.

"Had to repair my microphone," Markov explained. "And you are right, Cavanaugh, it *is* quite a sight. One I'm very grateful to be alive to see."

Jake sat rapt, his injuries forgotten, watching as the impossibly huge mountain grew even larger as they approached.

"'Where were you when I laid the earth's foundation?'" Randy heard Jake quote softly. "'Tell me, if you understand. Who marked off its dimensions? Surely you know! Who stretched a measuring line across it? On what were its footings set, or who laid its cornerstone—while the morning stars sang together and all the angels shouted for joy?'" Jake watched as moonrise fully embraced the mountain. "'Have you ever given orders to the morning, or shown the dawn its place? Tell me, if you know all this.'"

"That's too good for you to have thought up," Randy said after a moment's silence.

"It's from the end of the book of Job. Job is scared, sick, destitute, and forsaken. When he complains to God, God reminds him, in no uncertain terms, that he is, and always has been, in charge."

"Right now," Randy said quietly, "that sounds very good to me."

Chomolungma drifted out of sight behind them as they crossed the border into Nepal.

43

"Ready about!" Jake called. "Hard alee!" Everyone aboard *Turnstone* scrambled to the other side of the sloop as Jake pushed the tiller over. The freshening breeze brought the boom sweeping across the deck, and *Turnstone* swung around and started her run into the mouth of Pretty Marsh Harbor.

"Ease her off a bit," Joel suggested. "I expect us to run aground any second."

Jake glanced at the fathometer. "We've got thirty feet of water beneath the keel."

"True," Joel agreed. "But you're forgetting the amount of extra ballast we're carrying today."

"Huh? What extra weight?"

"All the food the women brought aboard." Joel winked at Pat, who was studiously ignoring him.

Turnstone's sails luffed as Jake pointed her into the wind. "Let go the anchor!" he called to Randy, who was waiting up at the bow. Randy heaved the anchor overboard.

"Sure you did that right?" Lee asked.

Randy leaned over the rail. "Looks OK to—," he began. Then he disappeared as Lee pushed him overboard.

Lee broke the water in a graceful dive, surfacing next to

Randy. "C'mon!" she said with a challenging smile. "Race you to shore!"

Jake paused in his loading of supplies into the Boston whaler *Turnstone* had towed. "Glad it's warm today," he remarked as he watched Lee beat Randy by a half length. He glanced at Anne, who was handing boxes of food down to him from *Turnstone*'s stern. "Don't even think about it," he warned her with a grin.

"Let's take a walk while Anne and Pat set out the food," Joel suggested to Markov as the Boston whaler scraped ashore. "I'll show you some of Mount Desert Island."

"And perhaps," Markov said, "you could also tell me more about something Cavanaugh mentioned on the plane here. He said they are found in every city in America."

"What's that? Churches?"

Markov shook his head. "Just what are these things called 'microbreweries'?"

❖ ❖ ❖

His hands in the pouch of his anorak, Randy walked beside Lee along the southern edge of the harbor. He stopped and turned to her. "I'm sorry . . ." he began.

Lee raised her hazel eyes to his. "For?"

"For pressuring you." Randy took a deep breath. "I apologize."

"I don't recall objecting too much at the time," she said softly. "I owe you an apology, too."

Randy watched as the three-masted schooner *Victory Chimes*, on a reach through the Bartlett Narrows, appeared beyond the tip of West Point. "Jake and I talked on the flight home. He gave me a lot of things to think about. I've got an assignment coming up, but when I get back, I'd really like to spend some time with you. If you don't mind," he added earnestly.

Lee smiled up at him. "I'd like that very much."

✧ ✧ ✧

Full and content, Jake stretched out on the beach in the spring sun. "What'd you call that stuff?" he asked.

"That *stuff*," Anne replied tolerantly, "is called frittata. Eggs, bread crumbs, spices, Parmesan cheese, and artichoke hearts. Did you like it?"

"Beats the heck out of yak tartare." Jake rolled over, then sat up suddenly. "I almost forgot this," he said, reaching into his pocket.

Anne opened the small box Jake handed her. She gasped as the sunlight ignited the ring's cabochon emerald.

"It's gorgeous," Pat exclaimed. "Where did you find it?"

"In a shop in Lhasa," Jake explained. "The old guy who ran the shop said it once belonged to the wife of Prester John."

"*Who* John?" Anne asked, turning the ring in the light.

"Prester John." Anne, Pat, and Joel listened as Jake described his encounter with the Tibetan jeweler. "I don't know if the story's true or not," he finished. "But there's the ring."

"You said the jeweler was old," Joel said. "How old do you think he was?"

"Good question. He had one of those timeless faces. Could've been anywhere between fifty and five hundred. Why?"

"Your friend might have been a lot older than even five hundred." Joel finished his soda. "I believe that in the Bible Jesus indicated that some of his disciples wouldn't die before his return. The Gospel of John seems to imply that it was John himself about whom Christ was speaking. Out of this belief rose the Prester John legend, which says that after Christ's ascension, John went off and established a Christian kingdom somewhere in the Far East. So instead of being Asiatic, the Prester may have been a very elderly former Jew."

391

"You know," Jake mused. "Now that I think about it, that shopkeeper didn't look very Tibetan. . . ."

❖ ❖ ❖

After her parents had gone for a walk, Anne took the ring out of its case. She looked at it, then beyond it at Jake. "Which hand should I wear this on?" she asked.

Jake looked at her for a long time, the tenderness in his eyes betraying the mirth in his voice. "That, lady," he replied, breaking into a smile, "is entirely up to you."

Out in the harbor, the water lapped softly at *Turnstone*'s hull.

THE END

If you enjoyed *Tigers & Dragons,* you'll want to read its companion volume:

TOURMALINE
Jon Henderson   0-8423-7287-3

More intriguing, contemporary fiction—from Tyndale House Publishers:

THE CASTLE OF DREAMS
Donna Fletcher Crow   0-8423-1068-1

CIRCLE OF DECEPTION *(New! Fall 1993)*
Roger Elwood   0-8423-1128-9

Christian Jr./Sr High School
2100 Greenfield Dr
El Cajon, CA 92019